Brenda Jackson is a *New York Times* bestselling author of more than one hundred romance titles. Brenda lives in Jacksonville, Florida, and divides her time between family, writing and travelling. Email Brenda at authorbrendajackson@gmail.com or visit her on her website at brendajackson.net

Joanne Rock credits her decision to write romance after a book she picked up during a flight delay engrossed her so thoroughly that she didn't mind at all when her flight was delayed two more times. Giving her readers the chance to escape into another world has motivated her to write over eighty books for a variety of Mills & Boon series.

Discover more at millsandboon.co.uk

CLAIMED BY A STEELE

BRENDA JACKSON

HER TEXAS RENEGADE

JOANNE ROCK

MILLS & BOON

First Published in Great Britain 2020
by Mills & Boon, an imprint of HarperCollinsPublishers,
1 London Bridge Street, London, SE1 9GF

Claimed by a Steele © 2020 Brenda Streater Jackson
Her Texas Renegade © 2020 Harlequin Books S.A.

Special thanks and acknowledgement are given to Joanne Rock for her contribution to the *Texas Cattleman's Club: Inheritance* series.

ISBN: 978-0-263-27922-1

0520

MIX
Paper from
responsible sources
FSC www.fsc.org   **FSC™ C007454**

This book is produced from independently certified FSC™ paper to ensure responsible forest management.

For more information visit: www.harpercollins.co.uk/green

Printed and bound in Spain
by CPI, Barcelona

CLAIMED BY
A STEELE

BRENDA JACKSON

To the love of my life, Gerald Jackson Sr.
My one and only. My forever-hubby.
My everything.

To everyone who enjoys reading about
the Steeles, this one is especially for you.

To the librarians of Mississippi.
Thanks for inviting me to your 2019 conference
in Jackson, Mississippi. It was wonderful and
you guys made it fun! Thanks a million,
and since this is the book that I was working on
in my hotel room, I am dedicating it to you guys.

"With all lowliness and meekness, with
longsuffering, forbearing one another in love."
—*Ephesians* 4:2

Prologue

"You may kiss your bride."

Gannon Steele held back a laugh as he watched his brother Mercury pull the woman he loved into his arms and give her a whopper of a kiss. It was hard to believe that his *I-will-never-fall-in-love-again* brother had done just that. Fallen in love again. Gannon knew no one was happier about it than his mother, Eden Tyson Steele, who adored Mercury's new wife and who'd been ready to see another son married off.

He glanced around at his family. They were probably thinking the same things about Mercury that he was. Sloan Donahue had changed Mercury's mindset about love and Mercury had changed hers about being fiercely independent. Like everyone else, Gannon was convinced Mercury and Sloan were meant for each other.

"Should we think that maybe you're next?"

Gannon glanced over at his oldest brother, Galen. Their parents, Drew and Eden Steele, had given birth to six sons. For years, all six had been known around Phoenix as the Bad News Steeles. Mainly because of their die-hard bachelor ways. Now all those previous die-hard bachelors were married—all except for Gannon.

Unlike his five brothers, Gannon had never wanted to stay single forever. He viewed marriage as a part of his future. However, he was in no hurry to claim a wife, and now that Mercury was married off, that meant more women for Gannon to enjoy. He couldn't wait.

"You all should know that I'm next, Galen, since I'm the last of the Phoenix Steeles. But I intend to have the time of my life before that happens, which I don't foresee happening for another ten years or more."

"Ten years?" Galen asked, raising a doubtful eyebrow.

"You heard me. Ten years at least. Now that I am the last single Steele left standing, I plan to enjoy being the number one player."

"Be careful, baby bro. You'll be singing a different tune if the right woman appears in your life, trust me."

Gannon chuckled, definitely not taking anything his brother said seriously. He was the master of his own mind and his own fate. There was no woman alive who could change him. "Who would have thought?"

Galen gave him a quizzical look. "Thought what?"

"That you would be sounding like Mom in your old age."

Galen frowned. "Be amused all you want, Gannon. Just don't say that I didn't warn you. Do I need to remind you about what happened to me when Brittany appeared in my life? I was the last person anyone expected to fall in love."

Gannon knew that to be true, but then, all one had to do was look at Brittany or any of the women his brothers had married to understand why his brothers had gotten love-whipped. Not only were the women beautiful, but they were also intelligent. However, with his current mind-set, Gannon figured that even if a beautiful, intelligent woman walked into his life right now, he wouldn't bite. Although he had discriminating taste, he still preferred changing bed partners. Now with his brothers out of the way, there would be even more women out there for him. He couldn't see settling down to just one woman anytime soon. He would stick to his ten-year plan.

Deciding to change the subject, he said, "So Zion is having a baby, huh?"

Galen laughed. "No, Celine is pregnant. Zion is strutting around like a damn peacock, like he's the only one who can make a baby. For him to have been the Bachelor in Demand to hold out the longest to get hitched, it's totally hilarious that he's now all in."

Gannon laughed, as well, watching the group of men and their wives standing together. For years those men had been pegged as the Bachelors in Demand. Now they were all married and seemed pretty damn happy about it. And none of them had wasted time getting their wives pregnant.

Gannon wasn't ready for all that.

A short while later, while at the wedding reception, Gannon's cell vibrated. He checked and saw the caller was Delphine Ryland. He frowned. How did he know that name? Why was she listed in his phone contacts? Was she a past bed partner? Although he tried remembering names, he couldn't always do so. Unlike his brothers in their man-whoring days, Gannon didn't have a special phone just for women. If he preferred not talking to one, he just didn't answer.

"When is your interview with *Simply Irresistible*, Gannon?"

He glanced over at his sister-in-law Nikki, who was married to his brother Jonas. The two had announced last week they were expecting a baby. Gannon's brother Tyson and his wife, Hunter, had announced the same thing a few weeks ago. Gannon figured those announcements were another reason his mother was beaming with pride. She'd seen five out of six of her sons married, and by this time next year she would have more grandkids to spoil. Hopefully she would give Mercury and Sloan time to settle into their marriage before waving baby booties in front of them.

"I believe it's this coming week," he said. In all honesty, with the excitement of the wedding, and all his family and friends arriving in town, he'd completely forgotten about the interview.

Simply Irresistible, a Denver-based magazine, was owned by Chloe Westmoreland, a woman they considered a cousin-in-law. Gannon had felt honored when Chloe contacted him to say the magazine would be doing a series of feature stories on CEOs making a difference within their companies. They wanted him to be one of those they highlighted. In fact, they intended for him to be on the cover.

Over the last forty years, Gannon's father had taken his small trucking company and turned it into a million-dollar business, with routes all over the United States. When Drew retired a few years ago, Gannon had taken over the company as CEO, and he still enjoyed getting behind the steering wheel of a rig himself to make cross-country deliveries and pickups.

He had no problem doing the interview and hoped the feature would help to give more respect to the profession of truckers on the road and their importance to a thriving economy. He figured most people didn't think about how much businesses depended on the trucking industry to deliver their products to consumers.

"When I talked to Chloe last month, she mentioned that Delphine Ryland would be doing the interview with you," Nikki said, breaking into his thoughts.

Delphine Ryland.

At some point Chloe had given him the woman's name and number, and he'd put the contact into his phone list. "Do you know her?"

"Delphine? Yes, I know her."

Gannon shouldn't have been surprised since he knew of Nikki and Chloe's past working relationship and current friendship. Before Nikki's marriage to Jonas, she had freelanced as a photographer for *Simply Irresistible* on occasion. It stood to reason that she would also know some of the people who worked for the magazine.

"I just missed a call from Ms. Ryland."

Nikki nodded. "She was probably calling to remind you about the interview. Making sure you didn't forget since she was to arrive in town this weekend."

"No problem. I'll return her call tomorrow."

"Delphine's a nice person and a great journalist. You're going to like her, Gannon."

He decided not to say anything to that because he was a man who liked all women, and he figured his feelings for Delphine Ryland would be no different.

Glancing at her cell phone, Delphine released a huge sigh. She had placed two calls to Gannon Steele over the weekend and he had yet to get back in touch with her. It was important that she do a good job on this project and Gannon Steele was the last CEO to interview.

So far, she'd done interviews with Ron Paulus, the pizza CEO who often dropped into his stores to make deliveries, Jack Zelle, the owner of a huge manufacturing company who had no problem rolling up his sleeves to help get orders out of his warehouse, and Nathan Beam, who owned a slew of restaurants and often worked as a waiter. All those CEOs had something in common. They believed connecting with their employees was empowering and that the best leadership style was to not ask their employees to do anything that they themselves wouldn't do.

From her research, she knew Gannon Steele was no different. Since taking over at Steele Trucking Company when his father retired close to five years ago, the thirty-three-year-old CEO had transformed the company. Steele Trucking Company was already a multi-million-dollar enterprise, and he'd not only grown the wealth tenfold, but had also made it into a family-oriented business.

Gannon had listened to his employees, and he himself had traveled the routes they'd driven when he'd occasionally left the office to get behind the steering wheel of a rig. Doing so had given him firsthand knowledge of truckers' challenges.

As a result, he had implemented a number of changes that made life better for the truckers and their families whenever the drivers were away. He had opened several schools for the children of his employees and made sure a support system was in place to assist the families when the long-distance truckers were on the road. He'd even offered a tuition-paid program, where his truckers could go back to school to get their GED, professional certifications or even bachelor's degrees. The tuition program extended to the truckers' families, as well, eliminating a big source of stress. Then, on top of everything else, he'd raised the salary for his workers, making them the highest paid in the industry and making Steele Trucking Company one of the most sought-after employers in the state of Arizona. Already Gannon had graced the covers of a number of professional magazines as the boy wonder of the trucking industry.

Simply Irresistible was a magazine that catered to today's up-and-coming woman. The magazine's most popular edition still remained the annual Irresistible Man issue. The feature included a cover shoot and an in-depth story about a man who the magazine felt deserved special recognition because he was simply irresistible in both looks and how he'd made a positive impact on society.

In the past, many notables had graced the cover, including sports figure LeBron James, wealthy rancher Ramsey Westmoreland, professional motorcycle racer Thorn Westmoreland and former movie star turned rancher Walker Rafferty. A few months ago, the board chose Gannon Steele for this year, not only because of his accomplishments, but also because of his sexiness. The staff at *Simply Irresistible* knew the man featured on the cover needed to be thought of by their readers as a fantasy lover.

From the research Delphine had done and all the photographs she'd collected of Gannon Steele, he could definitely be a woman's fantasy lover. He certainly got her vote. The man's green eyes would make any woman drool. So here she was in Phoenix, ready to do the interview, and yet she couldn't get in touch with the guy.

Her boss, Lucia Westmoreland, who knew Gannon personally because of family connections, had given Delphine his cell-phone number and told her that Chloe Westmoreland, the CEO of *Simply Irresistible*, had already given Gannon Delphine's. That made her wonder why he wasn't accepting her calls. Had he changed his mind about doing the interview?

That thought sent nervous chills down her body. The last thing she wanted was to let down Chloe or Lucia when they'd been so good to her. They'd given her a chance because they'd seen the same ambition in her that they'd seen in each other at the start of the magazine. Chloe had launched it right out of college, and when she expanded the business to Colorado, she'd called on her best friend from college, Lucia, to manage the Denver office. Chloe hadn't intended to remain in Denver, but she and Lucia ended up marrying two brothers, and now Lucia mostly ran the business fulltime, while Chloe worked from home while raising her family and assisting her husband in his sheep-ranching business. Like Lucia, Chloe also knew Gannon personally because of family connections.

Delphine would always be indebted to both Chloe and Lucia for giving her a job as a journalist. After her breakup with Liddell Bartley, it had been her plan never to return to Denver. She'd been heartbroken when the man she loved—the man she thought loved her in return—had sent her a Dear Jane letter a month before the wedding, letting her know he'd fallen in love with someone else.

But her mother's health made it necessary for Delphine to move back to Denver. She hadn't known just how ill her mother had been until Lucia had written to tell her. Lucia's mother and Delphine's own had been best friends while growing up in Denver. Although Delphine's mother hadn't wanted her daughter to find out just how bad her condition was and had sworn Lucia's mother to secrecy, Lucia hadn't felt that secrecy extended to her. She'd been compelled to let Delphine know the true nature of her mother's health.

No longer caring that returning to Colorado would place her in an awkward position when it came to Liddell, Delphine had quit her job in New York to return to Denver to become her mother's sole caretaker. Knowing the time and attention Delphine would need to give her mother, Chloe and Lucia had offered her a job as a freelance journalist so she could work from home while contributing to the magazine. That was what she'd done for three years.

After her mother passed away last year, Delphine took a full-time position at *Simply Irresistible*. She enjoyed her work and the assignments she'd been given. The thing she liked the most was that her assignments, more often than not, took her away from Denver for weeks at a time. That helped with the grieving process.

The two of them had been close ever since her father had left her mother for another woman and hadn't once looked back. Delphine had been six years old at the time. She honestly didn't know now if he was alive or dead, and frankly, she didn't care. That seemed to be the story of the Ryland women's lives.

The men they loved left them for other women.

The unexpected ringing of her cell phone made Delphine jump. The caller ID indicated it was Gannon Steele, returning her call. "Yes?"

"Ms. Ryland, this is Gannon Steele. I apologize for not returning your calls earlier, but we had a wedding in my family this weekend and I've been quite busy."

She suddenly recalled that Lucia had mentioned there would be a Steele wedding, but Delphine hadn't known it would be happening this particular weekend. "No need to apologize, Mr. Steele. I understand." She inhaled deeply to get past the sound of his voice, a deep, rich baritone that reminded her of Barry White. Unexpected tremors flowed through her.

"So when can we get together?" he asked her.

She knew his question wasn't personal. They had both agreed to meet for the interview. But at that moment the sound of his voice had her imagining other possible scenarios, too. She shook her head, knowing none were realistic. During her research she'd discovered more about Gannon Steele than just his business accomplishments. She also knew he was the last of what the women in Phoenix referred to as the Bad News Steeles. With another brother married off, he was the only single one left. His and his brothers' reputations with women were legendary. Now she wondered if Gannon Steele intended to carry the banner proudly as the last remaining one of the sexy Steeles.

"I'm available whenever you are." Too late, she wondered if her response had come off as unprofessional. Before he could answer, she added, "I'm available to meet with you to discuss the magazine's interview whenever you are, Mr. Steele."

"Okay, what about tonight over dinner."

Dinner? He wanted to meet over dinner? She swallowed deeply, reminding herself that the offer was only business. There was no need to freak out. Too bad he was the first man who'd gotten her attention since her breakup with Liddell five years ago. And he had grabbed her attention just from the photographs she'd seen and the research she'd done. A lot of women considered him a charmer.

"Ms. Ryland?"

Hearing him say her name made her realize she hadn't agreed to meet him for dinner. "Yes, Mr. Steele, just tell me where to meet you and—"

"Sorry, but thanks to my mother, I'm old-fashioned. Business or otherwise, if I invite a woman out, then I'm responsible for making sure she gets there and back. Just tell me the name of your hotel and I'll meet you in the lobby at seven, if that time is acceptable to you."

She also knew all about his mother, the beautiful and vivacious Eden Tyson Steele, a former international model whose face had graced the covers of such magazines as *Vogue*, *Cosmo* and *Elle*. She could see the woman teaching her six sons about the value of respecting women, even if their philandering behavior would tempt them to do otherwise.

"I'm staying at the St. Laurent."

"I know exactly where that is. I will see you at seven, Ms. Ryland."

"Okay. Thanks."

Delphine hung up the phone and wondered what it would be like to sit across from Gannon Steele and talk business. Of course, she would thank him for agreeing to do the interview. She'd heard it was often hard to get their subjects to agree to be on the cover of their Irresistible Man issue. It seemed Gannon Steele hadn't balked at the idea. Instead, according to Lucia, he had even been flattered that she'd asked. That would certainly make Delphine's job of interviewing him easier.

A lot of women considered truckers hot, and Delphine was curious about them, as well. Was it true that a trucker had a girl waiting for him at every truck stop?

And that the truck was often used for more than just hauling merchandise? Of course, she wouldn't ask Mr. Steele those specific questions, but she couldn't help wondering.

Glancing at her watch, she saw that she had five hours to kill before he arrived, and she intended to put them to good use. This would be the first time in nearly five years that she'd gone out with a man. Even if the evening was nothing more than a business dinner, she intended to look her best.

Gannon parked his car, quickly got out and headed for the entrance of the hotel. A traffic jam on the interstate had made getting here on time a challenge, but he'd arrived with ten minutes to spare. When he entered the lobby, he recalled that he'd been here a number of times before, with several women. All of whom had known the score and been well aware that he was not looking for a lasting relationship. He was a between-the-sheets sort of guy and the women he slept with knew it. Most weren't looking for anything more serious than he was.

Of course, there were always women with love and marriage on their minds. Those were usually the ones who were one-and-done. Rarely did he repeat an evening with them. Only three that he recalled could make that claim. Gannon knew that when he got married it would be because he was ready to settle down. Like he'd told his brother Galen yesterday, he didn't see that happening anytime soon. He was sticking to his ten-year plan.

According to his watch, he still had five minutes, so he let his mind wander to his upcoming plans. He was looking forward to getting on the road and out of the office for a couple of weeks. He knew his right-hand man, Ozzie Hazouri, would handle things in his absence. Gannon would be heading south to Florida. Once he parked his rig, he would get a rental car and drive to Miami to his beach house. A week there would definitely revitalize him. With this being the end of April, he was two months from the halfway mark of the year. There were still goals he wanted to achieve in his thriving business. He intended to…

"Mr. Steele?"

He blinked, going temporarily speechless when a woman stepped in front of him. Granted, he'd never met Delphine Ryland and hadn't really thought about what to expect, but he definitely hadn't expected the woman standing in front of him. Damn, she looked absolutely, positively beautiful. So beautiful that all he could do was stand there and stare. Or was he gawking?

She had large, expressive eyes that were chestnut brown, shoulder-length curly brown hair with streaks of golden blond, styled to complement her oval face, and strikingly high cheekbones. But what really had him spellbound were lips that looked so indisputably enticing that he was tempted to lean in and give them one hell of a kiss. He was what his brothers often called a "lips" man.

Her lips were perfectly shaped, appealing to everything male within him. Just looking at her mouth made it impossible for him to think straight. Hell, he honestly couldn't think at all.

"Mr. Steele?"

Her repeating his name made him quickly grab control of his senses. No woman had ever captured his attention like this before. "Yes, I'm Gannon Steele. Sorry for staring, but you remind me of someone," he lied, hoping that excuse would cover his initial reaction to seeing her.

"I do?"

At that moment, he appreciated his ability to think on his feet. "Yes, and the resemblance is uncanny."

He was satisfied with his response. If she ever caught him staring at her again, she would assume he was thinking of her look-alike, who didn't really exist, instead of being fascinated with her. And he would admit to being fascinated by her, but then, he was a man and, quite frankly, any man would be taken with her.

Even if her looks hadn't captivated him, the outfit she was wearing would have certainly done so. On any other woman the dress would probably have looked okay, but with her small waist, curvy hips and shapely legs, "just okay" wasn't even close. "A vision of mouthwatering lusciousness" would be more appropriate.

He extended his hand to her. "And you're Delphine Ryland, right?"

She smiled, and when she did, it seemed the lights in the hotel's lobby shone brighter. "Yes, I'm Delphine Ryland. I knew who you were the moment I saw your green eyes."

He couldn't help but chuckle. "Thanks to my mom, my brothers and I are easily recognized."

Gannon released her hand even as he thought it felt too good encased in his. "Ready?" he asked her.

"Yes."

"I hope you're hungry. The restaurant I selected serves the best steaks in town."

She chuckled and the sound was warm and inviting. "Yes, I'm hungry. I skipped lunch."

"Well, I didn't skip lunch but I'm still hungry," he said, walking beside her out of the hotel and toward his parked car. "I have quite a hearty appetite. According to my mother, it's because I'm still growing."

Delphine wasn't sure if Gannon Steele was still growing or not, but what she saw now was pretty dang impressive.

She couldn't help giving him a discreet glance as they walked toward the shiny black Tesla. She had to admit, he looked pretty darn good in a pair of black slacks and a white shirt. Almost too good. She had seen photos of him before in different kinds of attire—business suits, jeans, sweats, jogging shorts. She'd even seen him in a pair of swimming trunks when he'd been in one of those male calendars as part of a charity fundraiser. He'd been Mr. September. She remembered that quite well, since her birthday was in September, and she'd enjoyed seeing him pinned to the wall in her office. However, she was certain that seeing him in the flesh was altogether different. She preferred the real thing.

"Here we are."

She paused as he opened the car door for her and then she slid onto the smooth leather seat. "Thanks."

"You're welcome, Ms. Ryland."

He closed the car door and she watched him walk around the front of the vehicle to get into the driver's side. She noticed he had a manly stroll unlike any she'd seen before. It was a purposeful stride, filled with confidence, but not arrogance. After he backed out of the parking lot, he glanced over at her.

"When did you arrive in Phoenix?" he asked her.

"Friday evening. And again, I want to apologize for disturbing you at your brother's wedding. Lucia had mentioned a wedding in your family, but I thought it was last weekend."

"No harm done. I'm sure my brother Mercury wished it had been a week earlier."

"He was that anxious?"

Gannon Steele laughed. "Yes, he was just that anxious to tie the knot, and I'm happy for him and Sloan. They left immediately after the wedding for a three-week honeymoon to Paris, parts of Germany and Switzerland."

"Sounds nice."

"For them, I'm sure it will be. Now tell me about yourself, Ms. Ryland. And please call me Gannon. If you don't mind, may I call you Delphine?"

"No, I don't mind, and there's a lot to tell. I've been working for *Simply Irresistible* for a while now."

"Was it your first job out of college? You look rather young."

She shook her head, grinning. "I'm not all that young. I'll be twenty-six in September. After college I got a job with a small publishing house in New York as an editor. I worked there almost a year before my mother became ill. I left New York to move back to Denver to take care of her."

"I hope she got better."

She couldn't hold back the sadness she knew shone in her eyes. "She didn't. Mom had MS and died last May." It was hard to believe the one-year mark was coming up next month. There was never a day that went by that she didn't think of her. Miss her.

"I'm sorry to hear that, Delphine. That had to have been hard on you."

She nodded. "It was. Mom and I were extremely close." Delphine paused and then said, "Because of the nature of Mom's condition, she needed full-time care and I wanted to be the one to take care of her, along with the visiting nurses who came to check on her every week. Lucky for me, I was hired by *Simply Irresistible* as a freelancer, writing articles from home. I also became a blogger."

He nodded. "What about your father?"

She could understand Gannon asking about him. In the world he'd grown up in, both parents had been present. "My parents divorced when I was six. I never saw him again after the day he left." No need to tell him why her father had divorced her mom, or how both she and her mother had cried themselves to sleep for months after he'd deserted them.

"Do you still live in your mother's house?"

"Yes. It's been in our family for a couple of generations, since it used to be my grandparents' home. I love living there, although I've decided to give it a much-needed face-lift," she said. "While I'm gone, I'm getting my floors redone. Replacing the carpet with wood."

"Who's overseeing the project while you're away?"

"My best friend from high school, Mandy. She likes doing renovation stuff. I trust her to make sure things will be done to my satisfaction and within my budget."

Gannon nodded. "According to Chloe and Lucia, you're a good journalist—one of the best."

Delphine appreciated him changing the subject from her personal life to her professional one. "Oh, I don't know about that, but I appreciate them for thinking so. Lucia's mother and mine were best friends from their high-school days."

She thought about how much support she'd gotten from the Conyers family over the years and added, "During Mom's last days, I don't know how I would have made it without the Conyerses being there for me and for Mom."

He nodded again. "It's always great having good people in your corner when you need them the most."

He brought the car to a stop. "Here we are."

She glanced out the window and saw the restaurant. The Grip. There was one in Denver, although she could never afford to eat there. "Nice restaurant."

"One of my favorites," he said, opening the car door.

Just lovely, she thought. She couldn't afford to eat at The Grip and he considered it one of his favorites, which meant he probably ate here a lot. She tried not to think about the differences in their livelihoods. Instead, she watched him walk around the front of the car to open the door for her. Normally, she wouldn't sit and wait for any man to open her door, but she knew from articles she'd read about him that Gannon had impeccable manners.

When he opened the door, she took the hand he offered and got out of the car. It had rained earlier and the scent of damp grass and wet soil permeated the air. And then there was his woodsy scent, which suited him. It definitely suited her since she liked the fragrance on him. She thought it made him even more manly.

As they were walking side by side toward the building, he suddenly took hold of her arm to skirt around a couple of puddles. Why did his touch feel so warm and comforting?

When they reached the entrance, he released her arm and stepped back to smile down at her. She was wearing high heels, yet she knew he was at least six-two or six-three. "Welcome to The Grip, Delphine. I hope you enjoy dining here as much as I do."

She couldn't help but return his smile. "Thanks, Gannon. I'm sure that I will."

One

"Now I know why this is one of your favorite places. The food is delicious."

Gannon glanced at Delphine over the rim of his wineglass and smiled. "Glad you're enjoying it."

He liked a woman who didn't mind eating, and was glad Delphine fit into that category. She had suggested that he order for her since everything on the menu looked good. When he'd told her he was a steak-and-potatoes kind of guy, she'd said that was fine since she was a steak-and-potatoes kind of girl.

He had ordered them both juicy rib eyes, baked potatoes and a selection of mixed vegetables. To start things off, their waiter had delivered a basket of delicious bread to their table and a bottle of wine. Gannon had asked her more about herself. She'd obviously assumed he'd wanted to hear more about her work history with *Simply Irresistible* and not anything personal.

That was not the case. He was curious about whether or not she was involved with anyone, and if so, were they dating exclusively? Bottom line, there was no way a woman who looked like her wasn't involved with a man.

Why in the hell was he even interested? Did it have to do with the fact that his entire body sizzled each and every time their hands touched, or whenever he looked at her mouth for any length of time? He'd been attracted to women before, but never with this much intensity.

He'd listened while she'd told him about other articles she'd written, as if to assure him that she wasn't a novice. Although that hadn't been the information he'd been looking for, he couldn't help but be impressed with all she'd done. Nor could he not be impressed with how the light from the candle seemed to flicker on her skin, giving it a radiant glow. There was no doubt about it— Delphine Ryland was one hell of a beautiful woman.

"I'm sure I've bored you with all I've told you about myself, so how about sharing information about you," she said, breaking into his thoughts.

He leaned back in his chair. They had ordered dessert, which would be arriving shortly. Both of them had decided on slices of carrot cake. "I'm sure you did your research on me, but I'm not sure how much you know about my family, who I am extremely proud of," he said, smiling, letting her know this interview wasn't his first rodeo.

Journalists had interviewed him before, although he would be the first to admit that none had been as pretty as Delphine. In fact, most of the interviewers had been men, simply because most women weren't interested in writing tractor-trailer-related stories. However, from some of the things she'd mentioned during dinner, she

had done her homework regarding rigs and truckers—
yet another thing that had impressed him.

Gannon found himself doing something he normally
didn't do, which was talk about his family, but for some
reason with her, he felt comfortable enough to open up.
He told her about his parents and how they met, deciding to leave out his father's former Casanova reputation, and how Gannon and his brothers were convinced
they had inherited Drew Steele's philandering genes.

"My brother Galen is the oldest of the six and he's
thirty-eight. He's made millions as a video-game cre-
ator, something he started while still in college. He's
married to Brittany and they have twins, a son and a
daughter. My parents' first grandchildren."

He took a sip of his wine and then continued, "My
brother Tyson is the doctor in the family, a gifted heart
surgeon. He's thirty-seven and married to Hunter.
Brother Eli is thirty-six and a prominent attorney in
town. He's married to Stacey. Jonas is thirty-five and
owns a marketing business, and he's married to Nikki.
Last but not least is Mercury. He's thirty-four and is the
one who got married this weekend to Sloan."

A smile spread across her lips and Gannon could
feel a tightening in his gut. Why were her lips such a
turn-on?

"Nikki loves being married and speaks highly of
your brother," Delphine said.

Gannon nodded. "All my brothers are blessed to have
married really nice women."

"All six of you are pretty close in age. That means
your mother was pregnant practically every year."

He chuckled. "Mom and Dad wanted a big family.
She says she doesn't regret being pregnant so often since
Dad pampered her."

At that moment the waiter returned with their dessert. After the man placed the plates in front of them and left, Gannon smiled and gestured to their cake. "It's okay to dig in and it wouldn't bother me if you licked your lips."

She threw back her head and laughed. "Is that your way of letting me know this carrot cake is that good?"

"Yes, I guess it is." In truth, he wanted to see her lick those lips. It would be torture watching her, but he was convinced it would be well worth it.

"Thanks for a wonderful evening, Gannon," Delphine said, as he walked her back inside the hotel a couple of hours later. She had truly enjoyed his company.

"Glad you enjoyed it. We covered a lot of topics, but we didn't get down to the specifics of the interview, did we?"

No, they hadn't, even though that had been the intent of meeting for dinner. However, she had to admit she'd rather liked their unorthodox meal. It had seemed more like a get-to-know-you date than a business meeting. She knew from his schedule that he would be leaving on Friday for Florida. It would be one of those trips where he became a trucker behind the rig.

She could just imagine him removing his suit and tie for a pair of jeans, a T-shirt and trucker boots. She wondered if she could talk Nikki into taking some photos of him in that attire for the magazine's cover. Nikki was a great photographer and still did freelance work on occasion for *Simply Irresistible*. There was no doubt in Delphine's mind that seeing him as a trucker instead of a businessman on the magazine's cover would make it one hot issue. She would suggest it to Lucia the next time they talked.

"What time should I expect you in the office tomorrow?"

She glanced up at him. "When would be a good time to come?"

He shrugged. "On Mondays I usually get in around nine. It's usually my day to meet with my department heads to see how things are going."

She nodded. In addition to the interview, he'd agreed to let her shadow him around the office. "I can't wait to see how things are done. I hope you know that your way of doing things has made people take a different look at the trucking industry as a whole."

They stopped walking when they reached the spot in the lobby where they'd met earlier. "There are a lot of different ways to operate a trucking business. Mine is just one. My dad ran the company for years and made it successful. The people who worked for him thought the world of him, and he of them. However, I took over at a time when I knew the industry was changing. I established focus groups to determine what was important to the drivers, especially those who spent a lot of time away from home. One of the studies showed a high divorce rate among those truckers and that bothered me."

"And you were determined to do something about it?" she asked him.

"I was determined to try. I figured happy employees make better employees." He glanced at his watch. "I've bored you enough for one day. Besides, everything I'm telling you can wait until tomorrow. Good night, Delphine. I'll see you at nine in the morning."

"I'll be there. Good night, Gannon." She stepped on the elevator and noted he stood watching her until the door closed between them. That was when she released a deep sigh. She had enjoyed being with him tonight and she'd taken note of the times she'd caught him staring at her. She understood; she reminded him of someone. Delphine figured the woman must have meant something to him at one time. Was he pining for this woman? If so, he should resolve his issues with her before moving on. What if he got seriously involved with someone, but ended up returning to that other woman? The one she reminded him of. That wouldn't be fair, but then, when were men fair? She and her mom had certainly been the recipients of their unfairness. In her experience, men had no qualms about tossing aside a woman like yesterday's garbage.

She sighed deeply, refusing to let any resentment toward the male species ruin what had been a nice evening getting to know Gannon. What he did, or with whom, was his business, she thought, stepping off the elevator when it reached her floor.

A little later, Delphine had taken off her clothes, showered and was ready to call it a night when her cell phone rang. She smiled when she saw the caller was Nikki. "Hello, Nikki."

"Hello, back at you. Welcome to Phoenix. I understand you've been here a couple of days."

"Yes. How did you know?"

"Gannon. At the wedding he saw he'd missed a call from you," Nikki said.

"I forgot about the wedding and apologized about bothering him."

"The two of you did connect?"

Delphine eased into the wingback chair in the room. "Yes. In fact, we had dinner tonight." She thought she should clarify, so she added, "It was a business dinner."

"I understand. How did it go?"

"Okay, I guess. It was one of those getting-to-know-you kind of meetings, to sort of break the ice before to-morrow. That's when I start the interview process, by shadowing him and asking him questions."

"Well, the reason I called is because I'd like to invite you to dinner. Jonas is looking forward to meeting you. Is Tuesday okay?"

"Yes. What time?"

"How about six?"

"Six is fine. I'll just need the address. I have a rental car with GPS, so I shouldn't get lost."

Delphine and Nikki talked for another ten minutes, then ended the call. Getting up from the wingback chair, Delphine glanced over at the clock on the nightstand next to the bed. It was past ten already. She would get a good night's sleep and be ready to meet with Gannon again tomorrow.

And she couldn't deny she was eager to see him again.

Gannon entered his condo, went straight to the bar and poured a shot of brandy. He needed it. Being in Del-phine Ryland's company had challenged his libido to no end. Each and every time she licked her lips, his erec-tion would throb. And when she'd excused herself to go to the ladies' room, his gaze, along with several other men's gazes in the restaurant, had followed that perfect walk, that good-looking ass and those legs in stilettos.

He was glad that by the time they'd been ready to leave the restaurant, he had regained a semblance of control. Otherwise, she would have known the effect she had on him. Hell, anyone who'd seen him would have known and that would not have been good.

Gannon put down the shot glass and rubbed his hand down his face. The last thing he needed right now was for any one woman to hold his interest the way Delphine Ryland was doing. Like his brothers before him, he enjoyed women. He relished one-night stands. What he didn't do was allow his thoughts to linger on any one woman, like they were doing now. What was it about Delphine that affected him like this?

He had looked forward to the day when his five brothers would no longer be competition. And that time was now. He could have any woman he desired without wondering if she was using him to work her way up to one of his brothers. Of course, the Steele brothers never, ever shared women. But that didn't stop some women from trying.

Gannon figured the reason he was so taken with Delphine tonight was because he hadn't expected her to be so gorgeous. In all honesty, he wasn't sure just what he'd expected, but it hadn't been to gaze into her eyes, and then shift his gaze to her lips, and feel such an intense attraction—one that he had to work to control. Being attracted to a woman was nothing new, but there was something about his fascination with Delphine Ryland that was different. He just couldn't put a finger on what that difference was.

Gannon hoped like hell that his imagination was merely running wild at the thought that with all his brothers off the market, he was the last one standing. In fact, he couldn't wait until he visited his cousins in Charlotte over the summer to check out all the beautiful women there.

Feeling better that his mind was back on track, and his libido in check, he headed toward his bedroom to call it a night, certain that when he saw Delphine Ryland in the morning, he would be his old self again.

Two

"Well, Delphine, what do you think so far?" Gannon asked, as if he really wanted her opinion.

To say she was impressed was an understatement. She had arrived on the Steele Trucking Company lot at eight, determined to get there early, only to discover he'd already arrived. Not only was he there, but he had also gotten her through the security process in what she figured to be half the time, probably quicker than that.

He had given her a tour of his office before they'd taken a short walk to the company's cafeteria, where everyone was served a complimentary hot breakfast before the start of the day. He had introduced her to the cooks, the husband-and-wife team of Ms. Pearl and Mr. Sam. They were excellent at their jobs and breakfast had been to die for.

Before returning to his office, via a golf cart, he had taken her on a short ride around the lot to a huge mechanic shop where repairs were done. Then there was the terminal garage, where it seemed as if over a thousand or so trailers were stored. He had explained that some of their shippers used their own trailers and some did not. Then there was another huge lot where the cabs were parked. He said he would continue the tour after their next meeting.

She switched her mind back to his question. "So far, I think everything is overwhelming. The next time I pass a tractor trailer on the interstate, I will do so with a lot more respect."

And she meant it. She hadn't realized just how tightly the trucking industry was regulated. She would admit a lot of the laws were to protect both the truckers and regular drivers on the road. But there were some that were all political, and they varied from state to state. That meant the truckers needed to know the rules and laws of several states.

Gannon smiled. "Good answer. Now how about lunch?"

She rubbed her stomach and laughed. "Are you kidding me? Who can eat lunch after a breakfast like the one we had this morning?"

"I can. Remember what I told you yesterday. My mom claims I'm still growing."

Either that or he had a high metabolism. He also had a fantastic-looking body. All muscle and no fat. It was obvious he also used the gym he had installed on the premises for his truckers. She would admit to seeing quite a few nice-looking male bodies walking around. That dispelled the myth that most truckers had beer bellies. At least, not on Gannon Steele's watch. When she asked him about the state-of-the-art gym, he told her it was important to keep his drivers healthy.

Another thing she'd discovered was that there were quite a few female drivers. Gannon told her that he was constantly looking for ways to accommodate their needs while on the road. He also employed a number of team drivers that included husbands and wives.

When he asked her again to join him for lunch, she agreed, figuring it would give her a chance to ask him more questions. By the time they'd left the lot to go to a café a few miles away, she had pretty much covered everything on her list for today. She would use the rest of the day to shadow him.

It was obvious that, for a man of thirty-three, he was well respected by the people who worked for him, both young and old. "Has it always been this way, Gannon?"

He glanced over at her when he parked the car. "Has it always been what way?"

"Your employees. They like you a lot. Was it easy taking over for your dad?"

He shook his head and laughed. "Heck, no. Those who worked here twenty years or more thought Dad walked on water and didn't like him turning the company over to his wet-behind-the-ears son. You wouldn't believe the rumors that went around even before I took over. Some believed I would fire everyone over fifty, or that I would merge with another company, and some even thought they would come in the day after Dad retired to find I had shut down the place and hired all new people."

She nodded. "How did you win them over?"

"By being myself and giving them a chance to tell me how they felt. I also included them in my focus groups. I convinced them I was here to make the company better and not to get rid of it. I persuaded them to trust me and believe in me just like they had with Dad, because, after all, I was his son."

"That worked?"

"It worked."

When he opened the car door for her, they walked side by side toward the entrance of the café. They were about to enter the building when a very attractive woman came out. The moment she saw Gannon, she threw herself into his arms, nearly knocking Delphine out of the way in the process.

"Gannon! It's so good seeing you. I missed you at the ball game this weekend."

He politely removed the woman's arms from around his neck. "Hey, Trish. Mercury got married this weekend."

"Oh, yeah, that's right." That was when the woman turned to Delphine. "Oh, hi."

"Hello." Delphine returned the greeting, ignoring the woman's daggered expression. Delphine had seen such looks before, mainly from Liddell's wife, Agatha, whenever Delphine would run into them at the grocery store. It amazed Delphine that the woman could even think she'd ever want Liddell back after the way he'd humiliated her by calling off their wedding.

"Trish, I'd like you to meet Delphine," Gannon said.

The woman's eyes narrowed. "You're new to town?"

Delphine was tempted to tell Trish to pull back her claws because she had no designs on Gannon. In fact, she was surprised during the introduction that Gannon hadn't explained the nature of their relationship and let the woman know it was strictly business and nothing more.

Delphine was curious about something. If there was as much to the woman's relationship with Gannon as this Trish evidently wanted Delphine to assume, then why hadn't Trish been invited to his brother's wedding? Delphine quickly concluded that Trish was just one of a number of women who were vying for a top spot on Gannon's "keepers" list.

"I'm in town for only a short while," Delphine said.

"Oh? Did you come for the wedding?" Trish asked.

Before Delphine could answer, Gannon said, "That's none of your business, Trish. Now if you don't mind, Delphine and I would like to enjoy lunch."

Without waiting to see if Trish minded or not, Gannon took Delphine's hand, opened the café's door and escorted her inside. He glanced around, and when he spotted a vacant table in the back, still holding firmly to her hand, he led her to it.

"Gannon?"

He looked over at her. "Yes?"

"Maybe sharing lunch isn't a good idea."

He lifted an eyebrow. "Why?"

"I don't want to cause problems for you with anyone." Namely, she didn't want to cause problems with him and that woman named Trish.

"You're not causing any problems, trust me," he said, pulling out a chair for her. Before taking his own seat, he handed her a menu out of the rack on the table. "There's an assortment of great choices here."

She figured he meant it to be the end of that discussion when he added, "You're going to love their ribs."

Did the man honestly have room in that flat stomach for ribs? As he had yesterday, he was wearing a pair of slacks and a dress shirt. Also, like yesterday, the moment she'd seen him her nerves had jumped into overdrive, and had made goose bumps form on her arms. He definitely had an effect on women, and whenever he would level those green eyes on her, she wanted to melt right on the spot.

"I'll just have a salad. A small one."

He shrugged. "Just wait until you see my plate. I bet you'll ask to try one."

Instead of saying whether she would or wouldn't, Delphine glanced around. The place was crowded with the lunchtime crowd. She looked at the table next to theirs, where a waitress was delivering a plate of ribs to the couple sitting there. She leaned across the table and asked Gannon, "That plate of ribs is for two, right?"

He followed her gaze and a soft chuckle escaped his lips. "No, it's for one."

The ribs, oozing with barbecue sauce, were stacked so high on the plate that they nearly covered all the French fries and hush puppies. "Please don't tell me you plan to order something the size of that one."

He chuckled again. "Okay, I won't tell you. But before you have a panic attack, I'll level with you. I'll only eat some of it here. The rest goes home with me for dinner."

Delphine thought that made sense, but still…eating that many ribs in one day couldn't be healthy. She decided to keep those thoughts to herself.

The waitress came to take their order. Gannon ordered the rib plate and Delphine ordered a small salad. When the woman walked off, he said, "I need to apologize for Trish's rudeness."

She shrugged. "You think she was rude?"

"Don't you?"

She shrugged again. "She's just a woman who wanted to mark her territory."

"She has no territory when it comes to me. No woman has. I don't operate that way."

She wondered what way he operated, and then decided it wasn't any of her business. She was a journalist who'd been sent here to do an exclusive interview with him and nothing more. What he did in his spare time didn't concern her. But still, she couldn't help but wonder if he was one of those men like Liddell, who didn't give a crap when it came to breaking a woman's heart because they truly didn't value the concept of what a serious relationship was about.

She'd known her mother had never liked Liddell even when they'd dated in high school. Her mother thought they'd made the right decision in going to separate universities. It had always been Delphine and Liddell's plan to marry as soon as they finished college. He'd even encouraged her to begin planning their wedding when they'd both reached their junior year.

A month before graduation everything had been set. Even the invitations had been sent. They were to marry two weeks after his graduation, since hers was slated a week before his. His parents had even offered them the use of an empty apartment over the garage until they got on their feet. Both their mothers had worked together to make sure their wedding day would be one they would always remember. Then out of the blue, Delphine got the Dear Jane letter, and her world as she'd known it hadn't ever been the same.

"Delphine?"

She looked at Gannon when she heard her name. Had he been talking to her when she'd taken a stroll down memory lane, reliving those memories that still pained her to think about? Their broken engagement had become the talk among those who knew them—neighbors, classmates, friends and church members. It didn't take long for everyone to find out that there would still be a wedding. She just wouldn't be the bride. For her that had been the humiliating part.

She forced herself back to this conversation. "Yes, Gannon?"

"I asked what you plan to do for dinner tonight."

"I'm going to dine in that restaurant in the hotel. I understand the food is good. Then before going to bed I'll enter my interview notes onto my laptop. It will save time for me later."

The waitress arrived with glasses of water. When she left, Delphine glanced over at him to find he'd been staring at her. That wasn't the first time today she'd caught him doing that very thing. In the meeting this morning, when his dispatcher was covering all the things her job entailed, Delphine had felt someone looking at her and had glanced over at him to find his gaze intently on her. Again, she couldn't help but wonder about the woman she resembled who could cause such a reaction from him.

After taking a sip of the water the waitress had placed on the table before leaving, she said, "I understand you're taking a load down to Florida over the weekend. Tell me about it."

Gannon noted Delphine hadn't pulled out that little brown notepad or her cell phone to record. Did that mean she was asking because she was interested? Or had she merely asked about his on-the-road trip to change the subject? And he knew she'd caught him staring at her more than once today. Was she wondering about that? Or was she used to men being mesmerized by her beauty?

Today she was wearing a pair of chocolate-colored slacks and a pretty beige blouse. He'd glanced up this morning and seen her walking across the parking lot toward the main building, where his office was located. A number of his truckers, who were heading out with that day's load, had seen her, as well, and had stopped to watch. Married or not, they could appreciate feminine beauty, so he couldn't rightly blame them for ogling her. She had a confident stride and her outfit revealed what a curvaceous body she had. For a quick moment he had envied whatever man claimed her as his. What a damn lucky bastard.

"Gannon?"

He blinked as he realized that while he'd been sitting there staring at her like a nitwit yet again, she'd been waiting for a response from him. "Sorry, my mind was elsewhere," he said, hoping she would accept that and not question his sanity. "Yes, I have a load of merchandise to deliver to this huge clothing warehouse in Jacksonville, Florida."

"Do you do that often? Get behind the steering wheel of a rig?"

Although she didn't have her notepad or recorder, he could tell she was still in her interviewer mode. He had no problem telling her what she wanted to know. Talking would help him keep his mind on the questions and not on her. "I do it often enough. Not only does it give me a chance to get out of the office, but it also gives me firsthand knowledge of the challenges my drivers face."

"Such as?"

"Regulations, for one. Each state is different and if my drivers cross state lines they need to be aware of that particular state's laws. The Department of Transportation shows no mercy on violators, whether the violations are intentional or not. For instance, to get to Florida I have to travel through Texas, Louisiana, Mississippi and Alabama. Before hitting the road, I need to familiarize myself with their laws."

"Any reason you're doing this particular delivery?"

He nodded. "In addition to all I've said, I have a beach house in Miami Beach. After delivering the load in Jacksonville, I plan to drive to Miami for a short vacation. I figure a week at my beach house will be nice. I love the Atlantic Ocean."

She smiled. "That sounds nice. I've seen the Pacific Ocean, but never the Atlantic."

"It's beautiful."

At that moment the waitress returned with their lunch. They had to move aside some of the condiments to make room for his huge plate of ribs. "Are you sure you don't want to share these with me?"

"Positive. My salad is all I can handle. Besides, you're going to take the leftovers home for dinner, remember?"

He grinned. "Yes, I remember."

At the end of the workday, when Gannon entered his home, he was still remembering. In fact, he was remembering a lot of things. Going straight to the kitchen, he placed the package of leftovers on the counter. He wasn't hungry just now since he had eaten a lot of the meal at lunch…while trying not to openly stare at Delphine with every bite he took.

He had managed to get her to talking again after she'd asked several more interview questions. He had no problem with the interview because he'd never been shy about talking about his work. She had told him about her college days and her first job with that New York publisher. Then she proceeded to tell him about all the interviews she'd done since starting to work for

Simply Irresistible on a full-time basis and how much traveling the interviews entailed.

He had used that as the perfect opening to ask her how the man in her life dealt with her being away from home so often. She had, without preamble or pause, told him that after spending three years taking care of her mother, she'd been ready to include adventure in her life. She'd always wanted to travel, and being an on-the-road journalist for *Simply Irresistible* took care of her wanderlust cravings. With the issue of the man in her life, she stated that she chose not to date and didn't provide a reason why.

Gannon could understand a woman who traveled a lot not engaging in a serious relationship, just like he understood a man like himself who preferred one-night stands. But to say you didn't date at all was a bit much, especially for someone who looked like her.

Unfortunately, he didn't get a chance to ask *why* she chose not to date because he'd had to end their lunch to head back to the office for an important conference call. The call had lasted longer than he'd expected, and by the time it had ended, so had the workday. When he'd asked his administrative assistant about Delphine, he'd been told she had left for the day with a message that she would see him tomorrow.

Yes, he would see her again tomorrow. In fact, it would be her final day with him. In a way, that was good, since he wasn't sure how much longer he could control himself when in such close proximity. And he still had that fascination with her lips. Each and every time she'd smiled at him today, he'd thought of all the things he would love doing to her mouth.

He was about to leave the kitchen when his phone rang. Checking caller ID, he saw it was his sister-in-law Nikki. He picked up and said, "Yes, Nikki, what's going on?"

"Not much. I'll be glad when the morning-sickness part of my pregnancy is over, though."

"I bet you will be." Jonas had mentioned how bad Nikki was feeling in the mornings.

"The reason I'm calling is that I invited Delphine to dinner tomorrow night and thought that since it's her last day here, you'd like to come, as well."

He leaned back against the counter, thinking that he'd spent the better part of the day with Delphine Ryland and she hadn't mentioned anything about dinner at Nikki's tomorrow. But then, it wasn't as if he needed to be privy to her every move.

Blowing out a deep breath, he knew what his answer would be. What it *had* to be. It was bad enough not acting like himself around her while being interviewed, but the last thing he needed was for that behavior to extend past his work hours. There had not been a single moment in her presence today that his entire body hadn't been on high alert.

"Thanks for the invite but I have something planned already," he said.

"You sure?" she jokingly asked. "I've never known you to turn down a meal."

He smiled. His family knew of his hearty appetite. "I'm positive."

"Okay. If you change your mind, just drop by. As always, there will be plenty."

"Thanks, Nikki."

Delphine stepped out of the shower to dry off, thinking the interview with Gannon that day had gone well. In her line of work, she'd discovered that some people, when being interviewed, placed a high importance on themselves. She categorized those as the "me" people. It was all about them and they didn't believe in giving credit to anyone. Then there were others, like Gannon, who preferred acknowledging everyone but themselves.

It was easy to see that Gannon admired his father and credited him with not only starting the business, but also working hard to make it into a financial empire to pass on to his sons. Gannon had shared with her that, initially, Drew Steele had assumed all six of his sons would one day work the family business. When it became apparent that five had other plans, he was grateful when his youngest son had shown interest.

According to Gannon, his love of tractor trailers began at an early age. One year, Drew Steele needed to deliver a load of supplies to Texas on his birthday. A young Gannon had been determined not to let his father be alone on his birthday and had done what his mother had done years ago—stowed away on his father's truck. By the time his father had found him it had been too late to return him home, so Gannon had continued the route to Texas with his father and had the time of his life. From that day on, Gannon had looked forward to summers when he could take road trips with his father.

When the time came for college, Gannon made the decision to attend a university in Phoenix to be available to help out his father on the weekends. No one was surprised that Gannon had majored in transportation management and logistics and later acquired an MBA.

She could just envision a twelve-year-old Gannon hiding in the back of his father's truck just to make sure his father wasn't alone on his birthday. He'd told her birthdays were important to him. As a result, he implemented a policy at the company where no one worked on their birthday. They got it off with pay. Now she understood why the Steele Trucking Company was such a sought-after employer.

She also understood why Gannon Steele was a sought-after man with the ladies. Trish hadn't been the only woman vying for his attention at the café. Others had stopped by their table just to tell him hello. Several times his phone had rung, and without answering it, he would press the decline button.

Being around him for the past two days had reminded her that she was a woman who could appreciate a sexy man when she saw one, and he was definitely sexy. While being her mother's caretaker, she'd pretty much lived a secluded life. Lucia and her mother had tried encouraging Delphine to get out and enjoy life, and they would volunteer to look after her mother while she did so. She soon discovered that most of the single guys in town preferred not hooking up with a woman who had a sick mother; very few men asked her out. However, she would be the first to admit she hadn't often made herself available to be asked.

After her mother died, that was when the guys began calling. First they'd give her their condolences, and then in the next breath they'd offer to help her get over her loss. Most tried convincing her that a night in their bed would do it. She had no problem letting them know she wasn't interested. And she'd even told a few to lose her number.

She wondered what Gannon had thought when she'd told him she was not dating. Had he assumed constant traveling was the reason, or did he think there was more to it than that? There was no way for him to know that, thanks to a man name Liddell Bartley, she was a woman who was scared of giving a man her heart again.

She tried pushing thoughts of Liddell from her mind, and instead, she thought about her beautiful, sweet mother. Till the end, June Ryland had been concerned about her only child. Delphine had known her mother assumed the reason Delphine had refused to date was because she hadn't gotten over Liddell. June hadn't been happy with the idea of that. Her mother had wanted Delphine to move on with her life, find someone to make her happy so she wouldn't be alone. Delphine hadn't been able to convince her mother that being alone worked well for her. Even now, she could recall the last coherent conversation the two of them had. She would never forget how her mother had pleaded with her not to let Liddell win by never loving again. Breaking one's heart did not necessarily mean destroying it. June believed there was a man out there worthy of her daughter's love, and that when she found him, that man would give Delphine unconditional devotion and be true to her. Only her.

Delphine had not spoken to her mother about the skepticism she'd felt. Nor had she pointed out that her mother was asking her to believe in something that June hadn't believed in for herself. Her mother had been a beautiful woman, yet when Theodore Ryland up and left her for someone else, she hadn't picked up the pieces of her life and moved on. At no time had Delphine recalled her mother going out on a date. Instead, her mother became part of singles group at church, preferring group activities.

Deciding to think of other things after slipping into her gown, she turned her thoughts back to Gannon. Things were different with Gannon compared to other interviews she'd conducted. He didn't act as if she was a bother, or like this was free publicity and nothing more. At no time had he made her feel that she was disrupting his day, or that her questions had been intrusive. That had definitely made things less stressful for her and more relaxing.

Tomorrow was her last day with him and she was beginning to feel a sense of... She wasn't sure what. She was certain these mixed emotions were due to the fact that Gannon had never made her feel like he was the superior being and she the lowly person sent to interview him. Instead, he had taken her out to dinner, shared breakfast with her this morning and taken her to what he said was his favorite place for lunch.

Not feeling the least bit sleepy, she moved across the room to sit on the love seat and grabbed the remote off the table before folding her legs beneath her in a comfortable position. All during her shower she had thought about Gannon. It was unusual for her to think about any man. But how could she not think of him, when he was so good-looking? But she knew his good looks were just part of what made Gannon Steele an irresistible man, worthy of gracing the magazine's cover.

She was about to find a news channel to watch when her cell phone rang. Leaning over, she picked it up off the table. Her heart began beating fast when she saw the caller was Gannon.

"Gannon?" she said, after clicking on.

"Delphine, I'm sorry to bother you. I know we're supposed to meet in my office first thing in the morning, but I just got a call from one of my shippers and I need to go meet with them. I should be at the office around ten. I look forward to seeing you then."

He looked forward to seeing her then? Although she

was certain he hadn't meant for his comment to be anything but professional, for just a quick second she pretended it wasn't. That he did look forward to seeing her and that his response didn't have anything to do with the interview. That was stupid for her to even pretend because *everything* had to do with the interview. That was the reason she was here and she must not lose sight of that.

She wished she could respond by saying that she looked forward to seeing him, as well, but she knew saying such a thing would not be appropriate. She figured the reason she was acting so unlike herself was because this was the most time she'd spent in a man's presence for nearly five years. Five years alone was beginning to take its toll, especially when being around a hottie like Gannon.

"Okay, Gannon, I will see you tomorrow."

When she ended the call, she reminded herself that after tomorrow, the chances were she wouldn't be seeing Gannon again. She would have to be content with the photos of him.

Three

Gannon listened to what the owner of Murdock Mart was saying, and he had to agree that the man's concerns were legitimate. For the past two months one of Gannon's trucks was routinely late to its destination. This wasn't the first time Gannon had received complaints about Lester Oakwood. The driver had been placed on probation twice and had been counseled several times. Gannon knew he couldn't put off any longer what needed to be done. He could not give Oakwood any more chances.

A divorce last year had nearly ruined the man's life and he hadn't gotten over it. Instead, he was spending way too much time at the truck stops and Gannon knew why. He'd gotten reports on that, as well. "Thanks for bringing it to my attention, Mr. Murdock. I will take care of it."

The older man nodded. "I know you will, son. And

I know you hate to do so. Oakwood has been around a long time. He started years ago with your daddy. One of his first drivers."

And that was why Gannon figured the man should probably want to go ahead and retire. However, Gannon was aware that the man's wife had left him in a financial bind when she'd wiped clean his bank account. Then she'd broken Oakwood's heart because the two had been married over thirty years and she'd left him for another man.

Anticipating what this morning's meeting with Murdock would be about, Gannon had already spoken with his father for advice. Drew had left the decision to Gannon as to how to handle it. Oakwood would be turning sixty-seven this year and was eligible for a darn good pension, but Gannon knew the man needed more than that. Driving trucks was Oakwood's life and had been for close to fifty years.

Not wanting to think about what he had to do when he returned to the office, Gannon instead thought about the person he would see when he got there. Delphine. There had been no reason for him to call her last night to tell her about the change in plans for this morning. His secretary could have given her the information when Delphine arrived at the office this morning. But for some reason, he had wanted to hear her voice one last time before going to bed.

He wasn't sure that had been a good thing because after hearing it, he hadn't been able to go to sleep. Instead, he had thought about, or rather fantasized about, Delphine the rest of the night. He thought back to how she'd looked at dinner Sunday night in that killer dress and how she'd looked yesterday in her slacks and blouse. He'd even gone further and imagined how she would look in a pair of Daisy Dukes, or just a bra and a pair of panties, and then with nothing at all. In other words, he'd imagined her as naked as the day she'd been born. Those fantasies had been what put him to sleep, although for the life of him he couldn't remember when he had finally dozed off.

It honestly didn't matter. What did matter was that whatever was happening to him because of Delphine had to stop. After tomorrow, she would be gone and there would be no reason for their paths to ever cross again…unless he decided to visit with his friends the Westmorelands. But just because he visited Denver didn't mean he would run into her. Denver was a big city and the Westmorelands had their own area on the outskirts of the town known as Westmoreland Country. To see her, he would have to intentionally look her up.

He shook his head, deciding not to be taken in by a beautiful face, a gorgeous body and a pair of lips that hit him hard whenever he thought about them. He wasn't supposed to be so attracted to her. So why was he? Maybe it was just a phase he was going through, because his five brothers were now happily married. The last thing he should be doing was feeling curious as to whether there was a perfect woman out there somewhere for him. It was too soon. He had ten years to worry about such a thing. So why on earth was he wondering if perhaps that woman could be Delphine?

Not liking the way his thoughts were going, he decided to call and talk to the one brother who'd always kept it real—Eli Steele. Although Gannon hadn't imagined any of his brothers getting married before forty, Eli had been the biggest shocker. Namely because Eli had been the one most resistant to the idea of wedded bliss. However, he'd ended up being the second one to succumb to love when he'd married Stacey.

Pressing the button on his car's steering wheel, Gannon instructed, "Call Eli Steele."

Moments later his brother's voice came on the line. "What do you want, kid?"

Gannon shook his head. It used to annoy him whenever his brothers would call him that. He soon decided not to let it bother him. He was the youngest, and he figured no matter how old he got, his five older brothers would see him as the kid.

"When did you know you had a thing for Stacey?" Gannon decided to come right out with his question. There was no reason to beat around the bush. Besides, the attorney in Eli wouldn't let Gannon do such a thing, anyway.

There was hesitation on his brother's end of the phone. Then Eli asked, "Why do you want to know?" The attorney in Eli also often drove him to counter-question.

"Just answer, Eli."

Gannon could picture his brother rubbing his chin, trying to decide what to tell him and how much. "It wasn't love at first sight."

"I didn't say it was," Gannon responded.

Eli chuckled. "Stacey grew on me. Remember, she was Cohen's sister and I was in no hurry to get my ass kicked. We had womanizing reputations and Cohen was overprotective."

Cohen was their brother Tyson's best friend, so Gannon definitely understood the ass-kicking part. "How long did it take for her to grow on you?"

"Growth started from day one. I detected it but couldn't do a damn thing about it. I knew I was in big trouble when my desire for other women began fading. In fact, it started fading the moment I met Stacey."

Gannon didn't say anything. Had his desire for other women dwindled away? It'd only been two days, but he'd gone longer without thinking about women, if he was busy enough. He didn't need to be in a woman's bed every night. But he would admit that when he'd seen Trish yesterday, he hadn't felt anything but annoyance. And Trish had made it to his "keepers" list—the women he slept with more than once or twice.

Over the years, only three women had made the cut, and Trish knew she was one of them. Delphine had picked up on Trish trying to be territorial, so maybe it was time Trish was removed from his list. However, as it related to what Eli had said, Gannon hadn't desired another woman since meeting Delphine. No other woman had even crossed his mind.

"Whether you tell me why you're asking these questions doesn't matter. The fact that you are means something."

Gannon frowned. "Means what?"

"You've met a woman who has undoubtedly blown your mind."

Gannon's jaw twitched. He didn't like what his brother said. "I wouldn't go that far."

"I would. One thing I discovered in talking to Galen, Tyson, Jonas and Mercury is that we should have suspected something was up. We should have known our wives were our soul mates when we began doing things we didn't normally do. We definitely should have been forewarned when we treated them differently from the way we'd treated other women. We didn't pick up on the changes right away, but when we did, we were smart enough to know what to do to seal our fates. The last thing you want is to lose the one woman who is meant for you."

Frustration swept through Gannon. He'd heard enough. "I'll talk to you later, Eli."

"So when will we get to meet her?"

Gannon lifted an eyebrow. "Who?"

"The woman who got you calling me in the middle of the day asking questions," Eli said, sounding amused, which only frustrated Gannon even more.

"There's no such woman."

"If you say so. When you discover there is, let me know. I can't wait to meet the woman who made you rethink your ten-year plan. Goodbye."

Gannon cursed under his breath. Eli was crazy. There was no woman alive who could make him do that. Not a single one.

"Mr. Steele has arrived, Ms. Ryland, and he's ready to see you."

Delphine smiled over at Gannon's secretary, not sure if she was ready to see him. "Thanks."

In reality, she'd already seen him. From where she sat in the lobby, she had a good view of the parking lot. She had known the exact moment Gannon had parked his car in his designated CEO spot, and later entered the building through a side door.

She had sat there fascinated by seeing him wearing a dark suit and could barely keep her heart from racing. The man looked good no matter what he wore. Drawing in a deep breath, she stood and headed down the long corridor to his office. When she reached the closed door bearing his name in huge print, she inhaled and then exhaled before knocking.

"Come in, Ms. Ryland."

He'd called her "Ms. Ryland" instead of "Delphine." Did that mean they were back to being formal again? Was that how it was supposed to work when he was in more businesslike attire? she wondered. She would find out soon enough and decided to follow his lead.

When she opened the door, their gazes connected. For a second, Delphine felt weak in the knees. He stood when she walked in and she immediately noticed that he had removed his jacket and loosened the tie around his neck. And, of course, she didn't miss the one button at the top of his white dress shirt that was undone. Why did seeing him so relaxed have an effect on her?

But then, she could say the same for him. He was staring at her the same way she was staring at him. She knew she was fully dressed and the last time she checked her hair was in place. What was going on here?

She knew the answer. Lust. Something she definitely wasn't used to. It was kicking both their butts. Lustful vibes had been strong yesterday, but they were even stronger today.

That wasn't good. Whenever he looked at her, she got overheated. Today his look was almost setting her on fire. This was her last day and she needed to take control of the situation or burn to a crisp right in front of him.

Clearing her throat, she said, "I hope things went well at the meeting you had this morning with your shipper."

As if the sound of her voice broke whatever spell he'd been in, he blinked and then said, "Yes, they did." Then, shoving his hands into his pockets, he added, "However, there's a matter I need to handle."

She nodded. "I understand. I can come back—"

"No. Let's wrap things up with the interview now because I'll be busy for the rest of the day."

Was that his way of letting her know he was tired of this process? Tired of her doing the interview? More than anything, she wanted to believe his change in attitude had nothing to do with her, but was connected somehow to that meeting he'd had earlier.

"I'll be quick," she said, taking the chair in front of his desk. The same one she'd sat in yesterday. "I just have a few more questions."

"Fine," he said, moving to sit down at his desk. "Ask away."

While fighting to keep his concentration on the questions he was being asked, Gannon noted that Delphine never failed to bring out the sexual beast in him. He tried keeping his focus on her eyes, but his gaze would slip to her lips time and time again. If she'd noticed, she wasn't letting on. In fact, she was acting like the professional in the room. He was the one sitting there getting more aroused by the minute.

And he didn't like it one damn bit.

He didn't like that she had this pull on him. When she had walked into his office, he'd stared at her, trying to get his breathing under control. The mere sight of her had done something to him, made him feel things, want things and need things. She had to have felt the sexual tension between them because it had sparked all over the place. She had held his gaze with as much intensity as he'd held hers. At least the attraction wasn't one-sided.

At least, he wanted to believe that it wasn't.

Beginning to feel annoyed again that she could so easily get next to him, he tossed his pen on the desk.

"Are you about through with your questions?" He'd thought she'd said she only had a few. Well, she'd asked more than that. It wasn't the questions that annoyed him since they were typical interview questions—it was just the fact that she was the one asking them. He wanted to do more with their time together than answering questions. He didn't like that she was ignoring what he knew was going on between them, when he was about ready to climb the walls.

"I can end the questions now if you'd like."

It was on the tip of his tongue to tell her exactly what he would like—first would be her sitting in his lap; then he'd taste her delectable-looking lips. "No, you can finish your questions."

The only reason he told her that was because he knew that when she asked the final question, there would be no reason for her to hang around. He knew from Lucia and Chloe that she wasn't leaving town until Thursday, but asking the last question would truly be the end for them. Unless he made a special attempt to do so, he wouldn't be seeing her again. He wasn't ready for that to happen. So when she asked two more questions, he took his time answering, in an attempt to keep her there a little longer.

"Well, that's it, Mr. Steele," she said, standing.

He wished his gaze hadn't followed the movement, but it had. His breath hitched at the way her hair fell to her shoulders. The perfect fit of her breasts against her blouse.

Damn, he had it bad.

"Why are you calling me 'Mr. Steele'?"

She then had the nerve to shrug her shoulders—shoulders she'd bared with the dress she'd worn Sunday. Shoulders he knew were sexy as hell. "I was just following your lead," she said.

He lifted an eyebrow. "My lead?"

"Yes. When I knocked on the door you addressed me as 'Ms. Ryland.' I figured that meant we were no longer on a first-name basis. I thought that's what you wanted."

Had he called her that? He didn't remember if he had and he certainly hadn't meant to change anything between them…although there really wasn't anything between them. He forced his gaze to lock on her eyes and not drift to her lips. "Then I apologize. That's not what I wanted."

Now was a good time to tell her exactly what he wanted. But he couldn't when he didn't know what he wanted himself. Other than to kiss her, and he knew that was a line he dared not cross. No telling what might happen if he did. He'd never been addicted to any woman, but he could see himself becoming addicted to her.

"Thanks for everything, Gannon," she said, extending her hand out to him. "You've been nothing but kind and I appreciate it."

Gannon stood and took her hand in his. Immediately he felt a flare of response in his chest. He figured it was twofold. One for wanting her as much as he did, and the other for knowing when she walked out his door that it was done.

Did she realize they were standing there staring at each other like two people who knew what they had to do but didn't want to do it? He knew he should drop his gaze from hers and release her hand, but he couldn't. Not now.

The sound of a door slamming somewhere in the building made them jump, and he immediately released her hand. Too late. If she hadn't noticed anything ooz-ing between them before, there was no way she could ignore it now. The heat of touching her was still evi-dent in his hand.

"I have to go," she said as she backed up a few steps, then turned around to quickly head for the door.

"I'll walk you to your car."

She stopped and turned back to him. She shook her head. "No, you don't have to. Besides, I need to say goodbye to a few people before I leave."

"Oh, I see."

He felt warmth spread through his body as he watched her head for the door. When she reached it, he willed her to turn and look at him one last time. She didn't. He watched her open the door, quickly step out and slide the door closed behind her.

Delphine entered her hotel room with her heart still pounding in her chest. What had happened in Gannon's office? She might not have dated in over five years, but she could detect attraction...couldn't she? Had it been there all the time and she'd just picked up on it? Or was her mind playing tricks on her?

After placing her purse on the table, she slid into the wing chair. She needed to think, something she hadn't been able to do on the drive from Gannon's company. Her mind stayed stuck on that handshake. She had felt something. If she was totally honest with herself, she had felt something as soon as she'd entered his office. Things seemed to skyrocket from the moment their gazes locked.

Never in her twenty-five years had she felt desire claw at her the way it had done today. Gannon's large hand had encircled her wrist and held on tight, yet it had felt gentle. Intense heat had spread through her like butter melting on bread. Standing, she checked her watch. She would be dining with Nikki and her husband tonight, and since she'd ended her interview early with Gannon, she had time for a nap before leaving.

She was about to head toward the bathroom to strip down to her bra and panties when her cell phone rang. Recognizing the ringtone, she quickly picked up the call. "Hey, Mandy, what's up?"

"You might want to extend your time away from Denver for another week, girlfriend."

Delphine lifted an eyebrow. "Why?"

"The company doing your floors suspects asbestos."

"Oh, great," Delphine said, a little agitated, although she knew she really shouldn't be. After all, she did have an older home. "What's next?"

"A building inspector will be coming out today to obtain samples, and it will be a couple of days before the results are known. In the meantime, all the work on the floors must stop until we know the results. If asbestos is found, then it will be removed. I got this, and there's nothing you can do for now. If you return home, you won't be able to stay in your house, so you might as well enjoy yourself in Phoenix for another week."

Delphine knew that was easier said than done, especially if it meant running into Gannon while she was here. Even though he worked close by, there was no reason she would run into him when he lived on the other side of town. "Not sure my staying in Phoenix is a good idea."

"Why not?"

Delphine nibbled on her bottom lip, not ready to share any of the details about her confusion over Gannon with anyone, even her best friend. And she *was* confused. She had felt something toward Gannon that she hadn't felt for a man in years. And the depth of her attraction to him was confusing.

"I was ready to come home."

"Why?"

She knew why her best friend was asking. With her mother gone, there was nothing in Denver for Delphine to rush back home to. It wasn't like she had a boyfriend, and she knew if she asked, *Simply Irresistible* would give her any time off she needed, since over the past year she hadn't taken any of her vacation days. "I just was."

"I thought you wanted to do as much traveling as you could."

"I do."

"Then do it, Del. If you don't want to stay in Phoenix, then you can really be adventurous and make the drive from Phoenix to Vegas. You'll get to travel through the desert and Navajo land."

"I'll think about it. Either way, I won't come home Thursday as planned after all."

"Fine, just let me know. And like I said, don't worry about things here—I've got this."

"So, there you have it, Dad," Gannon said. "I was able to talk Lester Oakwood into retiring."

Drew Steele nodded. "I'm glad. Had he been fired, which you had every right to do, considering Lester's work habits lately, he would have lost all his benefits and his pension. I'm glad Lester did what you suggested."

"I'm glad, too. I think that deep down he knows he's messed up more than a few times and there was no way I could give him any more chances."

Gannon had come straight here when the office closed. Although his father had retired, Gannon still consulted with him whenever he needed advice. As far as he was concerned, nothing could top Andrew Steele's experience and expertise.

He glanced around. "Where's Mom?"

"Out shopping with friends. I expect her back any minute so we can go out to dinner. By the way, how did your interview go this week?"

His father bringing up the interview made Gannon think about Delphine. Not that he hadn't been thinking about her anyway. Although he knew it was for the best, considering how attracted he was to her, it still bothered him that he wouldn't be seeing her again. Unless...

He shook his head, refusing to go there, namely Jonas and Nikki's place. Gannon knew Delphine was joining them for dinner tonight. He'd been invited but had turned down Nikki's invitation. At the time he'd figured it was for the best. But now...

"Gannon?"

He glanced at his dad. "Yes?"

"I asked how the interview with that magazine reporter went this week. I guess your mind was a thousand miles away."

He wished it *was* a thousand miles away, but it was right here in Phoenix and on a certain woman. "The interview went fine. We finished up today."

"I was hoping we'd get to meet her," Drew said.

"Who?"

"The woman who interviewed you."

Gannon studied his father, then asked, "Delphine Ryland? Why would you have wanted to meet her?"

"No special reason other than she interviewed you and you seem quite taken with her."

His father's words surprised Gannon. "What makes you think I was quite taken with her?" He knew for a fact he hadn't mentioned one thing about Delphine to his parents, or any of his brothers except Eli. And of all his brothers, Eli, being the attorney and used to confidentiality, was the one who could be depended upon to keep his lips sealed. And Gannon figured Nikki had no reason to suspect anything.

"The obvious."

The obvious? "Which was?" he asked.

"You mentioned to me and your mom on Sunday that you felt bad about not returning her calls and that you intended to invite her out to dinner as a way to atone, and to get to know her before the interviews began yesterday."

"Yes, and...?" he prompted, certain there was more, but he couldn't figure out what.

"And that's it. I talked to you last night and not once did you mention anything about her or the interview. The only reason we're talking about her now is because I asked."

Gannon stared at his father. Everything he'd said was true, and for any normal person, none of it would mean a thing. But he had to remember he wasn't dealing with just any normal person; he was dealing with Drew Steele, the man who'd been the original Bad News Steele.

In Drew's younger days he'd been so much of a womanizer that he'd been run out of Charlotte by a bunch of women out for blood—namely Drew's. He had fled from North Carolina, where most of the Steele family lived, and made his way to Phoenix. That was where he'd eventually met and fallen in love with Gannon's mother.

"I never talk about any of the women I date," he reminded his father.

"No, but you and Ms. Ryland aren't dating, are you?"

"No."

"In that case, you had no reason not to bring her up. If nothing else, I'd expect you to mention how the interview was going."

Gannon shook his head. There could have been a number of reasons why he hadn't mentioned anything about Delphine to his folks, and none of them would have had to do with his attraction to her.

He was about to say that, but his father's next words stopped him. "I know my sons. More specifically, Gannon, I know you."

Gannon released a deep breath, knowing his father was right. Drew was close to all his sons, so he knew them all well. But when it came to Drew and Gannon, there had always been a special relationship, a tighter-than-normal bond. Gannon was the one who'd worked alongside his father for years at the trucking company. As a teen, he had been his father's traveling partner when Drew would make his deliveries across the country. They had rolled up their sleeves together to tackle problems related to the company. And when he had begun dating, initially it had been his dad who'd answered his questions about girls rather than his brothers.

So, yes, his father did know him. "It's confusing, Dad. I only met her three days ago. Yet…"

"Yet what?" Drew asked.

"She is confusing me."

Drew nodded. "Three days is more than enough time for a woman to confuse a man. However, I'm sure you will eventually figure things out."

In truth, Gannon wasn't sure exactly what he was

supposed to figure out. But just in case his father was alluding to there being more to Gannon and Delphine's relationship than was really there, he said, "I have a ten-year plan."

His dad chuckled. "That's right. You don't intend to settle down for another ten years."

"Right."

Drew leaned back in his chair. "I had a twenty-year plan, and the woman who threw that plan right smack out the window just walked in the door."

Gannon knew whom his father meant when he heard his mother enter the house. Gannon stood, deciding he would leave before Eden Tyson Steele had a chance to grill him about anything. While growing up, he'd discovered his parents often thought alike. "I'm leaving now. However, we'll talk again before I hit the road Friday."

"Okay."

"Gannon. How are you doing, baby?"

He turned at the sound of his mother's voice. While growing up, he'd thought his mother was beautiful. She still was. "Hi, Mom. I'm doing fine. Glad you arrived when you did because I was just about to leave."

Crossing the room, he gave his mother a kiss on the cheek before quickly heading for the door.

Four

"Thanks for inviting me to dinner, Nikki," Delphine said, handing the bottle of wine to her friend and then giving her a hug.

Delphine had met Nikki the first year Delphine had begun working at *Simply Irresistible*. She knew Nikki had started out with Chloe years earlier, when she started the magazine in Florida, as a freelance photographer. When Chloe opened the Phoenix office, Nikki had been the one to do that magazine's inside photos and covers.

Although Delphine had been working remotely, and only part-time, she had written several articles for the magazine, and Nikki had taken the corresponding photos. Her shots were always right on point. After Nikki got married, she did less freelance work for the magazine so she could work more closely with her husband's marketing company.

"No thanks needed and welcome to our home," Nikki said, holding the wine bottle in one hand and hooking arms with Delphine. She led Delphine toward the living room. "And thanks for the wine."

"You're welcome. You have a beautiful home."

"Thanks."

"And congratulations on your pregnancy. I know you and your husband must be very happy."

"Yes, we are," a deep, masculine voice said behind them.

Delphine turned toward the sound then sucked in a deep breath. The smiling man walking toward her resembled Gannon. His green eyes were a dead giveaway that they were brothers. His were the same shape and shade as Gannon's. Both men were also tall, although she figured Gannon was an inch or two taller, but even their build was about the same.

"Delphine, this is my husband, Jonas."

"You favor Gannon," Delphine said, taking the hand the man extended.

Jonas chuckled. "Since I'm older, Gannon favors me. My brothers and I consider ourselves the perfect blend of our parents. The six of us have our mother's green eyes, our skin tone is a combination of the two, and the rest of our features are strictly our father's."

Jonas turned to his wife. "Dinner is ready, sweetheart."

"You cook?" Delphine asked him in surprise.

He gave her a smile that looked identical to Gannon's. "Yes. In our bachelor days, my brother Mercury and I took a cooking class. Every once in a while, I enjoy getting in the kitchen and putting what I learned to good use."

"Let's be honest, Jonas. You like putting it to good use more than every once in a while, and I definitely appreciate it. He's a fantastic cook, Delphine."

"Thanks, gorgeous," he said, leaning over to kiss his wife on the lips.

They seemed to be comfortable being affectionate in front of others. Delphine wasn't used to that. Since there had only been Delphine and her mother living together, the only married couple she'd known well while growing up had been Lucia's parents, the Conyerses. Since the Conyerses had had a long marriage, Delphine figured they were affectionate toward each other without openly displaying that affection, like Nikki and Jonas.

"Since the chef says dinner is ready, I'll take you to where you can wash up."

"All right."

Before they could head that way, the doorbell sounded.

"I'll get that," Jonas said. "That's probably my brother Tyson. He's a doctor and works at the hospital a few blocks away. His wife, Hunter, is out of town, so he's probably just getting off work and figuring he can drop by to get a free meal," Jonas added, heading toward the door.

A few minutes later, after having followed the directions Nikki had given her, Delphine made her way back toward the living room from the bathroom, thinking just how huge this house was. She could sit hers in this one several times. What she liked most were the double spiral staircases and how they joined at the landing.

Delphine walked into the living room and saw Nikki and Jonas talking to a man whose back was to her. She figured it was another Steele brother, the one who was the doctor. When Nikki saw her, she smiled and said, "Look who decided to join us, Delphine."

The man who turned around to face her was Gannon.

* * *

Gannon saw the surprised look on Delphine's face and knew why she'd reacted that way. He hadn't mentioned anything to her about coming here this evening. Hell, he hadn't known that he would come here himself until he'd gotten home and taken a shower. That was when he'd decided to come see what Jonas had cooked for dinner.

Gannon drew in a deep breath. Who was he kidding? Definitely not himself. The reason he'd come here tonight was because he had known Delphine would be here and he had wanted to see her again. He hadn't been ready for the goodbye they'd shared earlier.

"Gannon, I didn't know you were coming," Delphine said.

His gaze roamed over her. She was wearing a pair of jeans and a pretty pink blouse. This was the most casual he'd seen her. But then, she could say the same for him, since he was wearing jeans, too.

Jonas cleared his throat, making Gannon realize he hadn't yet responded to what Delphine had said. "I hadn't planned on coming. When Nikki invited me yesterday, I had already made plans, but those plans changed."

"Well, I'm glad they did," Nikki said, smiling brightly as she hugged her brother-in-law. "Now go wash up and join us in the dining room."

He grinned down at Nikki. "Will do."

Gannon knew where the bathroom was and headed in that direction. He wondered if Delphine had been aware of the way her gaze had bored into him just now. The intensity of it had messed with his senses and made him even more aware of her not just as a woman, but as a woman he wanted. He hoped he hadn't made a mistake in coming here. Nikki might be clueless about his motives, but Jonas wouldn't be. A Steele male understood another Steele male, and there was no doubt in Gannon's mind that his brother had recognized his male interest in Delphine.

At this point, Gannon really didn't care what Jonas did or did not recognize. He was too wound up to care and he honestly didn't know why. That was what he was determined to find out. Mainly, why a woman he'd just met three days ago could have him tied in knots in a way that kept him from pursuing his freedom. And yet he wanted to be free. He wasn't a serious-relationship sort of guy. He didn't want to commit to any woman. He was supposed to be having the time of his life with plenty of them. As long as he was selective and up-front with whatever woman he was with, the sky was the limit.

Then why had he declined six calls already today and four yesterday? What was there about Delphine Ryland that had him not thinking straight or not thinking at all? Knowing he wouldn't find any answers here in the bathroom, he left and headed toward the dining room, where voices could be heard.

"For a minute there I thought you'd gotten lost," Jonas said jokingly as he placed platters on the table.

Gannon didn't say anything as he slid into the seat across from Delphine. He could have taken the seat beside her, but he wanted to look into her beautiful face and study those delectable lips.

"I hope you're hungry, Gannon," Nikki said.

"He's always hungry," Jonas added.

He saw the way Delphine's lips curved into a smile. She wouldn't be so amused if she knew what else he was hungry for. Namely her. He would love to spread her on this table and make her his treat. He would undress them both and then he would spread her legs and sink into her and—

"Gannon!"

He jerked his head in Jonas's direction. "What?"

"I asked if you'd spoken to the folks today."

He wondered why his brother wanted to know. "I talk to them every day."

Jonas laughed. "See, didn't I tell you, Delphine. He's the good son."

Gannon wondered when Jonas had told her that. How much conversation had been going on around him, about him, while he'd been sitting there staring at Delphine, imagining doing all kinds of wicked things to her?

"It's a habit."

"And a good habit," Nikki said, as if coming to his defense. "I think it's wonderful that he talks to them every day."

"Only because he didn't have to worry about Mom drilling him about marriage every time he called. He was the youngest and she started from the top. Mercury and Gannon got reprieves for a while."

Gannon thought Jonas was talking too much, although he didn't mind the ribbing. He heard it on occasion from all his brothers because he was the youngest. He had lived at home the longest and he had a close relationship with his parents. He had no problem talking to them every day and enjoyed doing so. He knew his father liked knowing how well the truckers were doing and his mom liked keeping up with him, period. He knew how much to tell her and how much not to tell her. He and Eden had a system. There was no need for her to put pressure on him because he intended to stick to his ten-year plan regardless.

He was piling mashed potatoes onto his plate when Nikki asked Delphine, "You're still leaving on Thursday?"

He glanced over at Delphine when she nodded. "Yes, but I won't be returning home as planned."

"Where will you be going?" he asked, as if he had every right to know.

"Not sure yet. All I know is I can't go home. I was having work done on my house and the workers found asbestos. The inspector stopped work until it's all removed. There's no reason to return home until that's completed."

"So where will you go?" Jonas asked.

Delphine sighed deeply, then added, "I thought about driving to Vegas from here. I heard it's a scenic drive."

"It is," Nikki said. "But I don't know if you should do it by yourself."

Delphine smiled at Nikki. "I'll be fine."

Although Gannon didn't say anything, he agreed with Nikki. He wasn't sure it was a trip she should take by herself. He recalled her telling him about the work she was having done on her home. He also recalled her telling him about how she enjoyed traveling and wanting a life filled with adventure.

"So how did the interview go?" Jonas asked.

Delphine smiled again. "I thought it went great. Gannon was an intriguing subject."

"Nah, it went well because you're a good interviewer. You made things easy."

She smiled over at him. "I merely asked questions about you that I figured the readers would want to know."

"And like I said, you did an awesome job. You can interview me again anytime, Delphine."

"Thanks, Gannon."

Gannon was about to take a bite of his meat loaf when he glanced over at Jonas and noticed his brother staring at him. He recognized Jonas's look. Whether Gannon wanted it or not, he knew Jonas would be talking to him later. He didn't have to wonder what the conversation would be about.

He found it downright amusing that Jonas, who was once pegged by the society tabloids as being the city's number one womanizer, was giving Gannon the eye. Of course, at one point or another, all of his brothers had worn that title. And none of them had seemed ashamed of it. So why Jonas felt the need to talk to him about anything was beyond Gannon's comprehension. Just like Jonas had once lived the good life while he was single, Gannon felt it was his time to do the same.

During dinner it was hard to keep his eyes off Delphine and, frankly, he didn't care who noticed. He was beyond caring. It was what it was. He was attracted to Delphine and would finally admit that he hadn't desired another woman since meeting her. Granted, it had only been three days, but still, for him to be this into a woman had to mean something. Didn't it? Even if it meant he needed to get laid in a bad way.

The good thing was that there were no longer any business dealings between them. Not that it mattered, since he'd never been one to separate business from pleasure. When opportunity knocked, a man took advantage of it. Just as long as he stayed in control of the situation and both parties understood the limits.

"Dinner is great, Jonas and Nikki. Thanks for inviting me," Delphine said.

"You're welcome," Nikki said, smiling broadly.

"And I ditto what Delphine said. Thanks for having me over, guys," Gannon added.

"You know you're welcome anytime, Gannon," Nikki said.

"Yeah, Gannon, with you around we never have to worry about leftovers," Jonas said, chuckling.

Gannon grinned and glanced over at Delphine. She was grinning, as well. She knew about his voracious appetite. At least, she knew about one of his appetites. Before she left Phoenix it might be a good idea to introduce her to the other one.

Delphine finished off the last of her dinner while trying to ignore the intensity of Gannon's gaze. His stare was making her feel things she'd never felt before, even with Liddell. They'd been sexually active since their senior year of high school. When they'd gone to separate colleges, they'd only hooked up when they returned home for the holidays.

Delphine now realized how the infrequency of their lovemaking could have made Liddell an easy target for someone like Agatha…not that it excused his infidelity. Delphine had been faithful to him for those four years while attending the University of Wyoming. Liddell had attended a university on the East Coast and sworn he would be faithful to her, as well. He'd even promised to invite her to visit him in Virginia, saying he would show her the Atlantic Ocean. He never did.

Refusing to think about Liddell's unfaithfulness any longer, she glanced over at Gannon. He was staring at her, and when their gazes connected, she again felt a strong stirring in the pit of her stomach. She quickly broke eye contact and took a sip of her iced tea. She didn't know just how much longer she could handle the feelings she was experiencing around the very handsome and sexy man sitting across the table from her.

Maybe she should head out for Vegas tomorrow instead of Thursday, since there was nothing holding her here. She figured she could use the extra day to begin writing her article on Gannon from her hotel room. A hotel room in Vegas would work just as well as one here. She'd been to Vegas before and wouldn't be lured by the excitement of walking the Strip.

"I hope everyone is ready for dessert," Nikki said, grabbing Delphine's attention. "And it's my contribution to the evening's meal. A key-lime cheesecake."

"That sounds good," Delphine said, smiling over at Nikki.

Again, she thought about how happy Nikki was. Delphine couldn't help but feel a little envious that at one time she'd wanted the same situation for herself—a husband who loved her and to be pregnant with his child.

A short while later, she was pushing herself away from the table. The cake had been delicious. "I'm full," she said, grinning.

"I'm not," Gannon said.

She glanced over at him. She'd noticed his slice had been double the size of hers and he'd eaten all of his dinner. Where did the man put it all and how did he keep his body stacked so nicely? This was the first time she'd seen him in jeans and he looked fine, with the best-shaped tush she'd ever laid eyes on. And then there were those sinewy thighs and firm hips… He could be in a western-wear ad easily.

"Well, I'm glad everyone enjoyed dessert. I couldn't have you think Jonas did all the cooking while I didn't contribute at all," Nikki said, laughing.

Jonas stood. "And this is the part she never volunteers for," he said, smiling over at his wife. "The cleaning up. But that's okay since Gannon is going to help me."

Delphine saw Gannon switch his gaze to his brother. "I am?"

"You are. Seems only fair since you ate most of the food."

"I'm a growing boy, what can I say?" Gannon said, standing and following Jonas's lead as he began clearing off the table.

"If you guys need additional—"

"Don't you dare volunteer for kitchen duty," Nikki interrupted Delphine with a huge grin on her face. "The guys can handle things. Besides, I can't wait to tell you about the decorating plans I have for the baby's nursery."

Gannon helped Jonas load the dishwasher and then tackle the pots. Although he did use his own kitchen on occasion, he never had as many pots and pans to clean as Jonas did whenever he cooked. He recalled when Jonas and Mercury had taken that cooking class. That had been in Jonas's before-Nikki days.

Gannon knew that neither Mercury nor Jonas had really been interested in learning how to cook. Their main interest had been the single women they figured they would meet in the class. For months the two had bragged about all the invitations they'd gotten for free home-cooked meals and no-strings-attached sex.

"What's going on with you and Delphine, Gannon?"

He'd wondered how long it would take for Jonas to get around to asking. His brothers usually had an agreement of don't ask, don't tell. At least, the five oldest ones did. For some reason they hadn't included Gannon in that agreement. Since he was the youngest, they felt it was their God-given right to know what he was doing at all times and with whom. Of course, he never told.

They claimed if they didn't watch out for him, their parents would never forgive them. There were times they seemed to forget that, at thirty-three, he was a grown-ass man who could take care of himself.

"What makes you think something is going on?" he asked, not bothering to glance at his brother while drying another pot.

His brothers always said they could look in his eyes and tell if he was truthful or not. This time it didn't matter. He was being truthful. There was nothing going on between him and Delphine. Had Jonas asked what he would *like* to be going on, then he would have given his brother an entirely different answer.

"I've seen the way you've been looking at her."

Jonas was right—he had been looking at her and hadn't tried hiding it. "So what of it?"

"It can only mean one thing."

He glanced over at Jonas. "What?"

"I've noticed how you stare at other women, but this was different. You want Delphine bad."

Gannon wished his brother would tell him something he didn't already know. "And?"

"I think you need to find out why."

"I already know why. She's a good-looking woman, intelligent and has a nice body. All the things I look for."

"She's also all the things you're not looking for."

Gannon lifted an eyebrow. "Such as?"

"She's a woman a man should consider marrying."

The pan Jonas was handing Gannon nearly slipped from his hand. He had to act quickly to stop it from hitting the floor. "Marrying? Are you crazy? I'm not marrying anyone until after my forty-third birthday."

"Then you should mark Delphine off your to-do list."

After drying the pan and placing it aside, Gannon

leaned against the kitchen counter to stare over at his brother. "You just met Delphine today. What makes you so protective of her?"

"Because she's Nikki's friend and I know her story."

"What story?" Gannon asked.

"The one about how she's been hurt before by a man, and how she spent three years taking care of her sick mother and how she's just getting her feet wet in the dating scene. The last thing she needs is to get entangled with a guy like you, who means her no good."

Gannon crossed his arms over his chest. "By no good, you mean a man who isn't interested in settling down?"

"Yes."

Gannon didn't say anything for a minute and then walked over to the window and glanced out before turning back to his brother. "What did the guy do to hurt her?"

"That's for me to know and for you to find out. If she wants you to know she will tell you."

Gannon frowned, not liking that Jonas was trying to be all secretive, like Eli. "Well, I'm glad you've let me know where her head is. If it's in marriage, then it's definitely not where my head is." Although he would admit that since meeting her he had thought a lot about their heads joining on the same pillow. He guessed that wouldn't be happening now since the word *marriage* had slipped into the mix.

"Can I share something with you, Gannon?"

He wondered why Jonas was even asking. If it was something he wanted to say, Jonas would say it, regardless of whether or not Gannon wanted to hear it. "Go ahead."

"I've watched you with other women and I think there's something about Delphine that has gotten to you."

Gannon shrugged. "And what if it has?"

"Then I think you'd be making a huge mistake if you don't find out why."

"I already know why," Gannon said.

"Do you really? Did I ever tell you that one day Nikki and I shared an innocent kiss? We had gotten caught up in my getting this big deal, and the next thing I knew, we were kissing. Before then, our relationship had been strictly business."

"And?"

"I felt something in that single kiss with Nikki that I'd never felt in a kiss before with a woman. It scared the shit out of me."

Interested in what his brother was saying, Gannon asked, "What did you do?"

"I did what I thought was best for my peace of mind and my survival."

"Which was?"

"To put distance between us. When I left her office that day, I intentionally stayed away from her for eighteen months. A whole damn year and a half, Gannon. I was determined not to let any one woman interfere with the way I wanted to live my life, which was a life that would include plenty of women. For eighteen months I went through other women to get my desire for Nikki out of my system. I had convinced myself that what I'd felt that day while kissing her had been a fluke, and that I would eventually feel the same way if I kissed other women. It never happened."

Jonas didn't say anything for a moment and then added, "I think you owe it to yourself to find out why Delphine gets next to you in a way no other woman can. Otherwise, ten years from now when you're ready to settle down, you might realize the woman intended to be

Mrs. Gannon Steele will have gotten away and married someone else, with kids that should have been yours. And all because of that ten-year plan of yours. Take it from someone who's been out there, doing women and thinking the next will be better than the last, only to discover the woman destined to be mine could have been lost to me forever had I not come to my senses when I did."

A short while later, after he and Jonas joined Nikki and Delphine on the back patio, Gannon wished he could put Jonas's spiel out of his mind, but he couldn't. Hell, his brother had talked about the lasting effect of kissing Nikki, and Gannon hadn't even gotten that close to Delphine. As far as he was concerned, he didn't need to kiss her to wonder what it would do to him if he ever did. Just looking at her lips stirred his guts. If he ever tasted her—sinking his mouth into hers, ravishing her tongue with his, without any restraint or control—he would definitely be a goner.

What Jonas evidently hadn't figured out yet was that Gannon was a step ahead of him. There was a reason he'd shown up unexpectedly here tonight—mainly because the thought of not seeing Delphine again bothered him. That in itself spoke volumes. And now he intended on taking it from there. He wasn't sure *where* he was taking it, but he knew it had to happen within the next twenty-four hours because she was leaving town on Thursday.

He honestly didn't like the thought of her driving from Phoenix to Vegas alone, but he couldn't say that when she was a grown woman who could take care of herself. Hadn't she been doing so for twenty-five years already? And what information did Jonas know about Delphine's ex-boyfriend? What had the bastard done to her? She'd told Gannon she wasn't dating and he had suspected there was more to the story. Now he knew that there was.

When the doorbell sounded, Jonas grinned and said, "I bet that's Tyson. I figured he would drop by, so I packed him a to-go container."

It was Tyson, still wearing his medical attire. He met Delphine and she remarked how much Tyson, Jonas and Gannon looked alike. Tyson stayed to converse for a little while before grabbing his to-go bag and leaving. As he was walking out the door, Tyson gave Gannon a look that indicated they would talk. As far as Gannon was concerned, they didn't have to talk. Since marrying, his brothers had become saints, conveniently forgetting the times when they'd given the name Bad News Steeles special meaning.

"Thanks again for everything, Nikki and Jonas. I really enjoyed myself, and thanks for giving me an extra slice of cake. And it was good seeing you again, Gannon."

He blinked. He had been staring at her the entire time, but he hadn't been keeping up with the conversation between her, Jonas and Nikki. She was standing, clutching the bag he knew contained the slice of cake Nikki had given to her. Did that mean she was leaving?

He stood up, too. "Same here, Delphine, and since I'm leaving, as well, I'll walk you to your car." He knew what he said sounded ridiculous since her car was parked right out front in his brother's circular driveway and not off in a parking lot somewhere.

"You don't have to do that, Gannon," she said, looking at him.

"I want to." He really meant that. "Besides, I want to talk to you about something."

"Oh, okay."

He watched as she gave both Jonas and Nikki hugs, and then they walked her to the door. He followed. After thanking his brother and sister-in-law for dinner, he and Delphine went outside. Although it was still light out, the sun had gone down and dusk was arriving.

"What do you want to talk to me about, Gannon?" she asked, as they walked side by side.

He gazed down at her. "How would you like to see the view of the city from the Black Mountains tonight?"

Five

Not for the first time, Delphine thought the green eyes staring at her were as sexy as sin. She'd gotten so caught up in them that she nearly missed what he'd said. "The Black Mountains? Tonight?"

"Yes, tonight. I figured I could follow you back to the hotel and we can go in my car. There's a small section of the mountains on my brother Galen's property. That's the only way you can get to it, so it's considered private."

Delphine thought about what he was saying. He was basically asking her to go parking with him. She hadn't gone parking with a guy since Liddell in high school and she knew what parking with a guy often entailed. "Why?"

They had reached her rental car and she leaned against it.

"Why what?"

"Why would you want me to go to the Black Mountains with you?"

He smiled and she felt her legs nearly turn to jelly. "I thought you would enjoy the view."

Yeah, right, she thought. But had she really expected him to give her the same answer Liddell would have given her had she asked him why they would be parking up on one of Denver's mountains? Liddell would have told her in five words or less exactly what they would be going up there to do. But then, Liddell had been her boyfriend and they'd been sexually active. Gannon was just a man she'd been sent here to interview for the magazine she worked for. A man she'd only known three days.

Delphine was very much aware that times had changed since her high-school days, but was she ready to drive to an isolated mountain location with someone she barely knew? Did he assume she was open to such a thing now that the business part of their relationship had ended?

"To just enjoy the view?" she asked him, doubting that was all he wanted.

"And I figured it could be a place where we could also talk privately."

She lifted an eyebrow. "Talk privately about what?"

"I'd rather not discuss it here."

Delphine nibbled her bottom lip. Although she hadn't known Gannon long, interviewing him had revealed a lot. Namely, his integrity. She honestly didn't think she had to worry about him taking her up there to the mountain and then forcing her to do anything against her will. Besides, why would he when there were women like Trish just willing and waiting to get into his pants?

Then there was something else she should take into consideration. Could she trust *herself* with him? There was chemistry between them and plenty of it. If there had been any doubt in her mind before tonight, it had been squashed. Every time she'd glanced at him across the table, heat had flooded her insides. Parts of her were even tingling now from him standing so close. What if he kept his hands off her but she couldn't keep her hands off him? What if—

"Will you go, Delphine?"

Tilting her head back, she held his gaze and felt the heat slither through her already hot body. At that moment, her entire body stirred with an emotion that until now had been foreign to her. But she recognized it for what it was. Sexual hunger. She never would have thought she had it in her to feel such intense lust until Gannon.

Hadn't she said that with her newfound independence she wanted to be adventurous? Granted, a sexual adventure wasn't what she'd had in mind, but maybe she should consider it.

"Yes, I will go with you," she said, before she could change her mind.

Gannon sat in his parked car and waited for Delphine to come out of the hotel. She'd gone in to take the cake Nikki had given her up to her hotel room. He had watched her walk inside, admiring the sway of her hips and trying to deal with the throb of his erection with every step she'd taken.

For the first time in his life, he didn't have a plan when it came to spending time with a woman. Usually he knew exactly how he intended the night to end, and he and the woman would be on the same page. But tonight, he was entering uncharted waters, and he wasn't sure if he would sink or swim. No woman had ever placed him in such a predicament before.

Drawing in a deep breath, he picked up his phone

and punched in Galen's number. "You caught me at a bad time. What do you want, Gannon?"

He smiled, wondering if he had interrupted anything between his brother and his sister-in-law Brittany. If he had, it wouldn't be the first time he'd done so. They claimed that with twins under three they had to sneak in passionate moments whenever they could.

"I'll be on your property tonight, going up to the Black Mountains. Just wanted you to know so you wouldn't think it was trespassers."

"And why would you be going up to the mountains at night, Gannon? On second thought, don't answer. Maybe it's best I not know."

"Not that you were getting information out of me anyway. And don't use your telescope tonight." They all knew about Galen's powerful telescope.

"Um, I'm not making you any promises about that."

"Do me a favor and try real hard. Good night, Galen, and give Brittany my love."

"She doesn't need yours when she gets enough of mine. 'Bye."

Gannon chuckled when his brother clicked off. He then glanced back at the hotel's entrance to see Delphine walking through the revolving doors. When a jolt of sexual need rocked him to the bone, he gripped the steering wheel to steady himself.

Moments later, Gannon got out of the car so he could open the door for her. She smiled up at him. "You didn't have to do that, Gannon."

"Yes, I did," he responded as he gave her time to slide onto the leather seat before closing the door. He would offer to snap her seat belt in place, but figured he wouldn't last long enough to do so. Her scent alone would render him mindless.

As he walked back around the car to get inside, he refused to question his sanity in asking her to go to the Black Mountains with him. But he was too far gone now. He got in the car, closed the door and then buckled his own seat belt before glancing over at her. She seemed nervous and he figured he needed to reassure her that she was safe with him. "I don't bite, you know."

She met his gaze and a smile touched her lips. "I would not be going anywhere with you if I thought you did, Gannon."

Their gazes held for a moment and he knew there was no way she didn't feel the strong sensual vibes flowing between them. The passion. The need. The desire. Sexual awareness seemed to thicken the air between them.

When a low moan slipped from her lips, he knew she was as far gone as he was. Gannon was aware of everything about her—her nearness, her scent and the look in her eyes. Heaven help him. He didn't understand what was happening, but he figured she didn't, either.

A primitive force he couldn't combat had him reaching out to trace the tip of his finger around her lips. Lips he wanted to kiss.

"Don't know what's happening between us, Delphine, but it's worth exploring, don't you think?"

In all honesty, Delphine couldn't think.

In fact, she could barely handle Gannon's closeness and his touch. Intense desire clawed at her and they hadn't left the hotel's parking lot yet. She was tempted to tell Gannon to forget about the drive up the mountains, and ask him inside her hotel room instead. When had she gotten so bold to even think of doing such a thing?

What she should do was tell him she had changed

her mind about going anywhere with him and bid him goodbye. But something was keeping her from doing that. She hadn't been with a man in over five years, and until Gannon had come along, she could have gone without one for another five. But he had made doing such a thing difficult, nearly impossible.

"Are you sure that you still want to go with me up the mountains, Delphine?"

His question, spoken in a deep, throaty voice, sent spiraling sensations to her very core. Yes, she wanted to go up to the mountains with him, although she knew she shouldn't.

When she didn't respond right away, he said, "I promise not to do anything that you object to."

If he thought that would make her feel better, he was wrong, because she might not object to anything. "I believe you."

He reached out toward the console and soft music began playing. It was relaxing, definitely something she needed to hear. She'd never pegged him for a symphony type, but as the sounds of Mozart, Dvořák and Beethoven flowed in the car's interior as they made their way up the mountain, she concluded that evidently he was. Her mother had loved symphony music, so Delphine was familiar with it. She saw this as just another side of Gannon she was getting to know.

They had done enough talking for now, and she was satisfied to just relax and listen to the music.

"We're here, Delphine."

He knew she hadn't been asleep, although her eyes had been closed. The sound of a symphony could do that. He'd read somewhere that it could decrease a person's stress level, as well as stimulate the regeneration of brain cells. And then, according to his brother Tyson, the renowned heart surgeon, music could also decrease blood pressure and improve a person's memory.

Gannon had brought the car to a stop and shut off the ignition. Releasing his seat belt, he watched as she sat up and looked around. He wasn't surprised by her gasp of surprise. Down below you could see the scattered lights of a number of households, as well as a good view of downtown Phoenix, although they were miles away from it.

"Oh, it's beautiful up here, Gannon."

He'd known it would be since he'd been here with his brothers, cousins and selected friends. They had gathered up here to celebrate Galen's pending marriage to Brittany, Eli's to Stacey, Tyson's to Hunter, Jonas's to Nikki and, most recently, Mercury's to Sloan. It had been a guys' night with their favorite bottles of liquor. This was the first time Gannon had been up here with a woman.

"I think so, too. If you look to the left, at that place surrounded by so many lights that it actually looks like a lit Christmas tree, that's where my oldest brother, Galen, lives."

She leaned forward to look out the windshield. "His house seems isolated from all the others."

"It is, intentionally so. He likes his privacy, so he bought all the land surrounding him, which includes this private road up the mountains. He won't hesitate to report trespassers, trust me."

She glanced over at him. "Does he know we're here?"

"Yes, he knows," he said, sliding back his car seat to stretch out his long legs.

She didn't say anything for a moment and then glanced over at him. "Earlier you mentioned wanting to talk to me about something."

Yes, he had told her that. He had thought about what he wanted to discuss with her before leaving Jonas's house. "I'm leaving Friday on a road trip," he said.

She nodded. "Yes, I know. What about it?"

He opened his mouth to respond, when suddenly she nervously swiped her tongue across her bottom lip. The action caused a spike of heat to catch in the lower part of his gut. It would not have been so bad if he hadn't been thinking about them, dreaming about them, fantasizing about those same lips since meeting her, but he had. And if that wasn't torture enough, he was sitting close enough to breathe in her luscious scent.

Seemingly with a will not his own, he leaned in toward her and tilted his face close to hers. As if drawn to him, she tilted her head to move closer, as well. And when he reached out and took the pad of his thumb and angled her mouth even closer to his, she didn't resist. A part of him was glad they were on the same page, because he honestly didn't know what he would do if she denied him this kiss. He wanted the sweet taste of her mouth and a chance to devour those delectable lips.

His gaze shifted from her eyes to her lips and an intense arousal surged within him. Desire didn't just claw at him; it ripped him open, laid him bare to a need of the most intense kind.

Not able to resist temptation any longer, he closed his eyes on a groan and hungrily covered her mouth with his. He released another groan, this one of deep longing and satisfaction, while burying his fingers into the thick curls on her head, as if doing so would bring her mouth closer and lock it tight with his.

His tongue took possession of hers, claiming it like he had every right to do so, with a hunger he felt through his bones. The pounding of need in his groin made him groan again in raw male appreciation. His body was making demands and they were all for her. He felt like he was burning from the inside out.

His hands left her head and he wrapped his arms around her to pull her across the seat to him. From the very beginning, her lips had presented a temptation that made him question his sanity, while at the same time testing the bounds of his endurance. Never had the taste of any woman lit him up this way, overwhelming him to the point where raw male satisfaction was humming all the way to his soul. His body was throbbing while a hard shot of lust rushed through his veins.

Gannon knew if he didn't pull back from the kiss now, he would strip off her clothes and be inside her in a matter of minutes. But he didn't want that. He refused to treat her as a one-night stand when he had a gut feeling she was meant to be more than that.

And it was up to him to find out why he felt that way.

What Jonas had said to him had hit a nerve, rattled him. What if ten years from now he did discover that she had been the one, and he'd let her get away? He had to know for certain before beginning his life for the next ten years as the ultimate man-whore. Was she the woman destined to be claimed by a Steele? Namely, claimed by *him*? On the other hand, was he ready to walk away from all those other sinfully erotic women's beds just for a possibility?

He knew the answer the moment he adjusted his mouth to deepen the kiss. How could he think of Delphine as a mere possibility, when at this moment he was feasting on the most scrumptious lips ever tasted by a man? Definitely the most enchanting ones he'd had the pleasure of kissing. Their mouths were perfect for each other, as if they belonged together, were meant to be connected this way. Not just for tonight, but for always.

For always?

The sound of a wolf's howl pierced the night and Gannon reluctantly released Delphine's mouth, but not before giving her lips a sweep with his tongue. Never had he felt such primal desire for any woman. Never.

"Gannon…"

She said his name on what sounded like a breathless moan and he braced his forehead against hers. Now he knew how it felt to have his common sense hammered by passion. He was one short sentence away from suggesting they crawl into the back seat, strip naked and have crazy, mind-blowing sex.

"I've never been kissed like that before," she whispered, as if saying the words sucked up oxygen she desperately needed.

He heard the words and was moved by them. If that was true, some man hadn't been taking care of business like he should have. That made him even more determined to find out what part, if any, she could play in his life. Or was he just getting caught up in a very sexual moment with her?

She then tilted her head to look at him, to stare deeply into his eyes. As if she needed to regain control of her senses, too. Then she asked, "What did you want to discuss with me, Gannon?"

Her question heightened the beating of his heart, which he was convinced had skipped a beat or two while kissing her. "It's my road trip."

Her gaze roamed over his face before returning to his eyes. "What about it?"

He was tempted to lean in and kiss her again, but

he knew he needed to answer her question. "I want to take you with me."

She stared at him with a beautiful pair of wide eyes. "You want to take me with you on the road trip?" she asked, as if she needed to make sure she'd heard him correctly.

"Yes."

And Gannon knew at that moment, there was no way he could leave her behind.

Six

Delphine moved away from Gannon to ease back into her seat. She didn't say anything, just stared out into the darkness, and then beyond to the lights of the houses below. Just a few moments ago she had melted in his arms, had allowed her mouth to be ravished by his kiss. And for a few moments she had thought…

What exactly had she thought?

That for once in her life a man had appreciated her for being her, and not for what he could get from her? That was the story she knew all the other single women were bitching about, and rightly so. Men weren't interested in love and forever after. They wanted the here and now. To leave their mark and move on.

But then, did she really want forever after? She'd honestly believed she'd had that with Liddell, but he had proved her wrong in the most hurtful way. Could she really risk her heart on another man? She honestly knew she couldn't. It would be a cold day in hell before she would think about getting back into a serious relationship. If that was her story and she was sticking to it, why did the thought of a man like Gannon, known for changing bed partners so often he had a problem keeping up with names, bother her?

"Delphine?"

She pulled herself together, considering the man she was dealing with. His business mind was brilliant. His sense of duty to his employees was remarkable. The only time they'd covered his personal life was when he'd gone on record to say he was a single man and intended to stay that way for a long time. She figured that was his way of letting any single female readers of the magazine know what to expect.

When he said her name again, she slowly turned to look at him. Green eyes were searching hers and she couldn't help but remember how much she had enjoyed the passion they hadn't been able to keep in check.

"Why, Gannon? Why do you want me to go with you?" She knew the answer but wanted to hear him say it. To put things in perspective. To tell her outright that she meant nothing to him, but was just another woman to add to his list of many.

"I enjoy your company and figured you coming with me would be our way of getting to know each other better."

His response hadn't been good enough. She needed more. "Why would you want to get to know me better?"

He didn't say anything for a minute, and she watched his expression closely. He was thinking hard, as if what he said was important. Why? He was the ultimate player, who should have his lines down pat. Why did it seem as if he was searching for words?

"I've never met a woman quite like you before, Delphine."

She didn't say anything. To keep the promise she'd made to her mother about giving love another try, and to prepare herself for dating, she'd purchased a book entitled *Be Aware of Pick-Up Lines Men Use*. She wasn't surprised that the one he'd just used had made the list.

"Keep living because you will undoubtedly meet others," she said, looking away from him.

"I doubt that very seriously. I don't think you understand."

She looked back at him. "Then make me understand, Gannon."

He broke eye contact with her, and she wondered if it was because he was trying to come up with a new line. She was about to tell him to forget it, and that he honestly didn't need to answer because she wouldn't be going anywhere with him regardless, when he glanced back at her.

She wasn't always good at reading people, but at the moment a part of her felt that every emotion known to man was expressed in Gannon's eyes. Why she thought that, she wasn't sure. All she knew was that the man she'd interviewed for two days had been confident, self-assured, even a little arrogant. However, the green eyes staring at her were filled with uncertainty.

"I need to make sure that you aren't the woman meant for me, Delphine. The one woman in life I'm supposed to claim. The woman who is my destiny. If I don't make sure, then it will be a missed opportunity and you will be lost to me forever."

Delphine's jaw dropped slightly, because those particular lines hadn't made the list.

* * *

Gannon doubted Delphine was aware that the words he'd just said were the most serious he'd spoken to any woman. They had been heartfelt, sincere and truthful because he knew of no other way to be with her. Whether she realized it or accepted it, something was going on between them. Something powerful. He couldn't stop it and doubted neither could she.

"That's the most ridiculous thing I've ever heard."

Her words hit a nerve. Ridiculous? His jaw twitched in anger. "Do you honestly think I want to feel that way? That I want to believe there's a woman somewhere who exists for me? A woman for me to claim? Then let me set the record straight. I've never been into claiming women, just enjoying sex with them. But for some reason, you're different. You make me feel things, want things, need things, and I don't like it. I liked the path my life was taking before you came along just fine."

Gannon watched Delphine angrily cross her arms over her chest. "Then why change it?" she snapped.

"Because of you. Can you honestly say you can't feel the vibes we generate? That you don't think something strong is happening between us?"

He watched as she nibbled her lips and his gut clenched. At least he had her thinking.

"All I'm asking is a chance for us to determine why we are drawn together like we are. I'm not asking you to go with me on the road for a sexathon. I want you to go because I truly want you with me, to share that side of myself with you. Namely, my love for the road. It has nothing to do with the interview, but with me. I've never wanted to share myself that way with any woman."

"I think you're just confused, Gannon."

"Then unconfuse me. I honestly meant what I said

about needing to make sure that you aren't the woman meant to be in my future."

"Trust me, I'm not."

"Then prove it, Delphine. While we are together, I don't plan to pressure you into doing anything you don't want to do. Any ground rules or limitations you set I will abide by."

He knew he could say that because the force of passion between them was so strong, there was no way they could spend time together and not share intimacy. According to his now married brothers, intimacy was one of the purest displays of love between a couple.

Love...

He swallowed deeply, wondering how and when that one single word had entered the equation. But he couldn't worry about that now. Gannon saw from the bemused expression in her eyes that he needed to make her understand and he would use a new angle to do so.

"Didn't you say that you couldn't return home just yet?"

She nodded. "Yes."

"And didn't you say you wanted to experience different things? Adventure? To tap into your wanderlust side?"

She hesitated a second, then said, "Yes, I said that, too."

"Didn't you also tell me that you'd never seen the Atlantic Ocean and that it's always been your dream to one day see it?"

She broke eye contact with him for a second before relocking her gaze with his. "Yes, I said that."

"Then let me share those things with you, Delphine. Going on the road with me will be an adventure—I can promise you that. It will satisfy your wanderlust since we will be crossing several states—Texas, Louisiana, Mississippi and Alabama—and end up in Florida. And I want to show you the Atlantic Ocean."

What he wouldn't spring on her just yet was that he intended to invite her to spend a week with him at his beach house in Miami. That was an invitation he'd never issued to a woman and he wasn't sure why it was important that he invite her, but for him it was.

He studied her features, namely her eyes, when she said softly, "Someone else promised to do that once."

"Do what?" he asked her.

"Show me the Atlantic Ocean."

He saw the pain in her gaze and had a feeling that someone was the same guy who'd broken her heart. The one Jonas refused to tell Gannon anything about. "I'm not that person and I intend to keep my promise."

Their gazes continued to hold as Gannon drove home another point. "You were going to leave here and go to Vegas anyway, so why not share the road with me instead?"

Already thinking of the excuse she would use next, he said, "The cab of my truck is internet-ready, with everything you need to continue working on your article. Plus, I'll be there in case you discover there's something you should have asked me but didn't."

His goal was to make it nearly impossible for her to say no. She looked away again and licked her lips. "I need to think about it, Gannon."

"All right. Can I have your answer by noon tomorrow?"

She glanced back over at him. "Yes, I'll have an answer for you by noon tomorrow."

"Think about it? Honestly, Del, what's there to think about when a hunk like Gannon Steele invites you on a road trip? If it was me, I would jump at the offer in a heartbeat."

Delphine heard what her best friend was saying, but still, they were two different people. "Of course you would, Mandy. You've always been the self-confident one." Mandy had married a guy she'd met in college and they had two sons. Mandy, Roger and the kids were the perfect family.

"And so were you until Liddell did what he did. The woman who returned to Denver after that was timid, with less self-esteem. I told you that."

Yes, her best friend had. But how was Delphine supposed to be confident when the man she'd loved had dumped her and the entire town knew why? "Yes, but—"

"But nothing. Why do you continue to let Liddell win?"

"I don't know what you're talking about."

"Don't you?" Then there was a pause before Mandy said, "Then maybe you don't."

"What do you mean?"

"What I mean is that Liddell Bartley is an asshole. He is not the nice guy we knew in high school. He went to that college on the East Coast and someone must have convinced him he was God's gift to women. Even Jerome can't stand him anymore."

Jerome Applegate used to be Liddell's best friend while growing up. "Why?"

"Because of the lies he's telling his wife. Do you know that to keep her in line, he's telling her that he can leave her for you anytime and that you would take him back?"

"He definitely lied to her if he told her that. No wonder she gives me daggered looks whenever she sees me."

"And you aren't helping the situation."

Delphine frowned. "What do you mean I'm not helping the situation? I have nothing to do with Liddell. We don't even speak."

"Yes, but because you aren't involved with anyone, he's giving people, especially his wife, the impression that you're pining for him. Hell, I honestly think he believes it himself."

"That's not true and you know it, Mandy."

"Of course I know it isn't true, but others may not. I think everyone understood why you didn't date while your mom was ill, but they're probably wondering what's your excuse now, Delphine. I know guys have asked you out, but you've turned them down. You're making it easy for everyone to think that maybe you are carrying a torch for Liddell and hoping he will dump Agatha and come back to you. A lot of people remember how much you loved him."

Delphine's head was spinning. How could anyone think she could still love Liddell after what he'd done to her? If they did think that, that meant they must also think she was pathetic. "I'm rarely in Denver. I travel a lot."

"Yes, but you're here enough, and when you are, you don't date. How do you think that looks?" Mandy asked her.

"Like I'm not interested in the guys who asked me out. I have that right."

"Yes, you do, and it's nobody's damn business. But as your best friend, I thought you should know what Liddell is saying. I know how much he hurt you, but I wouldn't give him the pleasure of thinking he's ruined you for another man."

"He hasn't!"

"You sure? If he hasn't, then we wouldn't be having this conversation, Del. You would already have your bags packed for that road trip with Gannon Steele. The mere idea that you need to think about it means something."

"Yes, it means that I know what kind of women Gannon is used to."

"And we both know you're different. Evidently he knows that, too, if you're the first one he's asked to go on a road trip with him. I think Gannon sees something in you that Liddell ignored, which will forever be his loss."

Mandy's argument made Delphine remember what Gannon had said earlier tonight. She recalled his exact words… *I need to make sure that you aren't the woman meant for me, Delphine. The one woman in life I'm supposed to claim. The woman who is my destiny. If I don't make sure, then it will be a missed opportunity and you will be lost to me forever…*

With nothing else to be discussed, Gannon had returned her to the hotel. It was obvious that he intended to kiss her good-night, but she had opened her own car door and rushed inside the hotel without looking back. She had called Mandy the moment she'd returned to her hotel room.

"This is just a new thing for Gannon—it won't mean anything."

"Then let it be a new thing for you, as well. Do you plan on giving your heart to this guy?"

"Of course not!"

"Then go have some fun. Stop living in the past and begin embracing the present. And there's nothing wrong with sleeping with him if that's what you want to do, on your terms and not his."

"I'm not promiscuous, Mandy."

"No, you're not, but you have urges just like the rest of us, sweetheart, and please don't deny that you do. There's nothing wrong with satisfying those urges once in a while. The desire to do so doesn't make you promiscuous."

Deep down Delphine knew that to be true, and for the first time, she saw what she was doing. She was fishing for anything to legitimize her fear of being hurt again. "I still have to think about it, Mandy."

"Then do so, if you must. In the end I believe you will make the best decision for you."

Later that night when she went to bed, Delphine replayed in her mind everything about Gannon, from the time they'd officially met in the hotel lobby on Sunday night until tonight. How could three single days be so impactful on her life? Could she handle seven days in close quarters with him?

She closed her eyes when sleep overtook her with that question on her mind.

Gannon glanced at the clock on the wall in his office. Today was the day Delphine would give him her decision. He'd tried to keep busy, but every so often his mind would replay every single detail of last night in the Black Mountains...especially their kiss.

How could one kiss be so powerful? Leave a lasting impression on every part of his body? The more time he spent with Delphine, the more he was beginning to think...

No, he wouldn't go there.

He refused to do so. But then, it hadn't helped matters when Tyson had called this morning. According to Dr. Tyson Steele, who barely missed seeing a thing, he couldn't help but notice the way Gannon kept staring at Delphine last night. Tyson said it was a way he'd never seen Gannon stare at another woman. His brother felt it was obvious that Gannon was taken with her, and like Jonas, Tyson felt Gannon should find out why.

Evidently, Tyson had shared that opinion with Galen and Eli because Gannon had gotten calls from them, as well. That was just great, Gannon thought, annoyed that they felt the need to call to give him advice, as if he couldn't handle his business.

His cell phone rang, and his heart began pounding when he picked it up and saw the caller was Delphine. Swallowing deeply, he clicked on and said, "Good morning, Delphine."

"Good morning, Gannon. I'm calling to let you know I've made my decision."

He breathed in deeply, knowing her decision could either make or break him. He hadn't realized just how much he wanted her to travel on the road with him until after he'd asked her. "And what have you decided?"

There was a pause. Or was it a hesitation?

He swallowed deeply again and waited.

To him it seemed an eternity before she said, "I've decided to take you up on your offer and go on the road trip with you."

At that moment, Gannon couldn't stop the smile that spread across his lips.

Seven

Early Friday morning at seven, Delphine arrived on the lot of the Steele Trucking Company to find Gannon standing in front of a huge tractor-trailer rig. Over the past forty-eight hours she had constantly asked herself if she'd made the right decision. Now just seeing Gannon standing there made her believe that she had.

Even if she never again became involved with a man, seriously or otherwise, she would have memories of this trip with him. Mandy was right. It was time to start living in the present and not hang back in the past. And it was time to have fun…on her terms, of course.

But what were her terms when she'd never gone out of town with a guy before? Not even with Liddell. She refused to dwell on that now. Instead, she much preferred putting all her concentration on the man whose gaze had been on her from the moment she'd parked her car and gotten out of it with her carry-on in tow. The man whose gaze was still on her as she walked toward him, and he acted as if he never intended to break eye contact.

Delphine wished that thoughts of the kiss they'd shared weren't weighing so heavily on her mind. Memories of it were still having an effect on her. She was inflamed with intoxicating yearnings. It was as if she could still taste him on her tongue, as if his scent was in her nostrils, as if his touch would now be impossible to resist. But she would try.

He was wearing a pair of jeans and a T-shirt that said Living for the Moment. Was that supposed to be a reminder of his philosophy? Or was that an invitation for her to think the same way? She wasn't certain which it was, but she decided not to sweat the small stuff right now. Instead, she tried to focus her attention on the ultrahandsome man whose company she would be sharing for an entire week.

"Good morning, Gannon," she said, coming to a stop in front of him.

"Good morning." He glanced down at her luggage and smiled. "That's all you have?"

Delphine couldn't help but smile back, especially when she saw the mischievous sparkle in the depths of his green eyes. "That's not enough?"

"Not if you were Eden Tyson Steele," he said, chuckling. "Whenever Mom went on a road trip with Dad, he had to make room for all her luggage."

She nodded. "Since I travel a lot, I've learned to pack light. Besides, I've heard that a number of the truck stops have Laundromats."

"They do. You would be surprised at what all they have." He glanced at the clipboard in his hand. "I've got our orders and I'm ready to hit the road if you are."

"I'm ready." Delphine hoped that she truly was, because just being near Gannon was causing an incredible warmth to spread through her.

"Then follow me so we can get this show on the road."

She followed him toward the cab, which didn't have a trailer attached. She knew the trip from Phoenix to Jacksonville, Florida, would cover two thousand miles. The road trip would take thirty hours if they drove straight through. However, she knew it would take longer due to federal legislation requiring rest for drivers.

"Where's the rest of the truck?" she asked Gannon.

"At the shipper's dock, being loaded. Most of the time that's how it's done. My drivers are drivers—the shipper and the recipient of the goods have people in place at the starting point and destination to load and unload."

When they reached the cab, he used the key fob to unlock it. She also saw the way the steps seemed to appear miraculously by the door. "Hideaway steps. Nice touch," she said.

"It was a suggestion we got from our employees' opinion surveys. Because the truck is so high off the ground, climbing up into the cab isn't always easy, especially for shorter and older drivers."

"Definitely a good idea and a considerate implementation," she said.

"Thanks."

He offered his hand to help her get into the truck. Delphine had glanced inside a cab before, but now she was getting a full view. It was roomier than she'd expected, especially the area behind the curtain. That was more than just a bunk area—in fact, there were several compartments and cubbyholes where they could store clothes and other miscellaneous items. He showed her how the bunk bed could convert to a desk and table with a laptop and miniature television. There was also a small refrigerator and microwave. Everything was neat and tidy, and the space was utilized efficiently.

"As you can see, there's no bathroom facilities, so let me know when you need to go. I have no problem stopping," Gannon told her after placing her carry-on bag in one of the cubbyholes.

"Okay, and drivers actually sleep in the truck?"

"Most of them do, which is why I try to make things as comfortable and easy as possible. A lot of the truck stops are connected to hotels. That makes things convenient."

"I just bet it does," she said. She knew a lot of truckers indulged in affairs on the road. Since Gannon didn't ask what she meant, she decided not to expound on it. Besides, she was pretty sure he'd gotten her meaning. "What's the time frame for us to get where we're going?" she asked.

"The dispatcher will provide all that to us. Right now, the route we're taking and the states we're covering require at least a thirty-minute break after eight hours on the road. After the break we can do three more hours."

"And then?" she asked, buckling her seat belt.

"And then we have to rest for eleven hours."

That was a lot of time and Delphine wondered what they would do during their rest times. She glanced around the truck at the first-aid kit, map, GPS and all the other gadgets. "What do drivers do to keep themselves company?" she asked him.

He shrugged. "Listen to music, some make use of CB radios, books on tape, talking on their cell phones, as long as it's not handheld. Definitely no texting. Would you like some coffee?"

She saw the huge thermos. "Yes, thanks." He poured them cups of hot, steaming coffee.

"And I got a box of snacks if you get the munchies later."

"Thanks, Gannon."

He took a sip of coffee and then slid on his aviator-style sunglasses. Smiling over at her, he said, "Let the fun begin."

"This coffee is so good, Gannon."

He took a quick glance at her as he pulled the truck out of the lot. "Thanks. I made it myself. I discovered long ago that if you did a road trip with Drew Steele, you had to learn to make good coffee. He taught me. When it comes to making coffee for my dad, you have to be on top of your game."

Mixed with the scent of the coffee, already the truck smelled like her. He didn't mind since he definitely liked her scent. In fact, he liked everything about her. Today she was wearing a pair of jeans and a button-up olive green shirt. Her hair was pulled back, away from her face, and clamped on both sides to keep it that way. A cute pair of navy blue sneakers were on her feet.

He had watched her from the moment she'd gotten out of the car and had immediately known his testosterone level would be at an all-time high around her, but he would manage.

"Do you really talk to your parents every day?"

He had brought the cab to a stop at a railroad crossing to let a train pass. He glanced over at her and knew she was referring to a comment Jonas had made at dinner the other day.

It was a beautiful day, the last one in April. The sun was shining bright and seemed to highlight the golden streaks in her hair. He liked that. In fact, he had accepted from that very first night that he liked everything about Delphine Ryland.

"Yes, we either talk or text. Lately, we text. I lived at home longer than my brothers. After they left, I saw no reason to leave, even during college, since I went to a local university. My parents traveled a lot, so I had the entire place to myself a lot of the time." No need to tell her that taking a woman to a hotel for the night had been fine with him since he'd preferred one-night stands anyway.

He took another sip of his coffee and then said, "And when Mom and Dad were home, they still gave me space, even though I enjoy their company."

Being around his parents, he'd observed just how in love they were because they were both openly affectionate. Gannon knew he wanted that same kind of forever love in his life one day. However, he also knew it would be a while before he would be ready to make such a commitment. His father had enjoyed his bachelor days before marrying Eden, and Gannon wanted to follow in his father's footsteps and do the same.

"I agree with Nikki. I think it's wonderful. My mom and I also had a close relationship since it was just the two of us."

He recalled her telling him that her parents had divorced when she'd been six and that her father hadn't maintained a relationship with her. He wondered how many parents could disconnect from their child that way. How had she handled such a rejection? And that was how he saw it. Not only had the man rejected her, but he'd also obviously rejected the responsibilities of being a father.

"I'm sure you miss her a lot," he said.

"Yes, especially with Mother's Day coming up. It will be my first without her. And the first anniversary of her death will fall on Mother's Day this year, so that day will be especially difficult."

Gannon understood how it would be. He could hear the sadness in her voice. Although he hadn't told her yet, it was his plan for her to be with him on that day. He didn't want her to be alone. He couldn't ever remember a day when he and his brothers had not spent Mother's Day with their own mom, but he'd already told his mother of his plans and why. She had understood and felt he'd made the right decision.

A short while later, he was glad to pull the cab into the parking lot of the shipper. For the next thirty minutes, he noticed she was attentive to how the trailer was connected to the cab. He also noticed how other truckers were trying not to be obvious in watching Delphine with deep male interest, which he understood. But still, he didn't like it. That was another first for him, since he'd never been jealous when it came to a woman. But he grudgingly accepted that he was now.

"Time to hit the road again," he said, once the hitching had been done and they'd returned to the truck.

"I'm excited about the route we are taking." She looked at the map he'd handed her.

He glanced at her before putting his sunglasses back on. "Interstate Ten is a good one to take while traveling from Phoenix to Jacksonville, Florida, where the interstate ends."

She didn't ask what would happen after that and he decided not to say. He wanted her to get to know him better and feel comfortable with being with him before broaching the subject of her spending even more time with him in Miami.

"Tell me about some of your other assignments, Delphine."

She began talking and he loved hearing her voice. It was smooth, soft and seductive. He could tell she was excited about what she did and the people she got to meet. A couple of her stories had him chuckling and laughing out loud. He, in turn, told her some of his road stories and loved hearing her laugh as much as he liked hearing her talk.

Usually he preferred being alone on his road trips, but her presence was rewarding. He enjoyed having her with him. During their conversation, he got a call and declined it when he saw who it was: Trish. It was time to tell her to lose his number. Galen had mentioned that he'd run into Trish at the grocery store and she'd all but insinuated that she and Gannon were in a serious relationship. Now, that was BS.

He glanced over at Delphine and saw she'd fallen asleep. She looked as beautiful asleep as she did awake, and he wondered what time she'd gotten up this morning. His gaze landed on her mouth. He'd finally tasted it and he had not been disappointed. He could clearly recall the moment their lips had touched, when hers had parted for his tongue to slide inside. And the moment her tongue had touched his, a jolt of sexual energy had rocketed through every part of his body. Later that night, in his bed, he had decided that no woman's mouth should taste that delicious.

Knowing that thinking about her lips could get him into trouble if he wasn't careful, he checked his watch and saw he'd driven for nearly four hours now. In two hours, he would stop at a café in El Paso for lunch. Once on the road again he would drive another two hours before taking a second thirty-minute break. Then he would drive into Fort Stockton to hunker down for the night. There was a nice truck stop there with all the comforts.

She moaned and he glanced over at her again when there was a backup on the interstate, and every vehicle was at a standstill. He hoped the traffic jam wouldn't mess with their schedule too much. Even if it did, he, like other drivers, was smart enough to build in reserve time to use if needed.

"Gannon…"

She had mumbled his name in her sleep. Was she thinking about him? Dreaming of him? If so, what thoughts were going through her mind? Were they similar to those he'd had of her last night? The ones that had been so intense they had awakened him with one hell of a hard-on?

She mumbled his name again and the throbbing of his erection got even worse. And then she moaned again. Then his name again. Hell, the sounds were getting to him.

The sound of a police cruiser trying to get through the throng of vehicles was blasting loud. Like all the other vehicles, he moved to the right to let the emergency vehicles through.

"What happened?"

He glanced over at Delphine and watched as she wiped sleep from her eyes. His body ached even more with arousal. "I think there's an accident up ahead."

"Oh."

The truck came to a stop again and he watched her stretch, saw how her breasts pressed against her blouse. He would give just about anything to see those breasts. To touch them. Taste them…

"Sorry I passed out on you."

"Don't apologize. You evidently were tired."

"I was. I didn't get in bed till late and then got up early." She glanced out the truck's huge window. "Where are we, anyway?"

"Near El Paso. I figured we could stop there for lunch. I know a café that's known for its Mexican food."

"Great! I love tacos."

He chuckled. "So do I. If you get hungry don't forget I have snacks in the bunk area."

"Thanks for reminding me."

Traffic began moving again, slow at first and then a little faster. When they got farther down the interstate, they saw there had been an accident. A fender bender. Thankfully, no one seemed hurt.

"I downloaded a few movies on my phone last night. I think I'll watch one now."

"Sounds like a good idea. What's the movie?"

When she told him, he chuckled. "That's a romance. I think my mom has seen it a couple of times."

"I don't doubt that since I've seen it a couple of times myself."

He chuckled. "My mom would love you."

Too late, he realized what he'd said. But then, he knew what he'd said was true. Eden *would* love her. Gannon glanced over at her. She seemed not to have been fazed by his words. It was obvious that she'd gotten wrapped up in the movie on the phone screen. Maybe it was wishful thinking on his part, but he was looking forward to getting all wrapped up with her.

"You're right, Gannon. These tacos are the best," Delphine said, taking another bite. Her movie had ended just seconds before they'd arrived at the café. She thought that was perfect timing.

He flashed a smile that sent all kinds of sensations through her. "Glad you like them. This establishment has been here for years. When I used to take road trips with Dad as a kid, we would always make a stop here.

The original owners have passed away and their sons are now running things. I'm glad they got the family recipe for the sauce. That's what makes the tacos unique."

Delphine would have to agree with that. She had eaten a lot of tacos in her day, but had to say the ones she'd just had were the tastiest. More than once during their meal, Gannon's phone had rung. He would check the caller ID and then decline the call. She tried not to let the thought that he was in such high demand by the female population bother her. They were not in an exclusive relationship. In fact, they weren't even in a relationship. He had invited her to come along and she had said yes. As far as she was concerned, there were no expectations beyond that for either of them.

Gannon had told her they would drive for another two hours after lunch, then take another break, and would eventually reach Fort Stockton after that. So far, the trip had been rewarding for her. She wasn't sure how he felt about it since she'd gone to sleep on him and then watched a movie. He might see that as her not being much company.

"Gannon?"

He glanced over at her as he wiped his mouth after finishing off the last of his meal. "Yes?"

"Do you regret asking me to join you? I haven't been much company."

"I disagree. You've been a lot of company." He reached across the table and took her hand. "Your presence alone means a lot to me. I enjoy having you here, even if you never say a single word. Just knowing you are with me means everything."

She held his gaze, wanting so much to know why he felt that way. Despite how much she wanted to know, she didn't want to ask. She couldn't risk his answer being one that would make her fall for him even more. And, yes, she was falling for him, even when deep down she knew she should not. But she wasn't sure she could stop herself.

Just like he claimed he enjoyed being here with her, she definitely enjoyed being here with him. When she'd first arrived in Phoenix, she figured it would take two days to complete the interview and another two days in her hotel room to write it up. She hadn't counted on this road trip with him, or him getting to her like he had. He'd turned around all her plans.

A short while later they were headed back to their truck for the next few hours of road travel. He had parked his rig in the far back of the restaurant, and when they reached it, he touched her arm before she went to her door. "What is it, Gannon?"

Instead of answering her, she saw his gaze shift from her eyes to her lips. She immediately felt heat infuse her mouth. She swallowed, knowing he'd looked the same way when he had kissed her the other night.

"Is anything wrong?" The heat from her mouth was slowly spreading through other parts of her body.

"Nothing is wrong, Delphine. I just need this," he said, lowering his mouth to hers.

A part of Delphine was screaming that she should take a step back. But she couldn't. She didn't want to.

What she did was meet him head-on when he slanted his mouth over hers. She couldn't do anything but surrender, allowing him to devour her with the passion he'd introduced her to a couple of nights ago. There was no way she could resist the fact that this was what she wanted and needed.

She had gone nearly five years without being in any man's arms, without being tasted by one. Lord knew when she arrived in Phoenix, she hadn't expected this.

But her plans didn't matter. She would take this, and when she returned to Denver, she would have memories to take with her.

When the kiss ended, he pulled her into his arms and held her for a moment. She scanned the parking lot, grateful that he had parked the truck in a way that gave them privacy. Had he done so intentionally, knowing he would be kissing her? A thrill of excitement rushed through her at the thought. Were there any more plans in store for her?

"Thanks. I needed that, Delphine. Now I'm good to go for the next few hours."

Was he giving her a heads-up that he would be kissing her on a regular basis on this road trip? If he was, he would get a "yes, please" from her. "Glad I could be of service," she said, smiling.

He chuckled before leaning in and placing a quick kiss to her lips. "Damn, I've never seen a more gorgeous pair of lips before. I like them. I like them a lot."

Did he honestly believe that, or were those just words? She began to think that maybe there was truth to his words when he licked her lips in earnest, like they were a piece of candy he enjoyed. Goose bumps formed on her arms and heat filled her stomach. When she suddenly felt weak in the knees, she grabbed hold of his shoulders to stay balanced.

"I guess I better stop, or we'll be late arriving in Fort Stockton," he murmured against her lips, before lifting his head to stare at her. Then, smiling as if seeing how wet he'd made her lips had pleased him, he said, "I've given you fair warning about my fetish with your lips, Delphine."

Yes, he most certainly had, and in a most delicious way.

Eight

"Tell me about him, Delphine. The man who broke your heart."

They were less than twenty miles to the truck stop in Fort Stockton and already the sun had gone down. Conversation between them had been steady, interesting and, to his way of thinking, pretty darn enlightening. They had shared information about each other, their likes, dislikes and parts of their pasts.

He'd told her about living in the spotlight as one of Eden Tyson Steele's sons, the strength of his parents' marriage and his close relationship with his brothers. And he'd talked about his grandparents and how he'd never met his maternal grandmother because she'd died before he was born, but how he had spent time with his maternal grandfather.

Delphine had told him that she'd been a cheerleader in high school and how she'd taken piano lessons for a while. She'd shared her love for Denver and how she'd missed it while away at college. She'd told him about her college days in Wyoming and all the groups and activities she'd been a part of. It was obvious she'd been an outgoing person who loved having fun. He didn't quite see her as that sociable person now.

Granted, she was friendly enough, and he knew the employees who'd met her this week had liked her on the spot. However, she was nothing like the gregarious person she'd described. He'd been around enough women to tell when one was not only protecting herself from heartbreak, but also doing so by withdrawing from the happy-go-lucky life she'd once lived.

"What makes you think some man has broken my heart? I don't recall giving you that impression."

He could tell by her tone of voice that she hadn't liked his question and, as a result, she was copping an attitude. That didn't bother him because she had that right. However, he refused to back down in asking what he had. This was a woman who affected him in so many ways he couldn't even count them, and the more time he spent with her, the greater the impact. So the bottom line was that he wanted to find out every single thing about her.

They had come to a stop at one of the weigh stations and he had turned around in his seat to look at her, to stare into her eyes. Feast his attention on her lips. "No, you didn't give me that impression. In fact, you haven't given me any impressions, one way or the other. You're deliberately staying clear of mentioning any involvement with a man. Do you want me to believe there has never been a man in your life? A special man?"

"You didn't mention any involvement with a woman,

Gannon. Do you want me to think there weren't any for you, either?"

"You interviewed me, Delphine. I won't believe that you didn't research my life before you did so. I know what the magazines and papers have printed, and most of it I won't deny. I'm a single, heterosexual male who likes spending time with women. There have been plenty of them in my life. That's not a secret. However, none of my affairs have been serious and the women knew it."

She didn't say anything for a minute and then said, "My past isn't a secret, either. I just choose not to talk about it."

"Okay."

He decided he would back off for now. He didn't want her to feel cornered. They'd enjoyed each other's company for the past eleven hours and he had no intention of changing that. Besides, he was more determined than ever to build a relationship with her, whether it was as a friend, lover or both.

The inspector gave him the okay to move his truck back onto the interstate to continue on his route. It was hard keeping his eyes on the road when he wanted to glance over at her.

"Are you mad at me, Delphine?" he finally asked her when he'd driven a mile and she hadn't said anything.

"Should I be?"

"Nope. I asked because I care," he said.

"And why should you care?"

Gannon waited a moment before answering. Not because he didn't have an answer, but because he needed to make sure he worded it so she fully understood what he was saying. "You know why I asked you to come with me on this road trip."

"To make sure I'm not *the* one," she said with a little mockery.

He ignored her tone. "Or to make sure you are."

"That's not possible."

"I figure the reason you might feel that way is because of something in your past involving a man," he stated.

"Not necessarily. It could be because I live in a more realistic world than you do," she responded.

He chuckled. "Well, at least you didn't call me crazy."

"I would never do that."

"And I appreciate you for not doing so because I am totally sane. I just want to get to know you."

Maybe it was something he said, or maybe it was something he didn't say. Either way, she began talking, telling him what he wanted to know.

"His name is Liddell Bartley. His family moved to Denver in my junior year of high school and we began dating in our senior year."

Delphine said nothing for a while, and he was certain she'd told him all she intended to tell him, when she surprised him as she added, "After high school we decided to attend separate colleges, not because we wanted to, but because our parents convinced us that was the right thing to do. They felt we were too into each other's pockets in high school and the four-year separation would do us some good."

She paused again. "They felt if we truly loved each other, everything would work out fine and the separation wouldn't matter. As far as I knew, it didn't. We would see each other whenever we came home for the holidays and we spent all our spring breaks together on the beach in Galveston, where his parents owned a time-share condo. We were to marry a week after graduation. Everything was set. Invitations were sent."

He heard the way her voice trembled, either from anger, pain or both. "What happened?"

"I got a letter from him a month before our wedding day letting me know he was marrying someone else because she was pregnant with his child."

Gannon said nothing. The thought that this Liddell guy had been committed to her and yet got another woman pregnant fueled his anger. "Was she really pregnant?" He knew the game some women played to get a man to the altar.

"No, but he didn't find out until after the wedding that she wasn't. She claims she honestly thought she was, and her parents demanded that he marry her."

"Are they still married?"

"Yes, and are living in Denver."

He figured that had to be pretty damn uncomfortable for Delphine. "You're better off without him."

"I know that. But still, not in a million years would I have thought he would have betrayed me that way. That just goes to show that you never know who you can truly trust."

He had pulled the truck into the huge lot of Truckers Bay, the largest chain of truck stops in the United States. When he brought the truck into Park, he glanced over at her. "I guess you could look at it that way or you could look at it another way entirely, Delphine."

"And what way is that?"

"That it was never meant for the two of you to be together in the first place. He was never your destiny."

He was never your destiny...

Although Delphine hadn't responded, his words

hadn't been lost on her. He was into this destiny kick, so she'd decided to pretend to ignore what he'd said. In truth, he hadn't said anything her mother hadn't said, as well as those friends who knew her well.

One of the reasons she hadn't returned to Denver after college was because she hadn't wanted to see pity in anyone's eyes. That was why she'd taken the job in New York. Then when she heard Liddell and his new wife would make Denver their home, she'd known her visits back to see her mother would be less frequent. At least, that had been the plan until her mother had gotten ill.

For the most part, since Denver was a big city, her path hadn't crossed much with Liddell's, and she was grateful for that. But once she wasn't confined to the house as much, she saw him more frequently. The first couple of times had been awkward, but the more she saw Liddell, the more she accepted that she had been his loss and not the other way around. In a way, she knew what Gannon had said was true. Liddell hadn't been her destiny, obviously. She was convinced no man was.

"Do you want to go jogging with me in the morning?"

Gannon had parked the truck and they'd climbed out of it. "Jogging?"

"Yes. This place has a gym with an indoor track."

Although she had yet to take a tour of the facility, she would admit she'd never seen a truck stop as spacious or with as many amenities as Gannon said it contained. In addition to a restaurant, there was a Laundromat, gym, arcade and a number of other conveniences. Across the lot there was even a hotel, where Gannon said they would be spending the night. Although he hadn't specifically said so, she expected they would each have a room.

Knowing they would end up in Florida, she had brought along a pair of shorts and a T-shirt that she could jog in tomorrow. "Yes, I'll go jogging with you in the morning."

"Good. Is five o'clock okay?"

"Five in the morning? You're kidding, right?"

He flashed her a smile. "No kidding. The best time to use the facility is when others are still sleeping. That means we'll be finished before they arrive."

"That's fine."

"You're tired?" he asked, reaching out to tuck a strand of hair away from her face.

She wasn't sure why he was asking, but, yes, she was tired. Yet not in the way he assumed. Her body was exhausted from combating the urges she felt from being around him. And him standing so close to her, messing with her hair, letting her inhale his scent, wasn't helping matters.

"Yes, I am kind of tired," she said, faking a yawn. "When I check into my hotel room, I don't plan to come out."

"What about dinner?" he asked her.

"I'll pass. I normally don't eat after seven anyway. Besides, those tacos we had earlier filled me up pretty good." There was no reason to ask if he would be eating again because she knew he would. Gannon loved to eat.

"If you change your mind and get hungry later, I'll be glad to bring you something."

"I won't change my mind, but thanks." Backing up a step, she said, "I'll see you in the morning. We can meet in the hotel's lobby and stroll over to the truck stop's gym." She knew she needed to get away from him as soon as she could, before she was tempted to do something stupid like inviting him to her hotel room.

"Okay. Sleep well. Tomorrow is a long day. My goal is to make it to San Antonio by dinnertime. That's where we'll spend the night."

Spend the night...

His words caused a sizzle of heat to spread through her. It was definitely time to part ways with him. "I'll see you in the morning, Gannon."

She quickly turned and headed toward the breezeway where her room was located, not caring that she was walking as if fire was at her heels.

Despite the fact that it wasn't quite daybreak and was still dark outside, Gannon saw Delphine the moment she stepped out of her hotel room. He wasn't a fan of breezeway-type hotel rooms that faced the outdoors, but he knew this style was a favorite with other truckers. They didn't want to be confined in a building without having quick access to their trucks if needed.

For that reason, he'd known that if Delphine was to meet him at five this morning as planned, she would be crossing the parking lot to the hotel's lobby in the dark, by herself, and he didn't plan for that to happen. There had been no reason to tell her he would be coming to her hotel room to escort her over to the truck stop because she would have argued about it. He hadn't wanted to argue. At least, not last night.

As far as he was concerned, yesterday had been perfect. It had started on a high note and he'd wanted it to end the same way. The only time he figured he'd somewhat gotten on her nerves was when he'd questioned her about that asshole who had hurt her. She'd finally told him what he wanted to know, but that still raised even more questions. Namely, was she still carrying a torch for the dude? Was this Liddell the reason she hadn't invited another man into her life, even though she'd said he wasn't? Even though she'd admitted she was better off without him in her life? Knowing it and accepting it were two different things.

He could recall the woman who'd broken Mercury's heart back in college. It had taken his brother a long time to get over the hurt, the anguish and the betrayal. Then he'd met Sloan and allowed himself to fall in love again.

Gannon's attention perked up when Delphine began walking away from her door. He knew this particular hotel was usually safe. There were video cameras and policemen periodically cruising the parking lot, but still, he had decided to hang back in the shadows to make sure she was okay. He discovered doing so was worth his time and effort as she strode into a lit area and he could clearly see the sway of her hips with every step she took. In her shorts and top, he could see that she definitely had nice hips and thighs. Now he was glad he was following her, even if she didn't know he was there.

After she'd left him to turn in for the night instead of going to his room, he'd had dinner with a couple of his drivers who were on this same route. That was one of the things he appreciated about these road trips—maintaining the various relationships he had with his employees. One team consisted of a husband and wife who'd been working with him for around five years now. They worked well together and always made their deliveries on time.

Even after a lively dinner and spending eleven hours behind the steering wheel of his rig, he'd had difficulty getting to sleep. Horniness had overwhelmed any exhaustion he should have felt. Every time he closed his eyes, he remembered their kiss. The second one they'd shared. It had been even better than the first, and he'd thought nothing could top that one.

Deciding that if he continued walking behind her, the enticing motion of her ass would be his downfall for the rest of the day, he called out, "Delphine. Wait up."

She turned and her expression indicated she was surprised to see him. "Gannon? Where did you come from?"

"My room." That wasn't a lie. No need to tell her that his room was only a few doors down from hers and that he'd been standing beneath the stairs waiting for her to come out.

"Oh. Did you sleep well last night?"

"I did." At least, he had once he'd finally drifted off with thoughts of her on his mind. "What about you?"

"After my shower I thought I'd get a little work done on the article. At some point I called it a night and climbed into bed. Not sure when or how. I woke up this morning still lying on top of the covers."

Gannon wondered if she realized she'd painted a pretty good picture in his mind of that entire scenario. He would have loved to have climbed in that bed right along with her, and if he had, there was no way she would not have remembered when and how. And she would not have awakened this morning still lying on top of the covers. If anything, she would have still been lying on top of him.

"Ready to jog this morning?" she asked as they began walking together side by side.

"Yes. Are you?"

She shrugged her shoulders. "I guess. I'm not really a jogger or even a walker, for that matter."

"Then how do you stay in shape?" he asked as they passed the hotel's lobby.

She chuckled. "Who says I'm in shape?"

"I do." And he would say it again if he had to. If she wasn't into physical fitness, he couldn't tell it. She looked sexy as sin in jeans, slacks, a pair of shorts or a dress. He'd seen her in all of them. Now he wanted to see her in none of them. More specifically, he would love to see her naked.

"Thanks for being sweet by saying that, but I could use a membership at the gym. But…"

When she stopped talking, he glanced over at her. "But what?"

She hesitated, as if trying to decide whether to give him an answer. Looking up, she met his gaze. "There's a gym not far from my house, but Liddell's wife is a member, so I choose not to go there. The next closest is on the other side of town."

"Oh, I see." And he honestly didn't like what he saw. Her decision not to go to a gym convenient to where she lived was because of her ex-fiancé's wife. He wondered what else she avoided for that reason.

They reached the truck stop and there were a couple of guys hanging around inside. Truckers who'd just parked and were on their way to the shower room. Gannon led her in the opposite direction, to where the gym was located.

"Wow. This is nice," she said, when they entered the huge room that contained several pieces of exercise equipment.

"It is. That's one of the reasons I make sure this place is on my drivers' routes. Sitting behind the wheel of a truck for twelve hours and then not moving muscles isn't good for your body. Leg cramps aren't a joke."

When they reached the jogging track, she glanced up at him. "We don't have to jog together. I plan to go at my own pace. And it will be a slow one."

He chuckled. "Okay. Will an hour work for you?"

"Heck, no," she said, grinning. "I was thinking more like thirty minutes. I would do half of that if I thought you would let me get away with it."

"I won't. Like I said, leg cramps aren't a joke. If you finish up before I do, there are other pieces of equipment you might want to try out."

He smiled when she gave him a look that all but said not to press his luck. "We'll see, Gannon. We'll see."

Nine

"Ready to roll again?"

Delphine glanced over at Gannon as she snapped her seat belt in place. "Yes, I'm ready." And she would admit she was looking forward to today's adventure. She'd visited San Antonio a couple of times with her mother and had always loved the River Walk.

Earlier that morning, after she had taken her thirty-minute jog, she had strolled another thirty minutes to keep Gannon company. Not that she felt she needed to, since he would happily jog by her. He had walked her back to the hotel room to shower, and they'd met back up again twenty minutes later to head over to the café for breakfast.

Now they were in the truck and ready to ride. She watched Gannon as he backed the truck out of the parking spot with ease, admiring his ability to handle the huge rig. "Who taught you how to drive one of these?"

He glanced over at her and smiled. "My dad. I also went to truckers' school to get my necessary licenses."

"You like this, don't you?"

He glanced over at her. "Like what?"

"Getting out of the office and out on the road."

He gave a slight shrug. "I like running things at the office, as well. I guess you can say I have the best of both worlds."

Yes, she could imagine him thinking that. The look that had shone in his eyes during her interview with him whenever he talked about his work had touched her. He had the ability not only to put people to work, but also to change lives. He did both.

She decided to stay awake today after he'd told her of the different sites they would pass along the way. Besides, she wanted to be better company for him. They talked about a lot of stuff, some she'd learned during the interview, like how involved he was in several charity organizations in Phoenix.

"All my brothers are," he told her. "You can't be one of Eden Tyson Steele's sons and not be," he added.

For a short while they listened to his classical music, and he suggested she check out the bunk area. She did and saw how roomy it was for her to sit on the bunk and use her laptop on the small desk. She edited most of her work before she pushed back the curtain to go back up front.

Later, after they had stopped for lunch, they reentered the truck to head out on the three-hour drive to San Antonio. He glanced over at her. "We're going to eventually have to find a place to hole up for an hour or so."

"Why?"

"Word just came from dispatch. There's a bad thunderstorm up ahead. It came out of nowhere on a practically sunny day. Regardless of how good your tires are, you have to be concerned with traction. We'll ride through it for a while and then we'll head toward a truck stop nearby. It's not as big as the other truck stops, but it will work to wait out the storm."

They hadn't gotten too far before the rain began. She leaned forward to stare out the windshield and could barely see outside. She did see other trucks pulling off the interstate and wasn't surprised when Gannon did, too.

The words of the dispatcher were slightly choppy, but Delphine understood them just the same. A tornado was in the area. "We're making it to the truck stop instead of remaining out here in the open," Gannon told her.

She nodded, knowing Gannon was better equipped to deal with the situation than she was. He drove the truck at a slow rate of speed with his caution lights on, then exited the interstate a short while later.

The rain had let up some, but the wind was howling something fierce. When they reached the truck stop, he parked on the lot and unbuckled his seat belt. "For safety reasons we need to get away from these windows. Let's get behind the curtain in the bunk area."

He evidently saw the frightened look on her face. She had never been a fan of thunderstorms and had a feeling her fear was showing.

He reached out and undid her seat belt before taking hold of her hand. "Come on."

She followed him to the bunk area, and then he put the curtain back in place so she wouldn't see what was taking place outside. Rain—so much rain—pounded hard on the truck. The thunder was so loud it seemed as if the ground shook from the sound. He sat her on the bunk and placed a quick kiss on her forehead. "You're safe with me, Delphine. Usually these sudden storms pass as quickly as they come up," he said, sitting down beside her.

Delphine wanted to believe that, but when the sound of thunder hit again, even louder, and seemingly lit up the entire truck, she pressed her face into his chest. He wrapped his arms around her and gently rubbed her back. At that moment, a comforting warmth spread through her body and she did believe what he'd told her. She was safe with him.

He pulled back slightly, his concerned green eyes staring down at her. "You okay?"

She could barely hear his question for the sound of the torrential rain beating all around them. She was grateful for him closing the curtain so she wouldn't see it. Hearing it was bad enough. She nodded. "Yes, I'm fine."

She wanted to add…*since you're here with me, I feel safe and protected.*

He placed another kiss on her cheek and she glanced up at him. Was she imagining things or were the depths of his green eyes getting darker and darker? Was that heat she was feeling flowing from him to her?

Delphine began nibbling on her lower lip and he watched her. Then she remembered what he'd told her about her lips and his fetish for them. Suddenly, she felt hot all over and she couldn't stop her gaze from moving over Gannon's very handsome face.

"Like what you see, Delphine?"

The question was asked in a deep, throaty voice, causing more heat to suffuse her. She decided to be both honest and bold. "Yes. What about you, Gannon? Do you like what you see?"

A sensuous smile lifted both corners of his lips. "Yes. Most definitely. And do you know what I yearn to do? Right now?"

"No. Tell me." Then, deciding to go up another notch in boldness, she said, "Show me."

He leaned in and lowered his mouth to hers. The exact moment he did, she felt not only the warmth of his kiss, but also the intensity of it. When he slid his tongue inside her mouth, she became so caught up in what he was doing and how he was doing it that she forgot the sound of the fierce rain outside, and the loud clapping of thunder.

Instead, she wholly concentrated on how he was taking her mouth with an expertise she felt in every part of her body. And when he deepened the kiss, she moaned into his mouth and wrapped her arms around his neck. He began doing creative things to her mouth, making her moan even more. Even louder. She felt the hard pounding of her heart with every bold sweep of his tongue. He'd told her how much he loved her lips and he was showing her just how much he did.

She wasn't sure how long they kissed, but when they finally tore their mouths apart, their breathing was erratic. Her eyebrows drew together in a question. Why had he stopped? She would not have minded if they'd continued. Gannon had the ability to bring out desires in her that she hadn't known existed.

"I think we better stop, don't you?"

Did she? No, not really. She wanted more. She wanted what she'd denied herself for close to five years. What she'd gone without since Liddell. Gannon had awakened feelings in her that she thought were essentially out of sight and out of mind. He'd proved that theory wrong.

She wanted him.

As if he read what she wasn't saying, he leaned in and said, "You know you're welcome to join me in my bed at any time."

Was that the invitation he issued to all the women who wanted him? The thought didn't freak her out as much as it should have. Heck, it honestly didn't bother her because she was the one woman, by his own admission, who had him thinking there could possibly be more between them. Even if it wasn't true, which she was convinced it wasn't, the notion that she had gotten his attention in a way no other woman had made her feel good inside.

"I'll keep that in mind, Gannon." It was obvious her response surprised him by the way his eyebrows drew together. Good. Let him feel as off-kilter as his kisses were making her feel.

"Sounds like the rain has stopped now," he said.

Had it? She listened and discovered he was right. But little did he know he had essentially awakened a quiet storm within her, and she had a feeling after this road trip with him that her life would never be the same.

It was time for her to begin enjoying life. Her mother had died before her fiftieth birthday and the last three years of her life had been full of agony and pain. But, according to her mother, she had not had any regrets. June Ryland often told her daughter that even with the humiliating ways her father had treated her, she never regretted falling in love and marrying him because they had produced Delphine.

Maybe it was time Delphine had that kind of attitude. No regrets. Live for the moment.

By the time Gannon stood, Delphine's mind was made up. Whether he decided she was his destiny or not, that didn't matter. She honestly knew she wasn't, anyway. What mattered to her was that she thought of him as her knight in shining armor. He had helped her get through the storm and now it was time for him to show her how to dance in the rain.

Ten

Gannon heard the knocking on the door, glanced at his watch and figured it was Housekeeping bringing him another coffeepot since the one in his room wasn't working. He and Delphine had arrived at the truck stop in San Antonio a couple of hours ago. This stop wasn't as big as the one in Fort Stockton, but he liked this hotel a lot better since it wasn't the style with hotel rooms opening out to a breezeway. He'd taken a shower, changed clothes and lain across the bed to watch television until it was time to leave to meet Delphine. He'd told her he would be coming to her room at seven to walk her to dinner.

They would be heading out early in the morning. He figured they were making good time and would be in Jacksonville as planned on Monday, barring any more bad weather. But he would be the first to admit that being held up with Delphine had been rewarding. When they'd gotten on the road again, she'd told him of her fear of storms since she'd been a little girl and how even now, whenever a bad storm hit, she would close all the curtains in her home, darken the house and go to bed and cover her head until it was over. Storms had never bothered him and the thought that they made her afraid had brought out a protective instinct in him.

Using the remote to lower the volume on the television, he eased off the bed, strolled to the door and looked out the peephole. It wasn't Housekeeping. It was Delphine, and she was holding several bags in her hands. He quickly opened the door.

"What's going on here?" he asked her, relieving her of the bags. The aroma flowing from them was a dead giveaway. Food.

"And just what do we have here?" he asked as she entered.

"I noticed how crowded the restaurant was and thought it would be nice if I ordered the food and we ate in. I hope you don't mind."

"No, I don't mind," he said, taking the bags over to the desk. "Something smells good."

"I hope you like everything I ordered, and I think they were generous with the portions."

He chuckled as he began removing containers. "Most truck-stop restaurants are. They know how hungry truckers can get."

He glanced up from the food to see Delphine looking around the room. He figured his was identical to hers and wondered why the interest. Instead of asking her, he said, "I'm ready to dig in. What about you?"

She laughed. "If your brothers had your hearty appetite while growing up, I don't envy your parents one bit."

He chuckled. "All six of us love to eat and we were

lucky that Mom loved to cook. That's why we have Thursday nights at her house."

"Thursday nights?"

"Yes," he said, pulling a couple of chairs closer to the desk. "When everyone left home, Mom didn't want to feel out of touch with her sons, so she implemented Thursday nights at my parents' house. She cooks dinner and expects everyone to show up so she can see all her sons together in one place. Namely, under her roof."

He watched Delphine slide into her chair before he took his. Like him, she had showered and changed clothes. He liked the tan-colored top and slacks she was wearing. But then, he'd liked the jeans she'd worn earlier, as well.

"Everyone usually shows up?"

"Anyone in their right mind knows not to miss it. She figures if you miss one that means she needs to spend extra time with you. Trust me, Eden Tyson Steele has no qualms about showing up at your place unannounced at the worst possible time."

Delphine laughed and he liked the sound. "You're kidding, right?"

"Nope. Several of my brothers have received Mom's unexpected visits when they were entertaining lady friends."

Gannon liked the choices she'd ordered for them. Pork chops smothered in delicious gravy, wild rice, an assortment of mixed vegetables and what looked like the best-tasting corn bread ever.

"I hope you enjoy all the food," she said.

He smiled over at her. "Don't think for one minute that I won't."

As they ate, more than once, he complimented her on the meal.

"It's not like I cooked it, Gannon."

"No, but you were thoughtful enough to think it would be better to eat here instead of the restaurant. I like it."

She tilted her head to look at him. "And why do you like it?"

He decided to be honest with her. "Because I like sharing private space with you."

Gannon truly meant that. She was the best traveling partner a trucker could have. They'd covered a lot of topics during their conversations, but he knew she still kept parts of her life away from him. Even so, he knew the important parts, namely about her ex and the pain the man had caused her.

A short while after they'd finished eating, there was a knock at the door. "That's probably Housekeeping bringing me another coffeepot," he said, heading for the door. "I called for one when I couldn't get this one to work."

He opened the door and a woman from Housekeeping walked in. She looked to be in her early twenties and gave him a flirtatious smile, although he was certain she'd seen Delphine sitting at the desk. "Where would you like me to place this?" she asked him.

"You can grab the old one and replace it."

He'd never had a problem with flirtatious women before, but he'd discovered that lately he found them pretty damn annoying. Like Trish, this woman was attractive, and as she crossed the room to the coffeepot, she was deliberately swaying her hips with every step. He'd also noticed the top two buttons of her blouse were undone.

He wasn't biting.

Not one stir of desire flowed through his groin. The only woman he wanted with a passion was the one sitting at the desk pretending not to notice the other woman's bold antics. However, Delphine had to be very much aware of the not-so-subtle message the housekeeper was giving him.

"Will there be anything else?" the woman asked in a sultry voice while raking him up and down with her eyes.

If there was anything else, did she think he would disrespect Delphine by inviting her to come back to his room later? "No, there's nothing else, and there's no need for you to return."

After the housekeeper left, Delphine stood and began placing all the empty containers back in the bags. "It's time for me to go," she said, not looking at him.

He leaned back against the closed hotel-room door and crossed his arms over his chest. "Why do you do that?"

"Do what?" she asked, looking at him now.

"Feel the need to retreat whenever it comes to other women?"

She lifted her chin. "I don't know what you mean."

"Don't you? I noticed it that day with Trish. After meeting her, you thought that maybe we shouldn't eat lunch together. You've also admitted how you avoided going to that gym close to where you live because the wife of your ex-fiancé goes there, like you should care. Then just now, that woman came on to me, which I handled, yet now you want to leave. Retreat."

She shrugged. "I don't want to cause problems."

He didn't say anything for a minute. Dropping his arms to his sides, he crossed the room. "When it comes to me, you could never cause problems, Delphine. You're here because I want you here. Always remember that. And I also hope you're here because you want to be here."

He reached out, took the bags from her hands and placed them back on the desk. Taking a step closer to her, he wrapped his arms around her waist and felt her quiver from his touch. "Do you want to be here with me, Delphine?"

She didn't answer at first, and then she reached up to place her hands on his chest, gently rubbing against the cotton of his T-shirt with the tips of her fingers. She met his gaze. "Yes, I want to be here with you."

He figured it had taken a lot for her to admit that. "Convince me. Convince me you want to be here with me."

Delphine licked her lips and he felt a stirring in his groin. "And how am I supposed to do that?"

He continued to stare into her eyes, hoping they were encouraging her to be as bold as she could be. "Any damn way you want will be fine with me."

She hesitated and then she leaned into him. Her arms shifted away from his chest to loop around his neck. Then she stood on tiptoe. Deciding to meet her the rest of the way, Gannon lowered his head to join his lips with hers. He wanted her to take control and moaned when she slid her tongue into his mouth. Then she began maneuvering it, like he'd done when they'd kissed earlier, and the other times. He could only take so much before his control broke and he began devouring her mouth greedily, enjoying the sweetness of her taste and the feel of her warm body plastered to his.

Lifting his mouth from hers, he tightened his arms around her waist while gazing into her eyes. "Convince me some more, Delphine," he said, leaning in, zeroing in on her lips to lick around the corners. "Convince me some more."

* * *

Delphine had never convinced a man of anything and wasn't even sure she knew how. But she was determined to try.

She had to. Because at that moment her body was filled with desire for Gannon. He hadn't made any promises to her and she hadn't made any to him. She'd learned the hard way that when it came to love, promises could easily be broken. She much preferred things this way. Simple. Easy. No commitments. Gannon wasn't beholden to her and she wasn't beholden to him. They could walk away at any time, and no matter what he thought about her having a possible place in his future, they would separate at the end of their trip. She would be flying out of Jacksonville and heading back to Denver in a few days.

That was why she needed this. A chance to show him just how much she enjoyed being here with him. How much she wanted to be here. She hoped she could pull it off because the desire shining in the depths of his green eyes could not be ignored. He wanted her as much as she wanted him. And she did want him. More than she'd ever wanted another man.

She stepped out of his hold and tugged her blouse over her head, knowing he was watching her every move. Then she placed her hands on her waist to slide down her slacks.

"Let me help with those."

His husky voice had her watching as he moved toward her. He got on bended knees to tug the fabric all the way down her legs. She stepped out of her shoes and then her slacks, leaving her wearing only her bra and panties.

He leaned back on his haunches and glanced up at her. "We're almost there," he said.

She swallowed and then took a deep breath as she removed her bra and tossed it on the chair. Her hands went to her panties and Gannon said, "Let me. I want to help with those, too."

She nodded. It was obvious he liked undressing her below the waist. When he leaned in to tug her panties down her legs, the desire she saw in the depths of his eyes seemed to increase tenfold. Standing there completely naked, she stared down at him. He again leaned back on his haunches while his gaze raked heatedly over her body.

Then he met her eyes. "You're beautiful, Delphine."

Although she wished they hadn't, his words stirred something within her that made every bone in her body turn to mush. She could barely stand under the heat of his gaze.

"What about your clothes?" she finally asked him.

"What about them?" he asked, standing back up.

"Aren't you going to take them off?"

He shook his head. "No, but you can if you want."

Yes, she wanted, so she moved toward him. His T-shirt came off easily, but she figured his jeans would be a little more challenging, especially when it was quite obvious that he was aroused.

"Need my help, Delphine?"

She glanced from his midsection up to his face. "Yes, if you don't mind."

"I don't mind at all."

She watched as he unzipped his pants and then tugged both his jeans and briefs down his legs. When he stood before her, it was just like she'd figured. Gannon Steele was beautifully made. Tight abs, wide shoulders, broad chest, taut thighs. Her gaze moved from the soles of his bare feet all the way up to the top of his head. Of course, she'd allowed her gaze to linger on certain places. Just looking at that part of him had her heart beating fast and furious against her rib cage. This was the second man she'd ever seen naked and he looked more impressive, definitely more powerful, than the first one had. She hated to compare the two, but Gannon gave her no choice.

"Let me know when you've gotten your fill."

She looked up into his eyes and saw the twinkle in the green depths. He was teasing her, but all she wanted to do was get it on with him. The sooner, the better. She hadn't wanted a man this bad, ever. "I don't think that's possible. For me to get my fill."

Gannon chuckled. "Glad to hear you say that because I doubt that I can get my fill of you, either, Delphine."

Now he was scrutinizing her body again, which made her nervously nibble her lips. He was in perfect shape, but her, not so much. However, he didn't seem to mind that her breasts weren't as big as some women's and that she had more curves than she thought she needed.

"You look perfect."

She would accept his comment and appreciate that he'd made it. "Thank you."

And then he swept her into his arms and carried her to the bed.

She was light as a feather, Gannon thought, as he moved across the room, carrying a nude Delphine. Her naked flesh rubbed against his, sending even more desire racing through him. After placing her on the bed, he stood back, needing to look at her nakedness some more.

He felt eager at the thought of making love to her. Easing inside of her, rocking her with hard, deep strokes and hearing her moan his name. Pleasure pulsed through his veins at the thought of all he wanted to do to her. All that he intended to do.

After sheathing himself with a condom, he crawled on the bed with her, straddled her body and slid between her legs. But first he needed to taste her. He began kissing her breasts, thinking they were a perfect size and shape. He loved the way the nipple fit in his mouth, and wrapped his tongue around it. Then his mouth moved lower as he licked her stomach, while his fingers massaged her breasts. He liked licking her navel almost as much as he liked her nipples.

Intent on going lower still, he began licking his way downward. He could feel her squirm beneath his mouth. He placed a kiss on her womanly folds before lifting his head to meet her gaze. "Easy, baby. I love all kinds of lips. Even these."

"I can't take much more," she whispered as she dug her fingers into his shoulders.

Gannon smiled before burying his head between her legs and sliding his tongue inside of her. His tongue swirled. Then he nipped at her clit and tasted her with ferocious intent.

"Gannon… Gannon…" She whispered his name over and over while rubbing the back of his head. He knew when her body became even more aroused. It made heat flare through his groin. Desire for her heightened even more and his lips and tongue were wet from her juices. Then she screamed and he quickly rushed up to her mouth to drown out the sound.

There was a raw sensuality about her that brought out everything male within him. He knew the moment the spasms had subsided, and it was then that savage lust took over his mind and body.

Moving back between her legs, he eased inside of her, loving the tightness, the perfect fit, the connection. His desire to mate with her this way, filling her with all of him, could no longer be denied. He glanced down at her, appreciating her beauty. His brothers' warnings had been right. The flame of desire that had kindled between them from the first had been lit for a reason. A powerful male force passed through him and he began moving with a need that had been building inside of him since the first day he'd laid eyes on her.

As he thrust hard into her, with every stroke he claimed her. Hearing her chant his name over and over was driving him past the edge. Each time he would quickly snatch himself back, needing more and more from her.

Their mating was in perfect unison. He wanted to give her all he had because he knew she was the only woman with the ability to do this to him. The only one. Every thrust was shared pleasure that he wanted to last forever. Suddenly, he felt an explosion, and when she screamed his name again, he couldn't silence her because he was hollering out his pleasure, as well.

He leaned down and captured her mouth, needing her kiss, her taste. Their mouths mated in a way he was convinced was meant to be.

He pulled away and, with their lips just inches apart, she asked, "Did I convince you?"

A smile touched his mouth from corner to corner when he said, "Yes, baby, you convinced me."

Delphine cuddled in Gannon's arms, completely sated and depleted of energy. She'd never felt a sense of satisfaction like this before. All she had to do was close her eyes to remember orgasm after orgasm while he'd thrust into her, rocked his hips hard against hers and been gripped in the throes of passion. Her body had shuddered, and the more it had, the harder he'd thrust. The hotel room was quiet. She heard only the sounds of their breathing mingling with the low hum of whatever he'd been watching on television.

"Are you okay?"

If only he knew just how okay she was. He had kissed her all over, tasted her, made love to her in the most erotic ways, and then they had lain there, absorbing the sensuous aftermath before doing it all over again. She had screamed his name and he had hollered hers. Yes, she was okay, because tonight she'd experienced all that was Gannon Andrew Steele.

She shifted in his arms to stare up at him. "Yes, I'm fine. What about you?"

"I feel great. Now we need to get some sleep. Tomorrow is a long driving day. We need to make it to Baton Rouge by evening. Make up for the couple of hours we lost during the storm. Now go to sleep."

Sleep? He hadn't asked that she get dressed and go to her own room. "You want me to stay?"

He'd closed his eyes, but he reopened them to stare at her. "Of course I want you to stay. I love having you here with me." He then leaned in to kiss her forehead. "In fact, I'd like to ask you something."

"What?"

"I had mentioned to you that after I reach Jacksonville and unload the cargo, I plan to show you the Atlantic Ocean before I head to my beach house in Miami for a week. I'd like to invite you to go with me."

Delphine felt a deep pounding in her chest. She recalled him mentioning his plans. "You're inviting me to go with you to Miami?"

"Yes. You said you didn't have to rush back to Denver, right?"

"Yes, that's right."

"And I want to show you the Atlantic from Miami instead of Jacksonville."

"Miami?"

"Yes. I'd like to take you with me to Miami. That way I can do more than show you the Atlantic Ocean. I want to spend time with you in the water. I want to share that with you, Delphine."

That he wanted to do that for her filled her with a degree of happiness she hadn't felt in a long time. "Are you sure you aren't tired of my company?" she asked him, nearly overwhelmed with joy.

"Trust me, I'm positive. Like I said, I love having you with me. So will you go to Miami and stay on the beach with me?"

Delphine smiled. She knew she shouldn't let what he'd said get to her this way, but it had. Gannon wanted to spend even more time with her, and what was so amazing was that she wanted to spend more time with him, as well.

"Yes, I'll go to Miami with you."

Eleven

Two days later, Gannon pulled his truck into the lot of the Duval Clothing Warehouse in Jacksonville. The dispatcher had notified him that a crew would be there to unload the truck. Glancing over at Delphine, he saw she was still asleep, and had been since they'd left Pensacola a few hours ago. He knew she needed her rest since he'd been keeping her up at night and he couldn't help smiling when he remembered how. Those nights had had an impact on him, and he hoped they'd had an impact on her, as well.

Leaning over, he gently shook her awake, then watched her eyes slowly open and meet his. The smile that touched her lips appeared as one of contentment, but the smile he returned was one of total admiration. He'd decided that Delphine Ryland was every man's fantasy come true. She was certainly his.

"We're here?" she asked in a groggy voice, but it sounded pretty damn sensuous to his ears.

"Yes, we're here." Not able to help himself, he leaned in and placed a kiss on those lips he loved. Over the past two days he'd given her numerous demonstrations of just how much he loved them. He got hard just thinking about it.

Straightening back up in his seat, he knew he had to get control of the situation or he would be putty in her hands. And speaking of…it didn't take much to recall just how she used her hands on him, along with that mouth.

Forcing those erotic memories from his mind, he grabbed the clipboard from overhead. They had come to the final leg of their journey and he would admit he had enjoyed every mile of it because of her. As soon as he finalized things here, they would take the five-hour drive to Miami. He had called ahead and everything would be ready when they got there. He intended to make the time special for her.

He glanced over at her. "I've ordered a car to be delivered to us and I think that's it over there. I'll help get everything out of the cab and loaded into the car in a few."

He got out of the truck to take care of the final part of his business. A few moments later, he returned and unloaded their stuff from the cab into the trunk of the car.

"Are you sure you feel like driving to Miami after just arriving here?"

"I'm positive," he said before slipping behind the wheel. "I figure we can stop for something to eat in Daytona. Unless you're hungry now."

"Are you kidding? After all we ate for breakfast?"

They had eaten breakfast at a café in Pensacola and he was convinced they'd been the best pancakes he'd ever eaten. He had eaten more than he should have, and for once he'd noted she'd cleaned her plate, too. He glanced over at her and smiled. "I will admit that for once I'm full."

"Really?"

He chuckled. "Yes, really."

He had driven away from the warehouse and headed toward the interstate, feeling content in a way he'd never felt before. Being in a serious relationship with a woman was something he'd always avoided and now he thought doing so wouldn't be so bad if the woman was Delphine. They connected on all levels, both in the bedroom and out.

"And you're sure you don't want me to drive for a change?"

He glanced over at her. Warmth spread through him in a way it had never done before when he'd been with a woman. "Yes, I'm positive. I just want you well rested for tonight."

She chuckled. "Um, have you thought that maybe I want you well rested, as well?"

He laughed. "If you think for one minute I'm not on top of my game, then you're wrong. I intend to prove just how wrong you are over the next several days."

A huge smile lit her face. "We'll see."

"You said, 'you'll see.' Have you seen yet?"

Instead of answering him, Delphine looped her arm around his neck and stood on tiptoe to place a kiss on his lips. "This is simply beautiful, Gannon," she said, looking into his eyes and then switching her gaze back to the ocean.

Upon arriving in Miami, Gannon had driven straight to his beach house on the ocean. It wasn't just a beach house. It was a masterpiece. He'd told her on the drive to Miami that his parents had owned it, and when they'd decided to sell it, he was the only sibling interested in buying it. The five others had loved their summers here while growing up, but wanted to try other locations for a change. He had not. He'd told her how this place held special memories for him of his childhood summers and he'd wanted to keep the house to share with the kids he would have one day.

That had been the first time he had mentioned settling down, marrying and having a family. Of course, he had mentioned it when he'd given his spiel about why he wanted her to come with him on this road trip, claiming that a part of him believed she was his future, but she'd never really believed that. She figured he had wanted her with him and would have said anything that sounded convincing to get her here. That thought didn't bother her because she didn't regret coming.

Being here with him was helping her on a number of levels. It was showing her that she could share a relationship with a man, even when she knew it wasn't headed anywhere. She'd seriously doubted that she could, but she felt good in knowing it was possible. She would never give her love, heart or dedication to a man again. Liddell and her father had shown her men didn't know the meaning of loyalty to one woman. In accepting that fact, she knew what she needed to learn was how not to enter into a relationship blindly, or love so quickly, or give her heart so easily.

"I love it here, Gannon. Now I know why you wanted to come here to stay a week."

He smiled down at her. "Did you enjoy walking on the beach with me?"

She had. In fact, that was the first thing they'd done when they got here. He had laughed when she'd raced toward the water and gotten her toes wet. This part of the beach was private, and they didn't have to worry about others sharing their space. "I can see why you bought this place from your parents. I can't believe they gave it up."

He chuckled. "Only because they purchased something bigger a few miles from here. They said the new place was an investment in their future. They figured their sons would one day marry and have kids of their own, and they wanted to own a place that would accommodate everyone. It's been a long-standing tradition in the Steele family to spend the Fourth of July together with the folks, and it's usually here in Miami at their beach house."

She nodded. "What about your brothers? Did they tire of a place on the beach?"

He wrapped his arms around her waist as they stood on the patio and looked out at the Atlantic together. "No. They just wanted a different beach for a change. Galen and Tyson own beach houses on Hilton Head, Mercury likes the Gulf and bought a place on the beach in Destin, Florida, Eli couldn't make up his mind and bought a beach house in California and also one in the Keys, and Jonas also got a place on the beach in Destin."

He leaned down and nuzzled her neck. "I thought we would go out tonight, if you aren't tired. We have the rest of the week to fend for ourselves. I don't cook much but I do like to grill."

She smiled up at him. "Sounds like fun."

They ended up going to a restaurant within walking distance of the beach house. Gannon had to put up a good argument to get her to walk with him, but he'd been very persuasive. It was obvious the owner of the establishment, Mr. Tyler, knew Gannon and gave him

special treatment. They ate in a private room that overlooked the Atlantic with soft classical music playing in
the background.

Gannon had told her the restaurant had been in the
Tyler family for years and that it was the place his family would visit often while spending those summers on
the beach. They had grown up with Mr. Tyler's two sons
and three daughters, who were now partners in the restaurant business. They'd met one of the daughters earlier when they'd arrived.

"How is the food?" Gannon asked.

"Great. In fact, I feel stuffed. Walking back to the
beach house probably is the best idea."

He grinned. "That's one of the reasons I suggested
it."

On the walk back, he kept her close to his side with
his arms wrapped around her waist. She liked the way
they fit together and how they seemed to stroll in unison. It wasn't lost on her that every so often Gannon's
hand would dip lower and purposely squeeze her butt.
That didn't bother her, since over the last three days
he'd done more to it than that. She didn't want to think
of the passion marks probably covering it.

When they reached his beach house, he opened the
door and quickly ushered her inside. She soon knew
why when he said, "Watching you eat your food almost
drove me crazy. The way you tackled those oysters was
a total turn-on."

Delphine had discovered that practically everything was a turn-on for Gannon when it came to her. It
seemed just breathing turned him on. She had no complaints and rather liked it. In fact, she liked it a lot, although she refused to let it go to her head.

"What do you intend to do about it?" she asked him,

knowing the last thing she should do was encourage him or taunt him when she knew where it would lead. In the three days since first sharing his bed, she had discovered a lot about herself. She enjoyed making love with a man. More specifically, she enjoyed making love with Gannon.

"You should have learned your lesson about doing that," he said, backing her up against the closed door.

"In doing what?" she asked innocently.

"In making me want to show you anything. What usually happens is I end up showing you a lot. Some of the things I wonder if you're ready for."

She would be the first to admit Gannon was a man of various ideas when it came to lovemaking. So far, nothing he'd done had turned her off. In fact, without a doubt, everything they'd tried had turned her on. "I'm ready for anything and everything from you, Gannon."

Delphine meant what she said, wanting him to know the effect he had on her. He had managed to tap into her passionate side, and she couldn't stop her body from responding to him even if she'd wanted it to.

"In that case…" he said, before easing her up and then propping her back against the door.

"What do you think you're doing?" she asked breathlessly. Her heart was beating fast and the area between her legs was pounding just as furiously. Gannon was hot-blooded and he was bringing out the hot-bloodedness in her, as well.

He had managed to pull down her shorts and underwear, as well as tug down his own. She wanted to say they were behaving like a pair of horny teenagers, but she couldn't say that when she and Liddell had never acted this way. Somehow, even in their positions against the door, Gannon managed to remove her top and her breasts sprang free.

"Well, well, what do we have here?" Gannon said, and she heard the huskiness in his voice.

"Like you didn't know I wasn't wearing a bra," she said, and then moaned when he began licking his lips.

"Damn right I knew," he said before sliding a nipple into his mouth.

She released another deep moan and he began sucking hard. When the sucking motion became more demanding, she felt every nerve ending in her body electrify.

"Gannon..."

"Hmm?"

She couldn't say anything, not when he'd moved to the second nipple and was giving it just as much torture as he'd done the first. All that pleasure had made her wet.

"Did you want something?" he asked, when he finally let go of her breasts to look at her. The green eyes staring deep into hers were intense and held promises of more to come.

Before she could say if she wanted anything or not, he lifted her hips a little higher, tilted her toward him and drove hard into her while still gazing into her eyes. She saw how the intensity in the green depths transformed into lust of the richest form.

She wanted to close her eyes, but she couldn't. It was as if his gaze demanded that she continue to look at him while feeling him deep inside of her. She was transfixed, thoroughly captivated, by the beauty of the man making love to her.

Delphine was convinced she felt him all the way to her womb. And while their gazes remained connected, he continued to thrust hard into her, with a vigor and fierceness that had her quivering all over.

"You have no idea what you do to me, Delphine," he murmured. "You have no idea." His voice was thick with emotion.

He was right; she honestly didn't. Had he determined if she was truly any different from all the others he'd done this with, or had that been just a line he told every woman he'd wanted? That they were his destiny? She pushed the question to the back of her mind, refusing to let anything dim the pleasure he was making her feel. She wanted this. She needed this.

Although she wasn't new to sex, she was new to Gannon Steele's brand of sex. He had introduced her to a degree of passion she'd only thought could be found in romance novels. She'd figured it was all make-believe, the work of an imaginative author. However, she'd found Gannon had the ability to bring all that passion from the pages of a romance novel right into his bedroom.

He broke eye contact with her when he lowered his head to take the lips he claimed he loved, and like always, he was demonstrating just how much he loved them. How could he multitask this way, and kiss her while steadily thrusting hard into her?

Suddenly a shiver of intense pleasure took over her entire body, rocking it back and forth. She began squeezing her inner muscles together when the throb between her legs strengthened and the ache increased. "Gannon, please…"

He knew what she wanted. Suddenly, he broke off the kiss, threw back his head and hollered her name. The sound triggered every passionate cell in her body to react, and she was thrust into an orgasm of gigantic proportions. She tightened her legs around him when she felt him explode inside of her. Immediately, she realized they were making love for the first time without him using a condom. She knew the moment he realized it, as well. He opened his eyes to look at her, and when she murmured that she was on the pill, he lowered his head and kissed her.

And he kept on kissing her, long after the last of the spasms had ended. It was as if they needed their mouths to be joined this way, while a surge of passionate warmth joined their bodies.

When he finally slid her body down his and her feet touched the floor again, he stared at her with a serious expression on his face. "I know what you said about being on the pill, but nothing is one hundred percent. If anything happens you will let me know, right?"

The intense look on his face gave her pause. Or was it a worried look at the thought he might have gotten a woman pregnant?

"Nothing will happen, Gannon," she said to reassure him. And then she placed a kiss on his lips.

Gannon glanced over at Delphine and saw she was asleep. Ignoring the twitch in his penis from wanting more of her, he slowly disengaged their bodies and eased out of bed. After returning from the bathroom, he grabbed his shorts off the chair and slid them on. Glancing over at Delphine again, he was tempted to crawl back in bed with her, but knew he couldn't. He had to think.

Opening the French door, he stepped outside and noticed there was a full moon in the sky that appeared to touch the ocean water. The scent of the salty sea filled his nostrils, but nothing could clear his mind of what had happened earlier. For the first time ever, he'd made love to a woman without using a condom.

Protection had always been his strictest rule, no matter what form of birth control the woman claimed she was using. And he didn't use just any type of condom. He used ones that were custom-made for their fit, as well as their performance effectiveness.

He hadn't wanted any woman to ever claim he was her baby's daddy. To that end, the last thing he'd ever wanted to encounter was a condom malfunction. His brothers used to tease him about being so particular, but that was the way he was.

Yet tonight he had gotten so caught up in making love to Delphine, so caught up in the passion, the desire, the pleasure, that he'd done just what he'd sworn he would never do. And he had liked it. Damn, he had liked the feel of exploding inside of her a whole hell of a lot. He had liked it to the point that when he had swept her off her feet to carry her into the bedroom, he had made love to her again the same way—without a condom. What would make him toss caution to the wind that way?

He eased down on the lounge chair and stared out at the ocean. Everything about Delphine got to him. Her beauty, the way she would look at him when he wasn't supposed to know she was looking. Her scent, the way her body would take his into hers, and those sexy moans that flowed from her delectable lips right before she came.

He liked touching her, sharing his beach with her, and his home. And he definitely liked the way she would wrap her legs around his waist whenever he would slide inside her to make love. That was when her inner muscles would clamp down on him hard, while her body arched into his so the connection would be deeper, each thrust more meaningful.

"Gannon?"

He turned at the sound of her voice. She was standing in the doorway naked. His gaze roamed over her, lingered on her pert breasts and flat stomach before lowering to the juncture of her thighs. He was about to explode just seeing that part of her that had pleasured him so much over the past few days.

"Gannon?"

He swallowed deeply. "Yes, Delphine?"

"I woke up and you were gone. I just want you to know you were missed."

"That can easily be remedied," he said, and slowly moved toward her. He swept her into his arms to take her back inside, knowing he was about to toss caution to the wind yet again.

Twelve

Delphine ran faster knowing Gannon was right on her heels, intent on catching her to toss her into the water. For the past three days, they'd taken a walk on the beach every afternoon, but he'd yet to convince her to go swimming with him. Today he'd decided that would change and began chasing after her.

She refused to look over her shoulder for fear that would slow her down and he would catch her for sure. So she kept on running, even if she was running in circles. Hopefully, he would tire out before she did. But then, all she had to do was remember all their lovemaking sessions and how he had the stamina of a bull and…

"Got you!"

They tumbled to the sand and she inwardly admitted that, yes, he had her. But then, he'd been having her for the past few days now. Not that she was complaining. Now she was flat on her back—nothing new there, either. When Gannon just continued to stare at her, she said, "I hope you know I'm getting sand all in my hair."

He lowered his head toward her lips and said, "I'll help you wash it out."

"Will you?"

"Of course I will."

Gannon's mouth came closer and his lips touched hers and she knew she was a goner for certain. But she didn't mind. She never minded when it came to him. It could be because she had gone and done the one thing she'd sworn she'd never do again.

She'd fallen in love.

She felt his hands glide beneath her T-shirt to touch her breasts. At the moment, she truly appreciated that they were on a private beach. She knew what he was about to do to her and she knew she would let him. Gannon had a way of breaking down her defenses and robbing her of all common sense. How else could she have fallen in love with him when she'd known better? When she had known that regardless of what he claimed, she was not his destiny. She was certain that by now he knew it, as well.

She figured he was just waiting for the perfect time to tell her that although he'd enjoyed her company, both in and out of bed, she was no different from all the others he'd dated. The sexual chemistry between them might be strong, but that was all it was—strong sexual chemistry. Nothing more. Too bad it had taken him a whole road trip with her to find that out.

While it might end up being too bad for him, she would always consider it one of the best weeks of her life. She had needed it, and she appreciated him giving it to her. She would leave here on Monday knowing that although she loved him, he didn't love her. But for one week, they'd been together.

"I want to make love to you, Delphine. Here. Now. On my beach. So whenever I come back here, I'll remember."

Whenever *he* came back here. Not whenever *they* came back here… Was that his way of letting her know that there wouldn't be a *they* in his future? That she wouldn't be coming back here with him? She got it. She wasn't his forever girl after all, like she'd suspected. That meant all she would ever have was this and she would take it.

Gannon made beautiful love to her under a magnificent blue sky on his beach. Afterward, he picked her up in his arms and carried her inside the house so they could take a shower together. True to his word, he helped wash her hair. He also washed her body and then he made love to her again.

He held her while she slept. For some reason, she'd tossed and turned most of the night, to the point where he'd awakened her to ask if she was okay. How could she tell him that, no, she wasn't okay? She knew that at some point before Monday he would be letting her know where they stood. Instead of telling him anything, though, she'd asked that he make love to her again, and he had.

"You okay, Delphine?" he asked her the next morning before either of them got out of bed. It was close to ten already and they'd decided to make today a lazy day and sleep in.

"I'm fine. I just have a lot on my mind," she said. "No worries." After placing a kiss on his lips, she eased out of bed to go to the bathroom. That was when she heard the ringing of his phone. She quickly noted the ringtone was different from any of the previous calls he'd gotten. It was to the tune of a flirty love song.

Instead of declining the call, like he'd done with all the others he'd been receiving, he clicked on and she heard him say, "Hello, beautiful. If you're calling to see if I miss you, the answer is yes, and I can't wait to return to Phoenix to see you."

At that moment, Delphine's heart crumbled. She'd known he would be telling her at some point that she wasn't his destiny, but she hadn't expected him to already be planning to get together with another woman. Why couldn't he at least wait until after she left to make those plans? They only had three more days together.

She took several deep breaths as she entered the bathroom and closed the door behind her, fighting back her tears. She leaned against the vanity as her heart broke in a million pieces. She then recalled something she had conveniently forgotten.

He'd told her the first night they'd met that she had reminded him of someone. Was that the person who was calling him? Had he been with Delphine, but in the back of his mind he'd been fantasizing about that other woman?

The last thing Delphine intended to do was to say anything to him about the phone call she'd overheard. What had he told her just a few days ago when they'd been on the road together? He'd pretty much accused her of feeling the need to retreat whenever it came to other women. He was probably right. She had learned her lesson. She refused to let a man decide she wasn't worthy by selecting someone else over her.

"Are you sure you're okay, Delphine?" Gannon asked. He was concerned about her. She hadn't slept much last night for tossing and turning, and today she'd seemed withdrawn. He kept asking her what was wrong, but she refused to tell him what was bothering her. However, he knew something was. The first anniversary of her mother's death was Sunday, which was also Mother's Day. Maybe that was it.

"I'm fine, Gannon, but there's something I need to tell you," she said, looking across the table at him. He'd grilled steaks and they had decided to eat outside on the patio.

"What do you need to tell me?"

"I'm leaving tomorrow."

He frowned, certain he hadn't heard her correctly. "Excuse me? Did you just say you're leaving tomorrow?"

"Yes," she answered simply. Just "yes" and nothing more. And what bothered him more than anything was that she was looking at the food on her plate instead of him.

"I thought you agreed to stay until Monday."

"Nothing was definite," she responded.

The hell it wasn't, he thought angrily. How could she not know he assumed they would be leaving together on Monday…but not before he told her how he felt.

That he had fallen in love with her.

"Why, Delphine? Why are you leaving?"

She lifted her head to look at him. "It's time for me to go home."

He held her gaze. "Is your house ready for you to move into?"

"No."

"Are you needed back in Denver for some reason?"

She shook her head. "No."

"Then why do you want to leave?"

"I just do."

As far as he was concerned, that answer wasn't good enough. "Does it have to do with your mother?"

"My mother?"

"Yes. I know the anniversary of her death is Sunday. Is that it? Is that what's bothering you?"

Delphine said nothing for the longest moment and then she broke eye contact with him. He waited. Then she looked back at him and said, "Yes, it has something to do with my mother."

Reaching across the table, he took her hand in his. "Then let me help you get through this, Delphine. Let me—"

"No. I don't want you to help me, Gannon. I want to handle this alone. I don't need your help."

Her words should not have been such a blow to him, but they were. Why was she acting this way? He was trying to be understanding, but he couldn't help her if she didn't want his help. Granted, he'd never been around someone still grieving the loss of a loved one, but why couldn't she see he wanted to be there for her? Why was she shutting him out?

"And you don't have to take me to the airport in the morning. I've scheduled an Uber already. The car will arrive around eight."

He stared at her, trying to hold back his anger. He could understand her being upset because of her mother. He could even understand her wanting to be alone. But there was something called being considerate. She hadn't been considerate enough to let him know of her change in plans ahead of time, and now she was informing him that not only was she leaving, but she'd also scheduled an Uber?

"I'm taking a walk on the beach," he said, standing

up. Normally they would walk together, but he needed time to himself. It seemed she was deliberately pushing him away. He couldn't understand why. He wanted to be with her, do what he could to help her weather this difficult time in her life, but she was refusing to let him.

Maybe it was time to tell her that he'd fallen in love with her. He wanted to hold her in his arms, tell her how much he loved her and assure her that she would never have to be alone again because he knew she was his destiny. The one woman he was meant to claim, to share his life.

"In fact, I think it would be best if I left tonight."

He glanced over at her, shocked at what she'd said. "Tonight?"

"Yes. There's no need to wait until morning. I can stay at a hotel that's closer to the airport and—"

"What the hell is going on here, Delphine? Why are you in such a rush to leave? I thought you'd want to—"

"To what? Make love one last time for the road? I'd rather not."

He heard the venom in her tone and didn't understand why it was there. He knew women could be moody at times, but she was being downright difficult. "Talk to me, Delphine. What's going on? Why are you shutting me out? I'll even go to Denver with you and—"

"No," she said, and stood, too. "I don't need or want you to do anything for me, Gannon. Nothing at all. I enjoyed my time with you, but the bottom line is that it's over and I want to go home."

"Fine, suit yourself. I'm going walking," he snapped.

He walked the beach an hour longer than he usually did, trying to figure out what was going on with Delphine. If it had to do with her not being able to deal with the anniversary of her mother's death, he wanted to be there for her. He would not accept her shutting him out like this. He would not.

He headed back toward the beach house, intent that he and Delphine talk. He would tell her he needed to be with her during this time because she was his destiny, the woman meant to share his life. She was the woman he loved and he would always be there for her. No matter what.

He knew something was wrong the moment he walked into the house. He entered the bedroom and saw the note she'd placed on the pillow.

Thanks for everything, Gannon, but it's time for me to go. I wish you the best. Delphine.

Gannon crushed the note in his hand as anger flared through him. She wished him the best... She couldn't even wait for him to return so he could say goodbye? What kind of crap was that?

Deciding to go for a swim, he grabbed a pair of swimming trunks from the drawer, intent on swimming away his troubles.

Thirteen

"So there you have it, Mandy," Delphine said to her best friend. "I left without telling him goodbye. At least, not in person. I left a note."

"Coward."

"Think what you want. There was no way I could have stayed and told him goodbye without crying a river of tears, and I refused to cry over another man."

"Yet it's been a week and you're still crying, and don't say you're not, because I can hear it in your voice. You should have called me."

"I told you why I didn't call you. I needed time to myself." Once she'd arrived back in Denver, knowing her house wasn't ready for her, she had checked into a hotel downtown and hadn't told anyone she was back. She had needed time to try to pull herself together. Instead, for the past seven days, all she'd done was cry even more.

She had gone to the cemetery on Mother's Day, the one-year anniversary of her mom's death, to place flowers on her grave. At least she'd kept the promise she'd made to her mother about giving love another try. She had fallen in love again, but, unfortunately, the man she loved didn't love her back.

"It doesn't matter that I'm crying or how long I've been crying, as long as Gannon never knows," Delphine said, sniffing. "I refuse to let another man know how deeply he's broken my heart."

Mandy was quiet for a minute. "Maybe you should have confronted him about the phone call you overheard, Del."

"It would not have mattered. Gannon had a right to talk to whomever he wanted to talk to. I didn't have dibs on him." Delphine drew in a deep breath. Gannon hadn't called her, but she really hadn't expected him to. He had wanted to get back to Phoenix, to the woman who'd called him. He probably didn't remember Delphine existed now that he was back with her, whoever she was. For all Delphine knew, it could have very well been the woman named Trish.

The one thing Delphine decided not to share with Mandy was that her period was late. Now, on top of everything else, she had to wonder if perhaps she was pregnant. She was on the pill, so hopefully it was a false alarm, but what if it wasn't? What if she was pregnant with Gannon's child? It was too soon to tell, and she honestly didn't want to consider that possibility.

"Do you need me to come over, Del?"

"No, I'll be okay." Wanting to change the subject, she said, "And the house looks great, by the way. Thanks for taking care of everything for me."

"What are your plans today?"

"I don't have any. I am going to just lounge around and enjoy my new floors."

A short while later, after ending the call with Mandy, Delphine wiped her eyes. She'd gotten over Liddell and she intended to get over Gannon, too.

"I hear you've been in a bad mood."

Gannon glanced over at Mercury. He and his wife, Sloan, had returned from their honeymoon a couple of days ago. It was Thursday evening and, as usual, everyone had shown up to his parents' home for dinner. The women were in the kitchen helping his mom, and his brothers, those with the good sense to leave Gannon alone, were in their father's man cave watching a baseball game with Drew. His brothers had informed Mercury correctly. Gannon wasn't in a good mood and hadn't been for almost two weeks. That was why he'd come outside to sit in his mother's courtyard, which contained every type of flower imaginable.

"What of it?" Gannon asked.

"You want to talk about it?"

"Nope." Gannon's response was quick and simple.

"I think you should."

Gannon rubbed his chin and stared at his brother. "You've been married all of three weeks and you think you're an expert on relationships now?"

"No, but what I do know is that if it hadn't been for your visit to my office that day suggesting that I make some decisions regarding Sloan, I might not have had three of the best weeks of my life. I never thanked you for that and I don't want you to make the mistake I almost made, Gannon."

Gannon didn't say anything as he took a sip of his

beer. He then looked over at his brother and said, "It might be too late for me, Mercury."

"What did you do?"

Gannon shrugged. "As far as I know, I didn't do anything. At least, she didn't say I did anything." He then told Mercury what he remembered. Delphine's sleepless night, the way she'd suddenly begun withdrawing from him and her sudden rush to leave.

"And you think it's all related to the anniversary of her mother's death?" Mercury asked.

"I think so. This was the first year of her mother's passing and it happened to fall on Mother's Day."

Mercury shook his head. "That's a sad situation for her to be in this year. But why shut you out when you wanted to be there for her? You told her that you'd reached the conclusion that she was your soul mate? Your destiny, right?"

Gannon rubbed a hand down his face. "No, I hadn't gotten around to it. She left before I had the chance."

Mercury stared at him for a moment. "Let me get this straight. You convinced a woman to take a road trip with you, to get to know her better, because there was a chance that she was your soul mate. And when you realized that she was, you didn't tell her?"

"Like I said, she left before I got a chance."

Mercury glared at him. "It's been almost two weeks, right? So what are you waiting for? You know your way to Denver."

"Yes, I know my way to Denver, smart-ass, but—"

"But what?"

Gannon took another sip of his beer, then said, "She left. What if she doesn't feel the same way about me that I feel about her? What if she—"

"Does it matter?" Mercury interrupted. "She's the woman you want to claim, right? The woman you love?"

"Yes, I love her." Gannon hadn't realized just how much he loved Delphine until he'd spoken his feelings out loud. He truly loved her.

"Stop fearing rejection, something you've never had to deal with before, and go after her. Do you think any of our wives made things easy for us? Once we determined who we wanted, that was the end of it, for them and for us. If you think she doesn't love you now, then use that Steele charm you're known for. If she's truly meant for you, then it will all work out. If I were you, I would let her know how you feel."

"You're pregnant?"

Delphine sat on the edge of her bed. The pregnancy test she'd just taken had confirmed her suspicion. "Yes, Mandy, I'm pregnant," she said, filled with all sorts of emotions. Both happiness and fear topped the list. "I suspected I was two weeks ago, but wanted to wait to take the test."

"Are you going to contact Gannon Steele and let him know?"

Delphine nibbled on her bottom lip. Was she? Other than knowing she was having a baby, she wasn't sure about anything right now. She felt so overwhelmed. However, she couldn't help but remember what Gannon had told her when the possibility of a pregnancy had been discussed. He wanted her to let him know.

"He has a right to know and I will tell him. I just don't know when."

And speaking of when, she'd racked her brain wondering how the pregnancy had happened when she was on the pill. Gannon had warned her that nothing was 100 percent. He'd been right.

"Well, I am happy for you, and I know you will make a wonderful mother."

Delphine intended to be that. She wanted to be the best mother to her child, just like her mother had been to her. "Thanks, Mandy. And you will make a great godmother."

Her best friend's scream nearly pierced her ears. Delphine laughed. "Come on, Man. Did you think I was going to let you off the hook? With two kids already, for which I am a proud godmother, you're the one with all the experience."

Later that day, after preparing more food than she could ever eat in a week, Delphine took a shower. She had a tendency to cook a lot when she was overwhelmed. Knowing she was having Gannon's baby had definitely overwhelmed her. She tried to think positively about the situation. Her mother had been a single mother and had done a great job raising Delphine. She would do the same for her child.

After her shower she had changed into a pair of shorts and a top. Grabbing a book off the table to read, she had settled into what had been her mother's favorite chair when the doorbell rang. She glanced at the grandfather clock on the wall and saw it was six. It was dinnertime for most people, and she wondered who would be paying her a visit.

After crossing the room to the door, she glanced out of the peephole and immediately caught her breath. Gannon was standing on her porch directly under the light. And as if he knew she was staring at him, he stared back.

She quickly backed away from the door. What was Gannon doing here? How did he know where she lived?

Why had he shown up when she hadn't heard anything from him in nearly three weeks? Although she honestly hadn't expected him to contact her. There had been no reason for him to do so. There was no way he knew about her pregnancy, since she'd just found out herself today. But what if he suspected it? What if...?

He knocked again and she jumped at the sound. Drawing in a deep breath, she opened the door. For the longest time they stood there staring at each other. If things were different between them, she would have rushed into his arms because she needed a hug. She needed his kiss.

But things weren't different.

One thing was the same. He looked good. He was wearing a pair of jeans and a white shirt. And he smelled good, as well. "What are you doing here, Gannon?"

"I think the reason for my being here is obvious, Delphine."

She frowned. If he thought so, then he was wrong. Since there was no way he could know she was pregnant, she said, "Well, your presence here is not obvious and how did you know where I live?"

He shrugged. "Finding you wasn't hard. Were you trying to hide?"

"Of course not."

"Then will you invite me in? There are a few things I want to say to you."

She wondered just what he had to say to her. She started to ask, but decided to let him say his piece. Besides, she could see Miss Anna's curtain moving, which meant the old lady across the street was curious about the car parked in Delphine's yard and the man standing at her door, whom she hadn't invited in yet.

"Come in, Gannon." She moved to let him inside.

* * *

Gannon thought Delphine looked beautiful. If he'd had any doubt in his mind that he loved her, it was erased now. But then, there had not been any doubt. The more he thought about how he felt, the more he was convinced he had fallen in love with her that day in the lobby of the hotel, when he'd seen her for the first time.

She smelled good, too. He'd picked up on her scent the moment she'd opened the door. It was the same scent he'd remembered waking up to, making love to. He had missed her and he hadn't realized how much until now.

He hadn't wanted to rush her. He'd given her three weeks. That had been time enough to deal with whatever she'd been going through without him. That would be her last time to go through it without him, because from this day forward, they would be dealing with things together. It was time she knew that.

After closing the door behind him, she turned to face him. "So what do you have to say?"

"A lot," he said, crossing his arms over his chest. "But first of all, I want you to know you aren't getting rid of me so easily."

She lifted an eyebrow. "What are you talking about?"

"I'm talking about the way you deliberately shut me out and didn't let me be there to help you deal with the anniversary of your mother's death. I wanted to be there for you."

"Yeah, right."

He stared at her, certain he hadn't really heard her flippant remark. "Are you saying you don't believe me?"

"Why should I? Let's be completely honest with each other, Gannon. You got what you wanted from me. I know you lied about thinking I was your destiny. That was just a line you came up with to get me to go on the road with you. You did say the first night we met that I reminded you of someone. You probably took me with you to Florida to pretend I was her."

What in the heck was she talking about?

He had no idea, so he asked her. "What are you talking about? Who are you supposed to remind me of?"

"I have no idea. The first night we met you said I reminded you of someone."

Gannon dropped his arms to his sides, remembering the excuse he'd come up with when he'd been caught staring at her beauty. He would address that later. Right now, he was focused on the other thing she'd accused him of. Lying about her being his destiny. "Would you care to tell me why you think I lied?"

"I overheard that phone call you got, Gannon. I heard what you told her."

Gannon frowned. *Her? Her who?* He searched his brain for what phone call he might have gotten. He knew for certain that although women had called him during the time he'd been with Delphine, not once had he answered a call from any of them. He had declined every single one.

"Women might have called me, but not once did I answer their calls."

"Yes, you did," she said, crossing her own arms over her chest and lifting her chin.

"No, I did not." He searched her face and saw the intensity in the depths of her eyes. He also saw something else. Pain. "I think we need to talk, Delphine."

"We are talking."

"No, you are accusing me of doing something I didn't do."

She glared at him. "I heard you."

It was beginning to dawn on him that the reason

she'd acted the way she had, the reason she had left, hadn't had anything to do with the anniversary of her mother's death after all. "What exactly did you hear, Delphine?"

For a minute he wasn't sure she would tell him.Then she said, "You thought I'd made it to the bathroom, but I hadn't. I heard your phone ring. First thing I noticed was that she had a different ringtone than the other calls you'd been getting. Then when you clicked on, you called her 'beautiful' and told her you missed her and couldn't wait to return to Phoenix to see her."

Gannon stared at her, saw the pain in her features as she retold what she'd heard. "You actually think I was with you, yet making plans to hook up with another woman when I returned to Phoenix?"

She lifted her chin. "Yes. I know what I heard, Gannon."

"You only know what you think you heard, Delphine. I'm trying real hard right now not to turn and walk out that door because of your accusations, but I won't."

While she watched, he took his phone out of his back pocket and made a single click. Then he said, "Please call me back." He then clicked off.

Within seconds his phone rang with that same ringtone Delphine was talking about. He clicked on and placed the caller on speaker. "Thanks for calling me back."

"No problem, baby. What's this about?"

Delphine frowned, wondering what point Gannon was trying to make. It had been the same ringtone she'd heard that night and it was a woman. A woman who had what Delphine thought was a very sexy voice.

Delphine was about to ask Gannon to leave when

his next words stopped her. "This is about me being in Denver with the woman I've fallen in love with. However, there seems to be a problem caused by your ringtone, Mom."

Mom? Had he just called the woman with the sexy voice *Mom?* Delphine was certain she'd heard him wrong. And had he admitted to loving her?

He obviously knew what she was thinking because he then said to her, "You heard me right, Delphine."

"Hi, Delphine," the woman—Gannon's mother—said.

Delphine swallowed hard before returning the greeting. She dropped her arms to her sides. "Hello, Mrs. Steele."

"Gannon has told me and his father all about you and we're looking forward to meeting you. Soon, we hope." Then she asked, "So what problem did my ringtone cause?"

Still holding her gaze with intensity in his green eyes, Gannon said to his mother, "I'm sure it's nothing Delphine and I can't work out."

"I certainly hope so," Eden Tyson Steele said.

"'Bye, Mom."

"'Bye, baby. 'Bye, Delphine."

"Goodbye, Mrs. Steele."

Gannon clicked off the phone and put it back in his jeans. He then looked over at Delphine. "What do you have to say now, Delphine?"

"But the ringtone…"

He shrugged. "It was Mom's choice. She assigned each of her sons a different ringtone. That particular one is mine because I am the youngest and she thinks I will always be her baby."

"Oh." Delphine then said, "You called her 'beautiful.' Who calls their mother 'beautiful'?"

He shoved his hands in the pockets of his jeans. "I do because she is beautiful. And I told her I missed her because I did miss her, and I looked forward to returning to Phoenix to see her."

Delphine threw her hands up in the air, as if frustrated. "Well, how was I to know the caller was your mother?"

"If the phone call bothered you, then you should have asked me about it instead of assuming anything. I recall pointing out to you before that you have a tendency to retreat whenever you feel somewhat threatened by another woman. This time the woman was my mother, but I have a feeling there is more to this retreating thing with you than I understand. So will you explain it to me?"

Delphine's head began spinning, and before she could answer his question, she knew she needed him to clarify what he'd said earlier. "You really love me?"

He took a couple of steps to stand directly in front of her. "Yes, I really love you. I also told you the truth about the reason I wanted you to go on the road with me. It wasn't a line or a lie."

"But what about the woman I remind you of?"

"You don't remind me of anyone. I just made that up the night I saw you to cover why I was so taken by you. Why I'd gone into a daze. The sight of you had overwhelmed me. Let me go on record now and say that you don't remind me of anyone but yourself. The woman I'm in love with."

Tears formed in her eyes. "But you didn't tell me that you loved me."

"I had planned to tell you, Delphine. I had decided on my walk on the beach that I would, but when I got back to the beach house, you had left. Without bothering to tell me goodbye."

She swiped at the tears she couldn't stop from falling. "I couldn't hang around to tell you goodbye."

He reached out and wiped away a tear that she'd missed. "And why couldn't you?"

"Because I really didn't want to leave since I had fallen in love with you, too," she said brokenly.

"Oh, sweetheart." Gannon swept her into his arms and carried her over to the sofa. He sat down with her cradled in his lap. He captured her mouth and began kissing her in ways that she had missed. Ways she thought she would never experience again. Ways that had her heart pounding in her chest. Then when he deepened the kiss, blood rushed through her veins and her pulse felt like it was on fire.

He released her mouth and held her in his arms. She could feel his warmth through his clothing. He looked down at her and touched her chin. "I love you, Delphine."

"And I love you, Gannon."

He was kissing her again, more passionately than all those other times, and then she felt him standing. "Which way, sweetheart?"

She knew why he was asking for directions. She had no problem giving them to him. "Down the hall to your right."

Gannon placed Delphine on the bed fully clothed, and he joined her there. They still needed to talk. Coming here, telling her that he loved her and accepting that she loved him, as well, were all firsts for him, and she needed to know that.

He pulled her into his arms. "Tell me, Delphine. Why

do you allow yourself to be threatened by other women? If a man tells a woman he loves her, then—"

"He can change his mind," she said, looking into his eyes. "Liddell told me that he loved me and asked me to marry him. I believed he did and agreed to marry him. I told you what happened."

Yes, she had, Gannon thought.

"And then my father left my mother for another woman and we haven't heard from him since. I don't know if he's alive or dead."

"And because of those two situations you think if I asked you to marry me that I would eventually call it off or leave you?"

She looked away. "I don't want to think that."

He reached out and touched her chin to bring her gaze back to his. "Then don't. Believe what I'm telling you, Delphine. I am asking you to not compare me to your ex-fiancé or your father. There is no excuse for what they did. I love you. I want you for my wife, as the mother of my babies, as my partner in all things. Will you marry me? If you say yes, I intend to make all those things happen."

She leaned against him and stared into his eyes. "One of those things you mentioned is already in the works."

He lifted an eyebrow. "What do you mean?"

She slipped out of his arms and scampered off the bed. "I need to show you something."

Before Gannon could ask what she had to show him, she had rushed out of the room. He glanced around, checking out her bedroom for the first time. He liked the way it was decorated, in yellow and green.

"I think you need to see this," she said, handing him a box.

He read it and then looked at her. "A pregnancy test kit?" When she nodded, he said, "Does this mean...?"

She nodded again as a huge smile appeared on his face.

"We're having a baby?"

She smiled, as well. "Yes. I don't know why the pill didn't work."

"It wasn't supposed to that time, for us." He couldn't contain the happiness and excitement in his voice.

She nodded for the third time and he pulled her back into his arms. "Will you marry me, Delphine, and believe that I will make a good father for our child and will love you forever? Will you trust me to do that?"

She smiled. "Yes, I will marry you and I trust you."

And then he pulled her down to him for another kiss.

Epilogue

Delphine smiled as she danced with her husband of two hours. It was their first dance together as a married couple and she had a feeling it wouldn't be their last. She was happy, and Gannon had told her several times today that he was happy and she believed him.

She had a wonderful husband and she was marrying into a wonderful family. She'd not only met all his brothers and his parents weeks ago, but today, she'd also met his cousins from Charlotte, North Carolina. And pieced together the puzzle of how the Steeles and the Westmorelands were semi-related. It had all started when Quade Westmoreland married Gannon's cousin Cheyenne Steele…

It seemed everyone was at the wedding, which was held at her church in Denver. The reception was in the ballroom of one of the city's largest hotels. Another reception would be held in Phoenix next month.

"Did I tell you how beautiful you look today, Mrs. Steele?"

Delphine smiled up at Gannon. "Yes, several times, but I appreciate every compliment."

If his family was curious as to why they'd wanted to get married right away, no one had asked. Gannon and Delphine decided they would announce the news about the baby to everyone when they returned from their honeymoon in two weeks. They would be leaving tonight for Barcelona, Spain, and she couldn't wait.

They would make Phoenix their permanent home and Delphine would continue to be a freelance journalist for *Simply Irresistible*. Everyone was excited about the issue containing the interview with Gannon that was coming out in September, on Delphine's birthday. She'd seen samples of the cover and thought the same thing everyone would think when they saw it—Gannon Steele was a very handsome man. She hoped everyone would enjoy her article, as well. The interview revealed just what a wonderful man she had fallen in love with and married.

"Happy?" Gannon asked her as they continued to dance.

"Extremely," she said, tightening her arms around his neck.

He smiled down at her. "There is another extremely happy person today, too. My mom. She has all of her sons married off and she is walking around with a huge smile on her face. And just so you know, now that you're mine, your life will never be the same."

"Um, more road trips?"

He chuckled as he brought her close. "More of everything. This I promise you."

Not caring that over three hundred people were probably watching them, he pulled her into his arms and kissed her. There was no doubt in anyone's mind that she was officially being claimed by a Steele.

* * * * *

HER TEXAS RENEGADE

JOANNE ROCK

For Marcie Robinson,
whose books I can't wait to read.

Prologue

Five months ago

Miranda Dupree Blackwood took deep breaths before the meeting with her ex-stepchildren where they would learn the contents of Buckley Blackwood's last will and testament. Miranda had flown from her home in New York City to Royal, Texas, because of Buck's highly unorthodox last wishes. Knowing what her wily ex-husband had planned for today made her ill, but she understood the role he wanted her to play, and she wasn't going to turn her back on it.

"Are you sure you want to be there for this?" Kace LeBlanc, Buckley's lawyer, asked her as the hour drew near for the meeting that she imagined would be like facing a firing squad. "You don't have to attend in person."

Miranda was upstairs in her former marital home,

Blackwood Hollow, where she was trying to make herself comfortable again after a three-year absence. Kace had been kind to stop by early to check in with her. She'd received the attorney in the upstairs den, the space she'd used as her office during her marriage to the wealthy finance mogul. So much had changed since she'd left Royal after her divorce. One thing that remained the same, however, was the animosity of her adult stepchildren, who would soon hate her more than ever once they understood the terms of their father's will.

"I'm committed," she assured herself as much as Kace, knowing that behind Buckley's unconventional strategy, his heart had been in the right place when he set up his terms. "I just wish he didn't have to be so damned secretive about his motives."

Kace shook his head, pacing in front of one of the windows overlooking the front gates of the sprawling ranch estate. "I urged him to make peace with his kids before his death, but he insisted this was the only way. You know how tough it was to argue with him."

How well she remembered. Miranda hugged herself tighter, bracing for the role she would have to play over the next few months until Buck's real motives made themselves apparent.

She'd had zero interaction with the Blackwood family since leaving Royal. Which, no doubt, was how of all three of Buck's grown children preferred it. Their combined venom toward Miranda for marrying their wealthy father in the first place hadn't subsided, not even when she left the marriage behind without taking anything of the Blackwood estate with her. She'd walked away with the same assets that she'd entered into the union, thanks to an ironclad prenup that they'd both wanted. Miranda did just fine for herself, and she preferred it that way.

"It's going to be a rough few months," she murmured, seeing a glint through the front window and guessing that the guests were already starting to arrive for the meeting. "I'll do my best to support Buckley's wishes, but you know there may be an uprising in the office once you tell them what the will says."

"I'm aware," Kace told her grimly, turning away from the window. "Just remember that Buckley believed in you. He saw what you were doing with Goddess and he was impressed. He knew you'd be a good steward for his estate until his kids are ready to take over."

She nodded, taking some comfort from that, at least. If only the family knew that they would receive their inheritances eventually. That one day, Miranda would hand everything back to the Blackwoods once each of his children was more settled. From the bank to the house, none of it would remain hers, although Buckley had donated an incredibly generous sum to her charity, Girl to the Nth Power, for her time and trouble in overseeing the distribution of his estate. She was humbled by the trust he'd placed in her, even if she hated that he was being so secretive with his true heirs.

Buckley may not have been the best husband, but he'd always supported her efforts to build her own business and their split had been amicable. Without his encouragement, she might not have driven her Goddess line of health and lifestyle centers into the level of nationwide success they now experienced. She'd pushed her way onto the *Forbes* list last year.

Now that she would be staying in Royal for at least the next several months, she had told her producer she couldn't be in New York when filming started for a new season of *Secret Lives of NYC Ex-Wives*, a reality show that had spurred the Goddess brand to huge new heights.

But Nigel had told her not to worry. She had a feeling he was making plans to film the show down here if he could talk her castmates into making the move. Which would bring a whole other level of chaos to an already complicated time in her life.

Still, she was going to forge ahead. First she just needed to get through today. Buckley Blackwood was about to deliver a devastating blow to his offspring, robbing them of everything he'd promised since they were children.

A cold sweat dotted Miranda's head. Buckley's children had called her the "step-witch" when she'd joined the family. What would they think of her today when they learned their father had left every shred of their inheritance to her?

One

Present Day

Miranda had hoped today's brunch could be a girls-only affair for her friends from the *Secret Lives of NYC Ex-Wives* show, but producer Nigel Townshend had convinced her he needed some footage at a more intimate gathering. Since the show had started filming in Royal, Texas, thanks to Miranda being tied to the town, their schedule had been packed with big, glitzy parties.

Especially engagement parties. Romance seemed to be in the air in Royal. Her stepson Kellan was now married with a baby on the way. Kellan's sister, Sophie, had married Miranda's producer, Nigel, just a few weeks ago. Their brother Vaughn had just gotten engaged, as had two of Miranda's castmates. And Darius Taylor-Pratt, her new business associate, had managed to find love, too—after he'd come to town to learn the stunning news that he was Buck's illegitimate son. The discovery had been a shock, but the love he'd found—or rather, rediscovered—with his former sweetheart, Audra, had softened the blow.

Weddings were all anyone wanted to discuss anymore. Even now, Miranda's castmate Lulu Shepard used the time as an opportunity to discuss plans for her nuptials to Kace LeBlanc, Buckley's lawyer.

"Do you have a venue in mind for the wedding, Lu?" Miranda asked her newly engaged costar.

They were seated at a table under the extended eaves that shaded the outdoor entertaining area near the guesthouse pool at Blackwood Hollow. In the five months that Miranda had spent in Royal since the reading of the will, she'd come to feel even more at home here than she had during her marriage to Buckley. Now that she and Kace had told the siblings about how their father had actually chosen to divide up his estate, her work here was almost done. That was why she was staying in the guesthouse at the ranch—the property belonged to Kellan and his wife now. She'd been surprised and touched when he'd invited her to stay in the guesthouse for as long as she needed while she wrapped things up in Royal. Her real inheritance had been the opportunity to mend her relationships with the Blackwood heirs, something she'd genuinely enjoyed.

Even if it involved enough weddings and engagements to make the most reluctant romantic a little envious.

"You *have* to marry in New York," Rafaela Marchesi announced, flipping dark, cascading waves over one shoulder to ensure her good side was visible to the camera. A five-time divorcee on the hunt for husband number six, Rafaela thrived on troublemaking and she played the diva for all it was worth. "Bring the party back where we belong."

Henry the cameraman lingered on the resident diva while Sam swiveled his second camera for a reaction shot from Lulu.

"No." Lulu tilted her champagne glass in Rafaela's direction, pointing it at her and showing off her amazeballs new diamond at the same time. "We're getting married in Royal, that much I know."

"Good," Miranda interjected, not wanting the brunch to turn into a snipe-fest. Audiences might love that kind of thing, but Miranda wouldn't let popular demand turn Lulu's wedding preparations into nonstop bickering. "It's only fitting to celebrate here when it all began in Royal for you two lovebirds."

Never let it be said Miranda didn't have a soft side, even if romance hadn't worked out well for her. She and Buckley had split on friendly enough terms, but the dissolution of her marriage still felt like a failure on her part. And lately, her thoughts were full of the man who'd held her heart before Buck.

Kai Maddox, the cybersecurity expert she needed to review the digital encryption measures at Blackwood Bank. No doubt that's why her long-ago lover had taken up residence in her brain this week after years of doing her best to forget him. Well, that and the fact that they'd shared a searing kiss the first time she'd asked for his professional help—right before he'd refused her outright. She'd have to swallow her pride and try asking him again. He might have a sketchy past, but no one could argue the man excelled at his job. Besides, his new company,

Madtec, was local, based in nearby Deer Springs, where he'd grown up.

"Cheers to being a Texas bride, Lu." Zooey Kostas, the youngest one of the ex-wives at thirty years old, lifted her glass to toast their friend, her diamond-encrusted bangles sliding down her slender wrist. Her honey-colored hair and green eyes gave her a fresh-faced appeal in spite of her hard-partying ways. "I want you to get married here anyway."

The five women at the table, including Seraphina "Fee" Martinez, who was also due to marry a local, lifted their glasses automatically to toast the bride. Miranda sipped her mimosa, savoring the fresh-squeezed oranges even more than the champagne, while Rafaela rolled her eyes.

"Zooey, darling, you've lost your mind," Rafaela declared, leaning in and piling on the drama for a good sound bite. "Why should we waste ourselves on cowboys in the Lone Star State when we can have our pick of Wall Street billionaires in Manhattan?"

Miranda slouched in her seat, so done with Rafaela Marchesi. Was this what her life had amounted to, trading barbs with frenemies over cocktails?

Lulu looked ready to fire off a comeback, but Zooey surprised them all with a wicked laugh that bordered on a cackle.

"Waste ourselves? You're just jealous you haven't bagged a rich Texan the way Lulu and Fee have." Zooey tossed her napkin on the table and then stood, her cream-colored halter pantsuit draping beautifully as she moved. "Excuse me, ladies, but I've lost my appetite."

The sudden diva-exit was so un-Zooey-like that Miranda and Lulu turned to one another at the same time, with Lulu looking as shocked as Miranda felt.

"Bitch," Rafaela muttered, studying her manicure. "Clearly, she's not getting laid enough if she's acting like such a shrew."

Miranda smothered a laugh while Lulu went back to brainstorming good places to exchange vows with Kace. No doubt the production team had filmed all the footage they needed for this week's episode anyway. And since the show had plenty of juicy moments for viewers, maybe Miranda stood a chance of sneaking away from the camera crew and Blackwood Hollow for the afternoon.

She needed to meet with Kai Maddox sooner rather than later to convince him to take on Blackwood Bank as a client, even though thinking about another confrontation with her former flame tied her in knots. What had she been thinking to allow that damned kiss to happen in the first place? Kai was the only man to ever shred her restraint so thoroughly.

Now that Vaughn knew he'd inherited the bank, it was time to pass everything over to him officially—but first, she needed someone to check into the irregularities she'd noticed while going over the books. She owed it to Buckley's family to pass over the reins of the company in good standing, especially now that she was only just starting to form real relationships with them. But she had no intention of letting her television audience see her fork up a bite of humble pie with her sexy-as-sin ex-lover to ask for his help.

Again.

He'd practically thrown her out on the street the last time she'd approached him. Right after the kiss that set her on fire every time she remembered it. Things were going to be complicated with Kai.

Assuming she even made it past the front door of Madtec.

This time, she'd simply have to make him an offer he couldn't refuse.

Kai Maddox strode across the rooftop terrace of Madtec's recently built headquarters in Deer Springs, lingering near the half wall and glass partition that overlooked the parking area as his afternoon meeting broke up. A light breeze blew from the west, but it did little to cool the afternoon heat. Soon, the days would be too warm for terrace meetings, but Kai planned to take advantage of the outdoor spot for as long as he could, knowing the benefit of fresh air and green space. He'd learned to make his health and mental wellness a priority since his teen years when he'd all but fallen into his computer screen, spending every waking moment honing his skills as a coder, a developer and, yes—occasionally—as a hacker.

Nothing prepared a coder for building the best digital encryption quite as well as breaking down someone else's.

Madtec had moved into its Deer Springs location shortly after the new year, as soon as work crews had finished the custom-designed, high-tech office building. With five floors and the rooftop terrace, it was more square footage than the Maddox brothers currently needed for their growing tech business, but the cost of real estate here was reasonable and Kai had faith that Madtec would only grow.

Even if he didn't return Miranda Dupree's phone calls.

He was doing just fine without taking business from a woman who'd dumped him the moment someone richer came along.

"Did you need anything else, Kai?" his personal assistant called to him from the steel-beam pavilion in the middle of the rooftop as he packed up his notes and tablet. Amad was new to the job, but the guy was efficient and eager to learn.

"No, thank you. I've got a meeting with Dane soon, but first I'm going to review the data penetration tests again." Kai and his brother, Dane, had new fraud-protection software almost ready to take to market, but first he'd asked his old hacking buddies to try to crack it.

So far, the issues in the software they'd uncovered had been minor, but he wanted to ask for one more opinion. He refused to rush the product to market without thorough testing.

"Sure thing, boss." Amad jammed everything in a leather binder and headed for the door leading back into the building, but he paused to look down at his phone before opening it. "The main desk says you have someone here to see you. Miranda Dupree? She's not on your schedule."

He cursed silently.

Miranda had cornered him at his hotel in New York last month and things had spiraled out of control fast. How he'd ended up kissing her was still a mystery to him, but that's just what had happened, even though he'd spent ten years hating her.

As much as he would have preferred to ignore her forever in light of their nasty breakup a decade ago, Kai suspected the knee-jerk reaction would be too damned self-indulgent. Bad enough that he'd been ignoring her calls. Now that she'd shown up in person, sending her away would be too visible, and might reflect badly on the company. She was a respected businesswoman. She'd made the *Forbes* list. He would at least do her the courtesy of a meeting before he refused whatever the hell she wanted from him.

"I'll meet her in my office," he said, deciding the quickest way to end this would be face-to-face—and one-on-one. He sure as hell didn't want anyone else around to see the chemistry that still sparked between them. "You can send her up in five."

"Will do." Amad shoved his phone in his pocket before he left the rooftop.

Kai followed him down to the penthouse office a few moments later. He shared the top floor with Dane, the two copresident suites separated by an executive conference room. Both Maddox brothers had private terraces on opposite sides of the building. On a clear day, Kai could see the roof of the humble house where he'd grown up.

There were a lot of unhappy memories in Deer Springs, but some good ones, too—and the hope for more in the future. Madtec had brought hundreds of jobs to the community that had shaped him, and that gave him a lot of satisfaction. Far more than he was going to get from this meeting with Miranda.

By the time Kai arrived in his office through the private back entrance, Amad was just opening the double doors to admit his guest in the front.

And damn, but she still had a potent effect on him.

Her fiery-red hair was cut just above her shoulders, with her curls tamed so that her hair swooped over one eye. She was dressed in a fitted black suit that showed off her figure—although not quite as much as the strapless red dress he'd seen her in last time. That dress had been... Damn.

Fantasy worthy. He was grateful to today's suit for covering more of her. She remained toned and athletic thanks to her lifelong commitment to yoga, and she had the lean limbs of a dancer. But her generous curves were more the pinup variety, giving her a silhouette that made men of all ages stop and stare. Including him, damn it.

He forced his gaze to her ice-blue eyes.

"Hello, Kai. Thank you for seeing me on such short notice." She smiled warmly at Amad before Kai's assistant left the room.

"You didn't leave me much choice," he informed her shortly, gesturing to one of the two wingbacks in front of his desk. "Please, have a seat."

She disregarded the offer, remaining on her feet as he did. Even in heels she was half a foot shorter than him, but her cool demeanor still commanded attention and exuded authority along with her smoking-hot sexiness.

She'd gained confidence along with over-the-top wealth from her marriage to Buckley Blackwood. Besides a national fitness empire and popular television series, he was certain that Miranda had access to a level of financial support that Kai had to wrestle and scrabble for from investors. The Blackwood name had unlocked a whole world for her. Kai's courtship, on the other hand, had consisted mostly of diner dates and motorcycle rides whenever he'd had a free moment from the endless stream of work that had claimed most of his time.

"You could have ignored me, the way you've snubbed my phone messages." She peered around the office.

He'd purposely kept it clutter-free and impersonal, a mostly soundproof haven for him to think. The walls were all gray stone except for the windows behind the desk. Lights ringed the tray ceiling, hidden in the molding to mimic the effect of daylight at any hour. His desk was glass-topped with steel underneath. Industrial and functional. He wondered briefly how it looked through her eyes.

If he was being honest, he wondered how *he* looked through her eyes, too. Ten years ago, he'd been knee-deep with the old hacker crowd, and skirting the law as he unraveled the most complex facets of data encryption. Miranda had been older than him, with a drive and ambition he admired and an ease with her sensuality that he'd found sexy as hell.

But she'd turned her back on him the moment she met Buckley Blackwood and his millions. And he wasn't about to take a trip down memory lane with her, even if memories of that rogue kiss in New York had put her in his thoughts all too often lately.

"Deer Springs is a small town, Miranda." He rounded the desk to stand closer to her, noting the way her eyes followed him. "I wasn't about to feed the local rumor mill with stories about me refusing to see the town's most illustrious native."

She laughed but it was a brittle sound. "Please. Deer Springs is practically Silicon Valley compared to Sauder Falls."

He'd forgotten she was technically from the next town over, a fact never referenced in her bio since Sauder Falls was a dingier town that had never recovered from a mill closing many years prior. When they'd met, Miranda had been working part-time at a diner in Deer Springs while she ran a local yoga studio and gave classes at another fitness center in Royal. Her big dreams and hard work to achieve them had captivated him since he understood that thirst to do something more.

"Nevertheless, your name is well-known around here." He was close enough to her to catch a hint of her fragrance, the same scent that made him think of night-blooming flowers. The sooner he sent her on her way, the better. There wouldn't be any surprise kisses this time. "And now that you've got your audience, what is it you want from me? I thought I made it clear I wasn't interested in doing business with you the last time we met."

Her lips compressed into a thin line at the reminder of their last meeting. After the kiss that had been so damned unexpected, he'd recovered by assuring her he wouldn't so much as cross the street for her anymore. Harsh? Not considering the way she'd dumped him.

No sense pretending they had much to say to one another anymore.

"I'm temporarily managing Blackwood Bank," she began, coming straight to the point as she tilted her chin. "And I need to update the security before I pass over the reins to the Blackwood heirs. You wouldn't be doing business with me so much as with the Blackwoods."

Surprise registered. He'd thought maybe she wanted help with Goddess, her line of fitness studios. Blackwood Bank was a client of a whole different caliber. Encryption for a financial institution was extremely complex. It might have been tempting, if not for the woman who made the offer.

She was tempting, too. But in all the wrong ways when he needed to focus on his business.

"But as you pointed out, you're managing the bank right now. You honestly expect me to work for you?"

Folding his arms, he leaned against his desk. Waiting. Willing his thoughts to stay on business and his boots to stay firmly planted.

No touching. No thinking about touching.

Even though the pulse at the base of her throat leaped frantically, drawing his eye and making him wonder what would happen if he ran his tongue over that very place. He'd be willing to bet she'd burst into flames. But then, he would too, and he'd be damned if that happened.

"Not for *me*. For the bank." Opening her purse, she removed a manila folder and placed it on his desk. The movement put her body in dangerously enticing proximity to his. "I have a contract ready, but if the terms aren't to your liking—"

"No." He didn't need to look at the terms.

"No?" She left the folder on the desk and her blue eyes met his. "Kai, this is a very good offer. The bank deserves the kind of data protection your company specializes in, and since you're local—"

"Madtec is busy." He was being abrupt. Borderline unprofessional. But he didn't like the way she affected him and didn't intend to tempt fate by spending any more time together than was absolutely necessary.

She gripped the leather of her designer purse tighter, her short nails and simple French manicure oddly reminding him she wasn't quite as high maintenance as the other women on her reality television show. There was still something more down-to-earth about Miranda.

Not that he'd ever watched more than a two-minute clip.

"I understand," she told him finally, inclining her head with the grace of a medieval queen. "But I'll leave the contract here and hope you'll reconsider. Perhaps Dane would feel differently."

Dane would kick his ass for turning down a client like Blackwood Bank. But Kai said nothing.

Realizing he was probably staring her down like a street thug, Kai shook off the frustration and straightened.

"Thank you for thinking of us," he said with too much formality, ready to get back to his work. "My assistant can show you out."

Not that Miranda Dupree had ever needed help walking away.

"I could assign someone else to be the point person for the bank." She tossed out the compromise, clearly sensing he wasn't going to budge. "You'd never have to see me once you agreed to the job."

He wasn't about to let her see that the offer had appeal. He managed a cool smile. "Afraid you'd end up in my bed again if we worked together, Miranda?"

"Not at all." She folded her arms and peered up at him like she knew exactly what he was thinking. "Are you, Kai?"

She let the question hang between them for a long moment before she turned on her heel and walked out of his office with the same quiet confidence that had accompanied her through the doors in the first place. Kai didn't breathe again until she was out of sight. And hell, he couldn't help but wonder if she had a point. Because she still tempted him like no woman he'd ever known.

Even if he couldn't trust her.

Shoving aside the contract she'd left behind, he pulled out his laptop from a hidden drawer in one gray stone wall, and got to work.

* * *

Humble pie tasted even worse when choked down with no results.

Miranda fumed on her way out of the Madtec offices, thoroughly irritated with herself for wasting time driving to Deer Springs only to have Kai Maddox reject her offer without even stirring himself to look at it. He'd been more concerned with making sure she knew how easily he could ignite the old attraction between them.

And she couldn't very well dispute it. The heat rolled off him in waves, melting her defenses like they'd never been there in the first place.

She took the stairs—she preferred stairs whenever possible to up her steps, especially when there was anger to be stomped out—and was surprised to discover the Madtec stairwell seemed to be designed for employee wellness. Motivational phrases were painted on the walls, and the stairs were wide enough to accommodate several people at once. There was even a "runners' lane" painted in red to one side. With vinyl walls and ventilation fans, the staircase implemented some of the same techniques she used in her fitness centers to keep the space clean and well aired.

And how frustrating was it to find something to admire about Kai when she wanted to stay furious with him?

"Ms. Dupree?" A young woman with a swinging ponytail yanked her earbuds free as she locked eyes with Miranda and halted on her way up the steps. "I love your show so much. Is it true the *Secret Lives of NYC Ex-Wives* is leaving Royal soon? It's been so fun seeing sites close to home on TV."

"Thank you." Miranda smiled warmly, knowing the

importance of connecting positively with viewers who invested their time in the program. "We will be filming in Royal for at least a few more weeks," assuming Lulu and the show's production team could pull together a big wedding in time, "but next season we'll be returning to New York."

"We'll really miss you," the woman said sincerely, digging in her messenger bag and pulling out a pen and paper. "Especially since you grew up around here and have ties to the area. May I have an autograph?"

"Of course." Miranda signed the back of the woman's grocery receipt before they went their separate ways, her thoughts snagging on the fan's words about being native to the region.

Miranda hadn't visited her mother since she'd been back in Texas. Nor had her mother come to Royal to see her, which was even more surprising in light of how thoroughly Virginia "Ginny" Dupree loved Blackwood Hollow. And how hard she'd once lobbied to have a role on *Secret Lives of NYC Ex-Wives*. She'd been angry at Miranda for not giving her that chance. Although not as angry as she'd been at Miranda for leaving her marriage in the first place. It had made her furious that Miranda signed a prenup—and walked away with nothing from Buck.

How stupid can you be? she'd shouted at Miranda over the phone, her diction sloppy from a prescription painkiller addiction that ebbed and flowed according to what was going on in her life at the time.

Breathe in. Breathe out.

Yoga, and all the mindful breathing that went with it, had been helping keep Miranda grounded her entire adult life. The teachings of Goddess centers everywhere weren't just about being physically fit. All that breathing definitely helped her emotional and mental health, too.

By the time she reached the main floor of Madtec, Miranda didn't feel quite as annoyed with Kai. Looking around at the design touches in the building, from the vintage video game posters that decorated the café walls to the courtyards and green spaces that seemed to give employees plenty of options for working outdoors in mild weather, Miranda had to admire the employee-centered corporate environment he'd given his workforce.

Kai Maddox might be a former hacker who'd skirted the law in the years he'd worked to learn the computer security business from the inside out, but there was no denying he'd turned his knowledge into an incredibly successful undertaking. Moreover, he'd given back to his hometown by building his corporate headquarters here. She'd read an article about a community center he'd built close to the diner where she used to work.

Where they'd met.

She wouldn't be driving by that on her way out of town, however. Shoving out the front doors of Madtec into the late afternoon sunlight, Miranda had enough thoughts of Kai crowding her head for one day. He'd packed on more muscle since they'd dated a decade ago, but there was no mistaking the always-assessing, smoldering green eyes and the scar on his jaw where he'd collided with the road on one of his motorcycle tours. The tattoos she remembered had been covered up by his custom Italian suit, but she found herself remembering every swirl and shadow of the intricate ink.

Stop.

She told herself not to give the reformed bad boy another thought. Clearly, he'd put her in his past and had no intention of spending more time with her than was absolutely necessary, no matter that she'd been prepared to pay him well.

She'd simply have to find someone else to review the Blackwood Bank digital security since Kai was determined not to help her. She'd been a fool to expect anything else. Maybe while she worked on bringing the cybersecurity of the bank up to snuff, she would have firewalls installed on her heart, too.

Two

"What the hell is the matter with you?" Dane Maddox stormed into Kai's office the next afternoon, a stainless-steel mug of coffee in one hand, and a sheaf of papers in the other.

Or, it *was* in the other hand until he slid the packet across Kai's desk.

The contract with the logo from Blackwood Bank emblazoned on the top pinwheeled across the glass surface before a corner lodged under his laptop.

Recognizing there wasn't a snowball's chance in hell of getting any work done until he addressed whatever had his brother fired up, Kai closed his computer and shoved back from the desk to meet Dane's glare. Dane might be two years younger than Kai, but he had all of Kai's tech smarts and a level of business savvy worthy of someone who'd been in the corporate world for twice as long. Kai was proud of him, even when he was being a pain in the ass.

"Let's see," Kai mused aloud, humoring him. "Depending who you talk to, it could be the chip on my shoulder. Or that I'm too much of a workaholic. And the whole thrill-seeking thing rubs some people the wrong way—"

"I'll tell you what your problem is," Dane continued, jabbing a finger on Kai's desk. "You're too damned bullheaded to recognize *this*—" he jabbed the contract twice more "—is everything we've been waiting for."

Tension bunched up the muscles in his shoulders, twisting its way along his neck.

"Madtec is thriving," Kai reminded him. "There's no need to affiliate ourselves with—" How to phrase his reservations about Miranda? About *himself* when he was around Miranda? "—people we don't care to work with just to make a buck."

Dane paced around Kai's office, his dark brown hair overdue for a cut and giving silent testament to how many hours he'd been putting into the new software testing.

"This contract is not with *people*." Dane loosened his tie a fraction although it wasn't even noon yet. "This is a contract to partner with one of the top ten privately held banks in the country, Kai."

He hardly needed to be reminded. But the knowledge didn't ease the knot in his throat at the thought of seeing more of Miranda. She might be easy on the eyes, but she'd been hell on his heart. Worse, Kai had been so thoroughly distracted by their affair and the thought of losing her that he'd taken his focus away from a project he'd been working on with his brother. The job had required a large-scale "almost" hack, since the first step toward preventing hackers from gaining access to any system is to learn how hacking is done. Quietly breaching a system—with zero malicious intent—had been a delicate task with devastating consequences if it was mishandled, but Kai had let Dane step up his role, confident his brother had the skills to monitor the program while Kai wooed Miranda.

The fact that Dane had done prison time for Kai's mistake would weigh on him forever. But bringing that up now would only tick off his agitated brother even more.

"When we started this company," Kai reminded him instead, "we agreed we would take the work we *wanted*—"

"I'm going to stop you right there." Dane charged toward the desk again to retrieve the paperwork. "When we came up with our mission statement, we agreed to work with companies that shared our values wherever possible, and I stand by that. But that doesn't mean we're suddenly going to turn down the chance to work with a reputable financial institution because an old flame happened to deliver the offer."

His brother laid the sheaf on top of his laptop and placed a heavy silver pen nearby.

"Does this mean you want us to take the project, even when we're already running at full capacity to get the new software to market?"

"We're only running at capacity because we haven't filled all the positions the new place can accommodate. We built this space to grow, and the Blackwood Bank account will allow us to do just that," Dane pointed out reasonably.

Kai blew out a frustrated breath, hating that his

brother was right. Hating that he'd thought about Miranda almost nonstop since she'd walked out of his office the day before.

"Kai, you know that a partnership with Blackwood Bank would give Madtec that final stamp of legitimacy we've been looking for." Dane finally dropped into the seat across from Kai's desk. Dane sat forward in his chair. "CEOs from major corporations across the country would be willing to take a cue from an institution as prestigious as Blackwood to take a chance on a business founded by a couple of ex-hackers."

"The affiliation would take us mainstream," Kai admitted, knowing he couldn't deny Dane this opportunity to cast off the last taint of his jail time.

How ironic that Miranda had been the one to give them that chance.

"You'll sign?" Dane pressed.

Kai picked up the pen for an answer, seeing no other choice. He'd bring the signed contracts to Miranda personally. Maybe then, he'd figure out a way to broker a peace between them long enough to fulfill Madtec's obligations to Blackwood Bank.

Dane was right about the need to accept the offer. But the sooner the job was done, the sooner Kai would put Miranda Dupree back in his past, where she belonged.

Miranda clutched a letter from Buckley Blackwood in her hands, eyes moving over the text. This was the third and final missive Buck had written to be delivered to her after his death. The first had explained the true intentions behind his will and the role he'd needed her to play. The second had included instructions on how to find his illegitimate son, Darius, and bring him into contact with the rest of the family. Now this letter included the last of his requests. She reread her ex-husband's final missive for her.

Dear Miranda,

Thank you for hanging in there with me to take care of these last tasks—the jobs I couldn't seem to pull off myself when I still had time. I hope this one last request will be a little easier than the others. I'd like you to organize a send-off for me, but not some schmaltzy memorial service—you know I hate things like that. I'm picturing an epic charity event, something like "Royal Gives Back," and I want you to organize it as only you can. I was thinking the proceeds ought to go to the Stroke Foundation or maybe the Heart Association since they study the underlying causes of strokes. It still weighs on me that my children lost their mother too soon because of a stroke. I wasn't the husband I should have been to Donna-Leigh before our divorce, but I'd like to do this in her honor. Now that I've been exposed for a philanthropist do-gooder, I might as well go all out one last time, right? I know you won't disappoint me. After this last favor, you can go back to your life in New York, and I'll rest easier. Yours, Buck.

Miranda returned Buckley's last letter to the small secretary desk in the guesthouse's second bedroom that served as her temporary office. She mulled over what it meant as she sat in front her laptop to review her work email for Goddess. Kace LeBlanc had hand delivered the note this morning, assuring her it would be the final note from Buckley.

That had been both good and bad news for her. While she was relieved there would be no more surprises from her ex, she would also miss Royal. She'd grown close to her stepchildren, people who felt more like her family these days than her mother ever had. Her gaze shifted away from her laptop screen to a new framed photo of the Blackwood heirs from Sophie's wedding—Sophie, Kellan and Vaughn with their half brother, Darius. Buckley would be so proud to have them all together at last.

Miranda felt glad she'd played a part in making that happen. Buckley hadn't been a great father, but he'd cared. Miranda's father had died when she was three, too young to be sure she remembered him, although sometimes she imagined she recalled his laugh or a feeling of being hugged by him. At first, her mother had worked two jobs after his death to provide for them, but she'd given up by the time Miranda was ten. The house fell into disrepair. The electricity was shut off more often than not. Miranda had only ever worn other girls' cast-off clothes. None of which was as troubling as her mother's decision to spend the little bit of money she brought in on a prescription pill addiction.

Ginny Dupree was a mean addict. She didn't hit, but she threw things, and she was verbally cruel. Some of her more cutting words had continued to hurt Miranda long afterward, which was why she drew firm boundaries with her now. But as she saw the Blackwood family healing, Miranda couldn't help a twinge of envy for the kind of companionship and support that came with family relationships.

The love.

She suspected that lack of love in her childhood home had been one of the driving forces behind her strong feelings for Kai Maddox. Being with Kai had opened a whole new world of possibilities for her heart.

Until he'd started to withdraw from her. She'd never understood it, but she'd felt his retreat in the weeks before their split. He might blame her for their breakup, but he'd pulled away long before she'd ended things.

Buckley Blackwood might have been richer and worldlier than Kai. But in many ways, she'd settled for him when she'd married him, telling herself maybe her quieter, steadier feelings for him were what more mature love felt like.

Lesson learned.

Except Kai Maddox was back in her thoughts now, stirring up feelings she'd thought she'd put to rest long ago. And stirring up a hunger for him that she couldn't possibly deny. She'd dreamed about his hands all over her the night before, bringing her intense pleasure while he whispered wicked, suggestive things in her ear. She'd awoken edgy and breathless, her heart beating fast.

Maybe organizing this charity event for Buckley was just what she needed. Instead of spending her final month in Royal working side by side with an old lover she couldn't stop thinking about, she would spend it planning something worthwhile.

With a frustrated sigh, she shut her laptop and changed into her workout clothes, knowing she'd never get anything accomplished with her thoughts spinning this way.

Lying on her belly in cobra pose, Miranda arched her spine and pulled her shoulders back while she moved through her afternoon yoga workout in the studio of the

Blackwood Hollow guesthouse. She inhaled deeply and slowly, matching her breath to her pose. The cycle of postures in the sun salutation was grounding for her during times of stress, and it took all her effort to focus on her breathing when memories of Kai clung to her thoughts.

With her mat positioned near the studio's big front window overlooking the grounds, she held the pose for five deep breaths, turning her head to one side and then the other as she tried not to think about how it had felt to stand near him. She would force his smoldering image from her mind by sheer will.

Except, was that him pulling into the driveway of the guesthouse? Parking a sleek silver sports car in front of the double bay detached garage?

She forgot all about her breath in the scramble to her feet as Kai emerged from a Jaguar F-Type coupe. Dressed in a deep blue jacket with a light blue shirt underneath, he looked more casual than the day before and every bit as compelling. Awareness and anticipation tingled over her skin. She had to remind herself that her sexy dream about him hadn't been real. That she couldn't afford to indulge those kinds of thoughts around him. She hurried toward the door, dismayed that instead of being dressed to impress, she wore capri-length leggings and a drapey tank shirt for her workout.

Not that there was any help for it now.

Slipping on a pair of beaded sandals by the front mat, Miranda opened the door of the studio attached to the rest of the guesthouse by a covered breezeway. The smooth stone path connected the buildings, outlined by native plants and shrubs. When she stepped outside, Kai's green gaze swung toward her.

He changed the trajectory of his stride, turning away

from the main house toward the studio building. She hadn't realized until then he carried a small box with an all-too-recognizable logo on it.

One that stirred nostalgia.

"Hello, Miranda. I hope I didn't interrupt you." He stopped a few feet from her under the shade of the breezeway, the spring air still fragrant with almond verbena.

Her breath caught to be close to him again, her heart rate picking up speed.

"I'm surprised to see you." She remembered how curt he'd been the day before, but if he was here to tell her he'd reconsidered, she couldn't afford to refuse. Still, there was no reason to make it too easy for him. She'd had to scarf down humble pie the day before—it wouldn't kill him to have a bite or two of his own. "I got the distinct impression you didn't want to cross paths again when I left your office yesterday."

"For that, I apologize." He lifted the white box in his hands. "I brought a peace offering."

Her gaze shifted to the parcel with the Deer Springs Diner label, a million memories bombarding her all over again. She used to waitress there, depending on the money to finance her first yoga studio. She'd met Kai there. They'd spent time plotting to take over the world from their favorite booth in the corner, and had shared many breakfasts there after long nights of lovemaking. Tentatively, she lifted the lid.

She suspected what would be inside before she even peeked under the top.

"Half lemon meringue, half caramel apple," she confirmed, the scent of their two favorites stirring nostalgia and longing she couldn't afford to feel around this man. Part of her wanted to send him away, escape what he made her feel. But she still needed him on a professional level. "Would you like to come in for a slice?"

She peered up at him and realized how close they stood. Close enough for her to touch the short bristles he'd always worn along his jaw. Close enough to breathe in the light spice of soap on his olive-toned skin and remember the taste of him. Hastily, she released the box top and took a step back.

"Thank you. I'd like that very much." His green eyes missed nothing. "We can celebrate our new venture together since I have a signed contract to give you."

The surprises continued.

"That's excellent news." For the bank, of course. But for her, the prospect of working with him proved equal parts tempting and daunting. "Although I'll admit I'm curious what made you change your mind after you seemed so adamantly opposed yesterday. Was it the prospect of me stepping aside?"

Turning, she led the way to the front door of the guesthouse, aware of his nearness every step of the way.

"No. That won't be necessary. I can separate my personal life from my business obligations." He sounded sincere. And yet both times she'd visited him recently, there had been enough sensual tension simmering to burn them both. Did he plan to ignore it?

Giving herself a few heartbeats to shore up her boundaries, she entered the cool interior of the guesthouse and paused in the entryway as Kai pulled the door closed behind them. The dark wood floor and white walls were simply furnished with rustic elegance. Sturdy leather couches and heavy iron pendant lamps were softened by an abundance of natural light, pale rugs and oversize yellow throw pillows. Drinking in the calming effects, she glanced at him.

"I didn't expect a warm reception after how we parted ten years ago," she admitted, pulse skipping erratically as she continued toward the open kitchen to retrieve plates and forks. "And how you reacted to seeing me in New York."

She hoped discussing it would dismiss the elephant in the room. They needed to put their old relationship behind them, so it didn't interfere with the bank's business.

Kai joined her at the kitchen island, setting the pie box on the white quartz countertop.

"That's all in the past now. I was needlessly abrupt yesterday, especially when you came to discuss a significant opportunity for Madtec." He reached into an interior pocket of his jacket and retrieved a folded packet of papers. He laid them on the counter, as well. "Dane and I look forward to a thorough review and revamp of the bank's digital security."

Miranda retrieved two bottles of sparkling water from the refrigerator and placed them on a bamboo serving tray along with the plates and silverware. While it would be easy to eat indoors at the kitchen counter, she thought sitting under the pergola in the backyard would help her keep boundaries in place. Especially when lemon meringue and caramel apple pie slices had the power to catapult her back in time to that diner with Kai. Feeding each other bites. Sitting so close her thigh pressed against his.

She would *not* think about his thighs.

"Dane convinced you to give this a chance?" she guessed aloud, her cheeks warm from the vivid thoughts she was trying to stifle.

"He was livid I hadn't already signed the papers," Kai

acknowledged. As she moved to pick up the tray, he took over the task, his warm hand brushing hers momentarily. "Lead the way."

She felt that brief touch long afterward. *Breathe in. Breathe out.* She opened the French doors to the patio where coral honeysuckle hung from the deep pergola. Hummingbirds bobbed around the vibrant trumpet-shaped blooms. Kai set the tray on the wrought iron dining table, then pulled out a cushioned chair for Miranda.

"Thank you." She tried to recall the thread of the conversation to distract herself from all the ways his nearness affected her. "I hope that Dane's insistence doesn't mean you're conflicted about working with us."

"I have no trouble opposing my brother when the situation calls for it." Kai took the seat next to her at the round table. "But in this case, Dane's instincts were correct. The software we're developing is tailor-made for a complex financial platform like Blackwood Bank."

Grounding herself in mundane tasks, Miranda laid out napkins and divvied up the waters while Kai opened the pie box and slid thin slices onto their plates. One of each kind for each of them. But rather than soothing her with routine, the familiarity of that simple act, something they'd done countless times and yet not for so many years, crowded her chest with feelings she wasn't ready for. Swallowing past the swell of emotion, she took her time smoothing the napkin over her lap.

"I have followed the rise of Madtec with interest. I suspected your company was a good fit for this role, Kai, or I wouldn't have approached you." She appreciated how the conversation anchored her in the purpose of the meeting. Because this was just business.

Something they both excelled at. Unlike personal relationships.

"I know that," he conceded, lifting his water bottle and clinking it lightly to hers. "Thank you."

Her gaze flicked to his as he held the pale green bottle in midair. She followed suit, clinking hers to his in a friendly toast that felt like a fresh start.

At least, professionally speaking.

"Here's to a successful partnership." Kai's green gaze lingered on hers, and she couldn't help but think she saw something simmering in their depths.

Old frustration over how things had ended? Or a hint of the lingering attraction that she'd been grappling with all day?

Neither one boded well for their venture. But she licked her lips before raising the bottle to her mouth. One way or another, she would figure out how to work with Kai Maddox for the sake of Blackwood Bank. "To new beginnings."

Three

She had the sexiest mouth he'd ever seen on a woman.

Kai tried not to stare at it, the top lip slightly fuller than the bottom in a perfect cupid's bow that made her look perpetually ready for a kiss. But the more he tried not to think about that incredible mouth of hers, the more he pictured it doing wicked things to him.

Being seated across from Miranda on a property that had once belonged to his rival for her affections felt damned surreal.

Kai had made the trip into Royal with his best professional intentions, hoping to make peace enough to take care of business together. But one look at her in the afternoon sunlight with no makeup on, wearing her yoga clothes, had stolen the breath from his lungs. Miranda was a beautiful woman no matter what. Full stop. Yet seeing her relaxed in her temporary home had reminded him of the woman he'd known, before she was a business mogul in her own right. The sight had catapulted him a decade backward in time, right down to wishing he could invite her for a ride on the back of his motorcycle, her slender thighs hugging his hips.

Except they were far different people now, no matter if he still saw shades of the woman he'd once loved in Miranda. That woman had been a myth—an illusion fueled by incredible chemistry. She'd made that clear when she left him for Buckley.

"We should discuss our next steps," he suggested as he pushed aside his plate. "The contract put a very condensed timeline in place for updating the bank's cybersecurity."

He glanced around to ensure their privacy. The patio behind the Blackwood Hollow guesthouse had a large, covered area for entertaining, complete with fireplace and outdoor kitchen. The table under the vine-covered pergola looked out over the pool shared with the main house. There was no one in sight.

Miranda nodded, bringing his attention back to the moment. To her. A few tendrils of red hair slipped from the clip holding the rest at her nape. "Because I have a reason to worry about it. Most aspects of the bank have been well managed since Buckley's death, but the internal data security director has flagged several concerns that haven't been addressed."

"The outside company Blackwood contracted with prior to us has had a few incidents in the past two years, which suggests to me they are failing to stay up-to-date." Kai had spot-checked Blackwood's system before making the trip to Royal to start familiarizing himself. "Our service niche requires continual, aggressive measures to keep current in a quickly changing marketplace."

"You and Dane have done incredibly well for yourselves, especially—" Her tone suggested she'd been about to say more but she stopped abruptly, then glanced back down at her plate. She speared her fork through a morsel of lemon meringue pie.

"Especially for former hackers?" he supplied, knowing he'd guessed accurately by the slightest tinge of pink in her cheeks. "You can't be a success at preventing cybercrime without knowing how the criminal element works."

"Madtec's rapid rise has been formidable," she amended before sliding her dessert dish to one side. "But remembering how protective you were of Dane, I know that it had to be hard for you when he got into legal trouble."

His jaw tightened. While he felt a small amount of satisfaction that she'd noticed Dane's arrest even as she'd been celebrating her engagement, Kai couldn't dodge the sting of resentment, too. He'd been solely responsible for his brother since their father died of pancreatic cancer when Kai was seventeen and Dane was fifteen. Their mom had been exhausted from the hardship of caregiving and her own grief, and she'd taken off to recover, leaving Kai in charge. She never returned.

"Mostly, I regretted that I hadn't been giving him my full attention in the months before his arrest. He'd only just turned eighteen." Instead of working with his brother on the weekend of the hacking incident that had first flagged an investigation into his brother's activities, he'd taken Miranda to Galveston for a few days at the beach even though her mother had already told Kai that Buckley Blackwood had started coming around the Dupree house. Kai had thought maybe devoting more attention to her would sway things in his favor, but in the end, he couldn't compete with Buckley's money.

Did she remember the timing of the events leading to Dane's arrest? It had been some months after the investigation began, but surely she remembered he'd been concerned about his brother's activities when Kai hadn't been around to keep an eye on him.

Her blue gaze broke away from his. Retrieving her water bottle, she took a long drink. "Dane was a prodigy. When someone is so gifted intellectually, it's probably easy to lose sight of their youth."

Leaning back in his chair, he weighed her answer. Told himself not to ruminate on the past. And still found himself asking, "Speaking of family, how's your mother?"

Her lips pressed together momentarily. A fleeting reaction from this self-contained woman, but he didn't miss it. He'd never understood the dynamic between her and her mom, but then again, Miranda had been more focused on her future than her past when they'd dated.

"Honestly, I'm not sure." She folded the linen napkin that had been on her lap, matching the corners and smoothing the fabric. "She has battled an addiction to prescription painkillers over the years, and that's made it difficult for us to maintain a relationship."

"I'm so sorry to hear it." The news was unexpected. Jarring, even, considering Ginny Dupree had been the one to warn Kai away from her daughter. Had she been an untrustworthy source of information? "I never saw any sign of that kind of problem when we were dating."

"She used to hide it better than she does now," Miranda told him drily, moving the folded napkin to the table and laying it over her plate. "But the problem dates back to when I was a preteen. I started working at a young age since a lot of her paycheck went toward her problems."

His understanding of their past together shifted, the pieces falling together in a different way. Had Miranda's financial situation pushed her toward Buckley? Or had her mother seen a payday when the wealthy rancher had come calling?

It didn't matter now since their breakup had been so long ago. But damn.

"I always admired your ambition, but I didn't realize that it was partially driven by necessity." He reached across the table to lay his hand on hers before considering the wisdom of it, the movement instinctive.

Her blue eyes darted to his, awareness leaping between them when he'd meant only to offer empathy. Understanding.

"Circumstances help make us who we are—good or bad." She didn't move her hand beneath his fingers, but he could feel the leap of her pulse at the base of her thumb. Her skin was so soft. "I'd like to think I used her problems as a push in a positive direction for myself."

He forced himself to release her, but it took more effort than it should have. And he may have glided a touch along the pulse point of her wrist before letting go completely, wanting her to remember the way they could set each other on fire.

Her eyes darted to his. Aware. He didn't know what to make of the current sparking between them. No matter how much he wanted to tell himself this next phase of their relationship needed to be all business, he was still undeniably drawn to her. He wanted to know more about her and how she'd spent the last ten years, but since he suspected she wasn't any more eager to talk about her past than he was willing to revisit his, he let go of the topic.

"That sounds like some of the inspiration for your nonprofit." While Kai hadn't watched much of her reality television show, he had pulled up a speech she'd given about her charity when he'd seen a mention of it online a year ago. "I read about Girl to the Nth Power."

She'd organized the group five years ago and had since received national service awards for her efforts to create supportive environments for young women. In her speech, she'd referred to her organization as a girls' club for a new generation, complete with mentors in disciplines from the arts to STEM, with access to workshops on friendship and self-care.

Her whole face changed, her expression lighting with some of that ambition and passion he remembered from those conversations in the diner where they'd shared their dreams. "While I'm incredibly proud of the work I do at Goddess, Girl to the Nth Power is where my heart lies. It's exciting to make a difference in teens' lives."

He couldn't miss the spark in her eyes. The commitment to her cause.

"If your schedule permits, you should come down to the community center in Deer Springs sometime. Check out the afterschool program." He thought she might be interested in the operation because of her work with teens. Not because he wanted her to spend more time near him.

"I read something about the community center." She stacked their dishes back on the tray they'd used to carry everything outside.

Taking his cue from her, he lifted the tray and followed her back inside the house, his gaze dropping to her curves as she moved. A butterfly tattoo on the back of one ankle was a colorful new addition that called him to explore the rest of her. He placed the tray on the island and shoved his hands in his pockets to remind them not to wander.

"Dane and I built one at the same time we broke ground on the Madtec headquarters. We thought it would give back to the town and make it more inviting for potential employees." He liked the idea of giving local teens more support and opportunities than he and Dane had.

"Smart thinking of you." She slid the remnants of the pie in the refrigerator while he loaded the plates in the dishwasher. "And thank you for the invitation. I'd like to see the community center."

Sensing their time together was coming to an end, Kai wouldn't linger. It was enough to give her the signed contract and pave the way for a working relationship. No need to rehash the past.

"Excellent. We'll be in touch with the Blackwood Bank data security director today and get to work installing new encryption precautions." He should shake her hand and leave. Or maybe just leave.

Except spending time with her today had stirred up too much. His feet didn't move as he watched her lean a hip against the kitchen island.

"I'm glad you changed your mind about handling the cybersecurity, Kai," she admitted. "Thank you."

Walk away, his brain told him.

But he didn't think he could keep this facade of civility between them every time they saw one another if he didn't address at least one of the issues that still bugged the hell out of him after all this time.

"Kai?" Her brow furrowed as she looked up at him questioningly.

Standing there together in that quiet kitchen could have been any one of a hundred times they'd been alone. The past and the present merged.

"There's just one more thing." He shifted closer, lowering his voice. "It's strange for me to be in Blackwood Hollow with you after how things ended for us. But how does it feel for you to be living in Buckley's guesthouse and overseeing his estate surrounded by his sons and daughter?"

She bristled visibly. "I'm not their enemy. Buckley arranged for me to play a role helping them through the aftermath of his death."

"Still loyal to him even after the divorce?" The question came out crueler than he'd intended. But he couldn't help wanting to know.

Her eyes narrowed and she straightened from the island.

"That's not any of your business," she told him coolly, making it clear that he'd effectively erased any progress he'd made smoothing things over between them.

"You're right, it isn't," he agreed, suspecting he'd need Dane to be the one to interact with Blackwood Bank if Kai couldn't refrain from poking at the past this way. "But that doesn't take away the fact that things are bound to be awkward between us while we're finding our footing to make this deal work."

Her full lips pursed. She gave a clipped nod and leaned toward him.

"In that case, let me assure you that living here again is beyond strange for me." She stabbed one manicured finger into the quartz countertop to make her point, a diamond tennis bracelet quivering with the movement. "Discovering my ex-husband trusted me with all his worldly assets during this transition of power to his kids has been even more bizarre." Another finger stabbing the quartz. "But given how much time has passed since you and I shared a history, I don't think there's any need for *awkwardness*. I'm thirty-six years old, Kai. I don't do awkward."

He welcomed the passionate outpouring from her, another facet of Miranda he recognized better than the self-possessed control she'd exhibited in his office and throughout some of their talk today. He stifled the urge to smile at the reemergence of her fiery side.

"Point taken. I've long envied your maturity," he told her with 100 percent honesty. "But for what it's worth, I think what I'm labeling 'awkwardness' might be more accurately called *attraction*." He gave her a moment to process that, knowing he owed her the truth even if it made a working relationship more difficult to navigate. "I'll be on my best behavior with you, Miranda, but I think it's obvious the fire is still there."

This time, she had no comeback, her lips parted in surprise.

Hell, he'd shocked himself too with that admission. But he wasn't the kind of guy to sidestep the facts. He plowed straight through.

Now, he watched as her jaw snapped shut and she straightened.

"Then maybe we should wait for things to cool off and revisit this at a later date." She stalked past him toward the front door, clearly done with him for the day. She pulled it open and stood to one side of the exit, studying him. "Goodbye, Kai."

Had he overstepped the bounds of professionalism?

He didn't think so. She knew him well, no matter that their shared history was ten years old. She couldn't be too surprised that he would speak plainly about his feelings. The attraction was still there—it would be ridiculous to pretend otherwise.

Closing the distance between them, he moved toward the door. He stopped before stepping over the threshold, their gazes meeting.

"Come to Deer Springs," he urged, awareness of her inching over his skin. "If we can come to terms with the history between us, then we can get some closure. Maybe then the attraction will fade and it will be easier to work together."

Her breathing quickened, the stroke of each warm puff stirring an answering heat inside him. But he didn't wait for her to agree. He strode by her toward his vehicle, needing to put Miranda in his rearview mirror. Not just today.

This time, for good.

Three days later, Miranda sat outside on the guesthouse patio with her morning coffee and set aside her work to organize the Royal Gives Back gala that Buckley wanted. Instead, she scrolled through the latest photos from Sophie Blackwood Townshend's European honeymoon. Sophie, the baby of the Blackwood family, had married Miranda's producer last month and was living it up in Paris, Morocco and—most recently—Florence. The backdrop in every picture was stunning, but what captured Miranda's eye most was how in love the happy couple looked. Sophie had met Nigel while working under a false identity at Green Room Media in New York in an effort to dig up dirt on Miranda. Happily, she'd found nothing and had finally come to terms with their relationship. It touched Miranda's heart to be included on the family's message group each day and see what Sophie was up to.

Although, settling her phone back on the wrought iron table, Miranda had to admit that even as her comfort with the Blackwoods grew, the contrast made her more aware of how she'd failed to heal the rift with her mother.

Maybe she didn't need to since her mom had betrayed the most basic rules of family loyalty in the past. But since Ginny Dupree was an addict, Miranda still held out hope one day it might be different between them.

Kai's suggestion she visit Deer Springs echoed in her mind—along with his reminder about the attraction that still simmered. At first, she'd been angry with him for stirring up trouble. Yet a part of her couldn't help but admire his willingness to wade headlong into the topics most people would dance around. It made things frustrating since it would be more comfortable to pretend the spark they'd shared was long buried. But was it true?

She couldn't deny the flare of heat when he'd touched her, even in a moment intended to offer comfort. Maybe he had a good point about trying to get closure. Surely then she could put all her feelings for him behind her. But every time she thought about him saying it was obvious the fire between them was still there, her belly flipped just like it had the first time they'd met.

Miranda had been holding down two jobs at the time, overloaded by the lunch crowd in the diner where she worked as a waitress, and panicked about the duct tape holding together a split seam in her uniform, a tear she hadn't gotten around to sewing the day before after getting into an argument with her mother. She'd never forget how it felt to arrive at Kai's table to take his order and having his heart-stopping smile chase away all the stress until it evaporated like summer dew.

He'd insisted he didn't want to order until she could join him for lunch. She'd brought him a soda anyway. He hadn't touched it until two o'clock when her shift ended. After she took a seat, it seemed like they didn't stop talking for months except to kiss and make love.

But Kai ended things.

Not in so many words, of course. But in his actions. He'd been the one to retreat.

She'd always thought it was stress of his own that had made him pull away. He'd worked even more hours than she had, and some of the jobs had been shady. And yes, that had bothered her, given how many times she'd been burned by her mother's brand of flexible ethics. She'd had enough instability in her life. She wanted steady. Even if predictable wasn't some people's idea of happily ever after, to her it had sounded blissful. Kai was six years younger than her, and he lived more dangerously than Miranda ever could. And yet she'd put up with all of that, compromising again and again, until she'd felt him pulling away. That was when she'd decided to stop trying.

He hadn't even argued with her when she'd decided to end things, the final proof she'd needed that things weren't right between them. Was it any wonder she'd been aggravated two days ago by his insinuations of loyalty to Buckley?

The marriage hadn't been perfect, but she'd given it her best shot.

Leaving her coffee cup on the patio table, Miranda

grabbed her phone and put it in her pocket. She wasn't going to get anything accomplished on the Royal Gives Back event with her thoughts straying time and again to Kai.

He'd invited her to Deer Springs to put the past behind them, hadn't he? She intended to take him up on it.

Four

Lulu Shepard raised her fist to knock on the door of the guesthouse when Miranda opened it wide.

"Lulu." Miranda smiled warmly, wrapping her in a friendly hug that carried a whiff of subtle perfume. "I wasn't expecting you. Is everything okay?"

Stressed and anxious about her wedding plans, Lulu hoped Miranda could help her. Sometimes she wondered if the other woman had ever experienced a moment's indecision. She seemed so perpetually poised.

Designer purse in hand, Miranda wore a fitted navy blue suit with wide lapels. Raspberry-colored sling back heels were a nice touch. Miranda always managed to look feminine and badass at the same time.

"I'm fine. I just wanted some wedding advice, but I won't keep you if you're on your way out." Lulu stepped back, giving her friend room to join her on the porch.

Pulling the door closed behind her, Miranda pointed to a couple of Adirondack chairs to one side. "I always have time for you. Let's sit."

Relieved, Lulu dropped into one of the seats. "Thank you. I'm in a dilemma about the bridesmaids for my wedding. I worked out the details with your stepson and then Nigel texted me confirmation that we can have the wedding here at Blackwood Hollow, which is great. But he sent around a memorandum to the crew that our next episode will be shopping for bridesmaid dresses for all of the *Secret Lives* members."

"I remember seeing that," Miranda confirmed. "And I'm glad you're getting married here, but I do remember thinking that it's going to seem forced for you to have us in your wedding. The audience knows we're not all best friends."

Lulu bit her lip, hoping she hadn't offended Miranda, whom she'd grown close to over the last two seasons. "I want Fee, of course, and I'd love to have you in it, but Rafaela? Come on. Why would I ask her to stand up with me after some of the stunts she's pulled?"

Earlier in the season, Rafaela Marchesi had snapped a photo of Seraphina's fiancé, rancher Clint Rockwell, without his prosthetic leg and sent it to the media in an obvious bid for ratings. Fee had been hurt and furious, of course, so as Fee's best friend, Lulu had been doubly outraged. She still was. She'd go to the mat for Fee.

"You have every right to decide who you want in your wedding," Miranda assured her in no uncertain terms, stabbing the arm of the chair with an emphatic finger. "That's a given. But it occurs to me that maybe Nigel is setting us up for the usual show drama by putting you in the position of having to tell the others yourself—on camera."

"Meaning you think he wants a bridesmaid shopping show to turn into a bitch-fest about exactly that kind of thing?" Lulu hadn't considered that, but it made perfect sense.

"If I've learned one thing from doing this series, it's that we live or die by the sound bites." Miranda shrugged a shoulder. "That's why I don't get as much screen time. I'm less interesting for viewers because I don't go from zero to sixty with my emotions."

"Or with your mouth," Lulu added, thinking how grounded Miranda seemed. How unlikely to fly off the handle. Whereas the others—Lulu included—were all apt to say whatever came to mind. They didn't hold back.

"Exactly," Miranda agreed, leaning back in her seat with a thoughtful expression. "Still waters might run deep, but they don't make for good television. I'm okay with that, though. I'm grateful to be a part of the show for the friendships. I hadn't realized until I got involved with *Secret Lives* how lacking my life has been in female friendships."

Touched, Lulu squeezed Miranda's hand. "I'm glad to have you in my life, too," she told her honestly, appreciating the different perspective. "What would you do about the bridesmaids if you were me?"

"The simplest option would be to just go along with it. You wouldn't be the first woman to fill up her wedding photos with frenemies. At least with us, you'll be aware of what to expect. How many friends do you know who were coerced to put cousins they hardly knew in their ceremony in order to placate an aunt or mother—only to then get in trouble anyway when the cousin couldn't stand the other bridesmaids? We've gotten through a few seasons and haven't killed each other yet, so you'll be safe on that score." Miranda shrugged, making it all sound so reasonable. "Personally, I don't think it's a big deal to have Rafaela in your wedding photos, but it's not about me, Lu. It's your day. Yours and Kace's."

Lulu's heart warmed all over again at the thought of marrying Kace. Having the day free of drama and artifice had become so very important. This was about their future. Their love. Not ratings.

"And at the end of the day, that's all that really matters, isn't it?" Lulu felt a tension slide away at Miranda's gentle wisdom and she decided she needed some more of that brand of Zen in her life. Or maybe she was already experiencing it now that she felt loved and appreciated by a man she wanted to spend the rest of her life with. "At my first wedding, I got all spun up about the details—seating arrangements and a whole lot of superficial stuff that didn't really matter."

"What counts is the marriage, not the wedding." Lulu caught the shadows in her friend's eyes. Was she thinking of her own marriage to Buckley?

Lulu knew Miranda hadn't had an easy road, no matter how much of a placid facade she tried to present to the world.

"I'm going to do it right this time," Lulu agreed, already imagining the future she'd have waking beside Kace every day. "The marriage, that is."

Miranda nodded approvingly, a few darting birds chirping a happy echo to the sentiment. "I know it's right when I see you two together. I think it's obvious to everyone around you."

Lulu held tight to the knowledge. She didn't need anyone else's approval, but she liked the idea that her friends backed her decision. "He makes me happy." It was as simple as that. "And the wedding can be as over-the-top as Nigel wants it."

"Are you sure?" Miranda asked, leaning forward, a diamond pendant swinging out and reflecting the sun. "Because you can tell him that you don't want Rafaela— or any of us—in it."

"I'm sure." At peace with her decision, she accepted that the wedding was a one-day party. The marriage was what would last a lifetime. "I wouldn't have met Kace without this show, and I don't mind celebrating that. Once the reception is over, I'm going to have a good man in my life forever, and that's what counts."

Standing, she thanked Miranda for helping her think things through. Before she left, however, she couldn't help but ask, "Where are you headed? That suit looks stunning on you."

Even before Miranda answered, Lulu's instincts told her Miranda was going to see a man. There was a hesitation. The briefest moment of uncertainty that Lulu didn't remember ever seeing before in this supremely poised woman.

"I'm heading to Deer Springs to speak with the tech company helping me bring Blackwood Bank's security up to speed." Miranda rose, walking Lulu to her rental car.

"My female intuition is screaming that there's a person of interest on the other end of this meeting," Lulu said lightly, not expecting much of a reply. Trying to pin Miranda down wouldn't yield results anyway.

Opening the driver's side door, Lulu remembered clearly how it felt to be circling Kace when they were getting to know one another. How alive she felt. She still did, just thinking about him.

She hoped Miranda's mystery man was worthy of her.

"He's interesting, all right," Miranda admitted, standing by the tall pots of flowering trees that lined the porch. "I'll give him that."

Lulu whistled low under her breath as she started the car, intrigued at the thought of Miranda navigating a new relationship. "For what it's worth, you look sizzling hot. Thank you for the advice, Miranda."

"Always," Miranda assured her, closing the driver's door before blowing her a kiss as Lulu put the car in Reverse.

Her heart felt happy. She would have Seraphina as her maid of honor in her wedding. As for Rafaela, Lulu knew Miranda would be right there next to her to intervene if their fame-chasing costar stepped out of line. Because while the audience might see Miranda as the grounded one who didn't cause a stir, Lulu had no doubt that her quieter friend would do whatever was necessary to make sure the wedding went smoothly. She just hoped Miranda knew that her friends would have her back in return, no matter what she was going through on her own.

Kai had just finished helping one of the kids in his coding class at the community center when a teen in the back of the room let out a quiet wolf whistle.

"Is there a problem, Rhys?" he asked the boy seated closest to the window. The teen's eyes were fixed on something outside in the parking lot.

Normally, Kai had the blinds lowered since the first-floor tech room had a view of people coming and going from the building, but today he'd opened one to let in some natural light.

"Sorry," Rhys muttered, swiveling in his chair to face his laptop screen. "Got distracted."

The teen went back to work without Kai having to say anything else, and Kai was about to dismiss the class when he spotted a feminine figure striding closer to the building's front doors.

Miranda.

Anticipation fired through him, even as he experienced a moment of understanding for the teen student's loss of focus. No doubt, Miranda had the power to distract. She entered the community center's front doors, out of sight once more.

"We'll finish our projects next time," Kai announced. "The tech lab will remain open for another hour if anyone wants to keep working."

Kai nodded his thanks to the lab's afternoon monitor, a local graduate student earning some internship credits. About half of the students gathered their backpacks and dispersed to the gym or the game lounge, but the rest stayed behind, including the wolf whistler.

Kai clapped Rhys on the shoulder before leaving the class. "Whistles and catcalling can make women uncomfortable," he reminded. The kid was working on a sophisticated program for someone his age—but when it came to emotional maturity, he still had a lot to learn. "A definite no-go."

"It won't happen again," Rhys assured him quickly, straightening in his chair.

Nodding, Kai let the kid off the hook, then headed toward the door to find Miranda. He could only assume she was here because she'd taken him up on the offer to put the past behind them in the town where they'd met. The town where their affair had set them both on fire.

He spotted her just outside the tech lab door, her fitted blue suit skimming her memorable curves, the skirt revealing toned legs. Hunger for her stirred. Not just because she was an extremely attractive woman. Some of his best memories were with her at his side.

"Hello, Kai." She tucked a slim handbag under one arm, her gaze fixed on his.

"I wasn't sure you'd come." He'd been waiting for days, wondering if he'd overstepped by suggesting they had unfinished business between them.

"I wasn't either," she admitted, her gaze taking in the huge common area of the community center. Couches were filled with groups of teens talking and laughing. The area was ringed by meeting rooms, a game room, gym and a snack counter. "When it comes to a business decision, I'm sure of myself. But the way forward in my personal life never seems quite as clear."

He appreciated her honesty, and repaid her in kind. "I'm glad you're here."

While it might be easier for them both, from a business perspective, to ignore their history for the sake of Blackwood Bank, Kai found himself wanting more resolution with Miranda. Or did he just want to bring her home with him and forget all the animosity to lose himself in her one last time? He couldn't deny that his thoughts about her ranged from sensual to explicit, and those thoughts were more and more frequent.

"You've done an amazing job with this place," she observed, not paying attention to the small commotion she was creating with her presence. A few girls seemed to have recognized Miranda's famous face, and the news spread in audible whispered conversations from group to group.

"Thank you. But it seems I've underestimated your show's popularity with the teen crowd. Looks like I created quite a stir by inviting you here." He slid a hand under her elbow, guiding her away from the lounge toward an unused meeting space in the back of the building. "Would you consider continuing our discussion at my house? I live close by."

She glanced over her shoulder briefly, as if to gauge how much of a commotion she was causing. Yet she never slowed her step, allowing him to lead her away.

A surge of misplaced possessiveness—or perhaps it was simple desire—made him want to wrap her in his arms. Tuck her even closer.

"Perhaps that would be for the best," she agreed, her voice quiet beside him so that he had to lean nearer to hear. "I'm parked out front."

"I'll drive you," he assured her, as he quickened his pace through the empty room sometimes used for local speakers or book clubs. There was a back entrance that opened onto a separate parking area. "My vehicle is right outside."

Today, no one else was in the rear lot as there were no special events planned for the evening, so they arrived at his Jaguar quickly enough.

"This is the second time I've seen you without a motorcycle," Miranda observed lightly while he unlocked the passenger door and opened it for her. "I will confess I'm surprised to see you behind the wheel of a car."

Watching her lower herself gracefully into the leather seat, Kai latched onto the topic of discussion to distract himself from her legs.

"While the Bluetooth systems available in helmets have come a long way, it's still easier to conduct a business call from a car," he admitted, closing her door and then letting himself into the driver's side. He started the engine once they were buckled in, heading west toward his house through the relatively quiet streets. "However, if you have an urge to roam Deer Springs on the back of a bike, it would be a pleasure to take you for a ride. I still keep two of them in the garage for when the restless urge strikes."

He shifted into a higher gear, remembering the feel of her arms wrapped around him, her breasts pressed against his back when they used to ride together. As her throaty laugh floated between them, he wondered if she was recalling some of those same times.

"I thought we were going to put the past to rest, not relive it." She slanted a glance his way, blue eyes assessing.

That's what he'd thought, too.

But his relationship with Miranda had never lacked for complications. And he found himself tossing out a far thornier solution.

"There's more than one way to fix a simmering awareness." He knew better than to label the chemistry "awkwardness" this time. She'd been very clear about that. "We could appease it."

Just saying the words made the idea shimmer with real possibility. If she agreed, they could indulge themselves as much as they wanted. Let the heat consume them both. Visions of her naked and eager for him practically crowded out his view of the road.

"I don't think I can appease your restless urges, Kai." She shifted in her seat, crossing one leg over the other in a way that snagged his gaze. "I never was very effective at that. And now that we're older..."

She let the thought slide, as if he knew the rest of what she'd say. He had to refocus on the words since his brain lingered on her legs. He wanted to part her thighs and lay between them. Kiss her until they were both breathless.

"Now that we're older, what?" he prompted, needing her to spell it out for him while he battled enticing images in his head. He turned down a side street that led to his private drive.

"If I couldn't keep your attention when I was a twenty-six-year-old, chances are good I won't be enough of a diversion for you at thirty-six." Her words were so unexpected—so unwelcome and wrong—that he pulled to a stop the moment he turned onto his private driveway even though they hadn't reached the house yet.

He shoved the car in Park.

"You were all I could think about when you were twenty-six, Miranda." Hell, thinking about her to the exclusion of all else was what had cost Dane his freedom. That had been the final blow to their faltering relationship. "Holding my attention has never a problem for you."

Surprise colored her eyes, her expression thoughtful for a moment before she spoke.

"You checked out on our relationship long before I ended things," she reminded him.

"Only because I knew we were a lost cause once your mother told me Buckley Blackwood had started coming around." He'd never forget the force of that blow. The kindness shaded with pity in Ginny Dupree's eyes when she'd informed him he had a powerful—rich—rival for Miranda's affections. "Six weeks later, we were finished. Dane was under investigation. Buckley Blackwood was shopping for diamonds and you were out of my life for good."

He heard Miranda's quick gasp. Saw her brow furrow. But she knew how that story turned out as well as he did, so he couldn't imagine what she seemed surprised about now.

For his part, he welcomed the reminder that this meeting between them wasn't about appeasing the damnable attraction that hadn't faded. Better to confront it. Shred it apart if necessary.

One way or another, he was putting Madtec and his brother first this time. He wouldn't let his attraction get in the way. If it was a problem for her, then Miranda would have to figure out how to work with him. She'd always been good at prioritizing the bottom line ahead of everything else.

Miranda had come to Deer Springs to put the past to rest.

The idea had sounded a whole lot more peaceful than the process was turning out to be.

She'd made a misstep marrying Buckley—she could admit that now. Had it been rooted in her relationship with Kai? She'd forgotten how being with Kai had always felt like someone turned the flame on high beneath her normally mild emotions. With him, feelings were more intense. Anger and passion were hotter. Pleasure deeper. Hurts more painful. She'd have to sequester herself in her yoga studio to breathe through all the tumultuous sensations pinballing around inside her.

But the revelation that her mother had intervened with Kai—effectively chasing him off the moment Buckley had shown up at the Dupree house to ask if he could see

Miranda privately—had rocked her. Kai had never told her about that before, but it made so many other perplexing moments from the past suddenly make sense.

Not that it mattered now.

As Kai drove the Jaguar the rest of the way down a winding drive and through a wrought iron gate flanked by brick columns, Miranda reminded herself to focus on the present. She needed to smooth things over with the copresident of Madtec and pave the way for a good working relationship with Blackwood Bank. That was why she was here.

Not to contemplate motorcycle rides with a hot guy from her past. Not even when he'd told her that she had been all he could think about back when they'd dated.

Pull it together.

"Here we are," he announced pulling around a copse of trees so she could see a house.

An incredible, modern marvel of a house. Because as the car arrived in the driveway, the lights around the place—inside and out—turned on.

"It's beautiful, Kai," she told him honestly, taking in the expanses of glass between sleek black stone walls.

The lights—perhaps motion-detection or connected to whatever security system he had in place—made the whole place glow. She could see into the huge rooms decorated in minimalist style. Designed in an L shape, the house wrapped around a pool that became visible only as he drove deeper into the property toward a detached garage. He didn't open any of the bays, however, leaving the sports coupe parked outside while she took in the details of the house.

A second-floor deck with a firepit and hot tub overlooked the pool area. From master suite to kitchen, guest rooms to office, the whole floor plan was visible thanks to the windows and abundant light.

"Thank you." He shut off the engine and came around to help her out of the car. "I worked on the design for almost a year before I was happy with it."

She braced herself for his touch before placing her hand in his, that current of awareness ever-present. Rising to her feet, she withdrew her hand quickly, but the memory of how he felt lingered long after.

Her only consolation was that Kai seemed ready to drop the idea of acting on their attraction after their conversation in the car.

"You designed this?" She shouldn't be surprised. She'd always known he was a gifted Renaissance man, his agile mind hopping from one project to the next, fascinated by the inner workings of things and studying them until he found answers that satisfied him.

"It was easier that way." His hand landed at the base of her spine briefly, guiding her toward a walkway leading around the pool. "At first, whenever I wanted to modify someone else's design to use recycled materials, I got a long song and dance about why it wouldn't work."

The feel of his touch called to her. She refocused on the house, grounding herself in the physical space to keep her thoughts off the ever-present awareness of the man.

"So you developed your own design instead." She admired the black, glittering stone walls, idly wondering where he'd sourced the material.

Small talk was a whole lot easier than what she'd come here to discuss.

"It's my home. Why should I compromise?" A hint of a smile curved one side of his lips. "Although my builder did call my blueprints the most obnoxiously detailed he'd ever seen, I took it as a compliment that the end product is exactly what I'd envisioned."

He stopped in front of a sliding door that opened into the kitchen, and de-armed the security system with an app on his phone. The system chimed twice before he slid the door wide, then wider still, opening the wall to the outdoor area and letting in a warm breeze. The lights that had flickered to life while they were still in the driveway dimmed now, leaving only the pendant lamps in the kitchen, which Kai had flicked on with a conventional switch.

"You did an incredible job. Your house, Madtec, the community center—they're all a testament to how much you've invested in Deer Springs. The town must be very happy with you." She set her purse on a padded barstool with sleek chrome legs that was tucked under the marble island.

Kai retrieved a pair of small bottles of seltzer from the built-in refrigerator and set them on the island near two glasses.

"This community was good to Dane and me after our father died and our mother left." He'd never spoken much about his family when they'd dated, but Miranda knew that his mom had taken off not long after their father had lost his protracted battle with cancer. "I had a lot of anger about my dad's passing and the responsibilities that came with my mom's departure, but the people here gave me room to work through it, overlooking a few screwups, helping out when they could."

"You've paid them back and then some," she assured him. "You've done good work here."

He dismissed her words with a curt shake of his head as he poured their drinks and passed her a glass while she thought back to their first meeting. It had been only three years after losing his parents, but he'd been so sharp. Mature beyond his age. Ready to take on the world.

She hated to think her mother had helped sabotage things between them when Kai already had so much on his plate. He'd had big dreams to build his company and advance his software. Except he'd had to look out for his younger brother.

Of course, Kai could have opted to fight for their relationship, and he hadn't. Sipping the bubbling water, Miranda's eyes met his over the rim of her glass. The bubbly sensation shifted from her lips to her belly, the awareness of him tickling over her skin.

It made no sense that he could make her feel like that from nothing more than a shared look. No doubt it had to do with the way he affected her, turning up the intensity of everything she felt. She set her glass aside abruptly, trying to rein in her emotions.

"Speaking of good work." He rested his glass on the counter beside hers and covered her fingers with his. "How do you suggest we move forward, Miranda, when the thought of kissing you crowds out everything else?"

Five

Miranda stilled.

He felt that stillness where he touched her, an unmoving wariness that lasted a long, breathless moment before her pulse jumped hard enough for him to feel the kick of it under his thumb.

"You were never one to mince words," she said finally, her blue gaze tracking his, probing deeper as if she could pluck his thoughts from his mind.

"We're here to have a conversation about it," he reminded her gently, stroking his thumb over that telltale vein. "So we might as well come to the point."

He hadn't meant to rekindle this spark with her, but it leaped to life of its own free will whenever they were near one another. It seemed foolish to pretend otherwise.

Her gaze lowered, settling on the place where their

hands touched. "I think I had a different idea about what it would mean to settle our differences."

"Why don't you tell me what you hoped to accomplish today," he pressed. "You're not a woman who minces words either. So be honest with me. How do you suggest we go forward from here?"

She remained quiet for so long he wondered if she was going to answer. A breeze blew through the kitchen, stirring her red hair, a strand stroking along her cheek the way his hand longed to. When she lifted her chin, there was a determined glint in her eyes.

"With dogged resolve not to repeat the mistakes of the past."

He couldn't help but admire her, but he'd be damned if he was going to let her off the hook when he knew he wasn't the only one feeling tempted by what they'd once shared. "I couldn't agree more. But I can't say I ever viewed touching you or kissing you as a mistake. Far from it."

"That brand of thinking isn't going to solve the problem." She withdrew her hand from underneath his, but her restless gaze roamed over him in a way that eased the sting of rejection.

The caress of her eyes was far bolder than his hand had been.

"Neither is ignoring what we both want." He folded his arms, daring her to contradict him. Craving the chance to prove her wrong.

Miranda didn't oppose him, however. "As temporarily satisfying as it might be to indulge ourselves, Kai, I think we have too much painful and complicated history for any good to come from falling into old patterns. We can't just pretend the hurtful parts didn't happen."

Had it been hurtful for her, too?

Her expression seemed to confirm it, but at the time, he'd viewed their breakup as one-sided. She'd moved on without him, turning her affections toward someone more successful. He'd thought he'd been doing her a favor by giving her up. The idea that there might have been more to it gnawed at him.

"You think renewing our affair is too risky." He summarized her point, winnowing it down to the bottom line. He paced away from her as he thought it over, his gaze shifting to the silent spill of water at the edge of the infinity pool on the patio.

"Yes." She sounded relieved that he seemed to understand.

But a good negotiator always had a backup plan.

"I disagree." He strode toward her again, liking the vision of her here, in his home. "We're both older and wiser. We wouldn't fall prey to the false illusions we had about one another ten years ago."

He stopped just short of her, his chest so close to her he could feel the heat radiating off her, the heat of their desire for each other. Except she looked ready to argue again.

"What about a compromise?" he suggested, before she could speak, still not touching her even though the ache for her was a tangible thing inside him.

She arched an auburn brow, questioning.

"One last kiss," he suggested, presenting his real agenda.

For now.

"I think that's a bad idea," she said quickly, reaching for her water glass again. She took a sip, then kept the cut crystal in one hand, a barrier between them.

Her lips glistened with moisture. His heart slugged faster.

"Is it?" He leaned closer, but didn't touch her. "Let me tell you why I think it's the best idea."

"Um." She shifted, her knee grazing his as she moved.

The brief feel of her stoked a fire inside him, but still he didn't touch her, needing her to make the decision. "It would let us end on a good note. Give closure to that chapter."

She set her glass on the counter, the tumbler clinking unsteadily on the granite. "I don't think so. And I'm not sure this is a fair discussion."

"Good debate calls for supporting arguments." He eased back enough to look into her eyes, a far deeper blue than the pool outside. "But if you're not interested in hearing how a kiss might clear away the thoughts that cloud my head when you're around—"

She closed her eyes for a moment, and he thought she was trying to shut down the conversation. But then she nodded. It was a gesture so slight it was almost imperceptible, but he'd seen it. Somehow that nod told him she was conceding the point. His pulse sped.

"If we're going to do this, make it count." Deliberately, she curved a palm around his neck and lowered his mouth toward hers.

She began by brushing her lips over his with a feather softness that made him groan.

Or maybe it was the feel of her luscious curves pressing into him that tore the sound from his throat. Either way, the sweet satisfaction of her hands on him, urgently gripping his shirtfront to draw him closer, was the best possible outcome.

Her lips parted, welcoming him, and he took his time savoring her, licking his way inside. He lingered in the places that made her breath hitch, remembering what she liked, reminding her what they could do to one another. He wrapped her in his arms, sealing her to him, positive no man could make her feel the way he could. The orange-jasmine scent of her skin fired through his senses while her fingers skimmed over his shoulders and down his back.

He tried telling himself it was just a kiss. That he couldn't handle any more than that. But the soft swell of her breasts against his chest, the shift of her hips muddled his thoughts. Her hips rocked, seeking, and he was lost.

The kiss went wild. Out of control. The needy sound she made in the back of her throat undid him. Her hands slid over his shirt and then her fingers made quick work of the buttons. She slipped one hand along the heated flesh of his bare chest, her nails lightly scoring. He forced himself back, knowing he needed to end this. Remembering she hadn't signed on for more than a kiss.

But before he could pull away completely, she captured his lower lip with hers, drawing on it in a move so sexy he had to grind his teeth together to keep from leaning her over the kitchen counter and pulling up her skirt.

"Miranda." He said her name, almost in a plea—needing her help if he was going to regain control.

Her blue eyes sprang open, but she didn't move away from him. Their heartbeats pounded wildly against his chest, and for a second, he couldn't have said which rhythm belonged to him. Need for her crowded out rational thought for long moments afterward.

Finally, her hands fell away from his chest.

He mourned the loss of her touch even as he said a prayer of thanks that he'd enlisted her aid. He'd never lost his head so fast for a woman.

Except with Miranda the first time.

Hell.

"I did warn you it was a bad idea," she reminded him, stepping back enough to give them both some breathing room.

She combed restless fingers through her red hair and then gave her suit jacket a tug, straightening it. A bright emerald cocktail ring on one finger was a welcome reminder that she was no longer the ambitious waitress with dreams of a big future.

This Miranda was independent and successful, with a whole life waiting for her in New York. And she'd made it clear she didn't want to retread their past.

"We have very different ideas of bad." He was in no mood to argue now. Not until he had his head screwed back on straight. "Because what just happened there was so damned good it hurt. You know it was."

"You wanted a last kiss. You got it." She finished her seltzer water and walked over to deposit the glass in his sink. "Now we can close that chapter and focus on the bank's business."

He slanted her a sideways glance as he refastened a few of his shirt buttons. "You realize how ludicrous that sounds. I think it's safe to say I was dead wrong about a kiss settling the tension between us."

She peered out over the patio area, a warm breeze filtering in. Her cheeks were flushed pink, her lips softly swollen from his kiss. Huffing out a sigh, she turned back toward him.

"Until we figure out what that means, why don't you show me the highlights of the house while we shake off the aftereffects?"

Her legs still felt shaky.

One kiss and she'd been ready to peel off all her clothes to relive the past with Kai. The rush of adrenaline must be what was making her skin buzz now. Maybe she should have just told him to take her back to her car.

But Miranda hadn't grown her business by being a quitter, and it bugged her to leave Kai's place without accomplishing what she'd come here for—to resolve the past so they could move forward with their professional partnership.

So even though the memory of the out-of-control kiss was still simmering in her veins, she followed him through his home, taking in the details of upcycled materials that had been used to achieve the sleekly modern aesthetic. Maybe her subconscious would tackle the problem of the kiss while she tracked the work Kai had done over the years.

She wasn't sure what impressed her most—the solar panels and collection of rainwater that made him far less dependent than most on conventional utilities, or the repurposed stone collected from teardowns around central Texas. He opened the last door on the bottom floor for her now, gesturing her inside a pale gray office space or lab of some kind, full of humming computers, a huge locked server cabinet and monitors everywhere.

"And this is my tech room," he announced, following her inside across the travertine floor. "I work on new software and gadgets in here. It's not so much an office as grown-up play space."

Her brain supplied a whole different set of visuals for a play space with Kai. She squeezed her legs together against the ache for him, but that only made it worse. Huffing out a pent-up breath, she focused on what she was seeing instead of what she felt.

"It looks a little high-tech for play," she observed, noting the electronic parts in various states of assembly at a counter along the far wall. There was a huge overhead lamp on one swing arm for easy movement, and a magnifying glass the size of a dinner plate on another.

"I come here when I get burned out on coding," he admitted, following her deeper into the room as if drawn forward by his favorite things. "I love my work, but when the thing you're passionate about becomes your primary means of income, it robs you of a good creative outlet."

Surprised by the keenness of the insight, she remembered another thing she'd enjoyed about Kai. No matter their other differences—his bad-boy ways that flirted with danger while she stayed firmly on the straight and narrow—they were both wired for high productivity and ambition. They'd been able to share their dreams and their passion for their work.

"I couldn't agree with you more." Walking through the space, Miranda recognized shades of the man she'd known. An artist's rendering of a futuristic-looking motorcycle hung on one wall. A framed photo of the groundbreaking for Madtec's headquarters rested on another. "I couldn't wait to share the peace I take from yoga with other people, and I get to do that in a big way with Goddess. But the business means I don't get to be in the studio as much I would like."

She felt his presence close to her shoulder, her whole

body keyed in to his no matter how hard she tried to forget about that kiss in the kitchen.

He didn't linger by her, however. Instead, he moved toward the door as if ready to move on. He waited there for her. "We're lucky to have those kinds of problems. But I hope you make taking care of yourself a priority, too."

The simple sentiment lodged in her chest, touching her, affecting her as much as his touch. When was the last time someone in her life had urged her to put her wishes first? Even Buckley—a great champion of her ambition—had measured her success by her profit margin. Shaking off the draw of the old bond with Kai, it occurred to her that relating to him physically was a whole lot simpler than acknowledging the deeper chemistry.

"I try." She strode toward the door as he made way for her in the gray stone corridor.

He nodded. Leaned a shoulder into the doorframe as he considered her, his arms folded. "The only places left to show you on the tour involve…beds." His green eyes darkened. Even the word sounded silky on his lips. "Places I don't dare take you with the aftermath of that kiss still singeing my insides."

She did that to him?

Her gaze dipped to where the fabric of his gray dress shirt went taut around his biceps. Tendrils of desire teased her, tangling around her legs and rooting her feet to the floor.

Breathless at the thought of him needing restraint around her, she posed to him the question she couldn't answer herself. "What do *you* think we should do to fix this?" She hesitated. "To get us to a regular working relationship, that is."

"I wish I had a clear answer for that." Sincerity colored his words, leading her to believe he'd thought long and hard about it, too. "But all I know is that ignoring the attraction is only making it worse."

Her heart beat so hard it felt like her whole body pushed her inexorably toward him. Fighting what she wanted demanded all her energy. All her focus.

The memory of what it felt like to be in his arms roared through her. The seductive answer to her question seemed impossible to ignore when he stood so close to her, more appealing than any man she'd ever met.

"At least we agree on what's *not* working," she murmured, as much to herself as to him.

"Why don't you let me make you my priority for the rest of the day, Miranda?" he suggested, reaching out to skim a knuckle along her cheek.

The touch melted any argument she might have made, any thought she might have had that didn't involve being with him.

Closing her eyes, she let herself focus on the place where his skin brushed over hers, the scent of him stirring her need while he continued to speak.

"We could step away from the problem of work for a while," he added, spinning a vision too enticing to resist. "And just…be."

Being with him would be so much more complicated than he was making it sound. But when was the last time she'd put what she'd wanted ahead of everything else? Her whole life had been about work and responsibility for years.

Opening her eyes, she found his.

"Yes." The affirmation of what she wanted felt like a step off a precipice, but it also felt damned good. She would take ownership of her choice. "I want to do more than see a room with a bed. I want to be in one. With you."

His knuckle stilled against her cheek as he seemed to absorb the words. Process them. And then, all at once, both hands cupped her face, lifting her chin for his kiss.

She stepped closer to him, wanting no space between them, needing Kai to deliver on the sensual promise he'd made. Now that she'd committed to this, she was going all in.

His mouth covered hers, claimed hers. His tongue stroked her lower lip, teasing a shiver that coursed through her whole body. She wrapped her arms around his neck, wanting to feel him everywhere.

He lifted her against him, his body a sensual friction against hers as her feet left the ground. She steadied herself with her hands on his shoulders while he turned them down a hall and up a stairway, his thighs stroking hers as he walked with her in his arms. His chest a warm weight against her breasts, his hips rolling against hers as they moved together.

Flames licked their way up her body, anticipation making her ready to come out of her skin by the time he shoved through a door into the master suite dominated by a platform bed with a padded leather headboard. He set her on her feet a moment before he leaned down to jab a remote. On cue, electronic blinds lowered to cover the windows while sconces flickered to life near a stone hearth on one wall, the low golden glow turning Kai's olive-colored skin to warm bronze.

The sight only fired her urge to see more of it. For the second time that day, her fingers went to work on his shirt buttons, desperate to feel him. Taste him.

"Miranda." Her name on his lips made her insides quiver. "I've missed your single-minded focus."

A startled laugh bubbled free, but it didn't come close to distracting her.

"You know how I am about goal setting," she teased, bending to kiss his sculpted pecs, his skin clean and his scent woodsy.

"And I enjoy being the focus of your goals." His hands were steadier than hers, quickly undoing the jacket of her suit. "But I did promise to make you my priority, remember?"

The cool air of the room, stirred by an overhead fan, sent a pleasurable shiver through her before he flicked a bra strap off one shoulder. The emerald green silk tickled before he lowered a kiss to her collarbone.

She forgot everything else but how that felt, gladly giving herself over to his touch. His mouth. She'd tried to bury the memories of what it had been like to be with him, but the knowledge leaped to life now, adding to the anticipation coiling tighter inside her.

She lost track of how his skillful hands freed her from one piece of clothing after another, but her skirt slid down her hips even before her jacket fell away from her arms.

Kai edged back to look at her, his green eyes missing nothing while she tried to catch her breath.

"You're so incredibly beautiful," he informed her, shrugging out of his shirt. "It's unfair to other women."

Feminine pleasure danced through her at his over-the-top flattery. She toed off her high heels and then moved toward him, her bare feet silent on the cool stone floor.

"It's far more unfair that you get to see me, and I can't see you." Hooking a finger in his belt, she slid the leather through the buckle before unfastening his pants, his skin hot to the touch where her knuckle grazed his abs.

He bent to kiss her again, distracting her with a flick of his tongue. She wavered on her feet and he lifted her once more, turning to deposit her on his bed. The downy navy-and-white-striped duvet felt cool against her skin while Kai remained standing. She watched him strip off his socks and shoes before shedding his pants. His boxers.

Her throat went dry at the sight of him. At the reminder of how much he wanted her. A helpless, needy sound tore free from the back of her throat before she could stifle it. He covered her with all that warm, heavy muscle, and the pleasure of it nudged her closer to the edge of fulfillment. Every nerve ending vibrated. One strong thigh sank between hers and she gasped at the feel of it.

Her fingers flexed against his shoulders, drawing him down to her, but he wouldn't be hurried as he unfastened the front clasp of her bra. Sensation tingled and tightened, making her ache. He soothed it with his tongue, circling the tip of her breast, drawing on her until she pulsated with need between her legs.

That too he cared for, fingering her lightly at first, then harder, through the thin silk of her panties until she writhed for more. She was so close to finding release. So close.

Dimly, she thought of telling him. But before she could form words, his breath warmed her ear.

"Come for me," he urged her, the whisper of sound coinciding with a sweet, devastating stroke of his finger up the very center of her.

The orgasm spun through her like a whirlwind, seizing all of her and twisting pure pleasure from her. The sensations pulsed over and over, as if she hadn't found release in all the years since he'd last touched her. She gripped his wrist, holding him there, even though she knew she didn't need to. Somehow, he still understood her body so very well.

When her quivers subsided, he drew her panties down and off. Speechless still, she kissed him hard, pouring the feelings she couldn't name into passion. She felt him reach into the nightstand drawer and knew he returned with a condom. Not trusting her trembling hands, she let him take care of it.

Just the way he took care of her.

The thought captivated her for a moment as he slid inside her. Then, his green eyes met hers and she didn't think about anything but making him feel as good as he'd done for her.

Rolling him to his back, she rained kisses down his neck as she moved over him, rolling her hips into him. Softly at first. Then harder.

He wasn't the only one who remembered their old rhythms. She found the pace he liked as naturally as breathing. Desire built all over again. As if he hadn't just delivered a toe-curling climax for her moments before. Her hunger for him returned. Redoubled.

They moved in sync. Perfect. Blissful. Harmony.

Kai rolled her to her back, taking over with an urgency she recognized. The pleasure boiled over, seizing her once more, even harder than before. Only then did he let himself go, the shudder of his powerful body a testament to what he felt.

When he slumped to her side, dragging pillows under both of their heads and wrapping a quilt over their cooling bodies, he stroked her face and kissed her forehead.

He'd always been the most tender, caring lover she could imagine. And right now, he'd awakened feelings inside her that she couldn't begin to pick through with drowsy contentment weighing down her limbs.

"It's early yet," he said into her ear, skimming her hair away from her face. "You have a lot of hours of pleasure ahead before you're allowed to have any second thoughts."

It seemed he still knew how to make her melt with his words as much as his body, too.

"Ten years have made you a wiser man," she observed lightly, knowing she'd need to retreat to her own space before she could figure out what this time with Kai meant in the big scheme of things.

No sense overthinking it now when she was in a muddle.

"Ten years have made you sexier," he returned without missing a beat. "Do *Forbes* list executive women still like postsex backrubs?"

Already his fingers were trailing light circles around her shoulders.

"You know my weakness," she groaned, rolling over to give him better access.

For one night, she could indulge herself, couldn't she?

Closing her eyes, she promised herself she'd wade through the confusing questions in the morning. There would be time enough to figure out a way to work with Kai then so she could leave for New York with Blackwood Bank in good hands.

Too bad a little voice in the back of her mind told her that ten years hadn't made her one bit smarter when it came to resisting this man.

Six

As they pulled up to Natalie Valentine's bridal shop in downtown Royal later that week, Miranda asked the driver to give her a moment to refresh her makeup before she exited the car.

She should have done it on the way to the shop, but she'd been preoccupied with thoughts of Kai—the same way she had been pretty much every minute since the unforgettable night they'd spent together. So much for hoping that giving in to the attraction would help tame her runaway feelings.

With one hand, she raised the mirrored case of her eye shadow palette, and with the other, she swept powder over her nose. One of the perks of her role on *Secret Lives of NYC Ex-Wives* was having access to a makeup artist, and it had been kind of fun to sit back and let someone else do the work for the first few episodes, but as a woman with a lot of goals to tackle every day, Miranda soon found the time in the makeup chair felt excessively indulgent. As long as her face didn't shine and she had some mascara on her lashes, she was good enough. Why feed into the idea that women needed to spend hours on their makeup? Besides, she couldn't help but remember how nice it had felt to wash her face in the master suite at Kai's house the night they'd spent together and have him kiss every inch of her clean cheeks, swearing she'd grown lovelier in the last ten years.

She might have written it off as empty flattery except that his eyes had been sincere. His hands and mouth positively worshipful in their attention to every part of her...

Was it any wonder she couldn't keep her attention on something as mundane as what shade of lipstick matched her dress? Maybe time spent filming the show would help her corral her thoughts. She needed to tie up loose ends in Royal and head back to New York. Maybe it was just being back in Texas that had stirred all the old feelings for Kai. If that was the case, then leaving Royal should help her forget.

Satisfied she looked acceptable for the afternoon filming at the bridal shop, Miranda shoved the compact and makeup brush back in her bag and thanked the driver for waiting before she stepped out onto the sidewalk.

"Over here!" Seraphina called from beside the cameramen. She and Lulu looked like they were comparing shoes, their toes out like they were in ballet first position, their designer heels side by side.

"We're twinsies today," Lulu announced as Miranda got closer. "Fee bought the new Jimmy Choos in leopard print, and I snapped up the metallic silver."

"You'll set the new bridal trend for animal prints and glitter. I like it."

Lulu laughed, tossing her dark hair. "My wedding, my way, right?" She sounded more at peace with it since their talk earlier that week. "No sense going too conventional."

"Good for you." Miranda gave her a one-armed hug. She was thrilled for Lu, even if that meant being the tiniest bit envious. Who wouldn't want that kind of happiness in a marriage?

Miranda had tried marriage, putting all her considerable ambition and effort into making her union with Buckley a success, and it still hurt that it had been the biggest failure of her life.

A wicked smile curved Fee's lips. "You could do metallic cowgirl boots under your wedding dress and make all the bridesmaids match you. Rafaela would spontaneously combust at the thought."

Miranda relaxed into their chatter, soaking in the joy of being around her friends while they ramped up to the show's season finale. Rafaela and Zooey joined them a few minutes later and they took the wedding party into the bridal shop. Even Rafaela seemed impressed by Natalie Valentine, the knowledgeable shop owner whose inventory ranged from couture to vintage with plenty of interesting designers in between. Lulu spent a lot of time trying on international bridal gowns inspired by wedding traditions from around the world.

Miranda sipped champagne poured over fresh raspberries while she perched on a settee beside Zooey, watching Lulu twirl around in a beaded mermaid-style gown. The odd sense of envy nipped again, bugging Miranda, because she wanted to be a better friend than that to Lu.

Besides, it's not like Miranda believed she needed a

man in her life to be complete. Far from it. If anything, she'd known greater contentment in her life since her divorce from Buckley, spending her time on friends and projects that were important to her. That fulfilled her spirit and nurtured her soul. So why the unrest now when her friend practically bubbled with joy?

Kai Maddox.

The man's face appeared in her mind's eye, distracting her all over again, assuring her that her mood today was entirely because of him. All at once, it occurred to her that some latent romantic part of her heart was craving something more with Kai.

It was a thought so startling she reared back from the starry-eyed romanticism of it, nearly spilling her champagne. Only Zooey noticed.

"You don't like the dress?" Zooey started to ask after Lulu disappeared to try on the next gown. Zooey turned toward Miranda on the settee. As she saw Miranda's face, she frowned, her honey-colored hair dipping over one eye as she leaned closer. "What's wrong?"

One of the camera crew rolled closer to them. Maybe someone else had noticed Miranda's sudden unease.

Crap.

She could practically hear the camera zoom button whirring, knowing her face was coming into sharp focus. Any lie she attempted about would be dissected by viewers.

Knowing she wasn't ready to confide her thoughts about Kai to anyone, let alone their million viewers, Miranda trotted out the one other truth beneath her melancholy mood today and hoped it would be enough.

"It just feels like the end of an era, doesn't it?" She swallowed over the emotions causing a lump in her throat, focusing on the bubbles in her champagne. "Seraphina's staying in Texas with Clint. Lulu and Kace are tying the knot, and I'm betting they'll be here more often than New York, too."

Nearby, Rafaela and Fee were scrolling through their phones to read more about a bridal gown designer, though they looked up when they saw the second camera moving toward Miranda and Zooey.

"Like high school graduation," Zooey offered, the comparison making Miranda smile at the reminder of how young she was. "Happy and sad at the same time because things will never be quite the same. Plus, you know you'll never have the same amount of drama."

Maybe the high school comparison was more apt than she'd realized.

"Exactly like that," she admitted, her eyes lifting to include Fee and Rafaela as she set aside her drink. "I'm going to miss the girl time."

Lulu stepped out of the dressing room just then, wearing a simple white sheath dress that was understated enough to put all the focus on her. She stopped short on the pedestal, surrounded by mirrors and her bridesmaids, peering around at their faces.

"What did I miss?" she demanded. "Something good?"

"We're getting all sentimental about the wedding feeling like a last hurrah for us," Fee told her, hopping up on the raised platform to link arms with Lu before slanting a glance toward Rafaela. "Remembering that we like each other...most of the time."

Rafaela sniffed, but didn't argue, which was practically agreeing for her.

"I'm the *bride*," Lu reminded them, squeezing Fee's

arm tighter. "You can't get sentimental without me. Save all gooey love talk for when I can be here to savor it."

Miranda set down her champagne and moved closer to the dressing platform, fluffing the bride's skirt. "This one gets my vote, Lu. You look amazing."

"I like this one, too." Zooey stood, smoothing a hand over her green floral minidress that made her hazel eyes more emerald. "But don't let Miranda deflect. She was all *verklempt* about this being the end of an era."

Rafaela sighed. "So does that mean we have to group hug? Because I just had a blowout and I don't want it crushed." She flipped her long dark hair over one shoulder as she came to her feet.

"Get up here, you ungrateful wench," Fee blustered, holding out a hand.

Miranda wasn't sure if Seraphina and Rafaela had made nice for the bride's sake, or if they were genuinely burying the hatchet, but she was glad for the peace among the group as they all joined the bride on her pedestal. The five of them looped arms around each other's shoulders, and she looked around at the other four faces of the women she'd plotted with, laughed with and cried with on more than one occasion.

"This is more like it," Miranda said. "If it's our last hurrah, ladies, let's make it a good one."

The cameras loomed, a boom mic hovering overhead, the intrusion oddly startling since she'd been so focused on her friends.

"We're going to rock this wedding," Fee added, squeezing Lu even closer.

"Do you think this is what guys talk about in their football huddles?" Zooey asked, narrowing her green eyes. "They look just like this when they're on the field."

"Except their asses are more fun to look at," Rafaela deadpanned.

Her phone buzzed in Miranda's pocket even though she'd set it to not disturb her. Very few contacts could override that and get a notification through. Excusing herself as she waved to her friends to continue the fitting, she moved to a quiet corridor just outside the dressing area of the bridal shop.

She was surprised to see a text from Kai on the screen.

Major security breach of Blackwood Bank data during transition to Madtec's new software. Need to see you ASAP.

A chill ran through her. Of all the ways she'd been fantasizing about seeing him again, this wasn't one of them.

"Vaughn." Miranda blurted her stepson's name, grateful to have gotten through to Buckley's son and the inheritor of the bank as she fastened her seat belt in the back of the town car. She'd already told the driver to head to Deer Springs. "We need to talk."

She'd left the bridal fitting immediately, knowing her friends understood the demands of running a business. And right now, she wasn't just in charge of Goddess. During the transition of the Blackwood assets to the rightful heir, she was still responsible. The weight of that felt heavy on her shoulders while she contemplated the possibility of exposing customer financial information to hackers.

"I've already heard about the breach," Vaughn informed her, his voice brusque. "From what I can tell,

Dad's in-house security team has been running on fumes for too long. I can't say I'm surprised."

She stared out the window, focusing on her breathing to settle taut nerves as they hit the outskirts of Royal, the homes giving way to fields and farmland.

"I'm heading to Madtec now to assess the damage." She knew that hiring Kai had been the right move, but had it been too late to protect the bank's clients?

"Good. In the meantime, I'm going to have to call a press conference to get on top of this." Vaughn might have spent most of his life ranching, but he had the same good head for business as his father. "News like this leaks fast."

"Do you want me to be there for the press conference?" she offered, needing to make herself available to Vaughn. Kellan and Sophie had been the toughest of the Blackwood heirs to convince that she wasn't the step-monster they all once thought, but while Vaughn hadn't been as focused on fighting her and contesting the will, he'd been the most withdrawn of the siblings. In fact, he'd barely set foot in Royal over the past few months. It wasn't until he'd come back for Sophie's wedding and reunited with his sweetheart—and their surprise child—that he'd opened up to Miranda at all. Their relationship was friendly now, but still fragile, and Miranda wanted him to know that he could count on her.

"No," Vaughn answered quickly. "I'd rather have you at Madtec being our ears to the ground. Please loop me in on whatever measures they're taking to counterbalance this attack."

"Of course." She hesitated as her driver left Royal behind, heading south toward Deer Springs. And Kai. "I still feel sure that hiring Madtec was the way to go. The Maddox brothers are excellent at what they do."

There was a beat of silence before his reply.

"I'll admit their client list is impressive. But we're their first big financial customer, and they do have a hacking background—" Vaughn swore on the other end of the phone. "Look, Miranda, I'd better go. My public relations department is up to their ears in calls."

"We'll make this right," she assured him before disconnecting.

Grip tightening on her phone, she tried to gather her thoughts before seeing Kai.

She trusted him, despite the Maddox brothers' reputation as the bad boys of tech. She worried her lower lip, remembering how Kai had mentioned his regret over not giving Dane his full attention in the months before Dane to jail. She'd understood what he was saying. Kai been distracted wooing her.

No doubt Kai and Dane had something to prove.

Maybe she did, too. She might have failed at her marriage, but she would at least succeed in business. Blackwood Bank wasn't hers permanently, but she was in charge of it for now, and she would fight for this company to make sure it thrived.

She'd hired Kai because she believed he was the best. So if there was anything she could do to help him avert disaster, she was all in.

"Ms. Dupree to see you, Kai," Amad's voice came through a speaker in the on-site lab at Madtec.

"I'll be right out," he informed his assistant.

At any other time, Kai would have been glad to see her. But with the cybersecurity breach weighing on him like a lodestone, dread balled in his gut. This was no personal call. On this visit, Miranda represented Blackwood Bank, and the news from all sides was grim. He'd been pulled out of his bed at 5:00 a.m. on his day off to deal with the breach, alerted by Dane, who'd been on-site with one of the techs when the drama started to unfold.

Now, twelve hours later, Kai's eyes were beginning to cross from the stress and exhaustion of securing the site, assessing the damage and implementing a new system.

"I'll be back," he assured Jerrilyn, the systems engineer in charge of revamping the bank's cybersecurity. "Call me if you find anything."

"We're fine," she assured him, never looking up from her screen. "We'll take care of this."

The hum of the electronic equipment and cooling fans was broken only by the occasional keystrokes of technicians scouring every inch of the breached site. In a lab of fifteen workstations, three computers were projected onto big screens so all the techs could track the progress of the new security data's installation, a slow process considering the massive undertaking. The initial installation had been interrupted by the breach, and they'd needed to do some cleanup on the site before they could try a second time.

Kai's gaze went to the central screen before he walked out to find Miranda. The new software would take all night to install, and that was running at the absolute fastest possible capacity. Madtec hadn't been prepared for this level of client demand so quickly into the relationship with Blackwood Bank, but at least—so far—the bank's internal tech team had taken the blame for the breach. They knew their security measures had gradually fallen apart before Madtec came on board.

But what would Miranda think?

It bugged Kai how much that mattered to him right now. After taking the elevator to his office, he walked past Amad's desk and into his office. Miranda's back was to him as she studied a photo on his bookshelves. No doubt she recognized the backdrop since it came from their long-ago trip to the beach in Galveston. The photo showed only his motorcycle, but the two helmets on the seat never failed to remind him of who'd been with him that day.

A silent reminder to him not to let himself get distracted again.

Miranda replaced the framed photo, her movement drawing his attention to the sweep of her blue chiffon dress sprigged with daisies. It was an ultrafeminine choice, reminding him he'd bothered her on the weekend when she'd no doubt been enjoying herself outside work. Memories of being with her at his place—never far from his mind this week—redoubled. For a moment, the urge to speak to her on a personal level, to pull her into his arms, was damn near overwhelming.

He ignored it, knowing his first loyalty had to be to his business.

"Thank you for coming." He shut the door behind them, ruthlessly reining in the need to touch her. "I'm sorry to interrupt your Saturday."

She turned, the hem of her dress swishing softly around her knees as her blue gaze locked on him.

"I'm grateful you phoned," she assured him, shrugging off his apology. "The only reason I'm still in Royal is to oversee the distribution of the Blackwood assets. There is nothing more important to me than this."

While he appreciated her commitment to the project,

the reminder where her loyalties lay still stung. But it was just as well to remember their reunion had happened only because of business.

He gestured to the high-backed leather chairs in front of his desk. "Please, have a seat, and I'll walk you through what's happening."

Miranda smoothed the full skirt of her dress before lowering herself into one of the chairs. Kai took the other, hitting a button on a remote to reveal a built-in projector screen on a wall between the bookshelves. When not in use, the black background broadcast a digital clock, but now it mirrored his laptop, where he had multiple tabs open to demonstrate the damage done by late-night hackers into the bank's system.

The frustration of seeing the bank's data compromised helped keep him focused on the task at hand instead of Miranda's nearness, her rapidly shifting sandaled foot the only indication of the tension she felt as he explained how many customers' financial data might have been compromised. No matter what life threw her way, the woman remained cool. Composed.

Always looking for her next move.

Throughout the briefing he gave her, she asked few questions, but those she did were thoughtful insights, demonstrating her attentive eye for business. Not that he was surprised. She'd always excelled at extrapolating pertinent information, utilizing her resources to propel her work forward. Whether she was scouting locations for a yoga studio in downtown Royal the way she'd been doing when he first met her, or listening to a postmortem on a cybersecurity incident, Miranda could home in on the key points and carry forward a vision for her next move. That cool head of hers was always thinking, always working ten steps ahead so she didn't miss a thing.

All of which made her a formidable businesswoman, but it made her tough as hell to read on a personal level. And it made him wonder where the passionate woman who'd been in his bed earlier that week still lurked inside this self-possessed head of America's biggest fitness empire.

"So the hackers could have accessed financial data for up to ninety thousand customers." Miranda summarized the bottom line as she stared up at the projected screen. Then she turned to him. "How are we fixing that? What steps do we tell them to take, and what are we doing on our end to ensure it won't happen in the future?"

Tired from spending all day addressing the dumpster fire that was Blackwood Bank's cybersecurity, Kai knew he wasn't at his best. He couldn't restrain some frustration that she didn't seem rattled about the ninety thousand people who'd had their data exposed to fraudsters.

"For starters, tell the bank's customers they weren't being adequately protected by the last system, and that Madtec was brought into an impossible situation to try to fix it overnight," he pointed out, losing patience with the job, but also with Miranda's cool veneer that didn't reveal a hint of what they'd shared.

A frown pulled at her lips, and Kai rose out of his seat to stalk behind his desk, needing some distance from her.

"While I obviously can't do that, I realize this situation isn't of your making, Kai," she assured him, too damned reasonable to tell him he was being irrational and defensive.

Always a professional. And gorgeous. So desirable he ached to have her again.

He hauled his gaze away from the tempting sight of her and leaned a shoulder against the window looking out over a first-floor courtyard with the central fountain.

"The rest of the tech world won't be so gracious, I assure you." He ran a hand through his hair, blinking gritty eyes. "Madtec has put everything into steering our image away from our past, so a breach like this on one of our clients—our fault or not—is a huge setback if we can't get on top of this."

He needed to pull it together. The job. The meeting.

The desire for this woman who revealed so damned little of herself.

"You will," she said simply, rising from the leather armchair with the graceful movements that punctuated her every step. "I have every faith in you and Dane. But I can see you have your hands full with this situation right now. Should I leave you to do your job?"

How was it she could just shut down the attraction that still threatened to set him ablaze just looking at her? Nerves frayed and tension radiating through him—from work and personal things—he felt as overcharged as a live wire and yet exhausted at the same time. More than anything, he wanted to hold her, and the realization that he needed her with a tangible, physical hunger was more than a little daunting.

"No." He ground his teeth together to hold back words that might reveal the depth of that need.

When he didn't say anything else, she shifted her weight from one foot to the other, toned calves flexing. He thought he saw a hint of uncertainty in her eyes.

"Are you sure?" she asked, her manicured fingernails lightly resting on the black leather seatback, a bright blue cocktail ring winking in the slanting afternoon sunlight.

Something about her chiffon dress, so different from what she normally wore for work, gave him an idea. A way to appeal to her that might slip around those damned professional boundaries of hers.

"Actually, if it's just the same to you, the head of Blackwood Bank can leave." He straightened from his spot at the window, facing her head-on. "As for the woman I slept with? I'd like to speak to that Miranda right now."

Seven

A spark leaped between then, arcing in the quiet air of Kai's office.

Miranda exhaled as she stood next to his desk, some of the tension sighing from her lungs at his clear-cut directive.

She understood it. Empathized, even, because she felt the strain of reining in her feelings around him. No doubt he was exhausted. Stress and fatigue hung heavy on him, making her long to offer him some kind of comfort. But she could also see how dialed in he was to the task at hand. How engaged.

Leaving her leather bag on the back of the armchair, she circled the massive steel-and-wood workstation to face him, stopping just inches short of him.

"Speaking as the woman who slept with you," she began, threading her fingers through his because she couldn't resist touching him another moment, "you're seriously lacking imagination if you can't see past the bank executive to who I am underneath."

His green gaze darkened as he looked down at her. He shifted an inch closer, until there was just a hair's breadth of room between them.

"I can imagine every inch of the woman beneath. Vividly." His voice hit a gravelly note. "That may be part of the problem." He lifted their joined hands to his face and stroked the back of her fingers against his jaw. "But the other part of it is that you're the last person I want to let down right now, Miranda. Not because of the bank. Because of what's happening between us."

The honesty of those words sent a shiver of worry through her, because she didn't know where this relationship was headed either. Anxiety constricted her rib cage, a sharp confusion she still wasn't sure how to resolve. The uncertainty about Kai's expectations made it hard for her to simply enjoy the feel of him, even though she had an urge to lean into him, too.

She wasn't used to relying on anyone, and the neediness she felt scared her.

"Is there anything I can do to help...with the fallout from the cyberattack, I mean?" she asked, pulling her attention from his face to the big office around him, wary of falling into his arms while they were in the middle of a work crisis. If he noticed her dodging the subject, he didn't comment on it. "Vaughn is going to hold a press conference, but I told him I would update him once I knew more."

Unthreading their fingers, Kai stepped back, distancing them again. Her relief at sidestepping a thorny talk was overshadowed by disappointment at the loss of his touch. His expression shuttered, and she had the sinking feeling she'd disappointed him.

But she didn't know how to walk this line they were treading. She couldn't keep indulging a physical relationship when the business was her priority.

"Right." Kai nodded, moving past her to close his laptop. "In a perfect world, I would send someone to the press conference to represent Madtec, but unfortunately I need every available body on-site working on the Blackwood Bank problem." His gaze locked on hers, and there was no hint of the tender lover she remembered from their night together. "I've got to return to the tech lab to oversee things. Why don't you make yourself comfortable here, and I'll send up our PR rep to help you coordinate a statement from us for Vaughn. She can provide ideas for how to frame the news for your customers."

She bit her lip as she watched him retreat from her. Not just physically. She remembered how he'd withdrawn from her before they'd broken up ten years ago. It shouldn't hurt anymore, now that she'd stopped hungering for a romance to complete her.

And yet, the pang in her chest was undeniable.

"Kai—" she began, wanting to be more supportive of his work. Wondering if there was a middle ground for a relationship she wasn't seeing.

But he was already pushing through the double doors and out of his office. She glimpsed him leaning over his assistant's desk to give instructions before the heavy double doors swung shut again.

Later, she would figure out a way to make it up to him for not knowing how to be his lover in these circumstances. She was a better professional colleague anyhow. She wasn't leaving Madtec until she could see with her own eyes that the new security software was up and running. She would set up camp for the night in an office and provide whatever updates she received to Vaughn.

For now, she'd do what she did best. Take care of business.

"You should head home," Kai told his brother, Dane, eight hours later. "You look like roadkill."

Dane had just walked into the tech lab, his thick brown hair standing on end, his focus going straight to the overhead screen that broadcast the progress made on installing the new security software for Blackwood Bank. They'd wanted to test it further before rolling out the installation, but the breach had robbed them of that chance. They didn't have the luxury of time anymore.

Setting aside a fresh cup of black coffee, Kai swiveled in the ergonomic leather office chair at the center of the room, pushing back from his workstation. Three other systems analysts remained in the area with him, overseeing their own responsibilities in the implementation process, but the installation had all gone smoothly so far.

"You're just jealous you can't rock a beard like mine," Dane said absently, stroking a hand over the facial hair while he glanced at one of the other analysts' monitors on his way to the center of the room.

"Dude, you've been here so long there are probably small life forms setting up colonies in that thing," Kai returned, relaxing a bit at Dane's easy demeanor. It reinforced Kai's own sense that the crisis was abating.

If Dane was still worried about Blackwood Bank's system, he would be wired, no matter how little sleep he'd had. The zombie-like trudge of his brother's steps was reassuring as Dane reached the chair beside Kai's and lowered himself into it.

"Possibly. But if looking like roadkill keeps me out of the media, I'll take it." Dane tapped the screen to life at the workstation in front of him, refreshing a tab tracking the day's business news. "We're going to have to give in and get more aggressive about defending the Madtec image though, so someone will have to start speaking on behalf of the company."

A bad feeling crept up the back of his neck.

"What do you mean?" Kai asked.

"I mean we should have sent someone to the bank's press conference instead of just issuing a statement, because Vaughn Blackwood wasn't prepared for the technical questions about the breach." Dane hit a button to fast-forward a clip from the local network news, stopping when it reached the last third of the video.

The camera captured a weary-looking Vaughn looking like a deer caught in the headlights as he fielded detailed inquiries from journalists about the nature of the breach, the party responsible and the kinds of measures being taken to address the problem. He kept returning to his note cards, reiterating talking points that only partially answered the questions.

"Shit," Kai muttered as he stared down at Dane's screen, wondering if he should have encouraged Miranda to be there for the press conference. No doubt she would have done a better job holding her own. "I had our lone press relations expert working with Miranda on the statement. That mistake is on me."

Before Dane could respond, the news coverage swapped to footage of the Madtec headquarters, where news vans were camped outside with a graphic marked

"Live" next to the images. A reporter told viewers that they would obtain answers "as soon as possible." Kai had no idea they were out there since there were no windows in the tech lab at the center of the building.

"The vans only arrived about an hour ago," Dane informed him, switching off the tab to open a different program he'd been working on. "But since it's after business hours, they haven't been able to enter."

"No one told me." Kai wondered if Miranda knew. They'd exchanged a few texts over the last eight hours, but he hadn't gone back to his office since they'd parted ways. She'd settled in for the night, requesting periodic updates on the security installation, then feeding the information to Vaughn.

She'd refused to leave until Blackwood Bank was secured again.

Which Kai understood. But her rebuff had stung. Maybe it had been unfair of him to ask for his lover instead of his colleague though, given how important the fate of Blackwood Bank was to her. When she'd arrived, he'd already had hours to come to terms with the breach, but the news had still been fresh—and upsetting—for her.

"You might consider holding an impromptu meeting with the press of your own," Dane suggested, waving over an intern who'd just stepped into the tech lab with a fresh pot of coffee and a stack of cups.

Normally, they didn't allow food or drink in the lab, but the crisis of the big client breach had temporarily relaxed their standards.

Kai shook his head, even though he knew that meeting the media was inevitable. "No wonder you look like death warmed over," he observed wryly, understanding Dane wanted no part of the spotlight.

Grinning, Dane took a steaming cup from the local college student and set it carefully on his desk. "Method, meet madness."

Conceding the point, Kai was about to go up to his office to speak to Miranda about it when the woman herself burst into the tech lab, her cell phone in hand.

"Kai, I'm so sorry to disturb you." She hurried over, walking so fast that her lightweight skirt sailed behind her a bit. Face pale, her features were drawn into a frown. "It's Sophie Blackwood. She's been rushed to the hospital."

Concern for Miranda, for her family, quickly shifted his focus.

"Why? Is she okay?" Kai was already on his feet, alert to Miranda's distress. He understood the importance of family.

"I don't know. Nigel just texted the family to let us know. They were just returning from their honeymoon and she fainted at the airport—"

"I'll take you," he told her shortly, steering her toward the door. He knew she hadn't gotten any more sleep than he had, so there was no way he was letting her go alone. He nodded to his brother, knowing Dane would oversee things. "Let's go."

Grateful for Kai's certainty about the decision, Miranda gladly let him lead her out a private entrance to the building. The warmth of his hand on the small of her back was a comfort even more than a pleasure, and she stayed close to him.

The last hours had been exhausting, monitoring the implementation of the new data security while exchanging calls with Vaughn about Madtec's progress. And then, there was the media interest and customer outcry. The media she didn't care about so much. But she was frustrated on behalf of the bank clients and wanted to do better for them.

Although none of that compared to her worries for Sophie. She'd just repaired her relationship with Buckley's only daughter. And while she'd never fooled herself that she could be a stand-in mother for the fiercely independent woman who was only a handful of years younger than her, she meant to be the most supportive friend possible.

"What about the news vans?" Miranda asked Kai as she stepped outside the building, peering in the dark to try to orient herself. "The press is camped out waiting to talk to you."

Long after midnight, the executive parking area was quiet, with only three vehicles visible.

"They're on the other side of the building," he assured her, pointing to their left where the glow of fluorescent streetlamps cast a bluish glow.

No sooner had they gone five steps than a spotlight popped on a few yards away from them, accompanied by the rush of footsteps and a rolling camera dolly. Miranda had been around enough of them to become intimately acquainted with the sound.

"Ms. Dupree!" a woman shouted as the sound of high heels pounded nearer, a camera eye winking to life beside her as a red light flashed a recording signal. "Is it true you chose Madtec to provide digital security because of your romantic involvement with Kai Maddox?"

Beside her, she felt Kai tense as he muttered under his breath. "I should have had security escort us. I don't know how they got through the fence." Then, holding up an arm to bar the camera's view of her, he continued to hustle her toward his car. "This is private property," he informed the camera crew. "You're trespassing, and there's no statement at this time."

"It's okay," she assured him, seeing their way blocked by a second duo of journalist and camera operator. She turned to speak into Kai's ear so as not to be overheard. "If we give them two minutes, they might leave. It might be faster than if we try to bulldoze through them."

His green eyes met hers, his face clearly visible in the bright wattage of the media lights as he seemed to decide whether or not to agree with her. Finally, he lowered his arm from where it had been shielding her face from view.

Miranda looked directly into the camera, knowing what she wanted to say after having spent hours working on potential statements with Vaughn. "Blackwood Bank has full confidence in Madtec. We are grateful to be the first financial institution to benefit from their new encryption software, and it couldn't have come at a more opportune moment."

"Will your relationship with the Madtec copresident be a storyline on *Secret Lives of NYC Ex-Wives*?" the woman asked, jarring Miranda since she didn't know how Kai felt about the show or his company's potential connection to it.

"No storyline is needed because there is no relationship," Kai shot back, spurring Miranda into motion again as he resumed a determined pace toward the silver Jaguar sports coupe. "No more questions."

The light and camera crews followed them, a second group joining the first in shouting provocative questions meant to incite a reaction. One of the women asked Kai if he hoped Miranda would move back to Royal, while another asked Miranda if Kai's "bad boy" reputation in the tech world had appealed to her. A man's voice wanted to know if Miranda's marriage had ended because of her previous relationship with Kai.

But by then, Kai had opened the passenger side door for her, and as she lowered herself into the seat, she saw two security officers dressed in Madtec uniforms rounding the building. No doubt they would ensure the journalists were relocated to the front parking lot where the other vans were.

Freed to move faster with the arrival of the guards, Kai pulled open the driver's side door and started the engine.

"That wasn't the business media, that's for damned sure," he observed darkly, driving quickly out the back gate and distancing them from the building.

"Probably tabloids. There are paparazzi down here following the show. I recognized one of the women from a seedy outlet that reports on celebrity scandals." She hugged herself, the run-in more disconcerting since it had happened with Kai at her side. And because the real story was supposed to be about Blackwood Bank, not a relationship between her and Kai.

Which, according to Kai, they didn't have anyhow.

His words harkened back to her now, along with the cold tone he'd used. No doubt he'd been irritated to be caught on camera in the first place, which she understood. Except she'd thought that he was angling for more of a relationship.

Wasn't he?

The silence between them stretched as he navigated through the vacant Deer Springs streets in the predawn hours, toward the highway to head north to Royal.

When he didn't speak, she glanced over at him. His jaw flexed, his mouth set in a flat line.

"I hope it wasn't a mistake to speak to the media. It didn't occur to me that anyone would ask about the show, or anything personal." Although even as she said it, she realized how naive she'd been to think she could keep her personal life separate from the Blackwood Bank trouble. "I should have anticipated it, however."

He seemed to weigh her words before answering carefully, "For someone as determined as you are to keep your professional image at the forefront at all times, I'm surprised you decided to do that show in the first place."

The highway unfurled before them in an endless-seeming gray path outlined in yellow and white. No other cars were on the road, the farms dark and silent on either side of them. Inside the luxury sports vehicle, the dashboard lights were minimal, highlighting the angles of Kai's handsome face.

Miranda wasn't sure if she should be offended about his implication that the show was the opposite of "professional." She supposed she could understand why he'd feel that way.

"The show may be over-the-top, but the relationships are real. And viewers relate to seeing how we handle crises of friendship." She remembered the young woman on the stairwell in the Madtec building who'd asked for her autograph. "I think we give women hope that life can be rewarding and fulfilling even if romance doesn't work out. We have plenty of things to be passion about. And we have each other."

"From the promos, it looks more like the show is about catfights and competitive shopping." He adjusted the air conditioner, and she felt the chilly breeze around her legs subside.

A different kind of coolness ran through her at his words, though.

"Marketing hooks don't always reflect the substance of a product," she retorted, miffed at the way people could write off feminine art. And yes, what they created was a kind of art, even if she was too tired to march out that particular argument tonight. "That doesn't mean the substance isn't there."

"Fine." His words were clipped as he acknowledged the point. "I was just curious why you did the show. Now I know."

"I hated failing at my marriage, that's why," she told him honestly, too irritated and out of sorts to hold back the way she normally would. "*Secret Lives* shows another side of life for women. Not just their dating. But their businesses. Their friendships."

Frustration simmered as she remembered the way Kai had denied they had a relationship. Even though she'd been the one to ensure that new boundaries went up between them since their night together, his slight had still hurt tonight. She told herself it was probably because she was also worried about Sophie. She hadn't heard any updates since that first text from Nigel.

"Then it's a good thing I told that reporter we don't have a relationship," Kai mused as they saw a sign for the exit for Royal. "Since it's clear you don't plan on having one."

She couldn't argue with that.

She'd thought as much herself, hadn't she?

And yet, as they drew closer to Royal Memorial Hospital, Miranda couldn't deny that she'd thought about

Kai—and romance—every moment since she'd left his house earlier that week. The idea that he didn't see it as the start of a relationship caused an ache in her chest to deepen, and she didn't have a clue how to make the hurt stop.

Eight

An hour later, Miranda sat on the edge of the creaky vinyl chair in the emergency room waiting area, checking her phone for updates on a business meeting she needed to delay with AMuse, a rival fitness chain. When she'd agreed to the meeting, she'd hoped to be back in New York next week, but between the Blackwood Bank crisis, the Royal Gives Back gala she still needed to plan, Lulu's wedding and not knowing what was wrong with Sophie, Miranda didn't think the timing would work out.

She would just have to juggle things as best she could from here, delegating as much as possible to her staff while she waited for news about Sophie. Just as she started typing a message to her assistant to reschedule, Kai strode back into the waiting area. And how was it that even when she should be engrossed in work, she felt his presence? A cup of coffee in each hand, he dodged a toddler pushing a truck around the floor while the boy's grandmother read a paperback. That was all the action in the waiting room right now, since it was three in the morning. Vaughn had fallen asleep after the press conference, so she'd been unable to reach him. Kellan and Darius were both out of town, but she'd spoken to them both briefly to let them know about Sophie. Kellan hadn't wanted to wake Irina at this hour unless it was an emergency, but he'd promised to call her once the sun rose so she could be with Sophie either way. An ambulance had rushed in someone earlier, but there'd been no family with the older man.

How much longer until Nigel appeared with an update about Sophie fainting?

"Thank you." She took the cup Kai offered her, then met his weary green eyes. "You must be running on fumes."

"I'll sleep soon enough." He took the seat beside her, winking at the adventurous toddler who was slaloming his truck between chair legs now. "Dane said the download just finished. He's going to work for another hour and then he'll crash, too. We're in good shape."

Testing her coffee, Miranda tasted the soy milk she preferred. "Yum. You've got a good memory, Kai Maddox. Thank you."

How strange that something so small could make a person feel so well cared for.

"We shared enough breakfasts that I ought to remember," Kai said before he tried his own drink.

A nurse peered into the waiting room and then hurried back out, calling something to an orderly with a wheelchair. The loudspeaker squawked, paging a doctor. All normal activity.

Except life was far from normal for her right now.

Miranda's attention returned to Kai as she mulled over his words. "I shared more than a few meals with Buck, but he wouldn't have known my favorite color or song, let alone how I like my coffee."

"Green. And Sinatra's version of 'Summer Wind.' Or at least, it used to be." Kai pulled her favorites from his brain as easily as if he were citing multiplication table facts. "I never did understand what you saw in Blackwood beyond his money."

The warmth she'd been feeling toward him dissipated. Defensiveness prickled and she was tempted to snap at him, but another nurse appeared in the waiting room. Miranda's heart stuttered in anticipation. Kai shot to his feet. But the nurse waved over the grandmother and little boy. Leaving Miranda and Kai alone.

He sank back into his chair with a lengthy exhale.

"It was never about his money." She set aside her coffee, wishing Nigel would make an appearance soon and tell them what was going on with Sophie. "How could you think that? I married Buck because I thought our goals and interests were aligned. On paper, we made good, practical sense. He encouraged my business ideas. I helped him grow his empire. I thought we'd be a good team."

Kai shook his head before slanting her a sideways glance. "And you and I didn't make sense?"

His tone was challenging. But then they'd never cut each other any slack before. Why should now be different?

Did she *want* it to be different?

"We were passionate, not practical." She'd been happy with passion at first, but then she'd believed the passion must have been fading—on his side, at least—when Kai had withdrawn from her. She'd been devastated. Brokenhearted. Not that she'd ever confess the depth of that hurt to him.

"We were lovers and friends, too," he reminded her, his dark eyebrows furrowed. Clearly her view of the past didn't line up with his. "We had both."

Old regrets tugged at her, but she hadn't made the decision to end things lightly.

"You might have been enthusiastic about my ideas for Goddess, but you were more wrapped up in your coding world than anything." She smoothed the wrinkles from her filmy skirt. "I think you saw me as an escape from work, whereas I wanted to share my professional journey with you, and I wanted to know more about yours, too."

"You wanted a business partner?" he asked drily, stretching his arm along the back of her chair, his hand grazing her shoulder. "Being lovers and friends wasn't enough to get the job done?"

Had she expected too much from their relationship? Maybe. She'd been so in love with Kai, there was a chance she'd lost herself with him a little. Lost her bearings. Passion was exciting and heady, but it could be overwhelming, too. The realization—and the worry that she might have subconsciously pushed him away because of it—robbed her of a reply.

Just then, the double doors to the patient rooms opened, and Sophie Blackwood's new husband, Nigel Townshend, walked through them. Though he was impeccably dressed as always, the Green Room Media studio executive's expression appeared tired and—happy?

"Miranda." He gave her a slight smile as he caught sight of her and headed their way. The normally unflappable Brit looked decidedly worse for wear in his wrinkled suit. His tie was gone and his hair stood on end as if he'd raked fingers through it a few too many times. "Thank you for coming."

"How's Sophie?" she asked, coming to her feet. Then, as Kai rose beside her, she introduced the two men. "Nigel, this is Kai Maddox. Kai, Nigel Townshend works for the studio that produces *Secret Lives*."

The two men shook hands briefly, nodding acknowledgment. Then Nigel spoke.

"Turns out Sophie's fine," he explained, his blue eyes still a bit dazed. "The doctor thinks she got dehydrated because she's pregnant—"

Miranda drew in a breath, ready to celebrate the news, when Nigel finished his sentence.

"—with twins."

The news left her stunned, but overjoyed at the good news. Relief streaking through her that Sophie was all right, Miranda hugged Nigel, then turned to hug Kai without thinking—only to stop short. "That's wonderful news."

Kai cleared his throat and agreed, "Yes, it most certainly is." He shook the father-to-be's hand again. "Congratulations, man."

"Thank you," Nigel said with genuine joy. "I couldn't be happier. Although I really do need to return to my wife so we can process the big news together."

"You're sure you don't need us to do anything for you, Nigel?" Miranda asked, ticking through the possibilities in her mind. "You came here straight from the airport. Do you need food? Or should we stop by your house and get Sophie some clothes?"

"The doctor isn't admitting her." Nigel ran a hand

through his light brown hair, his Patek Philippe watch glinting in the fluorescent lighting. "We're just getting a referral to be sure she can see an obstetrician tomorrow, and then I'll take her home."

A silence took hold in the wake of Nigel's departure, leaving her standing alone with Kai. Clearing his throat, he gestured toward the door.

"Should we go?" he asked, startling her from her thoughts of babies and marriage. New beginnings.

"Of course." She nodded, happy for Sophie even as she wondered what kind of relationship she would have with the Blackwood family once she left Royal.

She wanted to meet the twins. More than that, she wanted to hold them. Be a part of their lives.

She blinked past the rush of feelings, telling herself she was just tired.

Leaving the hospital together, Miranda saw the sun was just rising as they reached Kai's silver sports car.

"I'm thrilled for Nigel and Sophie, but I've lost all track of time," she murmured, exhaustion kicking in now that she didn't have worry and stress driving her forward. And yet Kai had been awake for longer. She couldn't let him drive all the way back to Deer Springs. "I can't imagine how you're still coherent."

"I'll be fine. And I'll have you home soon," he promised, holding the door for her as she took her seat and buckled up.

Her eyes followed his broad-shouldered frame as he strode around to the driver's side, her hungry gaze tempered by the realizations in the hospital waiting room.

Had she given up on passion prematurely when she broke things off with Kai? Yes, he'd pushed her away, but now she knew why. Her mother had been moving him around like a chess piece to ensure Miranda ended up with Buckley. Miranda could have found that out back ten years ago—but she hadn't asked. She'd felt Kai stepping back, and she'd just let him go.

It was difficult to accept that what she had with Kai was well and truly over when she still felt so drawn to him.

As he settled into the driver's seat and started the car, she watched his movements. She could see the flex of his forearms where his shirtsleeve remained rolled up from working. His broad, capable hands wrapped around the steering wheel, and she was transfixed by the memory of what his touch did to her.

He caught her staring.

"I'm curious what you're thinking right now." He didn't put the car into gear, his gaze wandering over her.

That simple attention stirred her insides, her nerve endings flickering to life.

"It occurred to me that you can't possibly drive back home tonight. You can stay at the guesthouse." She would have made the offer even if she hadn't been genuinely concerned for his safety. There were no two ways about it. She wanted Kai in her bed. "With me," she added, her voice grazing over a husky note.

Desire darkened his eyes. She shivered from the awareness tickling over her skin.

"And just like that," Kai spoke softly as he put the car into gear, "I'm not the least bit tired."

Fifteen minutes later, Kai held Miranda snugly against his side, nuzzling her neck as she entered the security code on the guesthouse.

A night breeze blew through the filmy skirt of her

dress, lifting the fabric enough to brush his pant leg. A touch so subtle he shouldn't have been able to feel it, except that his nerve endings were wound tight, his senses keenly attuned to this woman.

The scent of her shampoo mingled with the light fragrance she wore that smelled like jasmine. Her red lacquered fingernail hovered over the buttons on the security panel, as if she was unsure what to press next. He wondered if she was distracted by the same fire in the blood that roared inside him.

While she searched for the next numeral to input, Kai bent closer to taste the skin exposed along the back of her neck. A breathy sigh erupted from her lips, her head tipping toward him as she leaned into the kiss.

As much as he couldn't wait to explore the rest of her, to indulge himself in her sweet responsiveness, he also knew they needed to be inside the house for what he had in mind.

"Did you forget the code?" he asked, sliding a hand around her waist as he kissed his way to the hollow beneath her ear.

"No." She hit another number and he skimmed his touch higher, brushing the underside of her breast. With a sharp intake of air, she jabbed the last number hard. "Just distracted."

The alarm chimed an agreeable tone, allowing her to open the door and step away ahead of him. He followed her inside, trying not to think about the fact that this place once belonged to Buckley Blackwood, the man who'd stolen Miranda from him.

The man he'd believed Miranda wanted more than him.

Thoughts of the man stilled Kai. Tonight, he'd learned

that she hadn't been wooed by his wealth. Yet ten years ago, Kai had been quick to believe the worst of her, probably because of his own insecurity about the hardscrabble kind of life he would have been able to give Miranda back then. He'd given her up too easily.

A mistake he wouldn't repeat.

Miranda called to him from the kitchen while he still stood in the entryway. "Can I get you a drink? Something to eat?"

The sound of her voice spurred him back into motion. "No. Thank you." He followed her into the kitchen where he'd brought her pie from the Deer Springs Diner.

She was already at the island, a hip leaning against the white quartz countertop, pouring two glasses of water from a green bottle before returning it to the refrigerator. Kai paused by the island long enough to tip the beverage to his lips, his eyes following her movements as she ran a hand through her gorgeous red hair.

"I'm not hungry either," she agreed, joining him at the counter to pick up her glass for a sip of the sparkling water.

"Who said anything about not being hungry?" he asked, setting aside his drink before he bracketed her hips in his hands. He walked his fingers down her thighs, lifting the fabric of her skirt as he moved, baring more of her legs to his gaze. "I'm starving for a taste of you."

A stillness took hold of her as her blue eyes locked on him while he rucked up the skirt. Then, lowering her glass, she steadied herself with her hands on his shoulders. He traced the lace fabric of her panties with his finger while she sucked in a gasp.

His temperature spiked. And then their hands were all

over each other, roaming and exploring. She smoothed a touch over his chest and shoulders. He pressed his palm between her legs and her hips arched into him. He kissed her deeply, liking the small sounds of pleasure that hummed in the back of her throat. He was so damned greedy for her, he all but forgot where they were. When she stepped back, it took him a moment to blink through the hunger for her and remember they were standing in the kitchen.

She drew him forward by the hand, and he recovered his wits enough to follow the hypnotic sway of her hips as she moved down a lengthy hall toward a bedroom. He could see the king-size platform bed through an open door. A gray coverlet that looked like crushed velvet beckoned.

As they crossed the threshold, the scent of fresh flowers wafted from the nightstand where a vase of coral honeysuckle and daylilies rested. Behind the bed, a black-and-white print of downtown Houston took up a whole wall. But these were details he only half noticed as Miranda peeled down the top half of her dress, letting the silky fabric fall to her waist. A statement clear as a gauntlet dropped, and he'd be damned if he'd leave it unanswered.

Stress from the last twenty-four hours evaporated. All thoughts and doubts faded. The only thing he felt now was hunger for her.

"Let me help," he insisted, reaching for the buttons on her skirt. "I want to feel you as I undress you."

"I'd like that." She shifted her fingers to his shirt, working her way down the placket. "I want to feel you, too." She rolled her hips in a way that shifted her thighs against his. "All of you."

His body responded instantly.

"Happy to oblige." He tugged her dress down and off, leaving her in just a whisper of silk and lace that shielded her from view.

He shrugged out of his shirt as soon as she undid the final button, then shed his pants, socks and shoes, tossing them in easy reach of the bed.

Her eyes followed his movements, locking on his body in a way that was damned flattering. And burned away his last reserves of patience.

Lifting her against him, he carried her to the bed and laid her down in the center. Taking only a moment to admire how beautiful she looked with her fiery-red hair in the center of the gray velvet, Kai fell on her like a starving man. He kissed his way down her neck to her breasts, nipping and licking her through the thin silk barrier of her bra. She wriggled out of one strap and then the other, tugging the cups lower to give him full access. Gladly, he savored her bare skin, finding the source of her jasmine scent in the valley between her breasts. When he kissed his way lower, he dragged her lace panties down with his teeth, listening to every nuance of her breathing as he touched the sweet, hot center of her.

He glanced up for a glimpse of her face. The flush spreading across her chest told him she was so close to release already, as on fire for him as he was for her. He licked her and kissed her, loving the taste of her. Her release hit suddenly, surprising him with how quickly she flew apart in his arms.

A few hammering heartbeats later, he took his time retrieving his pants where he'd tucked a condom in his wallet, needing a moment to regain his self-control. But

Miranda took over the task, ripping open the packet and sheathing him with eager hands.

Which totally worked for him.

Everything about her turned him on. Turned him inside out. When she reversed their positions, she climbed on top of him to straddle him. His breath came in a harsh rush, his heart slamming hard against his chest. He looked up at her in all her feminine glory and forgot everything else but being inside her.

And then he was.

Moving slowly at first, and then faster. She raked her nails lightly down his chest, a welcome counterpoint to the feelings that threatened to send him hurtling over the edge too soon. He rolled with her, putting her on her back so he could enjoy her that way, too.

"You feel so good, Kai," she murmured, her eyes half closed as she writhed beneath him.

It might have been the movement or her words, but something about the moment sent him hurtling toward completion long before he wanted. The realization slammed into him that he hadn't brought her to that precipice with him, yet at the same moment, her legs wrapped around his waist, and she found her own release with him. Fulfillment rocked him even as he acknowledged how thoroughly she made him lose control.

As the sensations continued to ripple through him, Kai couldn't remember the last time he'd been so consumed by passion. Probably, it had been with Miranda ten years ago.

Sliding to the side of her, he felt a wave of tenderness for the woman in his arms. A feeling he had no business having for Miranda given how soon she'd be out of his life again. But he ignored that thought as he wrapped her in the soft coverlet and tucked a pillow under her tangled red hair, thinking she'd never looked more appealing to him.

Emotions crowded his chest, but he pushed them aside for now and simply kissed her on her forehead. She had to be tired. And he was, too. He hoped that was why he felt the urge to invite her to Deer Springs and spend more time pursuing a relationship. He knew that would never work since she had a whole life away from him in New York.

He shouldn't trust her anyway, based on how fast she'd put him out of her life the first time.

They didn't make sense on paper, she said.

And no matter how much he might wish it otherwise, they still didn't.

Nine

Miranda paced the floor of the guesthouse office the next morning after slipping from the bed she'd shared with Kai. She hadn't wanted to wake him, knowing his sleep deficit had far surpassed hers when they'd finally dozed off. She'd done her morning yoga poses out in the detached studio, then she'd returned to the office where a pewter pitcher full of purple coneflowers and sunflowers rested on the narrow secretary desk by her laptop. She carried a mug of mint tea to the desk and took a seat, hoping to use this time to somehow untwine her messy knot of feelings for the man sleeping just a few rooms away.

She'd told herself that she could resist his charm enough to prevent herself from falling for him again, but the more time she spent with him, the more she wondered if that was possible. History seemed to be repeating itself. And with that thought, she realized it might help to call her mother.

A crazy idea, maybe, she acknowledged as she pulled out her cell phone and scrolled through her contacts.

But the need to reconnect with her mom—to confront her about interfering in Miranda's relationship with Kai ten years ago—had preyed on her mind ever since Kai had revealed the role Ginny had played.

Leaning back in the leather office chair, Miranda tried to breathe through her nervousness as the call rang. And rang. She was about to hang up when her mother's voice sounded in her ear.

"Hello?"

Even from that lone word, Miranda could hear the husky rasp of exhaustion in her mother's tone.

"Hi, Mama. It's Miranda. Did I wake you?"

"Miranda?" Shuffling noises sounded on the other end of the call. A brief coughing spell ensued before her mother returned. "I'm surprised to hear from you."

Guilt pinched, but not for long. They hadn't parted on good terms the last time they'd spoken.

"How are you feeling?" she asked, knowing her mother always had a litany of health complaints—and yet her mother's ailments only increased the more "medicine" she took. The prescription pill problem ebbed and flowed over the last fifteen years, compounded by Ginny's refusal to get help.

"Since when do you care how I feel?" Her mother's words came wrapped around a cigarette, spoken out of one corner of her mouth. Miranda knew her mother so well, the small distortions of her words familiar to her after living with her for over twenty years. The flick of a lighter sounded, then a long exhale. "I seem to recall you didn't want me anywhere near you the last time I came for a visit."

Defensiveness pricked along her skin.

Ginny had arrived on the set of *Secret Lives of NYC Ex-Wives* during the first season, determined to be a part of the show. Miranda had refused. She had enough trouble navigating a relationship with her mom privately, let alone having the bond subject to public scrutiny.

"I would have been happy to spend time with you," she reminded her, glancing over her shoulder to ensure the door to her office remained closed. She didn't want to wake Kai. "But I got the idea you were only interested in visiting if our time together was televised."

Ginny sniffed. "I forgot you only show the world your cleaned-up side."

Miranda clutched her mug of tea, inhaling the minty scent and focusing on her breathing to ease the sting of the gibe that hurt more than she would have expected, maybe because there was some truth in it. But she'd worked hard to become the person she wanted to be. Why should she have to dwell on the unhappy pieces of her past that refused to heal?

Her mom had chosen her path—and continued to choose it, over and over again. Speaking of which, Miranda had a question to ask, and hedging only increased the nervous tension.

"Do you remember me dating Kai Maddox? Back when I still lived at home?" She'd remained in Deer Springs well into her twenties, determined to help her mother get clean.

It took a long time for her to learn that no one could help an addict who wouldn't help herself.

"The motorcycle guy who was too young for you?"

Another puff on her cigarette, the exhale a long, protracted sigh. "Sure I do."

Closing her eyes against the wave of frustration she felt, Miranda traced the rim of the stoneware mug with her fingertip.

"I never thought he was too young for me," she reminded herself more than her mom. Only six years separated them, a difference no one would blink at if the older party happened to be male. "And I cared for him a great deal." She'd loved him. "Do you remember why things didn't work out for us?"

Her mother snorted dismissively. "Seriously? Buckley Blackwood and his millions came calling, Miranda. No one would blame you for having your head turned."

Clinging to her own memories of the past, Miranda felt sure that hadn't been the way it had happened. Buckley had liked her from the first—that much was true. He'd come to her yoga studio not long after his divorce from his first wife, Donna-Leigh Westbrook. He'd immediately asked Miranda out, but she'd declined. Unperturbed, he'd continued to take classes with her. He'd sent flowers. He'd been a gentleman, but he'd also been persistent, sending her invitations to exclusive local events and introducing her to a few key members of the Texas Cattleman's Club who'd been instrumental in building her business.

But she'd been in love with Kai.

"My head wasn't turned by his wealth." She couldn't swallow back the defensiveness, remembering how careful she had always been to make sure the world knew she hadn't married him for his money. "I signed a prenup, remember? When we divorced, I walked away with nothing." She'd been determined to prove to the world she could make it on her own after her marriage fell apart, and she had. But she hadn't phoned her mother to talk about that. With an effort, she breathed through the simmering resentment and asked, "What I want to know is did you say something to Kai to send him away? To make him think I cared about Buckley and not him?"

As soon as she asked the question, she regretted it. She knew Kai wouldn't lie to her about something like that. Yet it upset her to think her mom had quietly upended Miranda's life like that without her knowing.

Her fingernails bit into her palm.

"That was a long time ago," Ginny informed her after a long pause. "I don't think I ever had much to say to the motorcycle-riding boyfriend."

This was a mistake. Closing her eyes, Miranda heard sounds emanating from the kitchen and inhaled the scent of frying bacon. She grappled for a way to end the phone call that was only frustrating her and not providing any answers. She dragged in a breath, but her mother spoke again before she could get a word out.

"Although now that you mention it," Ginny continued, "there was one time when he stopped by just as the floral delivery truck left. He asked me about the huge arrangement, and I remember being frank with him about Buckley having his eye on you. Why all the interest in Kai now?"

Miranda needed to end the call. With the hint of fresh coffee wafting in the air, she knew Kai was awake. She just hoped she could still enjoy their time together now that talking to her mother had her tense and stressed all over again.

"No reason," she lied, feeling twitchy and anxious. "I'll call again soon, Mama."

Disconnecting the call, Miranda tried to shake off the knowledge that her mother had poisoned her relationship with Kai ten years ago. Understanding the role she'd played helped her to forgive—a little bit anyway—Kai's withdrawal. Now, anticipation curled through her belly and it didn't have anything to do with the food. Being around him made her feel like a twenty-something again, full of starry-eyed romantic notions that she knew better than to believe.

Didn't she?

As she padded barefoot toward the kitchen, she really questioned how much she'd learned from her previous relationships. She knew she shouldn't count on something as fleeting as passion, and she couldn't expect any man to be a full-fledged partner in her life. Yet with Kai, she found she was wrestling back the persistent beast of hopefulness all the time.

The thought gave her pause, slowing her steps just as she reached the archway leading into the kitchen. Was it too late to retreat?

"Good morning," Kai greeted her, making any attempts to escape a moot point. "I hope you're hungry."

Hungry? Absolutely. For more than food. The enticing man standing at the stove was most definitely a feast for her eyes as he carefully flipped an omelet in one frying pan while monitoring a second omelet and bacon in another. He wore his jeans and a black unisex T-shirt emblazoned with the Goddess fitness logo that she'd left out for him the night before. With his hair damp from his shower and his face unshaven, he looked clean and roguish, like a man who would taste delicious.

Shivery sensations tripped over her skin thinking about what they'd shared the night before. And not just in a physical sense. His presence at the hospital, his insistence on driving her there to check on Sophie, touched her. Finding him in the kitchen, making them both breakfast, reminded her of when they'd been a couple.

"It smells great. How can I help?" She was already moving toward the coffeemaker, pulling mugs out of the cupboard and wondering how she was going to find her equilibrium with him today.

She might be tempted to lean into his warmth and support as a lover and a friend, but where would that leave her if he pulled away from her again? Her mother may have played a role in their relationship's demise, but Kai had never let Miranda weigh in on that conversation either.

She needed to be careful.

"Just butter the toast and we'll be good to go." He slid crispy slices of bacon onto two plates, each decorated with an orange slice. Fresh juice was already poured in glasses on the kitchen table. "Have you been awake long? I saw you were on a call before I started breakfast."

After taking care of the toast, Miranda poured two cups of coffee, finding it far too easy to fall into their old rhythms of working together. Had she been wrong to write off what they'd shared as purely passionate and therefore impractical?

"I woke up about an hour ago and felt like I should touch base with my...office." That much was true as she'd checked in with her assistant at Goddess before she'd called her mom. But she wasn't ready to share about her uneasy conversation with Ginny. Instead, Miranda carried the mugs to the table, noticing Kai had already put the creamer she preferred beside her place setting. "I've been in Royal for so long. I feel guilty about leaving my staff, but they've handled what they can really well."

He brought over their plates. "That sounds to me like there are tasks you haven't given them to manage. Are there things you need to be there for personally?"

He held her chair for her, silently inviting her to sit. She told herself to relax and enjoy Kai's attentiveness while it lasted.

"I need to meet with my biggest competitor, AMuse." Settling into her chair, she laid her napkin in her lap while he took the seat across from her. Their knees bumped and the jolt of electricity had her skin tingling. "Their CEO has called twice in the last month and I'm curious what that's about."

"Do you think they might try to buy you out?" He sipped his black coffee, his green gaze finding hers over the rim of the stoneware mug.

"I wouldn't think so, but either way, I'd never sell." She had to look away from his assessing eyes, unsure where she stood with him today or what the night before had meant for him. Instead, she thought back to the early beginnings of her business and how hard she'd worked to grow it. "Building Goddess helped me find my own strength. Every setback taught me something."

"I feel the same way about Madtec." He pulled out his phone between bites of the omelet and tapped a few buttons on the screen. "I double-checked with my pilot—the Madtec jet is available. We could be in New York before the close of day. Why don't we go check on things at Goddess and put your mind at ease?"

The suggestion caught her off guard.

"Really?" While her own business was thriving, she had never had the need for a jet or regular pilot service, but she could certainly see the appeal. "What about the bank? Should we be overseeing anything more with the hacking incident?"

Nibbling on a bacon slice, she ran through a mental checklist of all they needed to do in Royal. Beyond ensuring Blackwood Bank and its customers were now well protected, she still had details to oversee with the Royal Gives Back gala that Buckley had requested, and she wanted to be available for Lulu as the wedding date neared.

"The new data protection software is in place for the bank." He spoke with reassuring confidence. "We can send out a joint press release about that as soon as you or Vaughn approve the copy my PR department submitted for your review."

Mulling over the idea, she had to admit it sounded good to set her mind at ease about work. But she voiced the concern that held her back.

"Assuming we do this—and I appreciate the generous offer—what does it mean for us? It bears discussion as we start spending more time together." She wasn't sure about his expectations and she didn't want to confuse the issue. "That is, we haven't spoken about where this relationship might lead. You know I'm not staying in Royal."

Reaching across the table, he laid his hand over hers. The touch was tender, yet it stirred butterflies and memories, a wealth of feeling in that simple connection.

"What if we simply enjoy the time we have instead of worrying about what will happen at the end of the month?" His words cast a spell separate from his touch, tapping into the secret wishes of her heart and old, dangerous longings. "You've got a lot on your plate right now without adding me to the list of things you have to resolve."

It felt reckless to run headlong, heedless of consequences, into something that could cause her a world of hurt. And yet she found herself wanting to agree, just so their affair didn't have to end. She didn't know what she wanted long term, but the thought of ending things with Kai right now caused a pain that was almost physical. Could she trust him not to pull away from her the way he had the last time? Or would she be the one to pull away when she finished her duties in Texas and returned to New York? They had only a few more weeks before Royal Gives Back.

Surely she could keep her heart safe for just a little longer.

"In that case," she began, threading her fingers through his where their hands rested on the table, "I'd love to fly to New York with you."

"You went *where*?" Kai's brother's voice was curt over the phone. Dane sounded more than a little agitated.

Kai juggled the cell while he continued to work on his tablet in a chauffeured Range Rover. He sat in midtown traffic at rush hour, having dropped off Miranda at the Goddess headquarters. He was doing his damnedest to stay out of her way and let her use the time in Manhattan to conduct her business, but the moment she exited the private SUV, he'd begun making plans for their evening together.

His window of opportunity with her was narrowing as the end of the month approached, and he planned to pull out all the stops to romance her. That meant dinner and dancing at one of the most beautiful and exclusive rooftop bars in the city. He'd asked an assistant to review Miranda's episodes of *Secret Lives of NYC Ex-Wives* to learn any intelligence about her favorite places, and the Chelsea restaurant was a spot she'd exclaimed over in the first season. Kai had spent a small fortune to have the place to themselves on short notice. But before he could finish making preparations for the evening, he needed to deal with his brother.

"I flew to New York with Miranda," Kai explained. "Madtec has two clients I can see while I'm here."

"What about Blackwood Bank?" Dane swore on the other end of the call, and from the rhythmic thumping in the background, Kai guessed his brother was taking out his aggravation by running the green stairwell they'd installed in their building to use like a gym. "Reporters have been breathing down our necks all day."

"The situation is well in hand or I wouldn't have left the office yesterday." Kai leaned back in the leather seat, glancing out the window to see if they'd made progress. He had a meeting downtown in ten minutes. "The joint press release went out, so if the newshounds want a story, just keep referring back to the talking points. The data breach is old news."

"Is it, though?" The thumping on Dane's end of the call slowed and then stopped. He was breathing hard now. "I don't like the resentful tone I'm picking up in the tech community about the way we rolled out the new software during a PR crisis."

Kai frowned, his nerves drawing tight with foreboding. "What do you mean?"

"Face it, Kai. The bank data breach might have catapulted our cybersecurity software into national recognition if it ends up working as well as we think it's going to." Dane huffed out a long breath and then lowered his voice. "There are bound to be detractors who'll suggest we pulled some kind of unethical stunt to put ourselves in the position to be the white knights—and gain lots of publicity—given our...er, *my* history."

Kai knew Dane was referring to his stint in jail—to their shared hacking history that had been well publicized. Yet he still couldn't believe what he was hearing. He double-checked the partition window between him and SUV's driver, stabbing it hard with his finger to ensure it was sealed tightly.

"Are you suggesting that people are saying we organized a major breach of one of our own clients in order to draw media attention to our bringing a new protection software product to market?" The repercussions of that kind of publicity nightmare could be devastating for a fledgling business. Madtec was only just beginning to realize full legitimacy in the tech marketplace. This could ruin their credibility with any business that might be thinking of hiring them.

For that matter, what would Miranda think of the rumors? She'd never been comfortable with the idea that many successful tech gurus had skirted the law to learn the business, testing the bounds of cybersecurity by quietly hacking it. Her opinion mattered to him, and not just because of their business affiliation.

"I'm saying it's an excellent possibility." Dane sounded weary and more than a little ticked off. "It's already being speculated about among the tech elite. It's probably only a matter of time before a story like that finds traction with a wider audience."

"We need to track those rumors and put a stop to them." Kai opened a new screen on his tablet and got to work, firing off a message to the overworked press relations advocate at Madtec. "I'll be back in Deer Springs tomorrow, but I'll see what I can find out from here to squash the story."

Disconnecting the call, Kai realized the SUV was slowing outside his appointment with the city's major public transportation provider. He'd been working with them for months to increase their cybersecurity and had been glad to wrangle a last-minute meeting today. But it would take a superhuman effort to redirect his thoughts to this project right now when the fear of negative repercussions from the Blackwood Bank scandal threatened Madtec.

And his relationship with Miranda.

More than anything, he simply wanted to focus on making tonight a memorable experience for her. Because somehow, she'd slid straight past his defenses for the second time in his life, and he refused to waste this opportunity to woo her and win.

Stepping inside the custom closet in her Brooklyn brownstone that evening, Miranda took pleasure in the sight of her full wardrobe for the first time in months. Being able to dress for her date tonight with Kai would be all the more enjoyable for having access to her things. Because yes, she wanted to knock his socks off. To feel feminine and desirable after the failure of her marriage and the loneliness of the years that followed.

Peering over the rows of shoes carefully stored in protective clear bins, Miranda couldn't shake the unsettling truth that her New York home felt strange to her after spending so much time in Royal. Lonelier, somehow, since she'd formed tentative bonds with Buckley's children.

Not to mention the much more exciting connection she shared with Kai.

Inspired by a pair of sunshine-yellow high-heeled sandals, Miranda turned toward the rack where she kept her gowns to thumb through them for a draped silk gown in a creamy color, printed with greenery and yellow flowers. Kai had texted that he was sending a car for her at seven and would meet her for dinner at a surprise location. He'd indicated the dress was formal for a special evening out, a caveat that only added to her enjoyment in getting ready.

In the days when they'd been a couple in Deer Springs, their dates had been diner visits where they'd sneak a few moments together on her breaks, or rides on his motorcycle. They'd always had fun together without spending money neither of them had, but she looked forward to seeing Kai in a tuxedo and standing next to him in the kind of couture gown she'd once only dreamed of owning. It had taken her a lot of years to give herself this Cinderella moment, but she couldn't deny she took pride in herself for the hard work that made it possible to slide into handmade Italian leather shoes and fasten a bracelet of tiny yellow diamonds around one wrist.

When the sleek black Cadillac arrived for her half an hour later, the driver greeted her warmly but only smiled when she asked for a hint about her destination, ratcheting up the suspense, anticipation...desire.

What did Kai have in mind?

She was glad to think about the night ahead instead of her earlier meeting with her competitor, AMuse. The offer they'd made for a joint venture to go global had been exciting, but it also added a new complication to her already uncertain future. There'd been a time when she wouldn't have had to think twice about an offer like that. The opportunity to take the Goddess brand to other countries was exciting. A natural extension of her business plan. Yet it would make seeing Kai all but impossible down the road. Bad enough she was based in New York and he was based in Texas. But if she began traveling internationally to make the new venture with AMuse happen, she wouldn't ever have time to work on a relationship.

Not that Kai had hinted he wanted to continue seeing her once she left Royal. For tonight, she simply wanted to enjoy whatever Kai had planned.

The driver slowed down in front of a brick building in Chelsea, and it took Miranda a moment to recognize the plain black awning and black double doors with a discreet pineapple insignia beside them. Anticipation swelled when she recognized the facade to her favorite rooftop venue in Manhattan. How had Kai guessed?

A warm spring breeze teased her bare shoulders as she emerged from the vehicle, and a doorman appeared to escort her inside. This time, she didn't try to pry hints from him. She merely stepped into the elevator he indicated, surprised that the building seemed quiet at this hour. The lower floors were home to a unique, immersive theater experience and the restaurant and bar on the upper levels were usually packed, especially when the weather was this ideal.

Reaching the top level, the elevator doors slid open to reveal the rooftop bar swathed in green just the way she remembered. Lightweight vines climbed high structural arches. White lights wound through the greens and stretched overhead to put a network of tiny stars almost in reach. Live violin music—more formal than the sounds of the usual bar scene—played softly from a duo in a far corner.

But, strangely, the bar was otherwise empty until a devastatingly handsome man stepped out from behind a row of potted flowering trees. His face was illuminated by the white lights overhead and the hurricane lamps that crowded a nearby table.

Kai.

Her heartbeat quickened at the sight of him. Clean-shaven and dressed in a tuxedo custom fit to his athletic frame, he looked like a man born to the finer things in life. Desire for him, and all the delectable ways he could make her feel, curled warmly in her belly.

"You look incredible, Miranda." He walked forward to greet her with a debonair kiss that lingered on the back of her fingers. He held her gaze as his mouth grazed her skin.

The feel of his lips on her skin stirred fresh longing. Tingly sensations zipped up her spine and back down again.

"Thank you." She noticed he didn't let go of her hand, keeping her fingers wrapped in his. Her gaze wandered over the lines of his black silk jacket where it skimmed his broad shoulders and tapered to his narrow waist and hips. "The tux suits you, Kai. I wasn't expecting such a special night when you offered a spur-of-the-moment trip."

"I thought it was time to make my intentions toward you known," he countered, leading her farther from the musicians to a spot near the edge of the rooftop terrace.

They had a clear view of the lighted spires from sky-

scrapers in lower Manhattan when he took her in his arms
for a slow dance. Her body followed his easily, one hand
landing on his shoulder while he kept hold of the other.

"What intentions might those be?" Her pulse hammered harder, uncertain what she wanted or hoped to
hear.

She thought she knew better than to get involved with
Kai again, and yet here they were, unable to stay away
from each other.

"I want to remind you how good it can be between us,
Miranda." His forehead tipped toward hers. "Last time we
were together, I let outside influences come between us."

A chill feathered through her as she remembered the
way her mother had interfered, planting the seeds of
doubt in Kai's mind about their future together.

As much as she wanted to make the most of their
evening and push aside outside concerns, she found her
current doubts harder to ignore. The offer from AMuse
circled around her brain.

"What happens when I leave Royal at the end of the
month?" she asked, peering deep into his green eyes, desperate for answers that had proved all too elusive to her.
"I have a whole life in New York. And today, my competitor suggested a joint venture that would take Goddess global."

Kai's smile was as unexpected as it was unmistakable. "That's fantastic, Miranda." He squeezed her gently. "Congratulations. You deserve this."

"Thank you." A surge of pride swelled. After all the
times she and Kai had sat in the Deer Springs Diner together, figuring out how to make their dreams come true,
it felt like she'd come full circle to savor this business
victory with him here, dancing on a rooftop under the

twinkle of white lights and the glow of the city's skyline. "I've been so focused on how it would work that I haven't taken a moment to really celebrate the achievement."

"That changes now," he insisted. "I hope you'll let me celebrate with you over dinner. We'll see what the server can find for a fitting champagne to toast the moment."

The lilting tune they'd been dancing to shifted, slowing down a bit. Kai's steps matched the cadence, easily guiding her while she tried to put her finger on what was bothering her about celebrating the news with him.

"I appreciate that. And I'd love some champagne. But I wonder how hard this would make things for work and—" she hesitated as her hair blew softly against her cheek "—for me, personally. It would mean a lot more travel."

She didn't spell out her concerns about seeing him after she left Texas, mainly because she wasn't sure if he saw her departure as an obvious end date for their affair.

"There was a time when we wouldn't have let logistics dictate our future." He seemed unconcerned. But did that mean he wasn't counting on a long-distance relationship in the first place?

She didn't ask because she didn't know what she wanted either.

"And yet we both have too much at stake to walk away from businesses we've worked hard to create." The fact that they were even discussing it worried her a little. But it excited her too, stirring a forgotten hopefulness.

Could they find a way to make it work?

The distant sounds of New York nightlife drifting up from the street provided a soft background to the violins' romantic melody.

"For tonight, it's enough if I can just prove to you that

we were meant to be together." He twirled her under his arm as the music stopped altogether. When it ended, he pulled her against him for a long, slow, thorough taste.

She sank into him, wanting to burn the memory of this moment into her brain to preserve it forever. To look back on when she left Texas for good and resumed her life in New York without him. With the end of their affair in sight, she was eager to keep the outside world at bay, the moment sweetly dream-like with the soft breeze blowing her silk gown against her legs, and Kai's strong arms holding her close. His lips were soft and teasing at first, then lingered until she felt breathless.

When he eased away, she opened her eyes slowly.

"Is that why you went to all the trouble of booking this amazing venue just for us?" she asked, curious about what this over-the-top evening truly meant. "To show me how well you know what I like?"

"To show you there's nothing I wouldn't do for you, Miranda." His green eyes were serious, and her heart turned over in her chest.

Romantic words. They fluttered around her with teasing promise like the spring breeze. But could she trust them?

"For tonight, I just want to be with you," she admitted, not ready to think beyond the here and now.

Because after her failed marriage, she couldn't afford to be wrong about love again.

Ten

With the temptation of Miranda Dupree seated beside him, Kai willed the driver to go faster as their private car sped over Manhattan Bridge later that night, leaving the New York skyline behind them. He'd enjoyed every moment spent with Miranda tonight, but the need to be really, truly alone with her burned hotter than ever.

"Thank you for celebrating with me tonight." Miranda turned her liquid-blue eyes on him as her fingers covered his on the expanse of leather seat between them. "Sometimes I get so caught up in achieving the next goal I forget to enjoy the milestones as they come. This was…nice. Better than nice, actually. It was an unforgettable night."

Her happiness made all the effort he'd put into the evening well worth it. He took his time threading his fingers through hers, relishing the simple connection even as he craved a far more intimate one. With his other hand, he stabbed the button to raise the privacy window to prevent the driver from overhearing them. Or seeing them.

"The celebrating isn't over, as far as I'm concerned." He lifted her palm to his mouth and pressed a kiss in the center. "I hope to make the night more memorable for you soon."

He heard her swift intake of breath as he kissed his way past her wrist. Over the delicate skin of her inner arm. The scent of her fragrant skin—soap and jasmine—teased his nose as she shifted closer, her knee brushing his.

Electricity crackled between them. He lifted his attention from her arm to the soft swell of her breasts over the low neckline of her cream-colored dress. Her chest rose and fell quickly. Her lips parted in silent invitation.

An invitation he couldn't afford to indulge until they were alone. Because once he started kissing her, he wouldn't stop. He settled for cupping her chin and running his thumb over the full softness of her mouth.

"How much longer until we reach your place?" he wondered aloud, thinking he could put the time to more satisfying use for them both.

She turned to peer over her shoulder and look out the window as they drove deeper into Brooklyn.

"My street is next," she replied, straightening in her seat. "We're in luck."

A damned good thing given the way the sparks between them flared hotter with each passing second. A few moments later, the vehicle slowed on a tree-lined street in front of a row of brownstones. After helping Miranda from the vehicle and exchanging a few words with the driver about the next day's itinerary, Kai forced himself to take an extra moment to admire her quiet neighborhood before following her up the steps to the tall, black double doors that served as the main entrance. No sense crowding or rushing her. She had to know how much he wanted her. She'd already disarmed the alarm on the keypad by the door.

He stood in the foyer while she locked and reset the alarm. The long, narrow foyer was dimly lit from the hall sconces, but Kai could see the whitewashed brick fireplace and pocket doors that gave the home a historic feel. The low, modern furnishings and industrial chandelier were obvious touches of the current owner, however.

Before he could compliment her on the house, Miranda was in his arms, reminding him exactly why they'd been in such a hurry to get here. Her arms locked around his neck, breasts pressed to his chest in a way that made him forget everything else. She kissed along his jaw while he molded her to him, his hands tracing her curves through the silky fabric of her printed gown.

"Where's your room?" he asked, his breath coming fast.

She unfastened two buttons of his shirt before pointing toward the staircase. "Second floor."

They ascended the steps together, her hand wrapped in his, legs brushing on the way up.

She led him to the left where the master suite awaited. Inside the open archway, her bed stood in front of another fireplace. Here, everything was white and gray. A color scheme that would normally be calming if he wasn't on fire to have her. A single orchid bloomed by the bed. The blinds over the bay windows were already lowered so that the room was lit only by the white glow spilling from the open door of the en suite bath.

A beautiful space for an even more beautiful woman. She had so damned much to be proud of. She was vibrant. Independent. Fearless. And Kai wanted her more than he'd ever thought possible to want any woman.

Not ready to vocalize that until he figured out what it meant for them, he tucked a finger underneath his bow tie and freed the knot before unfastening the top button of his shirt. Miranda's gaze heated. A small smile curved one side of her lips.

She answered him by slipping off the straps of her gown. First one. Then the other.

Damn, but he was crazy about her.

When he shrugged out of his shirt, she stepped out of her shoes, her toes disappearing in the thick white carpet beneath their feet.

"Turn around." He reached for her hips to bring her closer. "I'll unzip you."

She pivoted to present him with her back. He lowered the zipper slowly, stroking touches along each new square inch of silky skin he bared.

When the gown sagged and fell to her feet, he anchored her to him with an arm around her waist. Skimming her hair away from her jasmine-scented neck, he kissed a trail from beneath her ear to her shoulder and back again. Unhooking her pale green bra, he let that slip to the floor too, his attention fixed on the taut peaks of her breasts. She shimmied against him, her hips rocking back into his as a low moan vibrated through her.

The last shreds of his restraint disintegrated.

Miranda was on fire.

Spinning in Kai's arms, she couldn't undress him fast enough, desire fogging her brain and making her fingers fumble awkwardly with the fastening of his tuxedo pants. She needed him naked with an urgency she'd only ever experienced with him.

He peeled off her panties while she dragged down his boxers, their arms bumping and hooking. Not that it mattered. Nothing mattered but being with him.

He lifted her to deposit her in the middle of her bed, a smooth drop into the soft, thick comforter. She had a moment to savor the way he looked when he retrieved a condom from a pocket of the discarded clothing. His square shoulders were backlit by the light from the bathroom, the outline of him deliciously masculine. Unquestionably powerful. When he stepped closer, the rippled muscles of his abs caught her eye, but only for a moment before her gaze shifted to his hips and the rigid length of him that awaited her touch.

Yet when she reached for him, he pinned both her hands lightly, his gaze probing hers as he covered her.

"I need you too much to wait another minute." His ragged words made hot pleasure curl in her belly. "I've wanted you all night."

Anticipation and excitement twined together, rendering her breathless. Light-headed.

"No more than I've wanted you." She liked knowing what she did to him, relieved that she wasn't alone in this out-of-control hunger.

With his gaze locked on hers, he let go of her wrists to curve a hand around her hip, tilting her toward him. She bit her lip against the exquisite feel of him sliding inside her. Deeper.

When she realized her fingernails were digging into his shoulder, she let go, kissing the place where she'd left red crescent moons. Wrapping her arms around his neck, she held on to him, letting him set the pace while the rhythm of it carried her away. Each stroke was pleasure filled. Each breath brought her closer to a climax she wasn't ready for. Not yet.

She wanted this night to last and last. Not just because of how it felt to have him with her. In her.

But because she couldn't imagine letting go of Kai again.

The realization slid into her consciousness at the same time he whispered her name in her ear, the sound of it and the feel of his breath making her shiver. Sending her hurtling toward the release she couldn't possibly stave off another moment.

She clung to him, her body undulating with waves of sweet sensations she never wanted to end. In the midst of it, she registered that she'd taken him with her, her body teasing him to his own completion.

They held each other for long moments afterward, breathing raggedly, heartbeats pounding madly. When, finally, those slowed down, Kai settled on her right side. The overhead ceiling fan stirred cool air over them, but he tucked her closer. She felt around for the edge of the duvet and draped it over them both.

He sifted his fingers through her hair, relaxing her enough to chase latent worries about their future from her brain. She was almost asleep in his arms when he whispered to her.

"I hope you're going to take the deal with AMuse." He spoke softly, but her eyes fluttered open to fix on his in the dim light. "It's the culmination of everything you've worked so hard for."

It definitely wasn't pillow talk, or sweet nothings whispered in her ear. She held her breath for a moment, wondering what it meant for him. Why he'd shared that thought with her now. Was it his way of setting her free after her time in Royal was done? Or was it a genuine encouragement for her to embrace the dreams she'd always had for her business? Seeing nothing but warmth and thoughtfulness in his eyes, she forced herself to let out her breath.

"I know," she admitted, tracing circles on his chest. She felt grateful at least that he understood her even if he wouldn't always be a part of her life. But thinking about a future without him in it hurt. "I probably will."

His nod was a fraction of movement. His eyes closed then, as if he felt his role in the decision was finished. He'd encouraged her to do what she wanted.

For the first time, she acknowledged that Kai was more than just a passionate lover. She'd been wrong to write off what they'd shared in the past as simple chemistry that wouldn't stand up to the tests of time. He was her friend. And he wanted what was best for her.

But was that enough to keep them together through a long-distance separation? Her chest ached at the idea of leaving, but she also couldn't possibly stay. So for now, she closed her eyes and told herself to keep breathing. One way or another, she'd have to figure it out.

Kai awoke to his cell phone vibrating.

He'd been so deeply asleep beside Miranda that it took him a moment to orient himself and realize that he was still in her Brooklyn brownstone after their impromptu trip to New York City. Sliding from the covers, Kai reached for his phone and answered it, even as he tucked the duvet tighter around Miranda. He regretted leaving her side one of the few times he'd been able to sleep beside her.

He gathered up a fistful of clothes from the floor before he made his way into the adjoining bathroom so he wouldn't wake her. There, he closed the door silently before speaking.

"What's up?" he asked quietly, meeting his own gaze in the huge mirror over the marble vanity. He knew it had to be his brother since Dane's number was the only one allowed to ring through at this hour.

Well, Dane's and Miranda's. But obviously *she* hadn't phoned him.

"Disaster is what's up." Dane spewed the words like hot lava, voice raised and angry. "The rumors about Madtec orchestrating the Blackwood Bank breach have gone national. A major news organization picked up the story."

Dread enveloped Kai's gut. Juggling the phone, he stepped into his boxers.

"Rumors aren't news," he answered reflexively, hoping like hell his brother was overreacting.

"Seriously? Have you read what gets shared for news nowadays, man?" Dane spoke fast, each word punching through the phone. "It doesn't matter if it's true. The suspicions raised will cripple the business—"

"Hold up." Kai stepped into his pants, noting that the sun was rising, a low light filtering in through the stained glass window. He needed to get on top of this. Fast. "Send me a link where I can get up to speed, and I'll call you back."

His brother swore, but pinged him an address to read the story.

Disconnecting the call, Kai sank to the white tile tub

surround and scrolled through the article along with the comments before checking a couple of social media platforms. Dane hadn't overstated the case. Madtec needed a full-scale response to the bad press if they wanted any chance of overcoming this.

He texted his brother and his head of public relations to set up a virtual meeting in an hour. First, he needed to wake Miranda. He needed to be back in Deer Springs. Regret that their night together had to end this way stung hard. But she would understand.

Tossing his phone aside, he sat on the mattress near Miranda and touched her shoulder through the covers. Her eyelids fluttered, and he wondered what it would be like to wake up beside this woman day after day. He was falling for her.

Hard.

The realization threaded through the tension of the day, tightening it all into a hard knot. He couldn't afford to think about long term with her yet. Not when she was going to be building her brand overseas and working out of Manhattan while he was in Deer Springs.

"Miranda?" He watched as she came upright in bed slowly, dragging the covers with her.

"What is it? Is everything okay?" Her blue eyes darted around him, taking in his clothes before shifting to the clock on the wall.

More than anything, he wanted to slide back into bed beside her. To relive their incredible night together. But that was no longer possible.

He flipped on the bedside lamp.

"I need to fly home. Madtec is under assault in the press because of rumors that we someone how orchestrated the Blackwood Bank breach." Sharing the words made it hit hard all over again. Just when he'd finally thought Madtec had gained the legitimacy and credibility they needed.

Fighting to prove himself over and over again was getting old.

"I don't understand." Miranda shook her head, a crumbled red curl wavering as she moved. "Why would anyone suggest your company would launch a cyberattack on the business you were hired to protect? It makes no sense."

Frustration flared. "I wouldn't think so either. But it's been suggested that we fabricated the security breach in order to show off our new software. Our detractors have gained traction with the idea that our saving a giant like Blackwood Bank was perfect—and free—advertising for the new encryption software."

Miranda's blue gaze faltered, a shadow passing through their depths. But then she seemed to hide her reaction, her lips pursing in thought before she spoke again. "That's ludicrous."

A moment passed as he tried to process what he'd seen. But it damned well looked like she doubted him.

"You can't think I'd do something like that... Do you?" he asked, feeling like the ground had been yanked out from under him.

He'd worked his ass off to prove himself in the business world. But it had never occurred to him that Miranda would question his ethics.

"Of course not," she assured him, as if he hadn't seen her doubt with his own eyes. Perhaps being so newly awake made it tougher to hide her real feelings.

She glanced down at the duvet where she picked at the white binding on the cotton cover. "It's just—for a moment—I was remembering what you told me about the tech community. That most of the giants who understand the industry best are the people who started like you and Dane—hacking."

The sense of betrayal shook him. He stiffened his spine against it.

"So you figured it was only natural we'd undermine our own clients for the sake of some good press." He understood now why total strangers could think it of him and Dane, when the woman he cared about so much could come to the same sickening conclusion about him.

"No." She sounded more certain now, but it didn't erase the flash of doubt. "I came to Madtec because you're the best, Kai. End of story."

Woodenly, he stood. He refused to think about how close he'd come to losing his heart to this woman all over again. Only to be stomped twice as hard as the first time.

"Either way, I need to return to Deer Springs." His problems had only multiplied by sharing them with Miranda. Funny, now the potential loss of his business reputation didn't feel nearly as daunting as the loss of her. "The pilot can be at the airfield in an hour, so I'll call a car as soon as you're ready."

For a moment, he thought she'd argue. Or somehow try to retract the way she'd just leveled him with her lack of faith in him.

But then, she simply nodded.

Kai turned on his heel and left her to get ready on her own. The sooner he got back to Texas, the better.

He belonged there. As for Miranda Dupree and her global success? She'd have to pursue her dreams without him, the same way she always had.

Eleven

A week after the disastrous conclusion to the New York City trip, Miranda stood on the front steps of the Pine Valley estate that Sophie Blackwood Townshend now shared with Nigel. Miranda clutched a bouquet in one hand and a basket of cookies and pastries from a local bakery in the other. She was overdue to congratulate Sophie on her pregnancy news in person, but it had been a long, heart-wrenching week since her misstep with Kai.

He'd barely spoken to her on their flight back to Royal. Of course, she'd understood he was in the middle of a business crisis with Madtec's reputation under attack. But she suspected that he'd been more upset by her moment of doubt than any of the rumors, and that had given her plenty of pangs of conscience since then.

It wasn't that she believed he was unethical. It was

just… Well, she'd been waiting for the other shoe to drop from the moment they'd reignited their affair.

She shoved those thoughts to the side, however, as a young liveried housekeeper with a long blond ponytail opened the door of Sophie's pretty French country estate.

"Hello." Miranda smiled at the woman. "I'm here to see Sophie—"

"Thank God for a visitor," Sophie's unmistakable voice rang out from the back of the house. "Tell her I'm in the kitchen, Josephine!"

The petite housekeeper grinned at the same time Miranda did.

"I'll find her." Miranda nodded her thanks while the housekeeper shut the door. "Thank you."

"Miranda, is that you?" Sophie asked, peering out of the kitchen, a glass of water in her hand. At twenty-seven years old, Sophie had long auburn hair and brown eyes. She had killer curves and a quick wit, always ready with a smile. As the baby of the Blackwood clan and the only daughter, she'd been beloved by all. "I'm so glad you're here. Nigel practically keeps me housebound on a steady diet of constant calories, so I don't faint again." Her gaze went to the basket. "Although I'll bet whatever is in that basket is the kind of calories I'll actually enjoy."

Warmth suffused Miranda's heart to be welcomed this way by the stepdaughter she'd once feared would hate her forever. Sophie had still been a teenager when Miranda married Buckley, and Sophie had strongly resented their relationship. After the reading of the will, Sophie had put all her considerable efforts into proving Miranda was up to no good by infiltrating Green Room Media in New York to dig up dirt on her ex-stepmother. Dirt she hoped to use to get the will overturned in court.

The fact that they were finally able to put those years of ill will behind them was nothing short of a miracle in Miranda's book. She would always be grateful to Buckley for giving her this second chance to be a family with the Blackwoods.

"I got your favorites," Miranda announced, remembering her own efforts to get to know Sophie as a young woman, attempting to buy her favor with treats. She set the basket down on the island of the gleaming white kitchen where Sophie seemed to be preparing a pot of tea at the coffee bar. "And some flowers to congratulate you on your amazing news." Miranda hugged her tightly.

"Thank you." Sophie sniffed the bouquet of hydrangeas and roses. "The flowers are gorgeous. Can I make you some tea?"

"Sure. But why don't you let me do it? You haven't been home from the hospital for very long."

Sophie turned a dark scowl her way before peering into the basket of pastries. "Don't you gang up on me too, Miranda. I'm pregnant, not ill." She withdrew an almond croissant. "Oh, this smells amazing."

While Sophie loaded a plate with some of the pastries, Miranda quietly found spoons and napkins, eager to get the two of them everything they needed so Sophie could sit and rest. Because no matter what Nigel's new wife said, Miranda had just visited the two of them in the hospital, so clearly Sophie needed to be mindful of her health.

Of course, thinking of that visit made Miranda remember how thoughtful and kind Kai had been to personally drive her to Royal that night. She'd missed him to the point of pain this past week, but she reminded herself to focus on Sophie as she carried the mugs and spoons to the breakfast bar in the huge, open kitchen.

"So what did the doctor have to say, Sophie?" she pressed, gesturing for the younger woman to take a seat on one of the padded leather stools. "Why did you faint at the airport?"

"Probably because we were going through customs in a crowded airport with a crush of other people and I hadn't eaten since the night before. I slept the whole flight." Sophie slid onto one of the stools while Miranda carried over the teapot and pastries. "If I'd known I was pregnant I would have packed a protein bar or something. But as it was...*whoosh*. Down I went. I scared Nigel half to death."

"I'm sure you did," Miranda mused as she took the stool beside Sophie, enjoying the vision of those two very different personalities spending their lives together. Sophie was so bubbly and warm, while Nigel was reserved to the point that he could be mistaken for aloof—unless, of course, you happened to see him when he was looking at Sophie.

Clinking the pot against Miranda's mug, Sophie lifted it to pour, the pointed sleeves of a colorful caftan trailing over her hand.

"But now he's completely overcompensating, expecting me to eat constantly and stay close to home." She rolled her eyes. "Although the honeymoon was so amazing, I guess I can forgive him."

A sly, happy smile curved her lips.

"I'm so glad for you both." Miranda felt another pang of envy for all the love and happiness around her while she floundered around trying to get her own life in order.

She'd just finished celebrating one wedding and now Lulu's was the week after the Royal Gives Back gala. "I hope you'll both be at the Royal Gives Back event?"

"We wouldn't miss it." After pouring her own tea, Sophie slid into the leather counter stool beside Miranda. "I think of it as Dad's 'coming out' party, where the rest of the world will finally know his good qualities."

They drank their tea in silence for a moment, perhaps equally wrapped up in their own memories of Buckley Blackwood. He'd been a blowhard and a tough businessman, always hiding his softer side while he'd been alive, even with his family. And while Miranda was happy he was finally going to be celebrated for the good person he was underneath the unyielding facade, she knew it would have made a lot of people in his life happier if he could have been more giving—and forgiving—while he'd still been alive.

She didn't want to be the kind of person who made the same mistakes over and over again her whole life. And yet hadn't she ended up back in the same place with Kai as she'd been ten years ago? The new rift between them hurt even more than the first time.

Sophie broke the silence when she set her cup back on the granite countertop, the scent of chamomile and lemon rising from the tea. "I heard from Vaughn this morning that things are running smoothly at the bank again after the security breach."

Miranda's breath caught, her thoughts flying straight back to Kai, the man who'd steered the bank through the chaos.

"We were fortunate to have Madtec helping us through that nightmare," Miranda said, missing Kai even more.

She nibbled on a raspberry tart, wondering how she'd ever get over him.

Would he even speak to her again? Or had he checked out on her for good this time? She'd hoped he'd be at the Royal Gives Back gala, but maybe he wouldn't bother attending now.

"No doubt." Sophie slanted a sideways gaze in her direction. "How about you, Miranda? Did *you* feel fortunate to have Kai Maddox back in your life after so many years?"

Miranda didn't miss the arch note in Sophie's voice. She spun to look at her.

"You knew I dated Kai?" she asked. Had Sophie just learned about this when the tabloids showed her and Kai leaving Madtec's offices together? Or had she known before? But no, surely if she'd known years ago, it would have come up when Miranda had first married Buckley.

Back then, Sophie had been so eager to do anything that might get under Miranda's skin.

"Of course. You forget how eager I was to see you trip up as Dad's new wife when he brought you to Blackwood Hollow." She didn't sound proud of the fact anymore. She stirred more sugar into her tea, the spoon clinking softly against the sides of the mug before she withdrew it and laid it on a napkin. "I made it my mission to learn whatever I could about your past. I hoped to catch you cheating, but nothing ever happened. You stayed loyal, even when things weren't working out in your marriage. Even I couldn't find fault with how you treated Dad, as hard as I tried. You were good to him, Miranda."

She released a pent-up breath, grateful she felt that way. "I tried to be. But I failed as a wife to Buckley. And it looks like I failed with Kai again."

Sophie swiveled in her seat to look at her head-on. "What do you mean?"

"I mean we were seeing each other again. Up until last week." Miranda hadn't told anyone about what happened with Kai. Not even the other *Ex-Wives*. But she felt the need to share it with someone, and Sophie had always been candid with her—even in the years when she hadn't been kind. Maybe she needed that candidness right now. "I was rattled when he told me about the scandal surrounding Madtec and the rumors that he and his brother had somehow engineered the breach for the publicity."

"You believed that?" Sophie's auburn eyebrow arched.

Clutching the warmth of her mug with both hands, Miranda felt like even more of a heel.

"Not really. But for a moment, I suppose, it sounded like something he might have done back in the days when he walked the knife's edge between right and wrong." He'd been so desperate to learn back then, even if it meant crossing some lines. But he wasn't that desperate kid anymore. She knew how much the reputation of his business meant to him. Not to mention the reputation of his brother, who'd gone to jail for something Kai felt like he should have prevented.

"So tell him you were wrong." Sophie underscored the advice by pointing at her with a fig cookie. "No one knows better than me that sometimes a big, fat apology is in order. I've had to give a lot of them since I've jumped to my fair share of wrong conclusions. But if you're sincere—"

"There are so many more things that aren't right between us though, Sophie. My life is in New York and his is here. I have the show, and an offer to take Goddess global—"

She halted herself abruptly as Sophie was shaking her head, her long auburn hair swinging. "That's all a smokescreen. And none of it really matters if you love each other. First you apologize. Then you can see if any of the rest of it has any bearing on your relationship. My two cents says that it won't."

Miranda wasn't so sure. But she understood what Sophie was saying.

Reaching for her, she squeezed Sophie's forearm. "When did you turn so wise?"

"A miracle, right?" Sophie laughed. "I guess I had to make my own share of missteps before I figured out how to be a better person. I hurt you, and I hurt Nigel with my headstrong ways, so convinced I knew it all. But part of being a strong person means learning to back down when you're wrong."

Miranda felt the unfamiliar prick of warmth in her eyes and she swallowed back a lump in her throat. She wasn't sure if the knot of feelings were for all she'd been through in her role as the Wicked Stepmother to Buckley's kids, or if it was because of how she'd handled things with Kai. But she appreciated Sophie's words.

She needed to decide if she was going to take the plunge and come to terms with everything she felt for Kai. She'd been hiding behind her defenses and her boundaries for too long. Maybe all of it was a smokescreen, after all.

"You're right." Miranda nodded, glad she'd come. "Thank you, Sophie."

"Of course. That's what families are for." Sophie winked at her. "Do you need any help with the gala? I'm really ready for a new project—"

"Nigel would have my head, and we both know it,"

Miranda reminded her. "I'll just be happy having you both there."

"We're looking forward to it," Sophie assured her.

An hour later, Miranda left Pine Valley and headed back to Royal to finish her preparations for Royal Gives Back. It would be her last task in town on Buckley's behalf, but she planned to stay for a week afterward for Lulu's wedding. The wedding would be the season finale of their show.

After that, there would be no excuse for her to remain in Royal any longer. Unless, of course, she convinced Kai to take a chance on continuing their relationship. Something she couldn't deny that she wanted more than air.

Because she knew now—after this miserable week of hurting without him—that she loved him. Now, more than ever. She hadn't wanted to face it, fearing how much it might hurt, but she'd fallen for him anyhow.

Maybe she'd sabotaged things with him purposely so she wouldn't have to face the hurt of rejection a second time. Whatever her reason, she refused to let Kai think she believed the worst of him.

That wasn't fair to him.

She just needed to find the right time to tell him before the gala. Then, she'd hope for the best. No matter how much it hurt.

Kai ignored the phone messages from Miranda the day before the Royal Gives Back Gala.

Amad had walked into his office with two of them earlier in the week. And now, the day before the gala, there'd been another.

Kai couldn't say why he was avoiding her—out of a need to protect himself from hearing her say goodbye, or to maintain the anger he still felt that she'd believed the worst of him. Thankfully, he'd discovered the source of the smear campaign earlier in the week, and this afternoon he'd had the pleasure of seeing the same tech rival who'd started the rumors now under investigation for breaking the law himself. Alistair Quinn had been a thorn in the Maddox brothers' side for years, but it seemed he wouldn't be making trouble any longer. How ironic that he'd been charged with pulling the kinds of cheap stunts he'd accused Madtec of using.

It was damned satisfying to be vindicated. Madtec had two big job offers roll in just in the last day, their legitimacy cemented for good.

Now, shutting down his workstation for the night, Kai retrieved his jacket and slid his arms in the sleeves. He opened his office door to find Dane and Amad watching replays of a college basketball game on Amad's desktop computer, reviewing the video in slow motion to exclaim over a great basket.

The workday was done, and it was rewarding to see Amad stick around the office to socialize. That kind of atmosphere was what he and Dane had hoped for when they'd created a more employee-centered office space at Madtec. And now, the business was back in good stead with the public. It should have been a day of celebrating, capped off by the sight of his brother smiling and happy.

Except Kai's victory felt hollow without Miranda.

"Hey." Dane straightened as Kai walked into the outer office. "Ready to go out for a drink to celebrate the future of Madtec now that Alistair Quinn is under investigation?"

"I thought I'd take the bike out for a few hours." He

hadn't ridden his motorcycle in weeks. Maybe the fresh air would clear out his head.

Ease the red-hot burn in his chest where his personal regrets lived.

Dane frowned. He strode with Kai toward the private elevator that led directly to the parking area. "Let me walk down with you."

Kai nodded, but said nothing. He felt like a countdown clock was ticking in the back of his brain, every second a reminder that Miranda was a moment closer to leaving Texas for good.

As soon as the elevators doors closed silently behind them, Dane turned serious eyes toward him. "What gives?"

"What do you mean? Why would something be wrong just because I want to take the bike out instead of going out for a drink?" Kai pulled his keys from his pants pocket, agitated.

"I mean, the news broke that the company was the target of a deliberately malicious smear campaign by a rival. We're vindicated and we got two big-money offers from huge companies. Our human resources department can't hire people fast enough." Dane ticked off all the good news on his fingers. "Yet you're dragging yourself through the office like you lost your best friend."

Kai stifled the urge to scowl and snarl because he didn't need Dane sniffing around his private life. As the elevator settled on the ground floor, he charged out into the parking area. The late afternoon sun glinted off a windshield, making him blink.

"It's all good news, but I'm fried. I've been working more than not for the past two weeks." He'd poured all of his energy into clearing his name—and Dane's, too.

And to keep himself from thinking about Miranda.

"I'm not buying it." Dane stepped in front of Kai, making him pull up sharply so he didn't run right into him. "Where's Miranda been? You two went to New York together, yet I haven't a heard a word about her or what went down."

The urge to scowl wouldn't be quieted this time. Kai narrowed his gaze.

"Since when do we trade stories about women? You don't see me inserting myself in your private life." He stepped around his brother and continued toward his car, popping open the locks on the coupe from the key fob.

The executive parking area was quiet, deserted. Heat sweltered off the tarmac even though it was almost six o'clock.

"I didn't say anything when you let her go the first time," Dane countered. "But I know you regretted it then, and you're probably going to regret it this time, too."

Kai ground his teeth together, his jaw flexing. "She's the one walking away," he said finally, the words spilling out in spite of him. "She turned her back on what we had then, and she's never believed we could last this time either."

"How convenient you never have to put yourself on the line with her," Dane observed drily, folding his arms over his chest. "I guess if you don't really try, you can't ever fail. Good thinking, Kai."

The sarcasm dripped from his words. Shaking his head, Dane pivoted on his heel to leave.

"I've tried," Kai retorted. But even he had to cringe at the sullen tone in his voice.

Hell.

Dane spun toward him, arms spread wide. "Have you?

Because from my point of view, it looks like you've been dodging her since that first day she showed up here with a business opportunity."

He flinched a little at the direct hit.

"True. But I had my reasons." He stalked away from his vehicle, thinking and pacing. "Since then, I've committed to showing her we could be good together."

He'd driven her to the hospital when her family needed her. Flown her to New York. Supported her global expansion.

"I believe you showed her. But that doesn't mean she understood your message as anything other than being helpful." Dane leaned a hip into Kai's car. "Have you *told* her how you feel? Or have you even worked out for yourself whether you love her or not?"

Kai quit pacing, stunned. The words called everything in him to a halt.

Did he love Miranda? Was he *in love* with her?

He'd never acknowledged the idea openly, maybe because he'd been trying his damnedest not to have his heart shredded a second time. But his love for her was so damned much a bedrock of everything he felt that he couldn't believe he'd never brought the feeling up into the sunlight where he could appreciate it. Share it.

Tell her about it.

Hell yes, he loved her.

"I've got to go." He charged toward his car, his feet fueled with purpose.

"Is that a yes?" Dane drummed his fingers on Kai's hood, assessing his brother.

"She's everything to me," Kai told him simply, the truth settling over him with new clarity. "And I've got to make sure she knows it."

He didn't miss Dane's smug smile as he backed up a step while Kai started the car.

Later, he would thank Dane for helping him figure out what to do next. Right now, he needed to get to the Texas Cattleman's Club before the gala kicked off. He wasn't sure of the logistics for how he'd tell Miranda he loved her, and he didn't know if the sentiment would be returned.

But he understood one thing now thanks to Dane. Kai would regret it forever if he didn't at least try to win her back.

Twelve

Just outside the kitchen of the Texas Cattleman's Club, Miranda consulted with the head of catering an hour after the Royal Gives Back gala began. She was grateful to lose herself in the details of the evening to escape the heartbreak of her rift with Kai. She'd been at the venue for two hours before the event kicked off to ensure things ran smoothly, taking a break only to slip into a black crepe cocktail gown with subtly sexy keyhole cutouts at the waist and shoulder.

Once she approved two minor menu changes, Miranda left the caterer to return to the party, walking through an archway draped with white and gold flowers. A few attendees stood in front of the wall of petals taking photos of each other, and Miranda smiled at them as she passed. The musicians were playing a short set of big-band music in the warm-up hour before Miranda took the stage to thank the guests and make a few announcements about Buckley Blackwood's legacy.

She had her notes waiting on the podium, and she had a few surprises to share with the guests. But for now, she took a few moments to peer around the great room that had been outfitted for the night's gala.

Looking for Kai.

She'd counted on seeing him here so she could apologize in person for doubting him. Even though she knew it wouldn't change the pain she'd caused him. Her words would come too late anyhow, since he'd already been cleared of any wrongdoing. She wished she'd driven to Deer Springs earlier in the week—before the news story broke about his tech rival organizing a smear campaign against Madtec. Then, her apology might have meant more. Might have changed things.

Either way, she had to see him tonight once her obligations at the gala were complete. She owed him the words.

Swallowing hard, she tried not to think about him tonight when she had this one final task to manage for Buckley. With an event planner's eye, she went over the room again, noting the huge white and yellow-gold flower arrangements on the tables, with white roses, daffodils and ranunculus dominating the tall sprays. Black accents kept the theme quietly elegant, the wrought iron candelabra and chair backs picking up the more masculine decor that dominated the remodeled building of the Texas Cattleman's Club.

Couples milled around the tables and admired the appetizer stations while cocktail service circulated regularly with specialty drinks of the evening. Kellan Blackwood and his bride, Irina, circled the dance floor along with the other couples. Russian-born Irina had been the quiet beneficiary of Buckley's kindness when he'd given the down-on-her-luck former mail-order bride a job as his maid to help her obtain a work visa while she divorced an abusive ex. The woman's green eyes sparkled now as she clearly enjoyed Kellan's expert moves on the dance floor, a purple spotlight winking off the bangles on her fringed red dress. She must be nearly four months pregnant by now, but Miranda would have never guessed if she hadn't heard the good news from Kellan two months ago.

While Miranda watched the utterly devoted couple, Kace LeBlanc, Buckley's lawyer and the executor of his will, drew up to her side. "I'd call this an unmitigated success," he announced quietly. The attorney was an interesting match for Lulu with his by-the-book, quiet competence. "You did an outstanding job with the gala. Buckley would be pleased."

"Thank you." Miranda had been grateful to throw herself into the preparations over the last week when she ached with all she'd lost, missing Kai every moment. And yes, she'd truly wanted to offer up this last tribute to her ex-husband, to give herself much-needed closure to move forward with her life. If only there was a gala she could throw that would somehow fix the way she'd left things with Kai. "I'm thrilled with the turnout, but even more excited about the donations. I think Buckley's kids were all pleased he wanted to support the Stroke Foundation."

Donna-Leigh Westbrook had died too young from a stroke, and her three children—Kellan, Sophie and Vaughn—had reeled from the loss for long afterward. Miranda had witnessed the hurt in their family firsthand.

"And you can double that amount," Kace confided, leaning closer to make the comment for her ears alone.

"Nigel Townshend just told me Green Room Media wants to match whatever we raise tonight. You can announce it when you take the podium."

"That's fantastic news." She was pleased and overwhelmed. If only she didn't feel like she was missing a piece of herself tonight with Kai's absence. "Are you set for the wedding next weekend?"

A smile curved Kace's lips, his normally serious expression transforming. "Honestly? I can't wait."

As if on cue, Lulu hurried over to them, her hands already outstretched to take Kace's, her diamond engagement ring flashing under the lights.

"Hello, gorgeous Miranda," she drawled, even though she never glanced Miranda's way. She twirled in front of Kace, her sapphire-blue gown fanning around her ankles at the kick-pleat. "I must borrow my man for a dance."

"Lulu—" Kace sounded like he wanted to protest, but he stretched his hands out to hers and let Lulu tug him toward the dance floor.

Faced with all these happy couples, loneliness hovered over Miranda like dark clouds, even in the midst of all the partygoers. Actually, maybe being among these happy, smiling people only increased her own sense of loss. She'd hoped to see Kai here, but now that it seemed like he wasn't going to show, she suspected she could slip away unnoticed from the party after her announcements were made.

She would drive to Deer Springs and speak to him in person. She had an apology to make and some news to deliver about a decision she'd made about her future.

Course set, she spun away from the dance floor and headed toward the podium. She was about to give the bandleader a nod to end the set when Kellan Blackwood

intercepted her. Dressed in a tuxedo, Buckley's oldest
son had dark brown hair that he'd always worn short,
with blue eyes that crinkled at the corners. He looked
happy tonight.

"Great party, Miranda." He folded her in a quick hug
that reminded her how far she'd come with the Blackwood heirs in the last few months. There'd been a time
they'd been certain she was a gold digger. "I'm bringing
Irina something to eat, but I wanted to let you know we
found out that she's having a boy."

Touched that he'd sought her out to share the news
with her, Miranda smiled, genuinely happy for them.
They deserved every bit of happiness they'd found together and she refused to let her own sadness taint their
joy. "I'm thrilled for you both, Kellan."

"We're going to name him Trevor Buckley Blackwood," Kellan continued, his blue gaze growing serious. "In memory of all that Dad did for Irina."

Kellan excused himself while Miranda battled to get
her emotions under control. She was so happy for Buckley's family. So why did she feel on the verge of tears?

Breathe in. Breathe out.

Standing off to one side of the raised platform where
the podium had been stationed, Miranda focused on her
breathing while the bandleader brought the song to a
close. The partygoers clapped, and Miranda climbed the
carpeted steps to take her place in front of the gala guests.
Her small perch looked out over the dance floor, and to
the rest of the great room beyond. The lighting was a dim
violet, but she could still discern the faces in the gala,
even as a spotlight snapped on over the podium.

"Good evening." She spoke into the microphone, paus-
ing a moment to let the crowd take notice and tune in

before she continued. Once more, she searched for Kai and didn't see him anywhere, his absence emphasizing the emptiness inside her.

Part of her short speech was just for him.

Swallowing hard, she told herself to forge ahead anyhow so she could go find him once she was done. Clearing her throat, she spoke into the microphone.

"Thank you all for being here at Royal Gives Back. I organized this benefit at the behest of Buckley Blackwood, a secret philanthropist who came to understand that all the millions he made during his lifetime couldn't compare to the joys of doing good for others." Her gaze traveled over her notes and then lifted to the attentive crowd. "And his wealth certainly couldn't compare to the rewards of his family."

The room seemed to go even more silent as if everyone gave her their full attention now, even the servers and musicians. Miranda bit her lip to keep her emotions in check, knowing the importance of giving Buckley a proper send-off. The weight of responsibility he'd given her settled on her shoulders one last time, and she hoped she proved worthy of his trust.

"Buckley found it hard to admit his mistakes in life. But before he died, he came to terms with the things he'd done wrong, and he chose to leave a legacy of philanthropy that we're celebrating tonight. It's my pleasure to announce that every cent we raise at Royal Gives Back will be matched by Green Room Media, thanks to Nigel Townshend." She waited while the assembled guests whooped and applauded. The engineer working the lights searched the crowd to find Nigel beside Sophie at a table in the back, and the producer waved a good-natured hand.

Sophie beamed proudly beside him.

Miranda remembered her stepdaughter's advice about Kai. *First, you apologize.* Then she'd worry about the rest. All the more motivated to wind things up so she could get to Deer Springs, Miranda read the segment of her speech that was in memory of Buckley's first wife, then talked briefly about how the fundraising efforts would aid stroke research.

Then, Miranda tucked her notes to one side.

She was just about to conclude her remarks with a personal addendum when she thought she heard a stirring of movement at the back of the room. A shuffle of feet. Low murmured voices.

Movement in the crowd alerted her to a dark-haired man walking closer to the front of the podium.

Kai Maddox stopped in the middle of the dance floor, separated from her by only a few couples in black tie. Her heart pounded so hard she was sure the microphone would pick it up and amplify it through the venue. His green eyes gave away nothing. She felt shaky as she started to speak again.

"Finally," she continued, pulling in a deep breath and willing herself to get this part right. For Kai. "I am grateful to Buckley for giving me this opportunity to return to Royal. While I was as stunned as any of you at the initial terms of his will, I hope I have grown as a person over these last five months—" Her throat closed up. She had to pause for a moment. "And I'm so glad to feel like I have a family here. Now that Blackwood Bank and the other Blackwood assets are in the hands of their rightful heirs, I could officially head back to New York."

Her gaze locked on Kai's handsome face. The face of

the man she loved more than she could have ever imagined possible.

"But overseeing Buckley's estate has taught me not to take for granted the time with family and loved ones. So I'm going to stay in Royal a little while longer to open a local Goddess fitness center." There was a murmur of surprise in the audience. Guests turned to one another. But Kai remained motionless, his face a mask. Miranda dug deep, pulling out the words that were meant for him alone. "Besides, I have unfinished business with a certain technology CEO who means the world to me. A man who—I hope—understands the value of a second chance."

He made his way across the room and the crowd began to part for Kai, his gaze locked on her with every purposeful stride. A spark of hope ignited inside her as she wondered if there could be a way forward for them after all. Maybe putting her heart out there for him to see could be enough. Perhaps he could hear the genuineness of her apology and her love.

Kai took the stairs two at a time to reach her. To tell her he wasn't ready to give her that chance? Or to tell her that he wanted to work things out with her, too? Uncertainty made her hands shake as she switched off the microphone and the crowd applauded.

When Kai swooped her up into his arms, the applause redoubled to become thunderous. Miranda looped her arms around his neck, holding tight. He hadn't spoken yet, but surely the action—his being here and holding her—meant something.

"I'm so sorry I doubted you," she told him, hoping against hope that he liked the idea of a second chance. "Kai, I want to do everything I can to make things work between us."

"In that case, we can't possibly fail." His strong arms flexed beneath her, lifting her a fraction so that his forehead tipped to hers while the band resumed playing nearby and the spotlight faded from the speaker's podium. "I happen to know you can move mountains if you set your mind to it, Miranda."

Closing her eyes, she gave herself a moment to soak in the feel of his arms tightened around her, the warmth of his forehead where it rested against hers. She breathed in the scent of his aftershave. Then, Kai straightened and carried her through the parted curtains that led to a small backstage area where extra tables and chairs were kept for events. He ignored the sign that said No Exit on a rear entrance and backed them through it, landing them in the parking area of the Texas Cattleman's Club, close to one of the side gardens.

Lowering Miranda to her feet, he took her hand and led her down a stone path to a secluded garden bench near a fountain.

"When I didn't see you earlier tonight, I was afraid you weren't coming. I planned to drive to Deer Springs right after I spoke so that I could apologize to you in person."

"I'm glad." Kai threaded her fingers through his, one by one as he let out a ragged sigh of relief. He pressed the back of her hand to his lips for a moment, his eyes sliding closed before he looked up again, his eyes open now and alive with desire. "Not that I needed the apology, but it makes me happy to hear you were making it a priority to talk to me. I know I haven't done a good job communicating what's important to me in the past, but I'm determined to do better with you in the future."

Hope sprang to life inside her, green and bright. He'd

spoken exactly the kinds of words she'd longed to hear from him so many years ago.

"You're thinking about a future together, too?" she asked, turning more fully toward him on the bench so her knee bumped his.

He took her breath away in his tuxedo, his broad shoulders filling out the black silk and casting her in shadow as she gazed up at him. Music from the gala seeped through the walls and windows, a lively country tune that would have the whole crowd two-stepping in their tuxes and gowns.

"I'm doing more than thinking about it," Kai promised, his thumb rubbing over the back of her hand and making her shiver from the simple pleasure of it. "I'm going to do everything in my power to make sure the logistics of our relationship will work."

A relationship. Something lasting. He was meeting her halfway in this, the way a real relationship worked.

"I really do want to stay in Royal for a while," she assured him, eager to do her part, make their commitment a two-way street that would pay off so beautifully for both of them. She'd given a lot of thought to bringing a Goddess fitness center to town, and she knew it was the perfect way to spend more time cementing what she had with Kai. "I've been so happy here—except for the past week, of course. I've missed you every minute we weren't together."

"I've missed you, too. I knew I was missing the big picture, but it took Dane rattling my cage a little to make me see I was never going to be happy until I took a risk and laid my heart at your feet." He cupped her cheek with his free hand, stroking along her jaw. "Tonight, I'm doing just that. I love you, Miranda, so damn much."

Her heart soared. A smile curved her lips, relief and joy wrapping around her like a hug.

"Oh, Kai." Leaning into him, she kissed him gently, taking her time to feel the exquisite pleasure of this man's lips on hers, a pleasure she looked forward to revisiting as often as she wanted. "I love you, too. I regret that I didn't work harder to make things right between us the first time, but I'm not going to take what we have for granted ever again."

She'd meant every word of her speech at the podium. Seeing her first husband's mistakes up close and personal had helped her see that she would never be happy pursuing her business goals at the expense of everything else. She would make time for love in her life, even if it sometimes felt riskier than her career.

She trusted Kai with her heart.

When he eased back to look at her, his feelings were all right there for her to see. Full of love and a promise for the future.

"Maybe we both needed the time to grow and appreciate what we had to make it work this time," Kai reassured her, his words a soft whisper over her lips. He kissed her again with slow thoroughness that left her breathless. Then, he nipped her lower lip and backed away again. "But I promise you, we'll get it right now that we have this second chance."

"Even with you based in Deer Springs and my company in New York?" She didn't mind flying back and forth, but he'd said something about taking the logistics into account, and she was curious what that meant.

"Listen," he began, releasing her hand to cradle her face between his palms. "I want you to take the deal with AMuse and follow all your dreams, Miranda. I can open a

Madtec office in New York so we can have a life together there, too. We don't have to choose. We can have it all."

She believed him.

More than that, she believed in *them*.

Together, they could take on the world.

"I like the idea of sharing all our future plans." She remembered sitting in the Deer Springs Diner all those years ago, telling him about the life she'd imagined for herself. Listening to him spin lofty goals of his own. "We were always good at dreaming big."

"Now that we've established that we're sticking together forever, would you like to go back inside and dance with me?" Kai's green gaze tracked over her. "You look stunning tonight."

Her pulse quickened.

"Actually, I was already plotting my escape after my speech," she told him honestly. "I'd rather you take me home and make love to me all night long."

With a husky growl of approval, he drew her to her feet, a hand curving possessively around her waist, landing on the bare patch of skin where her dress had a cutout.

"I drove my motorcycle tonight. Can you manage the bike in that dress for a moonlight ride?"

"Are you kidding?" She began to walk backward toward the parking lot, tugging him with her. "I've been dying for an excuse to wrap my arms around you. Lead the way."

His teeth flashed white as he stepped ahead of her, guiding her through the parking area toward their future. It promised to be a wild and incredible ride.

Epilogue

One Week Later

"Do you, Lulu Shepard, take this man…"

Kai listened to the officiant's words at the wedding ceremony, but his eyes weren't on the bride as he stood under the huge white canopy erected near the pool at Blackwood Hollow for the televised nuptials of Lulu Shepard and Kace LeBlanc. Granted, the bride was a beauty in her simple white gown that showed off the natural beauty of her glossy black hair and almond-shaped brown eyes. But Kai's eyes kept straying to one of the lovely bridesmaids. He could manage only to glance over to the couple in question.

Miranda's costar from *Secret Lives of NYC Ex-Wives* glowed, rushing to answer the question with an emphatic, "I do."

Her groom looked at her like he'd won the wife lottery.

Kai noted their happiness—and then returned his focus to the redheaded bridesmaid. Miranda stood with Lulu's other costars at the front of the canopy, the hem of her pale yellow bridesmaid's dress blowing gently around her legs thanks to the cooling fans placed around the tent for the sunset exchange of vows. She carried a small bouquet of purple violets. As always, Miranda captivated him.

She was everything he'd ever wanted in a woman—smart and ambitious, but tender and kind. She devoted herself to her charity and her loved ones even more than she committed herself to her work. Considering how far she'd come as a businesswoman, that was saying something. Kai's heart damned near burst with love for her as a quintet of musicians launched into a triumphant wedding recessional. Lulu and Kace led the way, holding their joined hands up in victory as a newly married pair, but Kai's attention stayed on Miranda where she walked through the aisle, each step bringing her closer to him.

The television cameras moved smoothly with the wedding party, tracking their every step while keeping out of the way. The ceremony was informal enough that the bride and groom were skipping a reception line since the party would start straight away. Photos had already been taken before the vows, so Kai looked forward to Miranda being free for the rest of the evening.

Her blue eyes found his among the guests milling about to admire the wedding cake on a table at the back of the tent. A space for dancing was set up as a country band readied to take over for the chamber musicians now that the formal part of the evening was finished. Flashes popped on cell phones as guests all hurried to capture the bride and groom in their first moments of married life.

All of that activity around him was just a backdrop for his night with Miranda, the most important woman in the world to him.

He pulled her to him as soon as she reached him, indulging in a brief kiss to her cheek and neck, her jasmine scent an aphrodisiac after the tantalizing nights they'd spent together.

"Well, hello to you, too," Miranda murmured warmly, clutching his shoulder with one hand while she still held her bouquet with the other.

"Public displays of affection are allowed at a wedding, right?" He forced himself to step back a fraction, but he wound an arm around her waist, his fingers gliding along the pale yellow silk of her gown.

"Absolutely." Her smile lit her whole face as she gazed up at him. "It seems only appropriate to celebrate a new love match with a kiss."

She set down her flowers on a nearby folding chair.

"Would you like to step outside for a minute?" he suggested, nodding toward the pool area visible on the other end of the tent. "It's a beautiful night."

"Sounds good." She threaded her arm through his so he could escort her among the folding chairs to a spot where they could exit the canopy.

The spring Texas air was warmer, even with the sun going down and a breeze stirring. The landscape lights reflected in the pool and violet stars winked overhead in the fading twilight. Kai followed the smooth stone path behind the water feature. Here, trees arched over the path, their leaves fluttering softly.

The country band launched into its first tune, and a whoop went up inside the canopy.

"Are you sorry to see your show end for another season?" Kai asked as he twirled her under his arm in a silent invitation to dance.

Miranda fell into step with him easily, as if they'd been together for a lifetime. He still couldn't quite believe his good fortune finding her again after the past ten years apart. This time, nothing would come between them. He felt it with unswerving certainty.

"No." She shook her head, the red strands of her silky hair catching the moonlight. "The whole season has felt like a finale to me, not just the wedding episode. I've loved my time with the women on this show, but I think I'm ready to turn my attention to other things in the coming year."

He'd sensed the same thing in the way she'd talked about the other cast members. With both Seraphina and Lulu getting married and moving to Texas, the group seemed to be moving on. He smoothed a hand up her spine and back down, savoring the feel of her. Grateful as hell to hold her in his arms.

"You know I'll stand behind whatever decision you make," he assured her. "But if I have my way, you won't be an 'ex-wife' for much longer."

He didn't want to rush Miranda, but he also knew that he wanted forever with this woman.

Her breath caught and she blinked twice before a smile curved her lips. "Something tells me it's going to be an exciting year."

Kai tipped her chin up with his knuckle, looking deep into her eyes.

"Have I told you today how much I love you?" He

leaned in to kiss her and they swayed together, lips locked, for a long moment.

"No." Her eyes simmered with blue fire. "But I'm going to have you show me tonight instead."

With pleasure, Kai vowed to do just that.

* * * * *

COMING SOON!

We really hope you enjoyed reading this book.
If you're looking for more romance, be sure to
head to the shops when new books are
available on

Thursday 14th May

To see which titles are coming soon, please visit

millsandboon.co.uk/nextmonth

LET'S TALK
Romance

For exclusive extracts, competitions
and special offers, find us online:

MILLS & BOON

THE HEART OF ROMANCE

A ROMANCE FOR EVERY KIND OF READER

MODERN
Prepare to be swept off your feet by sophisticated, sexy and seductive heroes, in some of the world's most glamourous and romantic locations, where power and passion collide.
8 stories per month.

HISTORICAL
Escape with historical heroes from time gone by. Whether your passion is for wicked Regency Rakes, muscled Vikings or rugged Highlanders, awaken the romance of the past.
6 stories per month.

MEDICAL
Set your pulse racing with dedicated, delectable doctors in the high-pressure world of medicine, where emotions run high and passion, comfort and love are the best medicine.
6 stories per month.

True Love
Celebrate true love with tender stories of heartfelt romance, from the rush of falling in love to the joy a new baby can bring, and a focus on the emotional heart of a relationship.
8 stories per month.

Desire
Indulge in secrets and scandal, intense drama and plenty of sizzling hot action with powerful and passionate heroes who have it all: wealth, status, good looks…everything but the right woman.
6 stories per month.

HEROES
Experience all the excitement of a gripping thriller, with an intense romance at its heart. Resourceful, true-to-life women and strong, fearless men face danger and desire - a killer combination!
8 stories per month.

DARE
Sensual love stories featuring smart, sassy heroines you'd want as a best friend, and compelling intense heroes who are worthy of them.
4 stories per month.

To see which titles are coming soon, please visit

millsandboon.co.uk/nextmonth

MILLS & BOON

HEROES

At Your Service

Experience all the excitement of a
gripping thriller, with an intense romance
at its heart. Resourceful, true-to-life
women and strong, fearless men face
danger and desire - a killer combination!

MILLS & BOON

MODERN

Power and Passion

Prepare to be swept off your feet by sophisticated, sexy and seductive heroes, in some of the world's most glamourous and romantic locations, where power and passion collide.